*S*acred Ground

Sacred Ground

Writings about Home

◙ ◙ ◙

BARBARA BONNER

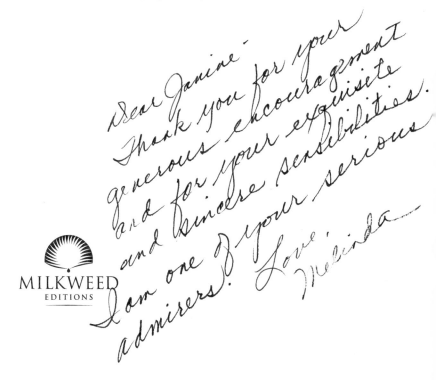

MILKWEED
EDITIONS

Dear Janine—
Thank you for your
generous encouragement
and for your exquisite
and sincere sensibilities.
I am one of your serious
admirers! Love,
Melinda

Published 1996 by Milkweed Editions
Printed in the United States of America
Cover design by Don Leeper
Cover art by David Lefkowitz
Interior design by Will Powers
The text of this book is set in Sabon.
96 97 98 99 00 5 4 3 2 1
First Edition

Milkweed Editions is a not-for-profit publisher. We gratefully acknowledge
support from the Bush Foundation; Target Stores, Dayton's, and Mervyn's
by the Dayton Hudson Foundation; Ecolab Foundation; General Mills
Foundation; Honeywell Foundation; Jerome Foundation; The McKnight
Foundation; Andrew W. Mellon Foundation; Kathy Stevens Dougherty and
Michael E. Dougherty Fund of the Minneapolis Foundation; Minnesota State
Arts Board through an appropriation by the Minnesota State Legislature;
Challenge and Literature Programs of the National Endowment for the Arts;
The Lawrence and Elizabeth Ann O'Shaughnessy Charitable Income Trust in
honor of Lawrence M. O'Shaughnessy; Piper Jaffray Companies, Inc.; Ritz
Foundation on behalf of Mr. and Mrs. E. J. Phelps Jr.; John and Beverly
Rollwagen Fund of the Minneapolis Foundation; The St. Paul Companies, Inc.;
Star Tribune/Cowles Media Foundation; Surdna Foundation; James R. Thorpe
Foundation; U.S. West Foundation; Lila Wallace-Reader's Digest Literary
Publishers Marketing Development Program, funded through a grant to the
Council of Literary Magazines and Presses; and generous individuals.

Library of Congress Cataloging-in-Publication Data

Sacred ground : writings about home / [edited by] Barbara Bonner. —
    1st ed.
        p.   cm.
     ISBN 1-57131-010-X
     I. Home—Literary collections.   I. Bonner, Barbara, 1939-
PN6071.H72S23   1996
808.8'355—dc20
                                                                    96-34814
                                                                        CIP

This book is printed on acid-free paper.

For Bob, for Tim,
and in memory of Jennifer Anne Bonner

I would like to thank all of the writers who responded to the call from Milkweed Editions for stories on home and homelessness; those people who contributed suggestions for reading on home, in all its forms: Deane Barbour, Lota Bare, Michael Chauss, Barbara Clark, Susan Cushman, Beth Davis, Ingrid Erickson, Gary Gach, Mike Kowalewski, Leone Lagervall, Eric Larsen, Sharon Locy, Jim McDonnell, Elizabeth McKinsey, Mark McKone, Kit Naylor, Ann Niles, Diana Postlethwaite, Spencer Reese, Lew Rosenbaum, Myra Sullivan, and Susan Wolff; Kirk Jeffrey and Nikki Lamberty, for their patience in helping me back to solid ground on the computer; Barbara Clark and Margaret Upshaw, who read parts of this manuscript during its preparation; Emilie Buchwald and the staff at Milkweed Editions for making this book possible; and, finally, and most of all, my husband, Bob, for his patience, support, and perspective during the preparation of this collection.

Sacred Ground

Introduction

How to think about home, this age-old center of human life that all people need but more and more people plainly lack? What is the essence of home, and why has it become less certain for us as we near the end of the twentieth century? In a time when magazines, books, and advertisements focus endlessly on home, and homeless human beings exist on the streets of all our cities, it is clear that the issue of home strikes troubling chords in our society. Have modern societies abandoned the ties with extended family and community, the natural world, ancestors, and the gods that provided meaningful connections of home in traditional times?

A call by Milkweed Editions for stories on home and homelessness brought forth more than seven hundred submissions from writers all over the country. These stories showed, overwhelmingly, the social, spiritual, and emotional dislocations we have suffered. From the time of Yeats and Forster, writers in this century have warned of the loss of binding communal connections; this consciousness informs the pieces gathered together in this book.

In attempting to represent the various meanings of home here, I have organized the book thematically in widening circles, moving outward from the most intimate experience of home to its broadest scale. If one is fortunate, this range of communal connections is accompanied by an inner growth or deepening of self, culminating in the "true home" of personal wholeness. At each point as our lives expand and we encounter these circles, the connections can be missed or destroyed, resulting in the inner homelessness of anger and alienation.

If this collection seems to dwell more on what has been lost than on what has been gained, I can only say that loss is what seems to be on the minds of writers these days. Besides the obvious losses of shelter and security revealed here in stories of life on the streets and of violence and sexual abuse in the home, there are other losses, such as divorce and fragmentation of families, as well as exile, abandonment, and social mobility.

Among the especially troubling losses portrayed in these pages is the loss of connection with a sustaining past, usually carried down through the generations. Many authors make clear that without these connections, our sense of who we are or who we might be has itself been threatened. Jim Wayne Miller in "A Felt Linkage" speaks of the pressures that work against putting down roots in our society:

> We are rewarded with money, prestige and success for pursuing nomadic existences, for our ability to pull up, take leave over-night, plug in quickly to new situations and size them up swiftly. We are rewarded for the exploitative grasp of new circumstances, the almost predatory reading of people and places. . . . There's little demand for the kind of knowledge that comes of living a long time in one place, knowledge gained slowly with the turning of seasons, in daily intercourse with neighbors. As a country storekeeper would say, "We don't get many calls for that."

Harry Crews turns that desire for rootedness in a particular community into a very specific personal lament. After following the trail of his long-dead father through the general stores of backcountry Georgia, he cries out:

> Listening to them talk, I wondered what would give credibility to my own story if, when my young son grows to manhood, he has to go looking for me in the mouths and memories of other people. Who would tell the stories? A few motorcycle riders, bartenders, editors, half-mad karateka, drunks, and writers. They are scattered all over the country, but even if he could find

them, they could speak to him with no shared voice from no common ground. Even as I was gladdened listening to the stories of my daddy, an almost nauseous sadness settled in me, knowing I would leave no such life intact. Among the men with whom I have spent my working life, university professors, there is not one friend of the sort I was listening to speak of my daddy there that day in the back of the store in Bacon County. Acquaintances, but no friends. For half of my life I have been in the university, but never of it. Never *of* anywhere, really. Except the place I left, and that of necessity only in memory.

Are we forced to the periphery of our own lives as we lose the physical and generational connection that home has always, unthinkingly, provided?

As we have lost our connection with place, we have necessarily lost connection with the creatures who share our world. The seasons and rhythms that once held us all in the same gentle or terrifying grasp have faded into insignificance. Works by Colette, Elisavietta Ritchie, Susan Gaines, and Paul Gruchow show our need for the connections of home in the natural world.

A number of the stories and essays I received showed that in our loss of these larger connections, we have also lost our place in the flow of time that allowed people in traditional societies to accept their deaths and their place in the cycle of generations.

John Berger has referred to the "vertical line" that connected people in traditional societies to the gods in the heavens and to the dead in the underworld. In Berger's view, "the dead now simply disappear; and the gods have become inaccessible." When some writers allude to twentieth-century essential home-lessness, they have this loss in mind. Naomi Chase, Hollis Seamon, A. B. Emrys, Susan Gaines, and Paul Gruchow testify to the difficulty of holding to any conception of the sacred in modern life. They show, at the same time, that a home lacking this concept of the sacred can never be more than a place. These selections suggest a link between the absence of spirituality from our lives and the presence of homeless people on our streets.

Writers, of course, deal with these problems in different ways. In "The Names of Women," Louise Erdrich recognizes her loss of the spiritual codes that governed the lives of her ancestors:

> I was not raised speaking the old language, or adhering to the cycle of religious ceremonies that govern the Anishinabe spiritual relationship to the land and the moral order within human configurations. As the wedding of many backgrounds, I am free to do what simply feels right.

For Erdrich, as for most of us in the twentieth century, "home is a collection of homes"; no single place or community magnetizes her or us. But for her, the urge to return home is satisfied by the urge to write, which she likens to her great-grandmother's urge to walk across the prairie to her ancestral home even when it lay one hundred miles away. S. Afzal Haider's story "Brooklyn to Karachi via Amsterdam" also deals with the loss of past traditions, but in this view freedom offers little comfort.

The works gathered in the last chapter portray the spiritual homelessness we have suffered in a time of technological revolution, when the electronic hearth of television dominates our homes. In contrast to the storytelling customs suggested by Harry Crews, intimate and familial, stories are now written by strangers for strangers.

Eva Hoffman has observed that with the death of the old hierarchy of heaven, earth, and hell, we live in a world where "dislocation is the norm rather than the aberration." Yet homelessness is not our inevitable lot. For John Berger, "it is on the site of loss that hopes are born." In many and various ways, the reading selections demonstrate connections of home that remain.

This collection ultimately makes clear that spiritual homelessness is not inevitable, nor is the breakdown in community often observed in our cities. In *Howard's End,* written near the beginning of this century, E. M. Forster foresaw the dislocation that seems to threaten us everywhere in our world:

London was but a foretaste of this nomadic civilization which is altering human nature so profoundly, and throws upon personal relations a stress greater than they have ever borne before. Under cosmopolitanism, if it comes, we shall receive no help from the earth. Trees and meadows and mountains will only be a spectacle, and the binding force that they once exercised on character must be entrusted to Love alone. May Love be equal to the task!

These selections speak to that hope, that love may bind our lives and the connections of home sustain us.

Today, as soon as very early childhood is over, the house can never again be home, as it was in other epochs. This century, for all its wealth and with all its communication systems, is the century of banishment.

JOHN BERGER

Sacred Ground

HOME

First Ties

I was still young enough then to be sleeping with my Mother,
which to me seemed life's whole purpose. . . . Alone, at that time,
of all the family, I was her chosen dream companion, chosen
from all for her extra love; my right, so it seemed to me.

. . . we two then lay joined alone. . . . It was a darkness of bliss
and simple languor, when all edges seemed rounded . . . and the
presence for whom one had moaned and hungered was found
not to have fled after all.

LAURIE LEE

ALLEN WHEELIS

An excerpt from

The Doctor of Desire

Five years old, too young for school. Skinny arms and legs sticking out from skimpy pants and short-sleeve shirt. When the older boys got back from school I went to Jimmy's house to play. Five boys had arranged themselves in a circle, were throwing a ball one to another in sequence. I put myself in the circle, but when my turn came the ball sailed over my head to the next in line. An oversight, perhaps; I waited the next round. When passed over again, I complained. They did not seem to hear. My complaint grew louder, became pleading. Again and again the ball flew over my head. I jumped but could not reach it, wailed, went to my friend who usually was willing to play with me, tugged on his sleeve, "Let me play, Jimmy! Throw it to me too! Please, Jimmy!" Jimmy shrugged, threw the ball over my head. I began to cry. "It's not fair!" I was enraged, wanted to retaliate, to walk away. But could not reject them so long as they would not see me, would not hear. And because they were denying my existence I could not give up trying to enter their circle. I began to run after the ball, tried to intercept throws, but when I managed to position myself before the next receiver, the order would change, the ball going instead to someone else. I ran back and forth, in and out, never finding a way to become a part. It was a magic circle, it joined them, excluded me. I was a non-person.

Eventually I gave up, sat down at some distance, exhausted, disheartened, watched the ball fly around, one to another, in sequences of infinite desirability. It was too painful to watch, I lowered my head, scratched in the dirt. When my crying stopped,

4

the boys tired of the game, stood about idly, bored, wondered what to do next. "Here, Henny," Jimmy said, as if to a dog, and tossed me the now unwanted ball. The boys huddled, came to a decision, set off together. "Where are we going?" I asked, following after. But again could not make myself heard. I ran to keep up, but they ran faster, and came presently to a thicket which, with their long pants, they could push through, whereas I, with bare legs, was turned back bleeding. The boys disappeared, their laughter grew fainter, died away. I extricated myself from the brush, walked back toward Jimmy's house. It was getting dark. There was a strong and cold wind. I was whimpering. Maybe crying.

Then there was my mother standing before me in her long brown coat. "A norther has come up," she said, taking my hand. "All of a sudden. That's why it's so dark and cold." I looked up. Black clouds were rushing across the sky. She wiped my nose. "We must go home." The pebbles hurt my bare feet; I hopped and lurched, holding her hand, trying to avoid the sharper stones. My teeth were chattering, the skin of my arms and legs became goose flesh. My mother stopped, opened her coat. "Come inside," she said. She folded me into the coat, buttoned it in front of me. We proceeded awkwardly, my shoulder against her thigh, my head alongside her hip, enveloped in darkness, in warmth, in the smell of her body. She was wearing an apron, and there was a smell also of food—onions and something fried. She must have been cooking supper when the norther hit. And stopped to come get me.

It was difficult to walk, we went slowly. I couldn't see anything ahead, but looking down could see the ground where I was putting my feet. I was getting warm in that germinal darkness. My teeth stopped chattering, my knees stopped shaking. I was aware of the powerful movement of her hip against my cheek, the sense of a large bone moving under strong muscles. Aware also that it was difficult for her to walk with me buttoned in. Occasionally she stumbled. And just then, for the first time, I became aware of goodness. Of goodness as a special quality, like evil, which a person may or may not possess. She doesn't *have* to do this, I thought. It's not necessary. I'm cold, but I could make it home all right.

What she gave me could not have been demanded, I would never have thought to ask. All afternoon I had been demanding something to which it seemed I had a right, and had been denied; yet here was a good to which I had no right, freely offered. No trade. Nothing asked in return.

The meaning of life is in that coat; it is the home to which one belonged as a child. If you're lucky you never lose it, it simply evolves, smoothly and continuously, into that larger, more abstract home of religion, or perhaps, in a secular vein, into clan or community or ideology. Meaninglessness means homeless-ness. When home is lost and the nightmares begin, that's when one goes in quest of meaning.

And one has the impression then of reaching outward and forward, of delving into something *out there,* of grappling with the world, trying to penetrate a mystery; and it seems that one has only just come to recognize the existence of this most funda-mental problem, a problem that has been there all along, but that only now, just possibly, one has arrived at the capacity to solve, or at least to try. But this is retrospective falsification. The problem has not been there all along; it came into being only with the loss of home, and the attempt to solve it is not an effort to create something new but to recreate something old. It is a quest backward. One is trying to refashion, in a form acceptable to an intellectualizing adult, the home of one's childhood.

KATHLEEN HOUSER

Without a Word Between Us

Maybe it's that I'm about to have a baby myself, or maybe it's the day, the wind attacking the windows, so horizontal and demanding, the same sort of day. But I've been thinking about my mother, Jean, and the day she almost lost her last baby, her last egg.

I won't tell you this tale is straight out of 11-year-old eyes. It's been tainted, or perfected maybe, by at least 10 years of interpreting, one thought laid over another. I'll admit I remember details only if they have something to do with me directly, not like my brother Jack, who was only 4 at the time and could name every billboard from Minneapolis to the Iowa border. The old house we lived in held all the families who had lived there before, and I heard them if I listened at night to all the creaks and thumps. Mourning doves, the last robin at dusk, which kids got to stay up—still screaming outside—later than me, my friends on the phone: These were the things I listened to. Certainly not the flow of words between my mother and father. They floated around me like the sounds from the radio when I was asleep in a moving car.

If there was nothing better to do, I hung around home, and the day Jack almost drowned the baby I sat on the back step writing with a chalk rock. I'd just read in the *Ladies Home Journal* that writing a clockwise circle meant something was very wrong with you. I was on the right side of madness, but at any time, I knew, this could change.

Jack ran the hose over his stomach to cool off. It was July of a summer hot enough for kids to take notice. The pool of water around Jack's feet forced some pretty big worms from the grass, something the robins saw, but he did not. The wind blew so hard it twisted the leaves inside out so the silvery white sides were flapping like crazy, which was what Jack started to do when he saw the worm bodies bloating up around him.

He screamed, threw the hose over the edge of the bassinet, and stood frozen in the middle of all that wet grass, pleading with his arms out for someone to pick him up. Mom and I both ran to his rescue. I grabbed his bulky, slippery body and bounced him over to dry ground.

Mother found the baby in the bassinet, lying in six inches of water. She scooped him out and ran with him to the front side-walk, screaming. By the time Jack and I reached her, a slow green car had pulled over, and a big man in a brown suit jumped out, took our baby, and breathed into him until he started to breathe himself, and then to cry. And then the man and that big fish of a car just drove off again.

On a normal day, my life was easy enough. My mother did whatever all people do, Jack roamed the neighborhood, came home to eat, and I rode my bike to the pool and climbed trees with my friend Sophie. Our welfare, Jack's and mine, was left in the hands of the world we felt we had made. It didn't occur to me to keep company with our mother, nor, I guess, did it occur to her.

But now she wanted us. "Come with me," she said, clutching the baby to her, "he needs to see the doctor," and without even changing his wet sleeper, she led the way to the car.

I held the baby as we drove, and concentrated on him, leaving no room for my mother to ask, "How could you have let this happen?" or even to cry. He was only four weeks old—he'd had no time to fatten up yet. He stared at me. His eyes were green as a lake in the sun. His hair was like my own, only wet it lost its cast of orange. His free arm waved randomly, like a wild branch, or a weed underwater. I lowered my face to his mouth— his breath smelled like butter, his hair like zinnias. The sun broke on his face as Mom rounded the corner to the clinic, and the baby started, closed his eyes. And right then I knew that this baby might have something to do with all of us, but he closed his own eyes, he made butter of his own breath, without us.

Mother took the baby and ran into the clinic. By the time we reached the waiting room, she was gone.

The nurse wasn't curious about Jack and me, didn't even lift her head when we walked in, until we tried the door to the inner rooms.

"I'm sorry. The doctor's with a patient right now."

Jack was no good in a situation like this. He'd already sat down and started playing with some king-of-the-hill marble game.

"Tell her your mom's in there," I commanded him.

He whined and jerked himself away from me. I decided to wait. Where was everybody else? Were there no other sick people? All I could focus on was the chubby, dirty, familiar body of my own little brother. I wanted to edge my foot over and kick him. Or at least the marble game he was so engrossed in. His brows puckered with concentration, he looked ready to drool.

Before Jack could finish the game, the door opened, Dr. Adams's smiling face bursting through first. He had his hand on my mother's arm, sort of helping to cradle the baby and keep her walking at the same time. She looked flushed and stiff.

"Your little brother's just fine," he boomed, and the nurse looked up at me. It made me sick that he was the one who should tell me that. "What do you know about it?" was what I would have said, if I had said anything at all. Instead, I stared at his hand, which had dropped away from my mother's arm and fallen to his side.

"You could have been friendly to the doctor. He's a nice man," my mother told me on the way home. "Bad enough to have to be there at all, but then you . . . ."

The grass along the boulevards was brown; even the dandelions were shriveling up. Everything looked colorless, the way things looked when you swim in chlorine for too long with your eyes open.

I turned my head as far toward the back seat as I could

without waking the baby, and hissed, "Quit kicking the back of my seat, stupid."

Jack started crying as Mom whirled us into the driveway, jerked the car into Park, took the baby, and left. "You two!" we heard her say before the front door closed.

We sat without a word between us for a long time before we dragged ourselves from the car and trooped into the house. My mother was on the couch with the baby, singing "Highland Laddy." "And it's woe in my heart," she sang, "that I wish him safe at home."

I went to the piano and pounded out the only piece I knew by heart. "Santa Lucia."

"Why don't you go to the pool?"

"No."

"Why not?"

"Because." I kept on playing. "I don't want to." Summer dust had settled on the keys. I played until the sun no longer cut across the dusty air and hamburger sizzled in a pan in the kitchen.

"Jack's going to Tina's for a while. Go with him, why don't you."

Tina was five years old.

The baby was sound asleep when Dad came home for dinner. He clapped his hands around my shoulders as I played. "Where's Mom?"

"In the kitchen." I got up and followed him. She was stirring something on the stove, he said hi.

"Molly. Run and get Jack for supper." I walked over, hollered his name out the back door, and sat down at the table.

"That's not what I had in mind."

"He'll come," I said.

Jack's noisy chomping, and his way of thudding his glass to the table, gave us all something to listen to during dinner. His food fell in clumps to the neck of his shirt, and his napkin stayed un-used under his knife.

"I'm goin' out," he said, and scraped his chair away from the table.

She had not yet told Dad about the baby, and now my dis-traction was gone. I could not stay at the table forever, nor could I hover around them once they got up.

I sauntered outside and sat on the back steps, but all I could make out was a smooth murmuring, then a chair pushing across the floor.

"Well, at least it's all over," my father said on his way into the living room. And then my mother's final statement, staccato and loud. "All over?"

After that, my days of privacy dwindled. Mother insisted we maintain our lives as always, something neither one of us was accustomed to her attending to. Sophie was at a lake cabin, and Mother tried for three weeks to foist me onto neighbor kids at the fringe of my territory.

"Why don't you go play with Susan?" she'd say, and when my only answer was a click of my tongue, "What about Craig? You always have fun with him."

If I left, I knew, things might simply do for themselves what I ought to be there to do for them. I spent a lot of time cruising between home and the Ben Franklin, buying penny candy and storing it in my room.

Mother would not take part in any of the quizzes Jack and I made up. "No!" she snapped one day. "I can't choose. Ask each other—I don't know!" She could not pick a favorite poolside garden from the *House Beautiful*. Nor could she guess the gesta-tion of an elephant baby from *The Nature Quiz Book*. In fact, she started to cry.

"Go on now," she said.

I watched her for a few seconds, then as quietly as I could

I went to my room and lay on the bed. The curtains blew in and out with the wind, lifting into the room, then sucking back against the screen. With concentration, I kept my breathing exactly at the pace of the wind's breath through the house.

It was the tomatoes she cried about. They were dying because no one ever watered them, but we never thought about it. It seemed to have always been her job.

That night, for the first time I could ever remember, my father stood behind the nozzle of the hose, jerking it up and down to keep the water from plastering down the frail bodies of our plants.

By August, we were all sick of each other. Dad worked or slept or held the baby. Mom could no longer stand any of us. Jack clung to her legs, or arched his back and whined to her like there was something he knew he wanted. I didn't speak to anyone; I perceived it as my duty.

Four days before Labor Day, Mom came into my room after supper with some change. "Will you take your bike to the store?" she asked me. "We need milk." She was puffy-faced, and not at all the person I wanted to look like one day.

It was early evening, and the two of them were trying to get me out of the house. As I saw it, now that they did not like each other, they had neither that pleasure nor the release of argument, since Jack and I hovered about, and for our protection words could not pass.

By the time I wheeled my bike from the garage and parked it next to the house, she was in the living room with my father, crying. I sat on the iron railing outside the front door, planted my feet inside the wrought-iron swirls.

"No! There's nothing you can do! What can you do?" she said to him, and then with greater force, "You tell me what you can do! You figure it out! You just figure it out!"

Ants were evenly roving the top step, carrying sand and dead bugs to their house near our welcome mat. I made a pattern of the hair that fell in front of my face, moving my head slightly to hold the ants within the road I had made.

Mother was crying again. She was displaced, she said, she was no good. I left for the store, bought some Nik-l-Nips, and saved the wax bottles for Jack.

The next day, my father came home from work just after lunch. Mother went on feeding the baby.

"Molly," she said, "you go swimming this afternoon—it'll be your last chance."

I protested. Sophie was gone, my bike had a flat tire, it was too hot to walk.

"Dad's here," she said. "He can drive you." So there I was, standing in a parking lot in front of the pool, boiling in a tea of hot tar and chamomile.

"We'll pick you up at 4:30," my father said, and drove off. I had no choice but to run for the water.

So many bodies were packed into the pool that there was room only to duck down and dolphin around all the floating legs that swelled about underwater. I flung myself around with little feeling for swimming, kept on moving anyway, diving under, coming up, squinting at the clock. Two forty-five. Three o'clock. I lay on my back, surging on the tide of the crowd of swimmers. I tried to make it from the rope to the three-foot end, from the three-foot end to the rope. As I came up short, the rope not even yet visible beyond all the bobbing heads, it was clear to me: When I got home, they would be gone.

This pool, so foreign anyway from anything they did, was now supposed to be mine, my solace. In the water, no one would know I was crying, but once I pulled myself from the pool I ran without stopping through the green shower rooms. My body was just then older, my stomach tightening around a thought only a bigger person could hold.

I walked home sobbing, swam with bloodshot eyes down the dry blocks of the town. I chewed and pulled at my towel, but saw nothing of the arc of old elms, the pink motel, the rows of old frame houses. I could have been anywhere. My body walked along, but my mind, maybe for the first time, was not there. I had the sense that any corner I took would leave me swimming down the same strange street.

On my own block, I could no longer deny that I was home. There it was, the house with the gray shutters and the spirea, plunked between two strands of picket fence. But this was no comfort, either, only a reminder of the distance between the world I could see and hear and my body, which had lost a feel for itself.

They would not be home. They would be gone to another place beyond my reach and I would never see them again. The doctors would tell them she needed to be away from us—from the children who could leave, or drown, or cry.

The house was closed up, hot and quiet. I ran straight to their closet, sticking to the wood floor like a magnet on the low pole of a globe. Their clothes were still there, the purses, the suits, the beautiful green shoes. How could I know what they would choose to leave with?

My voice shot through the empty house like the first bat through the yard in the evening. "Mom?"

"Mom!" I ran through the kitchen, up the stairs, shoved open the bathroom door. Then, my eyes scratching, my heart pounding, I walked into my room to decide what to do—and I saw her through the window.

She didn't leave. She was home all the time. I saw her through my window, sitting on a lawn chair in the backyard with the baby. She stared toward the line of lilacs, held the baby as if she were a hammock, fabric stretched together.

I knelt by the window and pushed my nose against the screen to smell the dust and fresh mowed grass. I watched her for a long time. I pictured my hand being the one that waved, slowly, insistently, toward my mother's face. I was not to know the layers of liquid that floated over and around her. I put my finger up to the screen and pressed it to her lips.

14

Leaving Home

Two of our aunt's three boys followed, without losing their foot-ing, the narrow path which leads across adolescence into normal adult life. But the middle one, Jake, repeatedly fell off into the morass. "Girl trouble," as the succinct family phrase put it.

DOROTHY CANFIELD

Self-realization requires leaving the orbit of the home, an excru-ciatingly painful experience fraught with many psychological dangers. . . . pain must be endured and risky chances taken, since one must achieve one's personal identity. . . . The child who understands . . . will find the true home of his inner self; he will become master over its vast realm by knowing his mind, so it will serve him well.

BRUNO BETTELHEIM

Over Doyles' Drop-Off

Mrs. Doyle leaned over the edge of the rowboat and raised her pole above her head to see if she still had a worm on. "When I was your age, my sister Alice told me she was going to hang herself from the track of the garage-door opener."

I was stirring the worms to find a big one, but when she said this I stopped. "What did you tell her?"

Mrs. Doyle turned to look at me. "I don't even remember."

"Did she do it?"

She lowered her line again and shook her head. "Alice would have liked the attention, but she couldn't solve the problem of not being able to enjoy it because of being dead."

I pictured it in my mind. "She probably had it planned that when your father drove in from the office and pressed the button"—I aimed an imaginary remote control toward the front of the boat and pressed—"she would ride up the track toward the back of the garage"—my hand hung limp with two fingers dangling and inched up the track—"until she jerked to a stop and her toes touched the windshield at exactly the spot where he was supposed to park."

Mrs. Doyle laughed. I liked the way her laughs rolled up inside her chest on their way out. "I would have become an only child," she said. She let out more line. "Where're the fish, Samuel?" She stuck her pole between her knees and pulled on the thin polka-dot blouse she wore over her bathing suit.

I pictured one of my brothers strung up in the basement. We

didn't have a garage. "Of course," I said, "becoming an only child at fourteen isn't like growing up being an only child." I was fourteen myself, with four older brothers, and there probably wasn't room to hang them all.

She saw me glance up to her house for signs of Mr. Doyle. We were anchored at the edge of the drop-off, ten yards beyond the end of Doyles' dock, waiting for him to get home from the office. This was last August, and we were having one of those hot spells we get. From where we sat you could see the whole lake. Most of the houses sit back in the trees and have steps to the shore and wooden docks sticking into the lake on posts. This was a Friday afternoon. Here and there you could make out people on the docks or in the water, and every so often you could hear a door slam across the lake or hear somebody holler.

Our house was put together by my grandfather from two summer cottages. The Doyles, who moved out from town, bought a cottage up the shore and tore it down so they could build a modern house that Mr. Doyle designed. He's a lawyer. It's a dark, one-story house with a flat roof and small windows, and when you're inside it's like you're stuck someplace, peeking out. Mrs. Doyle made him add a screened porch so she could have lawn parties for her bridge group. Their lawn goes right down to the water, but it's all spotted and brown from their two wiener dogs. The Doyles' dogs do their business wherever they feel like it except indoors. Mr. Doyle says the worst thing you can do to a dog is to shame it.

I thought I heard a door close, and had a feeling he was in there somewhere.

"Should be anytime," Mrs. Doyle said.

It drives my father crazy, the way Mr. Doyle spoils his dogs, but Mr. Doyle always says it doesn't cost anything to be nice, and that includes to dogs. When people are nice back to him, he seems a little surprised and really appreciates it. One time Mr. Doyle said he personally would rather be nice or be dead. Mrs. Doyle said that was bunk. Mr. Doyle said no nicer person ever walked the earth than his mother, but she was gone. Mrs. Doyle told me it was too bad Mr. Doyle couldn't have married his mother.

Mr. Doyle was in a situation at work that week. On Monday, his partner, Mr. Jacobs, had left in the middle of the night and took a lot of papers and some of Mr. Doyle's most important clients. Every day since then, when Mr. Doyle came home in the evening, he started drinking and told Mrs. Doyle the latest development. Usually it ended up having something to do with Mrs. Doyle. One evening he said that the clients who lost them money over the years were the ones he took as a favor because they were friends of Mrs. Doyle's, and now that it was too late he realized he should have been more concerned about whether they were quality clients than about making her happy. I wasn't there, but she told me about it. The next day, I hung around until he got home, and after his second drink he said it wasn't so surprising that some of his best clients had left. They were important people who were used to being paid some attention, but she never even entertained them. In thinking back he realized she had always been rude to his partner, and his partner's wife, too, as if the Doyles could afford to offend the Jacobses. He thought at the bottom of it maybe she didn't like Jews. She told him that he was full of baloney and the truth of it was, if he cared to admit it, with Mr. Jacobs gone Mr. Doyle didn't have anybody to blame his problems on but himself. That Friday Mrs. Doyle and I were out in the boat thinking that when he got home and discovered she wasn't there, we could lure him down to the lake and put him in a better mood.

I squeezed my forearm and let go to see if I was burning. I'd worked up a pretty good tan. I liked sitting in nothing but a bathing suit and smelling like Coppertone. I was completely brown except under my nails, on the bottoms of my feet, and under my trunks. Now and then I checked under my trunks to see how white it was. I turned around on my seat and put my other side to the sun. I moved the bait can to make room for my feet and set it down carefully, because in an aluminum boat like the Doyles' you could be very noisy without half trying.

Lydia Lake was clear as a cat's eye. Waves turned the sun into worms of white light that wiggled across the bottom and dissolved. You could see where clams poked up in the mud with moss on their shells and sunfish hung still in the slanty shadow of the swim raft with their gills going open and shut. When you go in, the water holds you up as gentle as warm air, and if you want you can let out your breath and nudge along the bottom past the sandy hollows where the crappies lay their eggs. The drop-off catches some people by surprise, but when I'm in the lake I always know where I am in relation to the drop-off. If you swim over it with goggles and a snorkel—and that means you have to swim through the weeds first to get there, unless you're very early in the season—you come out on the far side of the weeds like flying slowly through a forest, and then it opens up and you can see the soft muck slant away to black-green and no telling how far down.

I thought I saw something dart past a window inside the Doyles' house. "I think he's home," I said in a low voice.

"Shhh!" she said. She leaned over the edge of the boat again and raised her pole. "I feel a nibble." I leaned the opposite way to keep the balance.

"Play it a little," I whispered. I looked up at Doyles' and looked back at her. She held her breath and the tip of her pole twitched. She brushed her hair back from her forehead. Her hair is about half gray and half brown and she had it clipped in the back with a plastic comb. Mrs. Doyle is more than fifty years old, older than my mother, plus she smokes Salems. My mother never smokes except at parties. My mother has a normal body, but Mrs. Doyle's stomach kind of pooches out and she has long fingernails. She always has on lipstick and nail polish like she's expecting to be invited out or has extra she's trying to use up. I was teaching her that you have to let a fish work on your bait awhile before you set the hook. She looked at me and raised her eyebrows like a question.

"O. K.," I whispered. "Jerk it!"

She had the pole so high she didn't have any arm left to do the jerking and had to get up a little off the seat. She has a big butt, and it was all pale below her bathing suit, except where it had a flat red crease across it from the aluminum seat. The red crease stopped at the V-shaped part covered by her suit, which was turquoise, and started again on the other side. "There!" she said. When she was excited her voice got deep and she forgot to whisper. "Got him!" Her sleeve slipped off her shoulder and the loose part of her arm that would be muscle on a man jiggled as she worked the fishing pole. I grabbed the net. It was a pan-sized sunfish. I got out the stringer and put him on.

I looked down the shore toward our place. One of my brothers was doing something in waist-deep water, but I couldn't tell what. Maybe rigging his spear gun. I looked back to Doyles' and was sure I saw a face in the den window. I started to wave, but it disappeared. "Think we should go in?" I said.

"He'll think we're coming up. Better to stay put and hope he comes out." I watched the porch door. "When he's depressed like this it will take him a while to decide to come out," she said. "He's used to having things his way. It's what happens when you're an only child raised by a mother who would rather be drawn and quartered than let you suffer so much as a passing moment of unhappiness." She rolled out another laugh. I pictured Mr. Doyle as a boy being wrestled for fun by his mother. She probably had dark hair and creamy skin. Then I imagined him sitting in a long white chair on the lawn with his feet up while she served him lunch from a tray.

"What about his father?" I said.

"I never knew him. Willis says he only wore suits."

"Did his father spoil him?"

"His idea was to teach Willis self-discipline. If you ask me, what he should've done was make a couple more kids so Willis would've learned to work things out when they didn't go exactly his way."

"Maybe," I said. "But what if they just had fights?"

"Fighting's one way of working things out," she said.

"If you're oldest," I said. "If you're not, forget it."

Mrs. Doyle laughed and shrugged her shoulders. "Besides,"

she said, "if there are no other people around, it's harder than heck to get away with anything." She leaned over the side of the boat, stuck her hand out to make a shadow on the water, and tried to see if any more fish were near her bait. She made a laugh that was kind of a snort and said, "Knowing Willis, he never tried to get away with a thing in his life." I couldn't think of anything I tried to get away with, either. I didn't say so, though, because Mrs. Doyle made it sound like you should.

I wondered what he could be doing in there. Probably making a drink or digging through his drawers looking for his bathing suit. Usually, if I was there when he came home from work, Mrs. Doyle and I would be sitting on the porch and he would walk in and say something funny like "What's the gnus on the home front? Yak yak," and then, "Why don't you do the honors, Louise." While she poured him a bourbon-and-Coke, he would loosen his tie and fold himself—he's tall and soft—into one of those reedy, round porch chairs that look like upside-down Chinamen's hats, and then he would drink while we talked. He liked to tell me pointers about being in business, like having a grip on your fundamentals. He said if more businessmen had a grip on their fundamentals they would be putting money in the bank instead of going to the government with their hands out. If he was in a good mood he might tell some jokes, and I'd stay for supper, and afterward we'd play gin rummy. Other times when he'd get home he'd be in a really bad mood. You couldn't tell in advance. If you went by their house after dark sometimes they would be shouting things at each other that made you walk fast because you didn't want to hear it.

I started coming over to Doyles' when they hired me once to get a dead muskrat off their lawn. I took it home to my brother Martin, who collected dead animals at the time. He would store them in the freezer and then thaw them out so he could try stuffing them. Every dead animal was worth ten minutes using Martin's train set. Mrs. Doyle began hiring me to cut the grass. She brought lemonade out to the porch, and we talked. I was a little envious of Mrs. Doyle's situation for my own mother, not so much because Mrs. Doyle seemed particularly happy as because everything in her house was in order, and I could imagine what a comfort that might be for my mother. While Mrs. Doyle and I fished, or while we were sitting out on the screened porch, I told her funny things about my four older brothers, like how when I went through the house at night I slammed the doors open. I did this in defense from my brother Norman, who hid behind them and jumped out at me. I told her how in my family when you got up from your chair you had to shout "Get my place back" or anybody could take your seat. Sometimes Norman cheated by saying whoever's older gets best dibs. Once when we were waiting for my mother at the drugstore I had to get out of the car to see if a cat I saw was dead. I said, "Get my place back," but Norman slid right over to my window and said, "Best dibs." I tried to squeeze onto the seat, but he wouldn't shove back where he belonged. He gave me his stupid grin, and I decided I'd rather walk home than give in. Our turnoff was three miles up the road, and I kept checking over my shoulder for the blue Ford. Finally I saw them coming. When they stopped to let me in I was going to make Norman shove over, but they didn't stop. They just waved.

One time, when Mrs. Doyle and I were sitting on her porch, I told her that my father's philosophy for raising boys was to put them all out in the spring and not let them in until fall.

"Sheez," Mrs. Doyle said and laughed. She had on a green blouse with no sleeves, and when she poured the lemonade I could see the edge of her brassiere.

"My mother's philosophy is just to buy all our clothes in the same size," I said. I took the glass Mrs. Doyle handed me.

"If I was in her shoes, I'd do exactly the same thing," she said. She lit a Salem and blew out the smoke. "Your mother's a saint."

"I know," I said. "Sometimes I do secret things for her. Then I wait to see if she notices."

Mrs. Doyle adjusted herself in her chair and tugged a little on her blouse. "What kinds of things?"

"Well, a couple of times I slipped peanut brittle into her top bureau drawer," I said.

Mrs. Doyle laughed.

"She's crazy for it, but you can't have it in the house or somebody eats it."

"I can believe that."

"Or sometimes I get up early and sneak into the basement and match up the socks in the clean-clothes pile."

"Oh, go on. You do that?" The ash was getting really long on her cigarette, and I thought it might fall in her lap.

"She hates to sort socks. She tries to get us to pin our pairs together when we put them in the dirty clothes, but nobody remembers."

"Isn't she surprised when she finds them?"

"She's never mentioned it," I said. The ash fell and Mrs. Doyle just brushed it onto the floor. "But she probably know it's me."

Another time, the Doyles invited me to spend the night with them at a cabin they were going to, but my parents weren't home, so I couldn't ask their permission. John was in charge, since he's the oldest, and he didn't care, so I went. Mrs. Doyle called my mother right away the next morning to tell her when they'd be bringing me home. I could hear my mother laugh at the other end. She said she hadn't even noticed one was missing. Even though I wasn't on the phone, I can hear her exact words, and I can see her standing in her blue sundress at the breakfast counter with her brown hair curling over the black receiver that she has tucked under her left ear. She's wiping toast crumbs from under the toaster when Mrs. Doyle says that part about bringing me home, and she laughs in an easy way and says that she hasn't even noticed one was missing.

My father is editor for the local paper, but mostly he likes to invent things in his workshop. He invented a wire thing on a handle, which branched out so you could roast six hot dogs at one time, and he made a kayak that was just like the kind the

Eskimos had. We're always using inventions that other kids have never even seen, and when they ask what it is and where you got it, you say, "Made it," and they just have to hope you'll let them try it. My father invented a giant slingshot out of an inner tube and a tree branch once, but we had to take it down after the first demonstration because a rock we shot hit a car. Since my father knows how to do anything, people are always calling him up for ideas or coming by to see if he has certain tools. My mother says she hopes somebody in the family will grow up discovering how to make money. I told my father that to make money you have to practice the art of management, and the art of management is learning how to get other people to do things instead of having to do them yourself. (Mr. Doyle explained it to me.) Eventually all you have to do to make money is just spend it getting other people to do stuff. My father laughed and said he was sure I was probably right. I wondered whether Mr. Doyle had practiced the art of management on Mr. Jacobs. I could tell sometimes he practiced it on Mrs. Doyle, but it didn't always work the way he wanted.

The sunfish kicked up a small splash of water and scraped the stringer alongside the boat. The Doyles' porch door slammed and I saw Mr. Doyle walk slowly down the lawn. He still had on his suit pants and a necktie, and held a drink in his hand. He stopped halfway to the shore and looked at us.

"I suppose," he called, "since you-all are so intent on your fishing, I'm going to have to cook the supper around here."

"Gawd," Mrs. Doyle said to me. "Must be his third drink already." She called back to him, "We thought you might like a swim before supper." He stood watching us. I waved at him. He didn't notice and took a drink.

"Maybe we should go in," I said.

"Wait," she said. "Don't pull up the anchor until he comes down to the dock." She called to him, "We'll bring the boat in if you want to go for a swim." He stood and watched us like he hadn't heard. I held my fishing pole. Mrs. Doyle checked her worm. The waves were catching the afternoon sun like flames spreading toward us from shore. Mr. Doyle took another swallow and crossed the lawn a few more steps. The wiener dogs came around the house and circled him, sniffed his cuffs, and ran back up the hill. He looked at the dock. Finally he started walking toward it.

I was glad when Mrs. Doyle reeled in her line. I pulled up the anchor and put the oars in. We switched seats so I could row, and he was standing on the dock when we reached it.

"Must be nice to go fishing when the rest of the world's going all to hell," he said. I wished we hadn't tried our plan to lure him down. I grabbed hold of the dock while Mrs. Doyle climbed out, and then, without looking at Mr. Doyle, I climbed over the other side of the boat into the lake and made myself busy with the moorings.

"Wouldn't you like to cool off?" she said.

He leaned against a dock post. "I come home from another day trying to save our financial ass, nothing on the table when I walk in. You, out of consideration for me, are out fishing. Right?"

"Look," she said. "If you don't want to take a dip, I'll put the food out." She looked at him and waited but he didn't answer. She picked up the fishing gear and started toward the house.

"Can't find my bathing suit," he said.

She stopped and frowned at him. "Did you check the bathroom door?"

"Oh," he said. "I get it. You didn't have an opening in your busy schedule to straighten up the house?"

She sagged her shoulders and shook her head. "Willis?" He didn't say anything. He looked at me. I retied the rope on the boat.

"How's the water, Sambo?" he said.

"Good." I worked on my knot.

Then she said, "I'll go get it." She started toward the house again, but he kicked off his shoes. He walked up the dock toward shore and stepped off into ankle-deep water. "That's one of your best suits!" she said.

"It's a bathing suit now," he said. He drained his glass and tossed it onto the lawn. He stretched his arms, faking a dive, and looked at me. "Ready to swim, Sammy?"

Sometimes he says things in a way that makes it seem like you're taking sides when you aren't. I looked at Mrs. Doyle to see what she was going to do. She gave me a "what now" look and put down her stuff.

"O. K.," I said to him. I turned and looked down the shore toward our place. I could make out two of my brothers and my mother. She sat on the dock with her legs in the water, facing our direction.

Mr. Doyle put his hands on his hips and peered into the water. He began whistling to himself and taking small steps into deeper water. The wet ran higher up his pants with every step. I walked out until it was over my waist and then went under and stood on my hands with my feet in the air. When I came up, Mr. Doyle was in to his knees. I watched him lie back and let the lake sweep over his tie and dress shirt. He isn't a strong swimmer, and I could tell he was crab-walking on his hands, trying to make it look like he was swimming.

Mrs. Doyle got an air mattress from shore and walked it into the water. She launched herself on it toward Mr. Doyle. He made a grab for it and tipped her off. "Hey!" she said. He got on the mattress on his stomach and made funny little duck motions with his hands and feet. His white shirt looked pink, and you could see he had a hairy back. The long hair he combs over his bald spot hung down his cheek. His black socks were half off his feet and flopped when he kicked. I said maybe we should have some kind of contest, but Mrs. Doyle grabbed the edge of the air mattress and tried to tip Mr. Doyle off. He was too heavy. He backed away from her and she reached for his tie. "There!" she said, and began to tow him by the neck toward deeper water. She's a good swimmer. "Look what I caught, Samuel!" At first he squirmed and tried to splash her. Then he grabbed his tie and tried to pull it free. She laughed and kicked at the air mattress, and he had to let go of the tie to catch his balance. Then they were in the weeds.

"Not in the weeds! God damn it, Louise!" He got one leg on each side of the mattress the way you sit on a horse, but it folded in the middle and he had to lean forward because she still had a hold of his tie. They stayed that way for a minute, breathing hard, and she worked her legs and free hand to stay afloat.

"Samuel!" she called. "I got a big one. Help me land him!" Then she jerked the tie. All of a sudden Mr. Doyle turned over and went under.

"Willis!" She lost hold of the tie. "Willis!"

The mattress popped free and began to drift away. I swam to catch it. By now they were at the edge of the drop-off. I pushed the mattress to Mr. Doyle and he flopped an arm over it. His hair was in his eyes but he didn't wipe it clear. He coughed and breathed hard. Mrs. Doyle grabbed the other side and panted, too, and I hung on to the end.

They watched each other.

He tried to loosen his necktie. A breeze blew up and I kicked my legs to try to move us toward shallower water. I looked down the shore toward our beach. Now I could make out my entire family, including my father. Some of them were in the water and the others were on the dock, and it seemed they were all looking at something on the dock. I wondered what.

Mr. Doyle got his tie loose enough to pull it over his head, and at that moment Mrs. Doyle made a lunge and yanked the mattress under her. "Hah!" she said between breaths. Mr. Doyle had to let his tie float off.

"Haven't had enough?" he said. He grabbed her feet and started kicking the mattress further out. His socks were gone, and he made small grunting noises as he worked.

"Think we should go in now?" I said. Mr. Doyle pushed over the drop-off and kept working his wife into deeper water, helped by the breeze. I called after them, "This way," but they didn't look around. I treaded water. I heard barking and turned and there were the dogs on shore all excited about the Doyles' being so far out.

I raised my arms and began to sink. I leaked out my air and let myself fall free in the way I like to do. Silence flooded my ears and my feet fell ahead into the cool dark layers, and I let myself hang there until I was starved for air. Then I swept my arms down hard and pulled toward the light and at the very last possible moment pushed my head through the water's silver skin and grabbed air, rolled over and blew some bubbles and thought about Mr. Doyle. I wondered why he was kicking out so deep. Probably so Mrs. Doyle would be forced to stop messing around. I didn't know, and I let myself slip under again and turn like a slow question to aim along the edge of the drop-off toward our place. I stretched my arms ahead of me and swam with my eyes open. I hooked my thumbs together and flattened my hands like fins. With a turn of my wrists I could swim up or down, left or right, and I thought that the thing about water I liked most was how it always makes a place for you. When you sink it opens below and closes above, so smooth you don't know it's happening, and once you're under, nobody knows where.

I surfaced and looked back. Mr. Doyle was lying on the mattress with his legs crossed and his hands tucked under his head for comfort. He was pushing water through his teeth in small jets the way I sometimes do, and Mrs. Doyle was swimming behind and shoving him slowly over the weeds and in to shore. I slipped under again. I was thinking that if I steered myself in through the weeds and sneaked my breaths in quiet breaks I could return to my family undetected. If I surfaced under the dock and listened carefully to what they were talking about, I could say something remarkable and make them laugh.

Lisa Lenzo

Stealing Trees

We started stealing trees after the elms were dead and gone, when the city planted a twig in front of Frank's house. The twig had no branches and no leaves. It was as thin as a car antenna. From Frank's front stoop at dusk it was invisible.

So Frank and I started driving around at night and stealing thicker, bigger saplings, ones with branches and lots of leaves. We'd dig them up from the better neighborhoods in northwest Detroit, dump them into the trunk of Frank's Fairlane, and replant them on Frank's front lawn.

Frank refused to call what we did stealing; he was always correcting me: "Tree relocation, Stanley. The 57 Farrand Street Tree Relocation Project."

We could plant the trees at Frank's house because Frank's mother didn't live there and Frank's father never noticed what we did. Mr. Chimek played cello with the Detroit Symphony, and when he wasn't in concert he was upstairs in one of his rooms, either practicing music or listening to it. Occasionally he'd wander downstairs and fry himself some eggs, then go back up without turning the burner off. I can still picture him leaving the house for a concert: dressed in his black suit, white hair springing out of place, walking past the trees without turning his head. I lived five blocks over from Frank, and since my mother never passed by the Chimeks' house, she never saw our accumulating collection of stolen trees.

I suggested to Frank that we stop stealing trees after we'd bagged and replanted a half dozen. But Frank pointed out that stealing trees was less degenerate than setting tires on fire and rolling them down the ramp of the underground parking lot at Farrand and Woodward, something we used to do all the time in junior high. And by relocating lots of trees onto his front lawn, Frank said, and sneaking a few onto the lawns of our neighbors, we were helping to restore our city's reputation and name: "Highland Park, City of Trees."

We used to watch for the signs with these words—stamped in a circle around a tree silhouette—when we were little kids coming home from Detroit; crossing over the Highland Park border, we'd shout, "*Now* we're in Highland Park!"

In those days, the elms formed a ceiling of leaves a hundred feet up from Highland Park's streets. I didn't notice the leaves over my head as I grew older any more than people notice the ceilings of their houses. But when I was a little kid I used to look up past all the space to where the layers of green began, and watch the breeze stirring the leaves and imagine myself up there.

Ten years later, there wasn't a branch or leaf left in all of Highland Park's sky, but the signs were still standing. We watched for them on our way home from stealing trees, and though we still spoke out when we crossed over the border, our voices were quieter and our emphasis had changed. Most of the time we'd be smoking a joint or a pipe. "Now we're in *High*land Park," we'd say. "City of *Stolen* Trees," I'd sometimes add.

"Relocated trees, Stanley," Frank would insist.

Daytimes that summer, Frank and I worked at the rag factory at Woodward and Cortland, cutting up new rags and washing and drying old ones for the guys at Chrysler. Evenings we played basketball with Frank's neighbors, usually quitting when it got dark, but when we felt like it playing on into the night using the light Frank had rigged on his garage. (The guys we played with said Frank should turn the light off and just use himself as a bulb, he was so pale—blond-white hair, moon-white skin—that he almost glowed in the dark. They didn't comment on my whiteness, except for once when I was sunburned, and Dwight

Bates fouled me and I cried out, and Dwight said he thought all the tender white people had moved out of Highland Park.)

Besides stealing trees and playing ball, another thing we did at night that summer was sit around while Carol Baker corn-rowed Frank's head. Cornrowing was big then, but just among black people. This was before Bo Derek.

I'd sit on Frank's porch and watch Carol working through Frank's hair, and listen to her fuss and scold and threaten to slap Frank if he didn't hold still. As Carol got close to finishing, she'd swear she'd never braid such a fine-haired jumpity fool ever again. But Carol braided Frank every week all that summer, and whenever she went to slap him, her palm landed so lightly it was more like a stroke. Frank would reach up and take hold of Carol's hand, and Carol would pull away and threaten Frank some more. Frank just smiled and fingered his braids. He liked being fussed over, and the tight, close, pale braids kept his hair out of his face, which was perfect for playing basketball, and for stealing trees.

In August of that summer, Frank's father had a heart attack and died. Frank and I found him on the floor of his practice room with his tiger-necked cello lying beside him. My mom said Frank could come stay with us for a year—we had one year of high school to go—but Frank wanted to stay where he was. He'd lived in that house all his life.

Two weeks after Mr. Chimek's funeral, Frank decided that we should steal a tree from downtown. He had seen its picture in the paper next to an article about the new Blue Cross build-ing. The tree stood out in the foreground of the picture, a dome-shaped, leafy maple. So far we had stolen only locusts and oaks, the main kinds of trees being planted back then. The maple looked almost too big to steal, but we decided to check it out in person.

First we smoked some marijuana. Then we drove downtown. The maple looked even better in real life. Its hundreds of leaves were perfect and huge, and it looked as if its branches had been set in their upward, outward curves with a whole lot of planning and expertise. But there were too many cops cruising around down there—they never gave us a clean opening. At two o'clock in the morning we got on the Chrysler again, lit another pipe, and headed north, back toward Highland Park.

We hadn't gone a mile when Frank spotted the tree of heaven on the freeway slope. Later, planting the tree on his lawn, Frank said, "I've thought of another name for our project: The Otto Chimek Memorial Grove." But when he first saw the tree of heaven, Frank didn't mention his father—he didn't say anything at all—just pulled over onto the shoulder and looked at me with his high, shining eyes.

"What are you doing?" I said.

Frank pointed at the tree.

"What?" I said. "You want that tree?"

It wasn't the best-looking tree even from the car. Just your typical ghetto tree, that grows anywhere at all, but mostly in vacant lots and from between sidewalk cracks. Not the kind of tree that anyone plants, let alone steals. I looked at it, branches angling downwards like palm fronds, then at the green sign hanging from the freeway overpass just ahead: MACK ½ MILE. On our trips between downtown and Highland Park, we had seen the sign plenty of times, but we hadn't even thought of stopping here before. This was part of the city where black people didn't stop unless they knew someone who lived here, and white people didn't stop here at all.

The tree was growing close enough to the overpass that if a car crossed overhead we could hide below, and if a car came down the freeway, we could scramble up on top of the overpass. I tried not to think about what we would do if cars came by both places at the same time.

Frank pulled on the hood of his black sweatshirt and tucked handfuls of his long braids inside the hood until none of the dozens of plaits showed. I pulled on my black baseball cap. Then we got out of the Fairlane and started up the grassy slope.

Old, dry litter cracked like glass under our feet. I looked at the overpass to my left and felt like I was on another planet. All my life I'd seen freeway embankments and overpasses, but never from this angle, the overpass at eye level, the embankment slanting under our feet, nothing between the overpass and us, nothing between the grass and us, but the cool night air. Standing on that hill made the whole world seem tipped and slanted—it seemed like the world had been set on its edge.

I spread the garbage bag beside the tree. Frank pushed the shovel in to its hilt eight times, cutting a circle around the skinny trunk. He had just got the roots separated into their own private clump when we heard a raggedy car in the distance, up on street level.

Suddenly it seemed a bad idea to duck under the overpass. It came to me that every movie that ended badly had people getting wasted in closed-in, concrete places. Frank and I glanced at each other. Then he ditched the shovel and I dropped the bag, and we ran the rest of the way up the slope, and jumped out on the service drive and started walking along it as if we had not just run up there from the expressway canyon.

Soon we heard the raggedy car, or at least a raggedy car, approaching from behind us. We forced our breathing slow, tried to loosen our legs and shoulders. The car drew closer, and then alongside us. We turned our heads toward the car but kept walking. The driver, black as the car's upholstery, leaned his head out the window. "Can you please tell us how to get to the corner of Russell and Pearl?" he asked, his voice a perfect imitation of a prissy white man's. Four or five others inside the car laughed. All of them were black. At least one was a girl.

Frank smiled in the direction of the carload of people, trying to act as if he were relaxed enough to think their joking funny. He kept walking. I kept step with him, wondering where we were going. We were getting farther from our car.

"You boys lost?" someone from the back seat asked.

"No," Frank said.

"Oh yeah?" the driver said, sounding black this time, "You sure look lost." More laughter came from the others.

Frank glanced at the driver. "Yeah, I know we do," he admitted, just the right amount of blackness creeping into his voice— enough to let them hear that he was not a total outsider, but not so much that he seemed to be making any sort of claim. We still kept walking, but we didn't say anything more. It was better to say too little than to say something wrong.

"Where you boys from?" the driver asked.

This time Frank didn't answer.

I steadied my breathing. "Highland Park," I said carefully, trying to sound offhand and matter-of-fact, as if I didn't expect my answer to boost their opinion of us.

The girl shrilled something wordless from the back seat.

"Highland Park!" the driver said. "They let you boys stay in Highland Park?"

"For now, I guess," I said.

The driver eyed me more closely. Then he laughed—almost a friendly laugh—his lips breaking wide. He looked to be about twenty years old. He was wearing a light brown shirt zipped open at his throat. "And where you going later, man, when you got to move?"

"I don't know—*Romulus,* or somewhere," I said, with true dejection at the prospect. I'd never seen Romulus, but I had it pictured as rows of dirty white shoebox houses that collapsed when the jets flew overhead.

"*Romulus,*" someone from the back seat said. "Where the fuck is *Romulus?*"

"I know where Romulus is," the driver said. He jabbed his finger in the air. "Shit, you got to move, man, don't move to Romulus. The whites out there so mean they don't even like whites."

"If I was white," the man in the passenger seat said, "I'd move to Grosse Pointe, Bloomfield Hills, somethin' like that."

"If you was white," one of the men in the back seat said. "Listen to the nigger: 'If I was white.'"

The three in the back seat laughed loudly and easily. I let myself smile, but kept my own crazy laughter down in my belly.

"I got one other question to ask you," the driver said. The laughter stopped. I could feel all the ground I thought we'd gained slipping away from us. "Why was you digging up that tree?"

The trouble that had been floating around grew bigger and clearer, pressed at the quiet. My vision started shrinking inwards, I couldn't focus, I could hardly see. I didn't look at Frank or at the driver or anywhere.

"I know there's plenty of them raggedy trees in Highland Park," the driver said. "So what I want to know is, what do two white boys from Highland Park want with a tree that's as common there as dirt? I mean, that tree is as common in Highland Park as niggers are, am I right?"

"We've been digging up all kinds of trees, from northwest Detroit, mostly, and planting them in front of his house," I said, glancing at Frank. Frank was looking down at the pavement.

"You boys really are lost," the driver said. "This is not northwest Detroit."

Frank kept on looking down. I couldn't see his eyes. Frank! I thought, Do something! Save us! Frank had a way of winning people over to him, sometimes without saying a word. Too bad this wasn't a carload of old people or women or girls. But even among the guys at school Frank was well-liked, for a white person.

I thought of letting the men in the car know that Frank's father had just died. I thought of letting on somehow that he'd died just last week, just last night. But as soon as I thought of it, I knew it would be a mistake to bring up that subject at all.

"I don't think you boys really are from Highland Park," the driver said. "I think you're from one of them suburbs where they let the raggedy white folks live. Taylor, maybe. Or Romulus."

I thought of ways to refute this—name all the streets in Highland Park, show the eraser-burn tattoos our sixth-grade classmates had rubbed into our shoulders, at our request. But I thought that eraser-burn tattoos might be a Highland Park black thing rather than a black thing in general, and my and Frank's tattoos wouldn't have shown up that well anyway in the dark, being white on white.

In fourth grade, when our school was just about half black, the black kids in our class made plans to build a spaceship and fly to the moon, blowing up the earth as they left. They talked about it one day while the teacher was out of the room, said they wouldn't save a thing on earth except the people they took with them, and started calling off the passenger list. They named all of the black kids in the room, and then one of them said, "And Frank Chimek." "Yeah!" another boy said, "Frank Chimek is cool." After talking it over a little, they added my name, too—Frank and I were the only two white people on earth they thought deserved to be saved.

But of course I couldn't say this to those men in the car. I thought of all the times I'd wanted to convince someone of something—convince a girl that I was the guy for her, or a teacher that my excuse was really real, or some guys that wanted to beat me that I didn't deserve to be beaten.

The driver said something about taking us back to the tree.

A deep voice from the back seat called out, "What you going to do with 'em, blood, lynch 'em?" The whole group laughed hysterically. I couldn't help smiling, though it felt like the smile of a crazy man.

"Let's lynch them *and* that sorry-ass tree," another voice from the back said. "Hang 'em all three from the overpass."

The driver waited until the laughter died. "I don't like white boys stealing niggers' trees," he said, "no matter how sorry the trees is, or the boys. Y'all move over and make room for these boys."

There was movement inside the car. A door clicked open. I jerked as if the click had come from a knife or gun, and I guess Frank must have moved too. "Wait! Wait!" someone screeched. It was the girl. She scrambled forward so that her wide face and thick, round arms leaned over the front seat. "Take off your hood," she said to Frank.

Frank looked up from the street with that distant expression people and dogs wear just before they get beaten. "Fool!" the girl said, slapping at someone in the back seat. "Don't be pulling on me. Take off your hood," she repeated.

Frank looked at the driver.

"Go on," he said.

Frank untied the string and pushed the hood back, and his blond braids unfolded and fell all around him.

"I knew it!" the girl crowed. "They told me white folks couldn't do their hair like that, but I knew y'all could, I knew it. Come here—let me see."

Frank didn't move. He just stood there with his braids lying in lines against his scalp, snaking down around his shoulders, practically glowing in the dark.

"Damn, boy," the driver said, "did you get dunked in a tub of bleach?"

"Maybe he's an albino," the girl said. "Maybe he's really black." She and the man sitting in the passenger seat started arguing.

"C'mon, woman—a white black man? Give me a break."

"I saw a black albino once, man, in my social studies book. It was a purely white black man."

"Girl, you're talkin' about an oreo."

"I'm talkin' about an albino—don't you know what an albino is?"

"Why don't y'all stop talking stupid?" the driver said. "The man is obviously white."

"For real," the deep-voiced man agreed, "he's some kind of white freak."

"Naw," another man from the back said, "he just wants to be black."

"Is that it, man?" the driver said to Frank. "Do you wish you was black?" Everyone in the car looked at Frank.

Frank lifted his head, his blond braids tilting back, and looked at all the faces looking at him. "Right now I do," he said simply, his face serious, but hardly afraid, a hint of pleasure at his joke showing around his mouth and in his eyes.

The men in the car laughed suddenly, with surprise. "'Right now I do,'" one of them repeated, and everyone laughed harder, with the deep-voiced man saying "No shit! No shit!" over and over and between the laughter of the others.

When the laughter finally stopped, there was a floating sort of pause, like when you're standing on a teeter-totter with both ends off the ground. The driver said something to the others that I didn't quite hear—"Let's go," or, "Let them go." Then he turned back to Frank. "I don't know why in hell you want that tree, man," he said, "but if you still want it, go on and take it— then take your crazy asses back home to Highland Park or wherever it is you're from before you run into some mean niggers or the police. And next time you want to steal a tree, go on out to Grosse Pointe or Bloomfield Hills and steal yourself a nice *white* tree, something like a *pine* tree, all right?"

"All right," Frank said.

The driver spat out the window. The car rumbled off. Frank and I walked, fast, back to the freeway slope, and lifted the tree of heaven into the garbage bag. Then we walked down the slanting ground holding the bagged tree between us, checking the wide, grey freeway for cars.

The huge overpasses on either side were suspended at our level. We were leaning back against the pull of the slope, taking big strides. It felt like we were traveling between planets, like we were walking down from the sky. It felt like we were aliens— aliens in both worlds. But at least the world we were heading toward was home.

The Heart's Quest

In the presence of love, hearth and quest become one.

JEANETTE WINTERSON

This feels . . . like a much different love, an intimacy I've strained for but never quite reached before, as though some pieces of myself . . . had been discovered and restored. The "always" feeling, I call it. The movement from home into home.

NANCY MAIRS

MIRIAM LEVINE

Two Houses

I

The light at 31 Harwich Street was a miracle. There was nothing to block it. The two big deep-silled kitchen windows, which rattled in any kind of wind, looked out over the tiny trashy backyard and across the tracks of Back Bay station to the sloping roof of the armory. In bad weather, gulls would wheel in from the harbor and down the Charles River to hunch on the armory's long copper-flashed ridge. In early afternoon, a clear cool light washed in across the low nineteenth-century houses of the Back Bay. At those times, the kitchen was bright and shadowless. The previous tenant, a painter, had used the kitchen for his studio. Later, as the sun dropped, a rosy, then a wild red and gold light would shoot through the windows. The room lit up and seemed to float in another element. The woodwork seemed even heavier and the walls porous. I knew that the light was coming through the windows, but it seemed as if the brightness were actually penetrating the walls' secret invisible mesh.

For brief moments, inner life and outer life came together. It was enough to sit at the small bench-like table and watch the room fill and then gradually darken. I would feel the cool white coffee mug—I bought it for its thick heavy bottom—and I would experience a brief absolute clarity of sensation and peace.

The New England transcendentalists might have said that I was experiencing heaven's light. Emerson believed, "The sky was the daily bread of the eye." Thoreau preferred reflected blue—not these wild sunset reds and yellows—which gathered in the hollows in deep snow around Walden Pond.

The commuter trains would roar into Back Bay Station at dusk. Watching strangers get off and on—I could barely see their faces—I would feel I was sending them off like a friendly spy. In those brief moments, I wasn't lonely. Time stretched out, and there was plenty of time.

There were only three buildings left on Harwich Street in the sixties. The tight nineteenth-century row-houses, which formerly lined the block, had been knocked down, and the rubble cleared for a parking lot. I'm sure the demolition had undermined the remaining houses. The angles at Number 31 were so out of plumb that a friend told me he could never live there: it would make him dizzy. The stairs, which led to my second-floor apartment, leaned like a ship's stairs in bad weather, so although you were walking up, you were also leaning left, away from the wall. There was also a geological feel to it, but I never felt that things would spring apart. The shift had occurred, and the house seemed to be holding. In fact, it held until the wrecker's ball crashed through the walls in 1986.

31 Harwich Street house had been built around 1850 and, with the quick slump of Boston's South End before the end of the century, converted into three flats. The shallow black soapstone kitchen sink, its beveled edges cleanly cut like shelving, dated from that first renovation. Water turned the stone a darker slippery black. The brass faucets and copper pipes were stapled to a wide splashboard nailed above the sink.

I painted the one flimsy kitchen cabinet a terra-cotta brown, and repainted the walls in the same startling, uncompromising, flat white the painter had used. For the floor, I splurged on a bright "Daffodil Yellow." The tinder-dry boards soaked up paint, and even though I had laid on coat after coat—it took gallons—the pattern of the grain still showed through. There were wide gaps between the wide pine boards. The dark cracks, which would quickly fill with wooly matted dust, leapt out against the freshly painted floor. The kitchen was just large enough, so that if you looked down its length the floorboards seemed to narrow like railroad tracks in a perspective lesson.

The bathroom door, which was next to the soapstone sink, was usually open, making the view into the bathroom part of the kitchen scene. The massive claw-footed tub, big as a bed, bulked against the toilet. Because the floor tilted so wildly, the tub looked as if it would break loose from its moorings and smash the toilet like a tea-cup.

I was already spending a lot of time with John; we would marry in 1964. When he stayed over, he would sometimes soak in the big tub while I made breakfast. The door would usually be open. As I worked, I could see him in the steam, his damp head and bare wet shoulders resting against the sloping end of the tub. There was plenty of hot water, scalding water, in fact. We would eat mushroom omelettes—canned mushrooms were the most exotic item on my grocery shelf. I'd make coffee in a cheap aluminum drip pot, which I kept warm on a trivet placed over the gas burner.

Except for an old solid-chrome Sunbeam toaster bought second-hand, I had no electric appliances, and no t.v. They wouldn't have worked: the house ran on DC. (The refrigerator was on gas.) Electricity had been brought in around the time of the First World War, and the original wiring had never been changed. I was literally on a different current from most of Boston.

The landlord, Aaron Smith, who was black, lived just under me in the first-floor apartment. "You can do whatever you want," he said, "as long as there's no police." He was deaf as a post, and we communicated mostly through notes. His were formal: "Your note of even date enclosing check in payment of Sept. rent rec'd. I thank you and herewith enclose receipt for same." Before I left on a trip to Maine, he wrote: "I trust you will enjoy with much luck the fishing expedition to Northern Maine." (His epistolary style reminded me of my mother's, whose letters to me usually began, "Received your lovely missive.")

We never used first names with each other. When we passed in the hall, I would shout, "Hello, Mr. Smith," and murmuring, "Miss Levine," he would touch his hat, a beautiful pale gray fedora, carefully blocked, the fine nap smoothly brushed.

Over the black marble mantel, in what had formerly been the back-parlor and was now his kitchen, hung a large gilt-framed lithograph portrait of Abraham Lincoln. Mr. Smith voted Republican—Lincoln's party. The dusty heaped-up room, the clean pearly lithograph, each line like a dark gray hair, seemed encased in the must of another age.

Mr. Smith worked as a messenger for a Yankee business downtown. A friend said that Mr. Smith was a "house nigger." He had worked for white people too long. I didn't see him that way. He wasn't servile. He had style, Boston style. What else could it have been? He wasn't from down home.

When I knew him, he was already in his seventies, and there was something antique about his dress. He wore dark three-piece suits, which looked sculptured, and which seemed to gather their own atmosphere like the micro-climate around a plant. His stiff white shirts were immaculate, though a little worn. His ties were discreet, flecked with tiny nubs of gold or dark red. A gold watch chain looped across his midriff.

Mr. Smith stood very straight. He had the carriage of a much younger man, though sometimes, when I saw him coming down Harwich Street after work, I noticed he was moving very slowly. At those times he looked his age, bony instead of thin and wiry, and his magnificently constructed suit hung too loosely on the straight pole of his spine.

Mr. Smith was remote. That he was black and I was white must have been partly responsible for our shyness, yet I am sure he was solitary by nature. His deafness locked him in, but it had been his choice not to marry. He lived with his German shepherd, Blackie. Mr. Smith was correct, but not outwardly affectionate with the dog. They were like army friends of different ranks.

He had a nephew who would visit, usually on a Sunday afternoon or evening, and he had a girlfriend, who came occasionally to have dinner with him, a youngish woman with red hair, very light yellow skin, and bright make-up. I could hear her shouted conversation through the floorboards, and beneath her shouts—mostly about the food—his low speech, the words just out of my hearing. There was an habitual though loose formality to all of these meetings. Always they discussed the same things, as if to reassure each other. Or rather, she did. She had to work very hard to make Mr. Smith hear her. Sometimes, unavoidably I suppose, she sounded as if she were speaking to a dumb child.

Daily at B.U., where I was a student, I entered the "spiritual-heroic refrigerating apparatus." Sometimes it was thrilling. At home on Harwich Street, I would listen to the comforting minutiae of daily life. In one of his novels, Philip Roth has a young English instructor who would become a writer heroically correcting papers, his pencils sharpened, his mind clear. Control and order: he loves them. There's a different way to tell my story. The woman I once was sat in her kitchen. The faucet dripped. Mr. Smith's girlfriend asked again about the doneness of the roast beef, then it was, "He said . . . she said . . . Do you know what?" I lifted my book, a great book, and took my notes. I stopped and listened to the voices rising through the floorboards. I made myself a cup of coffee. Some water spilled on the stove. Sometimes I would hear a voice in my book, not exactly the language of souls, but a human voice, which seemed to come through time still in its flesh case; the words were flesh: I repeated them.

In our brief encounters in the dimly-lit hall, Mr. Smith was imposing. His reserve was monumental, almost taciturn. He was so like the immigrant men I had seen in photographs—my own grandfather, dressed in the same correct way, staring at the camera, his body stiff and slim, yet worn, a body that at one time had been worked too hard.

Mr. Smith's eyes advanced and retreated; there was a lot of pupil, a lot of burnt-out darkness, and also a smouldering light.

44

They were both full and vacant, both alert and exhausted—the
eyes of Poles at Ellis Island, the eyes of conquered Indians posed
in ceremonial dress, the eyes of Chinese railroad workers in the
American west staring at the camera. I never saw him smile.

Every night he would turn on Jerry Williams. (Williams is still
on Boston radio. His campaign against the seat-belt law, which
he said was fascistic, was responsible for its repeal. The other
day I heard him questioning a caller, "So you want mandatory
testing for AIDS? Let's just run right out and test every person
who wears an earring. Is that what you want? How about every
black baby? Is that what you want?") Mr. Smith's radio was
very loud. The bombastic hectoring voice of the popular talk-
show host would fill my apartment: Boston parking, civil rights.
For an hour, Mr. Smith and I would get some news of the world.

II

The two second-floor bedrooms of the house at 207 State Street
in Framingham were in the low wing, which had been added to
the older main house around 1830. The owners lived in the
older part of the house, and my husband John and I rented the
apartment, which had been created in the addition. The larger of
the two bedrooms, where John and I slept, was tucked under a
low ceiling, which slanted to meet two pairs of square eight-over-
eight windows. The windows faced each other like mirrors, or
pictures in a gallery. The sills were barely a foot above the floor.
The back windows, which faced southwest, were hot and bright,
the front-facing windows cool and pale. We put our bed between the front windows and faced the warmer light.

The huge headboard of the brass bed, which we bought from
our Yankee landlady, curved between two high bedposts like
a fabulous harp. The posts were square, rather than the usual
round columns, and gave the whole thing a neo-classical air. The
bed weighed a ton. The side-pieces reminded me of thick-gauge
railroad tracks. Yet with the harp-like or loom-like headboard
and footboard, the bed seemed about to float, to be just held
down by the sloping eaves.

We had rented in Framingham because I had just taken a teaching job at the state college, a block up the street. The house had belonged to the landlady's father. "We don't want any wild drinking parties," she said as we signed the lease. "They're teachers," her husband responded reassuringly. We were silent.

We had just come home from a year traveling across Europe. After living out of suitcases, suddenly we were owners, not only of the stupendous marriage bed, but also of a very white refrigerator and a washing machine. We understood that if you rented a place without these things, you had to buy them—Framingham was not a laundromat town—but we were dazed by the rapidity with which these heavy objects arrived. My husband's aunt gave us a rose-colored hooked rug for our pale blue bedroom, my parents gave us a blue velvet chair.

We did like the house, six rooms—more space than we'd ever had, paneled doors, and rustically delicate proportions measured out by a carpenter whose intelligent eye you could still feel.

The house had been done over before we moved in: the woodwork gleamed with good white oil paint, the floors shone. They had even had the windows washed. All that cleanliness could not obscure the oddness of the rooms, the way our bedroom lofted up against the ceiling, but was rescued from any sense of cramping by the four surprisingly generous windows—Yankees pouring out four glasses of delicious sherry, just one for each guest, our tight-lipped landlady lacing her baked beans with strong black molasses.

In a year I was pregnant. A month before I had bought a pants suit, dark green corduroy. The cut was slim, boyish, like a riding suit. How quickly the waist became too tight to button. Life was just happening. Although I wanted this child, the daily nausea of morning sickness made me feel unmoored and afraid. Even so I was stoical. I would eat a few dry crackers in bed before getting up. They would dull the nausea and I would go to work.

Our son David was born on May 1. He slept in the small second bedroom, which opened off our room. From my bed, I could see him in his crib a step or two away. He'd cry and I'd gather him up while my John slept. First I'd change his wet diaper—his legs were so thin, they looked like loose keys in gigantic white keyholes—then I'd nurse him; he'd suck and fall asleep, and I'd tuck him back in. The first night I accomplished this, I was elated. Sometimes I would bring him into bed with me and nurse him propped against the incredible headboard.

John, after hearing stories of babies being smothered in their parents' beds, dreamt that David had fallen asleep between us, and that he had carried him back to his crib. John woke up from the dream, bending over the crib holding a pillow, which he believed was the baby. He then became more frightened. "Suppose I didn't wake up, suppose I put the pillow down over him and went back to bed?" "But that didn't happen," I answered.

David thrived. One, two, three months passed. He woke less often. Two in the morning, then three, then four. Just before the first dawn light it is absolutely black. I'd wake to his signaling cry and stumble into blackness. I'd turn on the small light in his room. The light slipped like a heavy drawer through the door into the big bedroom, a sharp-angled slant across our bed. Just over the line, my husband slept in half-darkness.

Our nights were peaceful, but once, during the day, I had been downstairs working when David woke crying from his nap. I had left him too long. He had thrashed so that he had rubbed sore spots on his soft-boned fingers. I was horrified.

The cool nights of May and June when he had needed a light blanket were soon gone. Now when I picked him up, his new close dark hair, which grew through the gold down he had been born with, would often be damp, pressed against his head like wet fern. By then we were used to each other. He knew the sound of my rasping off-key songs.

By September he was regularly sleeping through the night, waking by six, sometimes by five. Our night scene changed. I would usually put him to bed by nine and get into bed myself. I'd leave the door to his room open, turn on the lamp next to my bed and read. He would fall asleep with his delightful round face turned toward the light. He saw me there composed, my then long dark hair spread on the pillow, my absorbed downward glance, my now familiar face. The light from the small blue and white lamp shone in a yellow circle; the headboard gleamed dully. The phone next to the bed was still. My friends reached me in the morning. Very little disturbed that votive half-hour, when gazing toward the light he fell asleep. "The Reading Madonna" was a title that could have described the scene.

There was a stack of books next to the lamp, a notebook. I relaxed against the pillows, and felt I was gently putting myself on view—like a living icon. It was a little like acting, mastering a technique, but at the same time my heart was loving. He fell asleep so quickly this way, in an instant. I didn't worry about his becoming too attached—Robert Frost was the only person I had ever heard of—besides peasants—who at sixteen was still sleeping in his mother's room.

So we had a moment of balance, my son and I. The rope that bound us became very light, invisible as an eye-beam. Seeing his face turned toward me in trust as he drifted off so easily into darkness made me understand myself: I was restless for adult words. There was the sound of turning pages. In those moments I was there for him, and not there.

Outside the walls of that low-ceilinged room, the night was thick and immense. There seemed to be nothing but that room. The windows were black. We could have been inside a cave. The bed might have been part of a theatrical dream-set. A bed and an altar both. The mystery of images: how potent they were. You could be a carrier, even a creator of images, and yet not be the thing you created, not completely.

And what about the rapt believer falling asleep with his face turned toward the light and my face? Perhaps, after years, he would learn that you could be more than one thing.

48

ANNICK SMITH

It's Come to This

No horses. That's how it always starts. I am coming down the meadow, the first snow of September whipping around my boots, and there are no horses to greet me. The first thing I did after Caleb died was get rid of the horses.

"I don't care how much," I told the auctioneer at the Missoula Livestock Company. He looked at me slant-eyed from under his Stetson. "Just don't let the canneries take them." Then I walked away.

What I did not tell him was I couldn't stand the sight of those horses on our meadow, so heedless, grown fat and untended. They reminded me of days when Montana seemed open as the sky.

Now that the horses are gone I am more desolate then ever. If you add one loss to another, what you have is double zip. I am wet to the waist, water sloshing ankle-deep inside my irrigating boots. My toes are numb, my chapped hands are burning from the cold, and down by the gate my dogs are barking at a strange man in a red log truck.

That's how I meet Frank. He is hauling logs down from the Champion timberlands above my place, across the right-of-way I sold to the company after my husband's death. The taxes were piling up. I sold the right-of-way because I would not sell my land. Kids will grow up and leave you, but land is something a woman can hold onto.

I don't like those log trucks rumbling by my house, scattering chickens, tempting my dogs to chase behind their wheels, kicking clouds of dust so thick the grass looks brown and dead.

There's nothing I like about logging. It breaks my heart to walk among newly cut limbs, to be enveloped in the sharp odor of sap running like blood. After twenty years on this place, I still cringe at the snap and crash of five-hundred-year-old pines and the far-off screaming of saws.

Anyway, Frank pulls his gyppo logging rig to a stop just past my house in order to open the blue metal gate that separates our outbuildings from the pasture, and while he is at it, he adjusts the chains holding his load. My three mutts take after him as if they are real watchdogs and he stands at the door of the battered red cab holding his hands to his face and pretending to be scared.

"I would surely appreciate it if you'd call off them dogs," says Frank, as if those puppies weren't wagging their tails and jumping up to be patted.

He can see I am shivering and soaked. And I am mad. If I had a gun, I might shoot him.

"You ought to be ashamed . . . a man like you."

"Frank Bowman," he says, grinning and holding out his large thick hand. "From Bowman Corners." Bowman Corners is just down the road.

"What happened to you?" he grins. "Take a shower in your boots?"

How can you stay mad at that man? A man who looks at you and makes you look at yourself. I should have known better. I should have waited for my boys to come home from football practice and help me lift the heavy wet boards in our diversion dam. But my old wooden flume was running full and I was determined to do what had to be done before dark, to be a true country woman like the pioneers I read about as a daydreaming child in Chicago, so long ago it seems another person's life.

"I had to shut off the water," I say. "Before it freezes." Frank nods, as if this explanation explains everything.

Months later I would tell him about Caleb. How he took care of the wooden flume, which was built almost one hundred years ago by his Swedish ancestors. The snaking plank trough crawls up and around a steep slope of igneous rock. It has been patched and rebuilt by generations of hard-handed, blue-eyed Petersons until it reached its present state of tenuous mortality. We open the floodgate in June when Bear Creek is high with snowmelt, and the flume runs full all summer, irrigating our hay meadow of timothy and wild mountain grasses. Each fall, before the first hard freeze, we close the diversion gates and the creek flows in its natural bed down to the Big Blackfoot River.

That's why I'd been standing in the icy creek, hefting six-foot two-by-twelves into the slotted brace that forms the dam. The bottom board was waterlogged and coated with green slime. It slipped in my bare hands and I sat down with a splash, the plank in my lap and the creek surging around me.

"Goddamn it to fucking hell!" I yelled. I was astonished to find tears streaming down my face, for I have always prided my-self on my ability to bear hardship. Here is a lesson I've learned. There is no glory in pure backbreaking labor.

Frank would agree. He is wide like his log truck and thick-skinned as a yellow pine, and believes neighbors should be friendly. At five o'clock sharp each workday, on his last run, he would stop at my blue gate and yell, "Call off your beasts," and I would stop whatever I was doing and go down for our friendly chat.

"How can you stand it?" I'd say, referring to the cutting of trees.

"It's a pinprick on the skin of the earth," replies Frank. "God doesn't know the difference."

"Well, I'm not God," I say. "Not on my place. Never."

So Frank would switch to safer topics such as new people moving in like knapweed, or where to find morels, or how the junior high basketball team was doing. One day in October, when redtails screamed and hoarfrost tipped the meadow grass, the world gone crystal and glowing, he asked could I use some firewood.

"A person can always use firewood," I snapped.

The next day, when I came home from teaching, there was a

pickup load by the woodshed—larch and fir, cut to stove size and split.

"Taking care of the widow." Frank grinned when I tried to thank him. I laughed, but that is exactly what he was up to. In this part of the country, a man still takes pains.

When I first came to Montana I was slim as a fashion model and my hair was black and curly. I had met my husband, Caleb, at the University of Chicago, where a city girl and a raw ranch boy could be equally enthralled by Gothic halls, the great libraries, and gray old Nobel laureates who gathered in the Faculty Club, where no student dared enter.

But after our first two sons were born, after the disillusionments of Vietnam and the cloistered grind of academic life, we decided to break away from Chicago and a life of mind preeminent, and we came to live on the quarter section of land Caleb had inherited from his Swedish grandmother. We would make a new start by raising purebred quarter horses.

For Caleb it was coming home. He had grown up in Sunset, forty miles northeast of Missoula, on his family's homestead ranch. For me it was romance. Caleb had carried the romance of the West for me in the way he walked on high-heeled cowboy boots, and the world he told stories about. It was a world I had imagined from books and movies, a paradise of the shining mountains, clean rivers, and running horses.

I loved the idea of horses. In grade school, I sketched black stallions, white mares, rainbow-spotted appaloosas. My bedroom was hung with horses running, horses jumping, horses rolling in clover. At thirteen I hung around the stables in Lincoln Park and flirted with the stable boys, hoping to charm them into riding lessons my mother could not afford. Sometimes it worked, and I would bounce down the bridle path, free as a princess, never thinking of the payoff that would come at dusk. Pimply-faced boys. Groping and French kisses behind the dark barn that reeked of manure.

For Caleb horses meant honorable outdoor work and a way to make money, work being the prime factor. Horses were history to be reclaimed, identity. It was my turn to bring in the monthly check, so I began teaching at the Sunset school as a stopgap measure to keep our family solvent until the horse-business dream paid off. I am still filling that gap.

We rebuilt the log barn and the corrals, and cross-fenced our one-hundred acres of cleared meadowland. I loved my upland meadow from the first day. As I walked through tall grasses heavy with seed, they moved to the wind, and the undulations were not like water. Now, when I look down from our cliffs, I see the meadow as a handmade thing—a rolling swatch of green hemmed with a stitchery of rocks and trees. The old Swedes who were Caleb's ancestors cleared that meadow with axes and crosscut saws, and I still trip over sawed-off stumps of virgin larch, sawed level to the ground, too large to pull out with a team of horses—decaying, but not yet dirt.

We knew land was a way to save your life. Leave the city and city ambitions, and get back to basics. Roots and dirt and horse pucky (Caleb's word for horseshit). Bob Dylan and the rest were all singing about the land, and every stoned, long-haired mother's child was heading for country.

My poor mother, with her Hungarian dreams and Hebrew upbringing, would turn in her grave to know I'm still teaching in a three-room school with no library or gymnasium, Caleb ten years dead, our youngest boy packed off to the state university, the ranch not even paying its taxes, and me, her only child, keeping company with a two-hundred-and-thirty-pound logger who lives in a trailer.

"Marry a doctor," she used to say, "or better, a concert pianist," and she was not joking. She invented middle-class stories for me from our walk-up flat on the South Side of Chicago: I would live in a white house in the suburbs like she had always wanted; my neighbors would be rich and cultured; the air itself, fragrant with lilacs in May and heady with burning oak leaves in October, could lift us out of the city's grime right into her American dream. My mother would smile with secret intentions. "You will send your children to Harvard."

Frank's been married twice. "Twice-burned" is how he names it, and there are Bowman kids scattered up and down the Blackfoot Valley. Some of them are his. I met his first wife, Fay Dell, before I ever met Frank. That was eighteen years ago. It was Easter vacation, and I had taken two hundred dollars out of our meager savings to buy a horse for our brand-new herd. I remember the day clear as any picture. I remember mud and Blackfoot clay.

Fay Dell is standing in a pasture above Monture Creek. She wears faded brown Carhartt coveralls, as they do up here in the winters, and her irrigating boots are rusted with yellow mud. March runoff has every patch of bare ground spitting streams, trickles, and puddles of brackish water. Two dozen horses circle around her. Their ears are laid back and they eye me, ready for flight. She calls them by name, her voice low, sugary as the carrots she holds in her rough hands.

"Take your pick," she says.

I stroke the velvet muzzle of a two-year-old sorrel, a purebred quarter horse with a white blaze on her forehead.

"Sweet Baby," she says. "You got an eye for the good ones."

"How much?"

"Sorry. That baby is promised."

I walk over to a long-legged bay. There's a smile on Fay Dells lips, but her eyes give another message.

"Marigold," she says, rubbing the mare's swollen belly. "She's in foal. Can't sell my brood mare."

So I try my luck on a pint-sized roan with a high-flying tail. A good kids' horse. A dandy.

"You can't have Lollipop neither. I'm breaking her for my own little gal."

I can see we're not getting anywhere when she heads me in the direction of a pair of wild-eyed geldings.

"Twins," says Fay Dell proudly. "Ruckus and Buckus."

You can tell by the name of a thing if it's any good. These two were out of the question, coming four and never halter broke.

"Come back in May." We walk back toward the ranch house and a hot cup of coffee. "I'll have 'em tamed good as any sheep-dog. Two for the price of one. Can't say that ain't a bargain!"

Her two-story frame house sat high above the creek, some Iowa farmer's dream of the West. The ground, brown with stubble of last year's grass, was littered with old tennis shoes, broken windshields, rusting cars, shards of aluminum siding. Cast-iron tractor parts emerged like mushrooms from soot-crusted heaps of melting snow. I wondered why Fay Dell had posted that ad on the Sunset school bulletin board: "Good horses for sale. Real cheap." Why did she bother with such make-believe?

Eighteen years later I am sleeping with her ex-husband, and the question is answered.

"All my wages gone for hay," says Frank. "The kids in hand-me-downs . . . the house a goddamn mess. I'll tell you I had a bellyful!"

Frank had issued an ultimatum on Easter Sunday, determined never to be ashamed again of his bedraggled wife and children among the slicked-up families in the Blackfoot Community Church.

"Get rid of them two-year-olds," he warned, "or . . ."

No wonder it took Fay Dell so long to tell me no. What she was doing that runoff afternoon, seesawing back and forth, was making a choice between her horses and her husband. If Fay Dell had confessed to me that day, I would not have believed such choices are possible. Horses, no matter how well you loved them, seemed mere animal possessions to be bought and sold. I was so young then, a city girl with no roots at all, and I had grown up Jewish, where family seemed the only choice.

"Horse poor," Frank says. "That woman wouldn't get rid of her horses. Not for God, Himself."

March in Montana is a desperate season. You have to know what you want, and hang on.

Frank's second wife was tall, blond, and young. He won't talk about her much, just shakes his head when her name comes up and says, "Guess she couldn't stand the winters." I heard she ran away to San Luis Obispo with a long-haired carpenter named Ralph.

"Cleaned me out," Frank says, referring to his brand-new stereo and the golden retriever. She left the double-wide empty, and the only evidence she had been there at all was the white picket fence Frank built to make her feel safe. And a heap of green tomatoes in the weed thicket he calls a garden.

"I told her," he says with a wistful look, "I told that woman you can't grow red tomatoes in this climate."

As for me, I love winter. Maybe that's why Frank and I can stand each other. Maybe that's how come we've been keeping company for five years and marriage is a subject that has never crossed our lips except once. He's got his place near the high-way, and I've got mine at the end of the dirt road, where the sign reads, COUNTY MAINTENANCE ENDS HERE. To all eyes but our own, we have always been a queer, mismatched pair.

After we began neighboring, I would ask Frank in for a cup of coffee. Before long, it was a beer or two. Soon, my boys were taking the old McCulloch chain saw to Frank's to be sharpened, or he was teaching them how to tune up Caleb's ancient Case tractor. We kept our distance until one thirty-below evening in January when my Blazer wouldn't start, even though its oil-pan heater was plugged in. Frank came up to jump it.

The index finger on my right hand was frostbit from trying to turn the metal ignition key bare-handed. Frostbite is like get-ting burned, extreme cold acting like fire, and my finger was swollen along the third joint, just below its tip, growing the biggest blister I had ever seen.

"Dumb," Frank says, holding my hand between his large mitts and blowing on the blister. "Don't you have gloves?"

"Couldn't feel the key to turn it with gloves on."

He lifts my egg-size finger to his face and bows down, like a chevalier, to kiss it. I learn the meaning of dumbfounded. I feel the warmth of his lips tracing from my hand down through my privates. I like it. A widow begins to forget how good a man's warmth can be.

"I would like to take you dancing," says Frank.

"It's too damn cold."

"Tomorrow," he says, "the Big Sky Boys are playing at the Awful Burger Bar."

I suck at my finger.

"You're a fine dancer."

"How in God's name would you know?"

"Easy," Frank smiles. "I been watching your moves."

I admit I was scared. I felt like the little girl I had been, so long ago. A thumb-sucker. If I said yes, I knew there would be no saying no.

The Awful Burger Bar is like the Red Cross, you can go there for first aid. It is as great an institution as the Sunset school. The white bungalow sits alone just off the two-lane on a jack-pine flat facing south across irrigated hay meadows to where what's left of the town of Sunset clusters around the school. Friday evenings after Caleb passed away, when I felt too weary to cook and too jumpy to stand the silence of another Blackfoot night, I'd haul the boys up those five miles of asphalt and we'd eat Molly Fry's awful burgers, stacked high with Bermuda onions, lettuce and tomato, hot jo-jos on the side, Millers for me, root beer for them. That's how those kids came to be experts at shooting pool.

The ranching and logging families in this valley had no difficulty understanding why their schoolteacher hung out in a bar and passed the time with hired hands and old-timers. We were all alike in this one thing. Each was drawn from starvation farms in the rock and clay foothills or grassland ranches on the floodplain, down some winding dirt road to the red neon and yellow lights glowing at the dark edge of chance. You could call it home, as they do in the country-and-western songs on the jukebox.

I came to know those songs like a second language. Most, it seemed, written just for me. I longed to sing them out loud, but God or genes or whatever determines what you can be never gave me a singing voice. In my second life I will be a white Billie Holiday with a gardenia stuck behind my ear, belting out songs to make you dance and cry at the same time.

My husband, Caleb, could sing like the choirboy he had been before he went off to Chicago on a scholarship and lost his religion. He taught himself to play harmonica and wrote songs about lost lives. There's one I can't forget:

Scattered pieces, scattered pieces,
Come apart for all the world to see.

Scattered pieces, lonely pieces,
That's how yours truly came to be.

When he sang that song, my eyes filled with tears.

"How can you feel that way, and never tell me except in a song?"

"There's lots I don't tell you," he said.

We didn't go to bars much, Caleb and me. First of all we were poor. Then too busy building our log house, taking care of the boys, tending horses. And finally, when the angina pains struck, and the shortness of breath, and we knew that at the age of thirty-seven Caleb had come down with an inherited disease that would choke his arteries and starve his heart, it was too sad, you know, having to sit out the jitterbugs and dance only to slow music. But even then, in those worst of bad times, when the Big Sky Boys came through, we'd hire a sitter and put on our good boots and head for the Awful Burger.

There was one Fourth of July. All the regulars were there, and families from the valley. Frank says he was there, but I didn't know him. Kids were running in and out like they do in Montana, where a country bar is your local community center.

58

Firecrackers exploded in the gravel parking lot. Show-off college students from town were dancing cowboy boogie as if they knew what they were doing, and sunburned tourists exuding auras of camp fires and native cutthroat trout kept coming in from motor homes. This was a far way from Connecticut.

We were sitting up close to the band. Caleb was showing our boys how he could juggle peanuts in time to the music. The boys tried to copy him, and peanuts fell like confetti to be crunched under the boots of sweating dancers. The sun streamed in through open doors and windows, even though it was nine at night, and we were flushed from too many beers, too much sun and music.

"Stand up, Caleb. Stand up so's the rest of us can see."

That was our neighbor Melvin Godfrey calling from the next table. Then his wife, Stella, takes up the chant.

"Come on, Caleb. Give us the old one-two-three."

The next thing, Molly Fry is passing lemons from the kitchen where she cooks the awful burgers, and Caleb is standing in front of the Big Sky Boys, the dancers all stopped and watching. Caleb is juggling those lemons to the tune of "Mommas, Don't Let Your Babies Grow Up to Be Cowboys," and he does not miss a beat.

It is a picture in my mind—framed in gold leaf—Caleb on that bandstand, legs straddled, deep-set eyes looking out at no one or nothing, the tip of his tongue between clenched teeth in some kind of frozen smile, his faded blue shirt stained in half-moons under the arms, and three bright yellow lemons rising and falling in perfect synchronicity. I see the picture in stop-action, like the end of a movie. Two shiny lemons in midair, the third in his palm. Caleb juggling.

It's been a long time coming, the crying. You think there's no pity left, but the sadness is waiting, like a barrel gathering rain, until one sunny day, out of the blue, it just boils over and you've got a flood on your hands. That's what happened one Saturday last January, when Frank took me to celebrate the fifth anniversary of our first night together. The Big Sky Boys were back, and we were at the Awful Burger Bar.

"Look," I say, first thing. "The lead guitar has lost his hair. Those boys are boys no longer."

Frank laughs and points to the bass man. Damned if he isn't wearing a corset to hold his beer belly inside those slick red-satin cowboy shirts the boys have worn all these years.

And Indian Willie is gone. He played steel guitar so blue it broke your heart. Gone back to Oklahoma.

"Heard Willie found Jesus in Tulsa," says Melvin Godfrey, who has joined us at the bar.

"They've replaced him with a child," I say, referring to the pimply, long-legged kid who must be someone's son. "He hits all the right keys, but he'll never break your heart."

We're sitting on high stools, and I'm all dressed up in the long burgundy skirt Frank gave me for Christmas. My frizzy gray hair is swept back in a chignon, and Mother's amethyst earrings catch the light from the revolving Budweiser clock. It is a new me, matronly and going to fat, a stranger I turn away from in the mirror above the bar.

When the band played "Waltz Across Texas" early in the night, Frank led me to the dance floor and we waltzed through to the end, swaying and dipping, laughing in each other's ears. But now he is downing his third Beam ditch and pays no attention to my tapping feet.

I watch the young people boogie. A plain fat girl with long red hair is dressed in worn denim overalls, but she moves like a queen among frogs. In the dim, multicolored light, she is delicate, delicious.

"Who is that girl?" I ask Frank.

"What girl?"

"The redhead."

"How should I know?" he says. "Besides, she's fat."

"Want to dance?"

Frank looks at me as if I were crazy. "You know I can't dance to this fast stuff. I'm too old to jump around and make a fool of myself. You want to dance, you got to find yourself another cowboy."

The attractive men have girls of their own or are looking to nab some hot young dish. Melvin is dancing with Stella, "showing off" as Frank would say, but to me they are a fine-tuned duo who know each move before they take it, like a team of matched circus ponies, or those fancy ice skaters in the Olympics. They dance only with each other, and they dance all night long.

I'm getting bored, tired of whiskey and talk about cows and spotted owls and who's gone broke this week. I can hear all that on the five o'clock news. I'm beginning to feel like a wallflower at a high school sock hop (feelings I don't relish reliving). I'm making plans about going home when a tall, narrow-hipped old geezer in a flowered rayon cowboy shirt taps me on the shoulder.

"May I have this dance, ma'am?"

I look over to Frank, who is deep in conversation with Ed Snow, a logger from Seeley Lake.

"If your husband objects . . ."

"He's not my husband."

The old man is clearly drunk, but he has the courtly manner of an old-time cowboy, and he is a live and willing body.

"Sure," I say. As we head for the dance floor, I see Frank turn his head. He is watching me with a bemused and superior smile. "I'll show that bastard," I say to myself.

The loudspeaker crackles as the lead guitarist announces a medley—"A tribute to our old buddy, Ernest Tubb." The Big Sky Boys launch into "I'm Walking the Floor Over You," and the old man grabs me around the waist.

Our hands meet for the first time. I could die on the spot. If I hadn't been so mad, I would have run back to Frank because that old man's left hand was not a hand, but a claw—all shriveled up from a stroke or some birth defect, the bones dry and brittle, frozen half-shut, the skin white, flaky, and surprisingly soft, like a baby's.

His good right arm is around my waist, guiding me light but

firm, and I respond as if it doesn't matter who's in the saddle. But my mind is on that hand. It twirls me and pulls me. We glide. We swing. He draws me close, and I come willingly. His whiskey breath tickles at my ear in a gasping wheeze. We spin one last time, and dip. I wonder if he will die on the spot, like Caleb. Die in mid-motion, alive one minute, dead the next.

I see Caleb in the kitchen that sunstruck evening in May, come in from irrigating the east meadow and washing his hands at the kitchen sink. Stew simmers on the stove, the littlest boys play with English toy soldiers, Mozart on the stereo, a soft breeze blowing through open windows, Caleb turns to me. I will always see him turning. A shadow crosses his face. "Oh dear," he says. And Caleb falls to the maple floor, in one motion a tree cut down. He does not put out his hands to break his fall. Gone. Blood dribbles from his broken nose.

There is no going back now. We dance two numbers, the old cowboy and me, each step smoother and more carefree. We are breathing hard, beginning to sweat. The claw-hand holds me in fear and love. This high-stepping old boy is surely alive. He asks my name.

"Mady."

"Bob," he says. "Bob Beamer. They call me Old Beam." He laughs like this is a good joke. "Never knowed a Mady before. That's a new one on me."

"Hungarian," I say, wishing the subject had not come up, not mentioning the Jewish part for fear of complications. And I talk to Mother, as I do when feelings get too deep.

"Are you watching me now?" I say to the ghost of her. "It's come to this, Momushka. Are you watching me now?"

It's odd how you can talk to the ghost of someone more casually and honestly than you ever communicated when they were alive. When I talk to Caleb's ghost it is usually about work or the boys or a glimpse of beauty in nature or books. I'll spot a bluebird hovering, or young elk playing tag where our meadow joins the woods, or horses running (I always talk to Caleb about any experience I have with horses), and the words leap from my mouth, simple as pie. But when I think of my deep ecology, as the environmentalists describe it, I speak only to Mother.

I never converse with my father. He is a faded memory of heavy eyebrows, Chesterfield straights, whiskery kisses. He was a sculptor and died when I was six. Mother was five feet one, compact and full of energy as a firecracker. Every morning, in our Chicago apartment lined with books, she wove my tangled bush of black hair into French braids that pulled so tight my eyes seemed slanted. Every morning she tried to yank me into shape, and every morning I screamed so loud Mother was embarrassed to look our downstairs neighbors in the eyes.

"Be quiet," she commanded. "They will think I am a Nazi."

And there was Grandma, who lived with us and wouldn't learn English because it was a barbaric language. She would polish our upright Steinway until the piano shone like ebony. I remember endless piano lessons, Bach and Liszt. "A woman of culture," Mother said, sure of this one thing. "You will have everything."

"You sure dance American," the old cowboy says, and we are waltzing to the last dance, a song even older than my memories.

"I was in that war," he says. "Old Tubb must of been on the same troopship. We was steaming into New York and it was raining in front of us and full moon behind and I saw a rainbow at midnight like the song says, 'Out on the ocean blue!'"

Frank has moved to the edge of the floor. I see him out the corner of my eye. We should be dancing this last one, I think, me and Frank and Old Beam. I close my eyes and all of us are dancing, like in the end of a Fellini movie—Stella and Marvin, the slick young men and blue-eyed girls, the fat redhead in her overalls, Mother, Caleb. Like Indians in a circle. Like Swede farmers, Hungarian gypsies.

Tears gather behind my closed lids. I open my eyes and rain is falling. The song goes on, sentimental and pointless. But the tears don't stop.

"It's not your fault," I say, trying to smile, choking and sput-

tering, laughing at the confounded way both these men are looking at me. "Thank you for a very nice dance."

I cried for months, off and on. The school board made me take
sick leave and see a psychiatrist in Missoula. He gave me drugs.
The pills put me to sleep and I could not think straight, just
walked around like a zombie. I told the shrink I'd rather cry. "It's
good for you," I said. "Cleans out the system."

I would think the spell was done and over, and then I'd see
the first red-winged blackbird in February or snow melting off
the meadow, or a silly tulip coming up before its time, and the
water level in my head would rise, and I'd be at it again.

"Runoff fever" is what Frank calls it. The junk of your life is
laid bare, locked in ice and muck, just where you left it before
the first blizzard buried the whole damned mess under three feet
of pure white. I can't tell you why the crying ended, but I can
tell you precisely when. Perhaps one grief replaces another and
the second grief is something you can fix. Or maybe it's just a
change of internal weather.

Frank and I are walking along Bear Creek on a fine breezy
day in April, grass coming green and thousands of the yellow
glacier lilies we call dogtooth violets lighting the woods. I am
picking a bouquet and bend to smell the flowers. Their scent is
elusive, not sweet as roses or rank as marigolds, but a fine fresh-
ness you might want to drink. I breathe in the pleasure and suddenly I am weeping. A flash flood of tears.

Frank looks at me bewildered. He reaches for my hand. I pull
away blindly, walking as fast as I can. He grabs my elbow.

"What the hell?" he says. I don't look at him.

"Would you like to get married?" He is almost shouting. "Is
that what you want? Would that cure this goddamned crying?"

What can I say? I am amazed. Unaccountably frightened.
"No," I blurt, shaking free of his grasp and preparing to run.
"It's not you." I am sobbing now, gasping for breath.

Then he has hold of both my arms and is shaking me—

a good-sized woman—as if I were a child. And that is how I feel, like a naughty girl. The yellow lilies fly from my hands.

"Stop it!" he yells. "Stop that damned bawling!"

Frank's eyes are wild. This is no proposal. I see my fear in his eyes and I am ashamed. Shame always makes me angry. I try to slap his face. He catches my hand and pulls me to his belly. It is warm. Big enough for the both of us. The anger has stopped my tears. The warmth has stopped my anger. When I raise my head to kiss Frank's mouth, I see his eyes brimming with salt.

I don't know why, but I am beginning to laugh through my tears. Laughing at last at myself.

"Will you marry me?" I stutter. "Will that cure you?"

Frank lets go of my arms. He is breathing hard and his face is flushed a deep red. He sits down on a log and wipes his eyes with the back of his sleeve. I rub at my arms.

"They're going to be black and blue."

"Sorry," he says.

I go over to Frank's log and sit at his feet, my head against his knees. He strokes my undone hair. "What about you?" he replies, question for question. "Do you want to do it?"

We are back to a form of discourse we both understand.

"I'm not sure."

"Me neither."

May has come to Montana with a high-intensity green so rich you can't believe it is natural. I've burned the trash pile and I am done with crying. I'm back with my fifth-graders and struggling through aerobics classes three nights a week. I stand in the locker room naked and exhausted, my hips splayed wide and belly sagging as if to proclaim, Yes, I've borne four children.

A pubescent girl, thin as a knife, studies me as if I were a creature from another planet, but I don't care because one of these winters Frank and I are going to Hawaii. When I step out on those white beaches I want to look good in my bathing suit.

Fay Dell still lives up on Monture Creek. I see her out in her

horse pasture winter and summer as I drive over the pass to
Great Falls for a teachers' meeting or ride the school bus to
basketball games in the one-room school in Ovando. Her ranch
house is gone to hell, unpainted, weathered gray, patched with
tar paper. Her second husband left her, and the daughter she
broke horses for is a beauty operator in Spokane. Still, there are
over a dozen horses in the meadow and Fay Dell gone thin and
unkempt in coveralls, tossing hay in February or fixing fence in
May or just standing in the herd.

I imagine her low, sugary voice as if I were standing right by
her. She is calling those horses by name. Names a child might
invent.

"Sweet Baby."

"Marigold."

"Lollipop."

I want my meadow to be running with horses, as it was in
the beginning—horses rolling in new grass, tails swatting at
summer flies, huddled into a blizzard. I don't have to ride them.
I just want their pea-brained beauty around me. I'm in the market for a quarter horse stallion and a couple of mares. I'll need
to repair my fences and build a new corral with poles cut from
the woods.

My stallion will be named Rainbow at Midnight. Frank
laughs and says I should name him Beam, after my cowboy. For
a minute I don't know what he's talking about, and then I remember the old man in the Awful Burger Bar. I think of Fay Dell
and say, "Maybe I'll name him Frank."

Frank thinks Fay Dell is crazy as a loon. But Fay Dell knows
our lives are delicate. Grief will come. Fay Dell knows you don't
have to give in. Life is motion. Choose love. A person can fall in
love with horses.

The Home Place

It is by knowing where you stand that you grow able to judge where you are. Place absorbs our earliest notice and attention, it bestows on us our original awareness. . . . It perseveres in bringing us back to earth when we fly too high. It never really stops informing us, for it is forever astir, alive, changing, reflecting, like the mind of man itself. One place comprehended can make us understand other places better. Sense of place gives equilibrium; extended, it is sense of direction too. . . . it is the sense of place going with us still that is the ball of golden thread to carry us there and back and in every sense of the word to bring us home. . . .

There may come to be new places in our lives that are second spiritual homes—closer to us in some ways, perhaps, than our original homes. But the home tie is the blood tie. And had it meant nothing to us, any other place thereafter would have meant less, and we would carry no compass inside ourselves to find home ever, anywhere at all. We would not even guess what we had missed.

EUDORA WELTY

JIM WAYNE MILLER

A Felt Linkage

The editor of a Kentucky weekly recently expressed concern about his county's loss of skilled and educated young people. He made a unique proposal. Let's tax the incomes of people who have been educated in the county but who went elsewhere to earn a living, he suggested. The tax ought to be levied on the incomes of teachers, doctors, lawyers, and skilled workers for the first twenty years of their employment outside the county.

This proposal didn't go unchallenged. A letter to the editor promptly pointed out that the county didn't educate a single teacher, doctor or lawyer; that the high school emphasized vocational training and, even so, seventy-five percent of its graduates had to go out of the county to find jobs. Also, most of those who went on to a college or university elsewhere couldn't hope to return to the county because opportunities for professionals and highly skilled workers were strictly limited there.

It's an old problem and there's no satisfactory solution. People have been drawn away from the place of their birth ever since Catullus went up to Rome, ever since German boys joined the Roman legions as mercenaries. And surely for centuries before that. If the writer of Genesis had been a sociologist, he would have noted there were unemployed men living down in the boondocks who got word they were hiring on at the Tower of Babel and so they struck out with wives and children and lived in a tent-jungle near the construction site. Living in London in the late 19th century, Arnold Bennett, the novelist, commented that he knew hardly any native Londoners. Almost everyone he knew had, like himself, come up from the provinces.

People leave home. Then at some point, for economic, professional, political or even spiritual reasons, they discover they can never return. Certainly since Thomas Wolfe wrote his last novel it has been axiomatic, for Americans, at least, that you can't go home again.

Obviously many people all over the country do leave home, are educated, and then return permanently to live just half a mile down the road from Mama. They return as teachers, doctors, administrators, social workers. They enter family businesses, the law firm with their father and three brothers. You can go home again even in Appalachia. Huey Perry went home. In his recent book, *They'll Cut Off Your Project,* he tells about some of the things he went home to.

But surely it's easier to go home to most other parts of America than to Appalachia. Unless you belong to a tiny mountain elite, you're apt to know more than other Americans the poignancy of that phrase, You can't go home again. If you were born in a coal camp, your home literally may not be there any longer. Actress Patricia Neal recently returned to Knoxville for a reunion of her high school class, but she couldn't go home to Packard, Kentucky, where she was born. The town ceased to exist in 1946 when the mine closed. Billy Edd Wheeler can't go home to Highcoal, West Virginia. The people, houses, post office—they're all gone. Where he went to school there's nothing but squirrels, birds and the creek running.

If you were born in a place like Packard or Highcoal, your family may now be in Cincinnati, Toledo, Cleveland or Detroit. Maybe your family were marginal farmers. They may still be on the land but actually earning a living from some 40-hour-a-week job at a paper mill, or a factory thirty-five miles away. If you are educated or trained for a particular skill or profession, there is less likelihood, if you are from anywhere in Appalachia, that you'll be able to return to the place where you were born.

Most of us just assume we won't ever go home again. We don't agonize over it. I doubt whether today an American could write about the realization of not being able to go home with as much feeling as Wolfe did in 1940. If Wolfe were in his late thirties and writing today, I doubt whether he could, either. In Wolfe's last book, George Webber seeks the help of America's "little people," realizing that greed and selfishness, purporting to be the friends of mankind, are keeping America from finding herself. More than thirty years later another George called, "Come home, America," but the Winnebago motor homes all headed for the territory.

The only other writer I know of who has recently written about leaving home and being unable to return who even remotely approaches Wolfe is Willie Morris, a former editor of *Harper's Magazine.* A Mississippian, Morris tells in his 1968 book, *North Toward Home,* how he felt both alienated from the South and yet drawn to it. But the tension is slacker than what is found in Wolfe or Faulkner. Morris's struggle, not particularly intense, is overcome and he is able to think of the American northeast as his home.

Many of us simply don't want to go home again. We have embraced varying degrees of transience and like it. This isn't such a break with the past, after all; it's very much in the frontier tradition.

We can get from one place to another so easily nowadays it's not necessary for us to define "home" as strictly as people once did. My grandfather's brother Will moved from Sandy Mush, in Buncombe County, North Carolina when my grandfather was about twenty, and for the next sixty-odd years my grandfather mentioned his and Will's exploits, but they never saw each other again, never even heard from one another. Now Will had moved down into South Carolina, what for us is a pleasant Sunday afternoon drive, a sixty-cent telephone call, a postage stamp away.

For the first seventeen years of my life I lived rooted in one place much as my grandfather lived all his life. I have just counted up all the different places I've lived during the second seventeen years and, not counting dormitories and temporary stays abroad, I find I've lived in more than twenty apartments or houses which, at the time, I considered permanent residences.

I haven't lived in the mountains since I was seventeen but I don't think of myself as having moved away from home, either. Home for me is an area vast in comparison to what my grandfather considered home, but still only a small part of the country. When Mary Ellen and I started thinking about where we would teach, we began to realize what we considered home. It wasn't Randolph Macon. It wasn't Haverford College. We realized home for us was a three-state area made of North Carolina, Kentucky and Tennessee. This was where our people were, people we knew and loved and, usually, understood. Home for us was among those people and in that place where we understood what Edward Sapir calls ". . . the thousands of feelings and ideas that are tacitly assumed and that constantly glimmer in the background."

Geography does still exist, contrary to what future-shocker Alvin Toffler maintains. But surely geography is less important than it once was. Easier and swifter means of travel and communication allow us to find community over greater distances and also make less likely our ever staying in one place for the span of our lives.

Geography aside, there are pervasive pressures to remain relatively rootless. We are rewarded with money, prestige and success for pursuing nomadic existences, for our ability to pull up, take leave overnight, plug in quickly to new situations and size them up swiftly. We are rewarded for the exploitative grasp of new circumstances, the almost predatory reading of people and places. The kind of knowledge valued is utilitarian and, being that, disposable. We re-tool. There's little demand for the kind of knowledge that comes of living a long time in one place, knowledge gained slowly with the turning of seasons, in daily intercourse with neighbors. As a country storekeeper would say, "We don't get many calls for that."

But if a permanent return to the place where we were born and brought up is out of the question for most of us, going home briefly, temporarily, and in our emotions is not less but more important. Going home is a spiritual experience, a confrontation with the self, an encounter with what poet John Hollander calls everything we are the upshot of. Willie Morris, the former *Harper's* editor, recognized the importance of going home for Americans. Four years ago he launched an unusual series called "Going Home in America" with this introduction: "Leaving home in America, and returning to it in one's dreams and emotions, are essential to what we are as a transient, displaced people; these have been main themes in our literature, and the very words, *going home,* have a special American resonance."

It is because we are confirmed transients that we need to be able to go home. We need to be capable of affirming our origins, a place, a people, a way of life, a set of relationships. Not to acknowledge these freely is to lose a part of one's self. Otherwise, we do massive damage to our inner images of self, confuse ourselves with our many roles. We get lost in the American Funhouse and wander among distorting mirrors. If we walked about in a funhouse long enough, we'd get accustomed to grotesque images of ourselves: a huge elongated trunk, a bulging wrap-around brow moving on stumpy legs, our belts just above our shoetops, our chins in our laps, our hands growing right out of our shoulders, no wrists, arms or elbows in between.

When we get used to walking around in our lives with similarly distorted inner images of ourselves, distorted because we have forgotten who we are or can't acknowledge who we are and where we came from, then we are profoundly confused. This confusion is the root of sickness, despair, alienation. We are then what Alan Watts calls "genuine fakes." Weird. Grotesque. Spiritual disaster areas. The sort of people who get together, men in one room, women in another, and have separate conversations about the relative merits of kitchen appliances and rider lawn mowers, the talk sounding like simultaneous editorial meetings at *Consumer Reports.*

To come home to the place of our birth and upbringing, to our school or college or university, is to return to a part of ourselves. The place and the people give us back our true proportions, help us to remember and see those parts of ourselves we may have forgotten. This is so even though our first awareness may be only of loss.

Predictably, when I go home to the place where I grew up, I am subjected to sudden weathers, showers of feelings; feelings with faces whose names I may have forgotten; feelings I enter into as a stranger might enter a house he once lived in; feelings like gray tobacco barns, empty of all but the sharp fragrance of last year's burley. I come upon feelings that, like cornplanters and cultivators leaning against locust posts in a toolshed, haven't been used for a time. Experiencing them again is like taking an axe by the smooth helve or gripping the handles of a plow again. At first I am a little saddened, aware only of loss, and admit to myself: you don't live here any longer. You're settled in a suburb, north of yourself.

Later, when I'm somewhere else, I'll know the sense of loss is at least partly illusory. I'll wake somewhere to a horn's beep, ship's bells, on a rising falling bunk out at sea, or to the sound of a strange tongue spoken outside my door—and realize I've been dreaming native ground. I recollect a vivid dream about my grandmother, who could conjure warts, who knew spells to make butter come, to draw fire from a burned finger, and how to settle swarming bees. I dreamt of her running under a cloud of swarming bees, beating an empty pie pan with a spoon until the swarm settled black on a drooping pine bough (was the dream set off by the clatter of garbage cans on the New York street below?). There she was, and nothing seemed lost.

Even more important than going home, maybe, is how we feel about home, no matter where we may be. (And though we wander far away / Thy chimes . . .) For we can't escape culture. We live in a culture but the culture finally lives in us. So what do we do? Do we let part of our life become an unacknowledged invisible companion? Are we contemptuous of it? It's easy to look down on people who have lifted you onto their shoulders. Are we to be slavish and servile, spiritual antiquarians? Or are we ready always to acknowledge those things in Appalachia that excite and inspire us, that are genuine and provide a felt linkage with past generations, previous human experience; that we feel akin to no matter how different our circumstances are now. We need this felt linkage, which is true culture, for it tells us who we are, and keeps us from getting lost in the funhouse where we are alone except for the grotesquely distorted images of self we keep meeting.

How would you describe your own childhood and adolescence? How do you feel about it? I think mine had some of the bleakness of *The Last Picture Show*. Viewing that film, I was afraid during several scenes that lights were going to come up in the theater, a spot would search around and discover me, and Ralph Edwards would step out proclaiming, "This is Your Life!" Most of the time, though, my childhood was as wholesome as *The Waltons*. And this was probably about the right mix for me.

I do regret that in grade and high school the images of people, work and lifestyle I got from textbooks had almost nothing to do with anything in my own experience. The result was that I suspected my own life, and the lives of everyone I knew were somehow inauthentic. I was starving for what Bill Best in a *Mountain Life and Work* article called "self-definition." Bill and I grew up not many miles from each other in North Carolina and we both have reported, independently of each other, the same felt lack. In his article he tells how excited he became when, after two years of Dick and Jane and their dog Spot, he found a story about Laplanders whose lives were similar to the life he knew in the mountains. He read the story and re-read it until the pages were ready to fall out. Why? Because he was starving to find his own experience somehow legitimized by the school. The school did give him something, finally, to get excited about. But this was the one memorable high point in a student's early education! Finding materials that excited him ought to have been an almost daily experience.

So we affirm our place and our people not always because but sometimes despite. Whatever was rich in the lives of our people enriches us, for we are sprung from the moist ground of their lives. Where they were manipulated in their pride and independence, exploited, tricked out of timber, land and coal, we stand robbed too. Where they burned, plowed and mined in ignorance, we are impoverished. Where they cut the future down, we are naked in our present. What they did in their private and collective darknesses is our dawn along a polluted river. Are we doing better? Debts they made to the earth fall due to us? What notes are we writing for our children? No, we can't separate ourselves from the lives of our people, except through delusion. Our lives flow from theirs as from a place where two creeks meet: if one comes tumbling muddy and trash-filled, the other enters quiet and clear.

SUSAN PEPPER ROBBINS

Red Invitations

In early December with Christmas looming, a cold spell cracked
dead limbs onto power lines and kept the snow so long on the
ground it turned yellow, almost translucent, like the plastic shell
of the old Zenith radio I had when I was a girl.

Between outages, we saw on television desperate things happening in Eastern Europe. In Virginia, December is often like
early spring, with warm rains blowing across the fields of
broomsedge and scrub pine. The bitter cold was unusual, and
we felt like the Eastern Europeans looked, bundled up and
ready to die. We expected something terrible to happen to us
and it did. Priscilla, our oldest sister, came home to go crazy.

She did not break down until she drove up into the yard. The
gravel was frozen hard as axe blades. We walked out to help her
bring her things in. She always brought us a lemon pound cake
and a plant she had grown for us from a root slip or leaf she had
gotten somewhere. We have a Kew Gardens azalea she grew
from a twig, a geranium from Zion Park, a snake plant from
Annette, her friend in New Mexico. Our table of plants has a
history like a nation of tribes. Some plants she stole, some were
given to her.

As we walked out to her car, we could see she was putting
her head back the way she always did to laugh. Then, her head
thrown against the headrest, she began crying. She did not stop
for five days. Her tears dehydrated her, her face swelled two
inches over its bone structure. She was a mess when the rescue

team, Joey and Tim, got her to Southside Memorial to start re-
placing fluids.

The year before, it was a very different Christmas—more the
typical Virginia December weather, for one thing. Priscilla gave
a party when she came home. She was celebrating her divorce,
three years later. She wrote "Come help celebrate my freedom" on
the red invitations she mailed out from her office in Baltimore.
Karo and I got one each—that's how we learned that the party
was at our place. When we saw where the party was going to
be, we knew we would be giving it too.

There was a ten-page recipe included in our invitations, five
pages folded twice in each envelope, xeroxed from the food
column in the *Baltimore Sun.* "Thompson's Turkey" called for
twenty-two spices, ones we did not have and had not heard of,
like memmi, and ones we had heard of but didn't have, like mar-
joram, turmeric, and coriander. We laughed when we read about
the truffles and sea salt. It called for water chestnuts and chopped
preserved ginger, which I had forgotten existed, and minced
chutney.

As soon as we got back in the house from the mailbox with
the invitations and recipe, we called Priscilla long distance to
protest. She told us we didn't understand what the party really
was, how important it was to her. Tell us, we said, as remote as
if we were calling from East Berlin. I was on the kitchen phone.
Karo was in the living room, talking. The party, we should
understand, was announcing something she couldn't write on
the red invitations. Something she would tell us when she got
home. She went on about how a party announces a new reality
without anyone having to say anything.

When she came home, the sheets of rain were drifting against
the green and brown hills. At the kitchen table, we heard what
the party would announce. To those who could take it, could
hear the announcement, the party would tell in the language of
drinks and candles in the windows, the incredible thirty-pound
Thompson's Turkey—could we have fires going in the double
fireplaces facing each other at opposite ends of our living room,

and some white pine sprays tied to the rafters and lashed to the porch columns?—that she was now lesbian.

"Maybe bi, I'm not sure yet, but probably not. And definitely not hetero anymore. I am finished with all that teenager stuff."

"I didn't know you could switch like that. What about your grandchildren?" Karo asked.

Karo was the youngest of us three. She said it was good in a way that we had to get the house ready to have seventy people in for Priscilla's party on the twenty-third. Our invitations came on the seventeenth. That's how, as I've said, we found out we were giving a party.

"You could have let us know," Karo had said to her invitation, holding it like a microphone in her work gloves when it came. Later to Priscilla, she said the same thing on the phone and again when she drove up in the yard, not waiting for her to cut the car off.

"Know about my whole new self?"

"About the party," Karo said, opening the door and taking a huge Norfolk pine out the back. I got the suitcases.

In our late middle age, we don't look like sisters. I have bushy white hair and broken vessels in my nose and cheeks, which give me a bluish-red, cheerful look. A lie. Karen, Karo, has only her startled eyes left from being young. Also a lie. Nothing startles Karo. She babied our parents, not just when they were old, but as long as I can remember. Then she was taking care of Mama, plus me, when I came home to dry out this last time. I ended up staying to help Karo build the prefab cabin and with some of the nursing. Mama was easy to nurse, which is a contradiction in terms to anyone who has done it, but for nursing a slowly dying person, it was easy.

"We all need a dying person to help us grow up," Karo likes to say. "Or maybe need the parents we had. Big, tall, beautiful babies."

Karo used to rehearse Priscilla and me about what to say to make Mama and Daddy happy. "It won't hurt you, Dumbbells," she would whisper to us. "Tell them you loved the trip to

Fincastle. You want to go again." We hated the visit to Aunt
Mary Mills, who lived in a dark little house by the chimney of
the house that had burned down. The one she had burned down
when she was four and had tipped the oil lamp over. We knew
the story by heart and didn't like seeing what had replaced the
raging fire, the rescued four-year-old Mary Mills, whose mother
had dropped the little girl by the tree, saying maybe her last
words, "Don't move, I'm going back for my sewing machine."
We used to play "Don't Move, I'm Going Back in the Fire." What
we saw in Fincastle was a chimney that looked like a backyard
cookout fireplace and an old Aunt Mary Mills who had long
drooping sections of her face and dirty fingernails. She wore a
dirty seersucker dress and men's work shoes. The oak tree in the
yard where our grandmother had left the four-year-old arsonist
had been cut down.

Sometimes I see a little of Mary Mills in my face.

"What happened to Priscilla? I thought it was the oldest
daughters of alcoholics who were more grown-up than God,"
I ask Karo as I am tying bundles of mistletoe I shot down from
the oak trees.

"Something didn't go right, I guess." Karo is skinning two
hams and boning them to slice.

Priscilla is fifty-eight. We thought about her news as we
worked toward the party that day, basting Thompson's Turkey
before it was sealed in its pastry crust, doing last-minute cleaning and adding fresh greens to the ones I had already hung, that
maybe she would make a successful lesbian. She had been a
good wife and a pretty good mother as far as we could tell. Her
sons, Fred and Charles, are free, at least, to lead their own lives.
Adult freedom is my highest standard for measuring childhoods.
Not coming back home is my next highest standard. Children
who move to Columbus, Ohio, say, are the ones I admire.

Karo and I, in our silly-looking, prefab cabin set on a hill,
the land that's left of our family's farm, six acres, are trying to
prepare, knowing we can't, hoping we won't have to, for our
old age, which scares the hell out of us. We hope, we say in the

evenings, that we'll wreck in our Bronco, together, have a double funeral and be buried side-by-side. Seeing what old age did to Mama, waving her in the winds around the planet, as if she were a rag, got our attention. Ten years she fluttered in space above the oceans and continents, her eighty-pound body anchored with us in the hospital bed we rented for the cabin we built around her bed, figuratively speaking, with ramps and invalid toilets and roll-in showers. When we saw her start to drift away from the earth and saw that I was staying sober, we decided to buy the Ayak Cabin Kit. A day at a time, that's how we did it. I like reading directions and then following them with wood and concrete. Karo likes not being surprised.

Priscilla sent out seventy invitations to people to come to our cabin on December twenty-third. She put little photocopied maps inside the envelopes. Forty-five people showed up. Mama had been dead four years. I'd been sober twelve. I have a dead son and husband. Karo is single. Her hands are a series of knobs, her fingers veer away from her knuckles with arthritis. She lives on Tylenol and Motrin.

So, last year when Priscilla drove up on the twenty-third, all high and bright, ready for her party that night, Karo said through the window, "You could have let us know."

"About my whole life? Or about the party? Why? You would have tried to say no. I don't have time for that. We're going to make the best of the rest of our lives, if you don't mind, and we can start now with my coming-out party here. Help me carry in this stuff for the party."

The party was loud and both hams were eaten with the hundred and fifty rolls I made. Thompson's Turkey was a big hit. We didn't think anyone knew what was being silently announced in all the noise. We could hardly believe Priscilla was lesbian, whatever that really meant. Did she invite her children? Yes, but Fred and Charles said they knew already, good luck with her new life.

Now our sister was a new person who went to bars to meet strange women and have relationships. She looked bigger and healthier. We looked, she said, a little worse than usual. She could see Mary Mills emerging in my face. Then she gave us a new kind of bear hug, a scooping forklift under our arms, lifting us up a few inches.

To our neighbors and the strangers who drove down from Baltimore, the forty-five who came, it was just another Christmas party, maybe better food and more of it. They missed the messages about a woman on the verge of early retirement turning lesbian. To us, the party was a lot of work, doing what we knew Priscilla wanted done. There had to be great garlands of running cedar made for the doors. We had waxed the polyurethaned pine floors—unnecessary work because the floors have a permanent sheen. Priscilla wanted us to remove the ramps we had for Mama's wheelchair, but we didn't.

The afternoon of the party, the rains began, warm and blowing, and the forsythia was blooming.

This year the cold is a steel blanket. We haven't had water or lights for two days. We are cooking dried beans—navy, pinto, kidney—on the woodstove we put up at one of the fireplaces. It throws out heat and the fireplace at the other end sucks it up the chimney. Even if Priscilla had wanted one, there couldn't be a party this year. No flushing toilets, no water to wash Mama's old wine glasses.

Priscilla has used the ramp to slide down to the driveway, to go, crying every step, up to the mailbox. I don't know what she is expecting. Last year, we had champagne stuck out in the old tin washtubs filled with ice. The black bottles in the ice were nice and people stood on the porch drinking iced champagne without their coats. Priscilla put a real candle in every window, that was the one thing she did for the party, if you don't count sending out the red invitations and photocopying the recipe for Thompson's Turkey.

This year Priscilla won't eat. Too busy crying. Her body is dissolving into air in front of our eyes. Fred and Charles have made it clear that we shouldn't call them, no matter what. I guess they don't mean a funeral. We're it. All she has left, Priscilla says to Karo and me, over and over, wrapped up in a blanket in a corner, far away from the stove.

She rocks back and forth. She wouldn't take a bath if we had any water. Karo brings in slabs of ice for me to melt in the biggest enamel pan we have, red-rimmed and at least forty years old. Then she leaves as fast as she can to work on the wood or feed our twelve cows, get the Bronco and pickup started: avoidance. I know that much.

Priscilla's shrink has sent us messages that boiled down to, as we translated Priscilla's sobs, if we wanted to help our sister, we should get ourselves shot. That might help. Sobbing, sobbing, Priscilla explains to us that such extremes probably wouldn't do the trick. Not by themselves. Maybe accompanied by other treatments. In conjunction, perhaps.

"Don't be simpleminded," she weeps. We always take things wrong. Not a firing squad of doctors raising their guns, saying professionally, you ruined her life, please pay with yours. We should remove ourselves emotionally, get lost, but still be there, be supportive. Her marriage, with its regular infidelities, was not her real problem; we were, are, always have been. Everyone has two or three sexual natures, but she guesses we don't know this. An old maid and a drunk, Karo and me, are her family now. Karo says "Ex-drunk." I want to hug her, using Priscilla's new hugging style.

Karo coughs when she hears Priscilla blame us for not letting her come take care of Mama. She recalls how Karo made her tell lies to Mama about the trip to Mary Mills. Karo gets up to put back on her insulated zip-up coverall. She can hobble into it, and while she is doing this geriatric circus-dressing act, Priscilla goes on crying over her life and how we have helped ruin it. Do we realize that? Other people have problems, sure, but we have deep, long problems. We are dysfunctional. Karo stops hobbling into her suit and coughs some more. Now Priscilla's tears are coming in flat clear sheets. Is she supposed to go it alone or with new people? Karo is now a camouflaged thorn branch in her suit. Her eyes are startled, like those of a deer caught on the highway by car lights. She claps her work gloves together softly, as if Priscilla has finished a speech, which she has.

I try to keep Karo from going out to check on the fences. The cows won't leave the shed in this cold. I don't want to be with Priscilla by myself. I don't want Karo to fall on the ice out by the shed. It's below zero out there. It's dark at four-thirty.

The next morning, still cold, the December sunshine is clear and startling, as if this little trouble brought to the country from Baltimore could be fixed in a minute. The sun rinses the pine table and the poly-treated pine floors in a lemon-juice solution, showing off the surfaces that I have waxed and polished for Priscilla's visit, thinking we might have another surprise party.

As it turns out, I'm right. In four days, Priscilla's sobs are drier and drier, sounding like cereal pouring out of the box into the bowl. In fact, my cleaning and waxing the house has been for a party, another party for Priscilla. A going-away party.

It takes the rescue squad to get Priscilla out of the cabin. They use the ramp. There are five of us at the party. Two men and three sisters.

Karo and I breathe carefully, apologetically, sorry, so sorry we are alive. No one lets the milk drip from the milk carton when I hand it around after pouring us more coffee. Joey and Tim have their names sewn on their white squad-team jumpsuits—that's how we know them. They don't look like the children of anyone we know.

Karo and I feel ready to follow the doctor's orders: hooded, ready to catch bullets for Priscilla. Our willingness hangs in the sunshine, which Priscilla must sense. She stops crying long enough to tell us how far up the line of family crimes the doctor has climbed in this series of visits.

"He seems stuck on us. Are we the worst?" Karo asks, looking surprised, but not at all surprised. Priscilla weeps, agreeing.

We understand that the doctor would like to have all of us show up: me, Karo, Fred and Charles, Priscilla's new and now ex-girlfriend, Paula. "Do 'group,'" he says to us through Priscilla. "Thursdays are good for him. How about it? Can we get to Baltimore in early January?"

Priscilla is tracing the lines of her silver necklace that looks like barbed wire. "Group" sounds better than the firing squad. She is crying the dry, flaked cries. Some of the people she needs shot the most are already dead. Write your parents letters, the doctor says. Tell them how they were cruel. Ask them how hell is. We can't believe a doctor talks this way. We are very careful with the milk and sugar. I wipe off the cream pitcher. Joey and Tim get Priscilla's lambswool coat and we all start for the door.

Words That Carry Us Home

It is not the property or the landscape any more than it is the physical structure that is important. . . . People who no longer have physical access to their homeplace seek solace in the power of narrative. Through their stories people may still travel home.

MICHAEL ANN WILLIAMS

LOUISE ERDRICH

The Names of Women

Ikwe is the word for woman in the language of the Anishinabe,
my mother's people, whose descendants, mixed with and married to French trappers and farmers, are the Michifs of the Turtle
Mountain reservation in North Dakota. Every Anishinabe *Ikwe,*
every mixed-blood descendant like me, who can trace her way
back a generation or two, is the daughter of a mystery. The history of the woodland Anishinabe—decimated by disease, fighting Plains Indian tribes to the west and squeezed by European
settlers to the east—is much like most other Native American
stories, a confusion of loss, a tale of absences, of a culture that
was blown apart and changed so radically in such a short time
that only the names survive.

And yet, those names.

The names of the first women whose existence is recorded on
the rolls of the Turtle Mountain Reservation, in 1892, reveal as
much as we can ever recapture of their personalities, complex
natures and relationships. These names tell stories, or half stories,
if only we listen closely.

There once were women named *Standing Strong, Fish Bones,
Different Thunder.* There once was a girl called *Yellow Straps.*
Imagine what it was like to pick berries with *Sky Coming Down,*
to walk through a storm with *Lightning Proof.* Surely, she was
struck and lived, but what about the person next to her? People
always avoided *Steps Over Truth,* when they wanted a straight
answer, and *I Hear,* when they wanted to keep a secret. *Glitter-
ing* put coal on her face and watched for enemies at night. The

woman named *Standing Across* could see things moving far across the lake. The old ladies gossiped about *Playing Around*, but no one dared say anything to her face. *Ice* was good at gambling. *Shining One Side* loved to sit and talk to *Opposite the Sky*. They both knew *Sounding Feather, Exhausted Wind* and *Green Cloud*, daughter of *Seeing Iron*. *Center of the Sky* was a widow. *Rabbit, Prairie Chicken* and *Daylight* were all little girls. *She Tramp* could make great distance in a day of walking. *Cross Lightning* had a powerful smile. When *Setting Wind* and *Gentle Woman Standing* sang together the whole tribe listened. *Stop the Day* got her name when at her shout the afternoon went still. *Log* was strong, *Cloud Touching Bottom* weak and consumptive. *Mirage* married *Wind*. Everyone loved *Musical Cloud*, but children hid from *Dressed in Stone*. *Lying Down Grass* had such a gentle voice and touch, but no one dared to cross *She Black of Heart*.

We can imagine something of these women from their names. Anishinabe historian Basil Johnston notes that 'such was the mystique and force of a name that it was considered presumptuous and unbecoming, even vain, for a person to utter his own name. It was the custom for a third person, if present, to utter the name of the person to be identified. Seldom, if ever, did either husband or wife speak the name of the other in public.'

Shortly after the first tribal roll, the practice of renaming became an ecclesiastical exercise, and, as a result, most women in the next two generations bear the names of saints particularly beloved by the French. *She Knows the Bear* became Marie. *Sloping Cloud* was christened Jeanne. *Taking Care of the Day* and *Yellow Day Woman* turned into Catherines. Identities are altogether lost. The daughters of my own ancestors, *Kwayzancheewin—Acts Like a Boy* and *Striped Earth Woman*—go unrecorded, and no hint or reflection of their individual natures comes to light through the scattershot records of those times, although they must have been genetically tough in order to survive: there were epidemics of typhoid, flu, measles and other diseases that winnowed the tribe each winter. They had to have grown up sensible, hard-working, undeviating in their attention to their tasks. They had to have been lucky. And if very lucky, they acquired carts.

It is no small thing that both of my great-grandmothers were known as women with carts.

The first was Elise Eliza McCloud, the great-granddaughter of *Striped Earth Woman.* The buggy she owned was somewhat grander than a cart. In her photograph, Elise Eliza gazes straight ahead, intent, elevated in her pride. Perhaps she and her daughter Justine, both wearing reshaped felt fedoras, were on their way to the train that would take them from Rugby, North Dakota, to Grand Forks, and back again. Back and forth across the upper tier of the plains, they peddled their hand-worked tourist items— dangling moccasin brooches and little beaded hats, or, in the summer, the wild berries, plums and nuts that they had gathered from the wooded hills. Of Elise Eliza's industry there remains in the family only an intricately beaded pair of buffalo horns and a piece of real furniture, a "highboy," an object once regarded with some awe, a prize she won for selling the most merchandise from a manufacturer's catalogue.

The owner of the other cart, Virginia Grandbois, died when I was nine years old: she was a fearsome and fascinating presence, an old woman seated like an icon behind the door of my grand-parents' house. Forty years before I was born, she was photo-graphed on her way to fetch drinking water at the reservation well. In the picture she is seated high, the reins in her fingers connected to a couple of shaggy fetlocked draft ponies. The bar-rel she will fill stands behind her. She wears a man's sweater and an expression of vast self-pleasure. She might have been saying *Kaygoh,* a warning, to calm the horses. She might have been speaking to whomever it was who held the camera, still a novel luxury.

Virginia Grandbois was known to smell of flowers. In spite of the potato picking, water hauling, field and housework, she found the time and will to dust her face with pale powder, in order to

look more French. She was the great-great-granddaughter of the
daughter of the principal leader of the *A-waus-e,* the Bullhead
clan, a woman whose real name was never recorded but who,
on marrying a Frenchman, was 'recreated' as Madame Cadotte.
It was Madame Cadotte who acted as a liaison between her
Ojibway relatives and her husband so that, even when French
influence waned in the region, Jean-Baptiste Cadotte stayed on
as the only trader of importance, the last governor of the fort at
Sault Ste. Marie.

By the time I knew Virginia Grandbois, however, her mind
had darkened, and her body deepened, shrunk, turned to bones
and leather. She did not live in the present or in any known time
at all. Periodically, she would awaken from dim and unknown
dreams to find herself seated behind the door in her daughter's
house. She then cried out for her cart and her horses. When they
did not materialize, Virginia Grandbois rose with great energy
and purpose. Then she walked towards her house, taking the
straightest line.

That house, long sold and gone, lay over one hundred miles
due east and still Virginia Grandbois charged ahead, no matter
what lay in her path—fences, sloughs, woods, the yards of
other families. She wanted home, to get home, to be home. She
wanted her own place back, the place she had made, not her
daughter's, not anyone else's. Hers. There was no substitute, no
kindness, no reality that would change her mind. She had to be
tied to the chair, and the chair to the wall, and still there was no
reasoning with Virginia Grandbois. Her entire life, her hard-
won personality, boiled down in the end to one stubborn, fixed,
desperate idea.

I started with the same idea—this urge to get home, even if I
must walk straight across the world. Only, for me, the urge to
walk is the urge to write. Like my great-grandmother's house,
there is no home for me to get to. A mixed-blood, raised in the
Sugarbeet Capital, educated on the Eastern seaboard, married in
a tiny New England village, living now on a ridge directly across

from the Swan Range in the Rocky Mountains, my home is a collection of homes, of wells in which the quiet of experience shales away into sweet bedrock.

Elise Eliza pieced the quilt my mother slept under, a patchwork of shirts, pants, other worn-out scraps, bordered with small rinsed and pressed Bull Durham sacks. As if in another time and place, although it is only the dim barrel of a four-year-old's memory, I see myself wrapped under smoky quilts and dank green army blankets in the house in which my mother was born. In the fragrance of tobacco, some smoked in home-rolled cigarettes, some offered to the Manitous whose presence still was honoured, I dream myself home. Beneath the rafters, shadowed with bunches of plants and torn calendars, in the nest of a sagging bed, I listen to mice rustle and the scratch of an owl's claws as it paces the shingles.

Elise Eliza's daughter-in-law, my grandmother Mary LeFavor, kept that house of hand-hewed and stacked beams, mudded between. She managed to shore it up and keep it standing by stuffing every new crack with disposable diapers. Having used and reused cloth to diaper her own children, my grandmother washed and hung to dry the paper and plastic diapers that her granddaughters bought for her great-grandchildren. When their plastic-paper shredded, she gathered them carefully together and one day, on a summer visit, I woke early to find her tamping the rolled stuff carefully into the cracked walls of that old house.

It is autumn in the Plains, and in the little sloughs ducks land, and mudhens, whose flesh always tastes greasy and charred. Snow is coming soon, and after its first fall there will be a short, false warmth that brings out the sweet-sour odour of highbush cranberries. As a descendant of the women who skinned buffalo and tanned and smoked the hides, of women who pounded berries with the dried meat to make winter food, who made tea from willow bark and rosehips, who gathered snakeroot, I am affected by the change of seasons. Here is a time when plants consolidate their tonic and drop seed, when animals store energy and grow thick fur. As for me, I start keeping longer hours, writing more, working harder, though I am obviously not a creature of a traditional Anishinabe culture. I was not raised speaking the old language, or adhering to the cycle of religious ceremonies that govern the Anishinabe spiritual relationship to the land and the moral order within human configurations. As the wedding of many backgrounds, I am free to do what simply feels right.

My mother knits, sews, cans, dries food and preserves it. She knows how to gather tea, berries, snare rabbits, milk cows and churn butter. She can grow squash and melons from seeds she gathered the fall before. She is, as were the women who came before me, a repository of all of the homely virtues, and I am the first in a long line who has not saved the autumn's harvest in birch bark *makuks* and skin bags and in a cellar dry and cold with dust. I am the first who scratches the ground for pleasure, not survival, and grows flowers instead of potatoes. I record rather than practise the arts that filled the hands and days of my mother and her mother, and all the mothers going back into the shadows, when women wore names that told us who they were.

HARRY CREWS

An excerpt from

A Childhood: The Biography of a Place

. . . some [friends and neighbors] would stay to sit by the fireplace late into the night, listening to the men talk, staying so late now and then they would end up staying all night, particularly if it was a weekend.

Because the only fireplace was in the living room where I lay, everybody gathered there after supper to watch the fire and eventually wash their feet and go off to bed. If it was a very cold night, they could carry a heated quilt from the fire to put over the icy sheets.

The stories start early in the night when the fire is as big as the hearth will hold, making its own sucking roar counterpoint to the roar of the wind under the shingled eaves of the house. Men and women and children sit in a wide semicircle, faces cast red and hollow-eyed by the fire. Auntie, who still stayed with me at night, floats into and out of the room, sometimes settling by my bed, sometimes going back to the kitchen to get something for me. Now and again, a woman or young girl will rise from her chair, back up to the hearthstone and discreetly lift her skirt from behind to receive the fire. . . .

The galvanized foot tub, holding perhaps two and a half gallons of water, captures the light on its dull surface. It is sitting in front of the first man in the semicircle. The water is getting hot. At some time during the evening, the man in front of whom it sits will slip his feet into the tub and wash. Then he will slide it to the person sitting next to him, maybe a woman, or a young girl, and that person will wash.

While the men talk, the tub makes its way around the line of people warming from the fire. After the last person washes his feet, it is only minutes before the other children will have to go off to bed and leave their daddies and uncles and older brothers to sit and talk late into the night. But I, safely in my fireroom bed, am privileged to hear whatever is said.

"Well, he was always like that."

"Had to happen like it had to happen."

"He jest had to win."

"He *would* win."

"Kill him to lose, jest kill'm is all."

"I remember. . . ."

Here the man would lean back and chew on a kitchen match, and the skin would draw tight around his eyes. He might not say anything for several minutes, but those of us sitting there, watching him chew on the match stick, didn't care how long he took to start the story because we knew that he was about to make what had been only gossip before personal and immediate now. The magic words had been spoken: "I remember. . . ."

One of my favorite places to be was in the corner of the room where the ladies were quilting. God, I loved the click of needles on thimbles, a sound that will always make me think of stories. When I was a boy, stories were conversation and conversation was stories. For me it was a time of magic.

It was always the women who scared me. The stories that women told and that men told were full of violence, sickness, and death. But it was the women whose stories were unrelieved by humor and filled with apocalyptic vision. No matter how awful the stories were that the men told they were always funny. The men's stories were stories of character, rather than of circumstance, and they always knew the people the stories were about. But women would repeat stories about folks they did not know and had never seen, and consequently, without character

counting for anything, the stories were as stark and cold as
legend or myth.

It is midmorning, and the women have been sewing since
right after breakfast when the light first came up. They are quilting, four women, one on each side of a square frame that has
been suspended from the ceiling to hold the quilt. When they are
through for the day, the frame can be drawn up to the ceiling
out of the way, but for now the needles and thimbles click over
the quiet, persistent drone of their voices.

I sit on the floor, and with me are two white-haired children,
brightly decorated with purple medicine used for impetigo, and
we sit there on the floor, the three of us, sucking on sugar tits,
trying to avoid the notice of our mothers, who will only stop
long enough to slap us if the noise of our play gets in the way of
the necessary work of making quilts.

The sugar tits we are sucking on are to quiet and pacify us
through the long day. They could not have worked better if they
had been opium instead of flour soaked with syrup or sometimes plain sugar wrapped in a piece of cloth. We chew on the
cloth and slowly the melting sweetness seeps onto our tongues
and it puts us into a kind of stupor of delight, just the mood to
receive the horror story when it comes.

"The Lord works in mysterious ways."

The needles click; the heavy, stockinged legs shift almost
imperceptibly.

"None of us knows the reason."

They start talking about God. We know the horror story's
coming.

"But it is a reason."

"Like the song says: Farther along we'll understand why."

"In heaven it'll all be clearer, but here on earth He works in
mysterious ways His many miracles to perform."

"It's no way to understand how things can sometimes be so
awful. We jest got to take the good with the bad."

"I reckon."

"A week ago tomorrow I heard tell of something that do make a body wonder, though."

Nobody asks what she heard. They know she'll tell. The needles click over the thimbles in the stretching silence. Down on the floor we stop sucking and have the sugar tits caught between our teeth.

Here it comes. . . .

The Kinship of the Living Earth

The country to the east of Derudeb was bleached and sere, and there were long grey cliffs and dom palms growing in the wadis. The plains were spotted with flat-topped acacias, leafless at this season, with long white thorns like icicles and a dusting of yellow flowers. At night, lying awake under the stars, the cities of the West seemed sad and alien—and the pretensions of the "art world" idiotic. Yet here I had a sense of homecoming.

BRUCE CHATWIN

COLETTE

My Mother and the Forbidden Fruit

The time came when all her strength left her. She was amazed beyond measure and would not believe it. Whenever I arrived from Paris to see her, as soon as we were alone in the afternoon in her little house, she had always some sin to confess to me. On one occasion she turned up the hem of her dress, rolled her stocking down over her shin and displayed a purple bruise, the skin nearly broken.

"Just look at that!"

"What on earth have you done to yourself this time, mother?"

She opened wide eyes, full of innocence and embarrassment.

"You wouldn't believe it, but I fell downstairs!"

"How do you mean—'fell'?"

"Just what I said. I fell, for no reason. I was going downstairs and I fell. I can't understand it."

"Were you going down too quickly?"

"Too quickly? What do you call too quickly? I was going down quickly. Have I time to go downstairs majestically like the Sun King? And if that were all . . . But look at this!"

On her pretty arm, still so young above the faded hand, was a scald forming a large blister.

"Oh goodness! Whatever's that!"

"My foot-warmer."

"The old copper foot-warmer? The one that holds five quarts?"

"That's the one. Can I trust anything, when that foot-warmer has known me for forty years? I can't imagine what possessed it, it was boiling fast, I went to take it off the fire, and crack, something gave in my wrist. I was lucky to get nothing worse than that blister. But what a thing to happen! After that I let the cupboard alone. . . ."

She broke off, blushing furiously.

"What cupboard?" I demanded severely.

My mother fenced, tossing her head as though I were trying to put her on a lead.

"Oh, nothing! No cupboard at all!"

"Mother! I shall get cross!"

"Since I've said 'I let the cupboard alone,' can't you do the same for my sake? The cupboard hasn't moved from its place, has it? So, shut up about it!"

The cupboard was a massive object of old walnut, almost as broad as it was high, with no carving save the circular hole made by a Prussian bullet that had entered by the right-hand door and passed out through the back panel.

"Do you want it moved from the landing, mother?"

An expression like that of a young she-cat, false and glittery, appeared on her wrinkled face.

"I? No, it seems to me all right there—let it stay where it is!"

All the same, my doctor brother and I agreed that we must be on the watch. He saw my mother every day, since she had followed him and lived in the same village, and he looked after her with a passionate devotion which he hid. She fought against all her ills with amazing elasticity, forgot them, baffled them, inflicted on them signal if temporary defeats, recovered, during entire days, her vanished strength; and the sound of her battles, whenever I spent a few days with her, could be heard all over the house till I was irresistibly reminded of a terrier tackling a rat.

At five o'clock in the morning I would be awakened by the clank of a full bucket being set down in the kitchen sink immediately opposite my room.

"What are you doing with that bucket, mother? Couldn't you wait until Josephine arrives?"

And out I hurried. But the fire was already blazing, fed with dry wood. The milk was boiling on the blue-tiled charcoal stove.

Nearby, a bar of chocolate was melting in a little water for my breakfast, and, seated squarely in her cane armchair, my mother was grinding the fragrant coffee which she roasted herself. The morning hours were always kind to her. She wore their rosy colours in her cheeks. Flushed with a brief return to health, she would gaze at the rising sun, while the church bell rang for early Mass, and rejoice at having tasted, while we still slept, so many forbidden fruits.

The forbidden fruits were the over-heavy bucket drawn up from the well, the firewood split with a billhook on an oaken block, the spade, the mattock, and above all the double steps propped against the gable-window of the wood-house. They were the climbing vine whose shoots she trained up to the gable-windows of the attic, the flowery spikes of the too-tall lilacs, the dizzy cat that had to be rescued from the ridge of the roof. All the accomplices of her old existence as a plump and sturdy little woman, all the minor rustic divinities who once obeyed her and made her so proud of doing without servants, now assumed the appearance and position of adversaries. But they reckoned without that love of combat which my mother was to keep till the end of her life. At seventy-one dawn still found her undaunted, if not always undamaged. Burnt by the fire, cut with the pruning knife, soaked by melting snow or spilt water, she had always managed to enjoy her best moments of independence before the earliest risers had opened their shutters. She was able to tell us of the cats' awakening, of what was going on in the nests, of news gleaned, together with the morning's milk and the warm loaf, from the milkmaid and the baker's girl, the record in fact of the birth of a new day.

It was not until one morning when I found the kitchen un-warmed and the blue enamel saucepan hanging on the wall, that I felt my mother's end to be near. Her illness knew many respites, during which the fire flared up again on the hearth, and the smell of fresh bread and melting chocolate stole under the door together with the cat's impatient paw. These respites were periods of unexpected alarms. My mother and the big walnut cupboard

were discovered together in a heap at the foot of the stairs, she
having determined to transport it in secret from the upper landing to the ground floor. Whereupon my elder brother insisted
that my mother should keep still and that an old servant should
sleep in the little house. But how could an old servant prevail
against a vital energy so youthful and mischievous that it con-
trived to tempt and lead astray a body already half fettered by
death? My brother, returning before sunrise from attending a
distant patient, one day caught my mother red-handed in the
most wanton of crimes. Dressed in her nightgown, but wearing
heavy gardening sabots, her little grey septuagenarian's plait of
hair turning up like a scorpion's tail on the nape of her neck, one
foot firmly planted on the crosspiece of the beech trestle, her
back bent in the attitude of the expert jobber, my mother, reju-
venated by an indescribable expression of guilty enjoyment, in
defiance of all her promises and of the freezing morning dew,
was sawing logs in her own yard.

ELISAVIETTA RITCHIE

Sounds

Great Aunt Eleanora is giving us trouble these days. She wants to stay on her farm. Alone.

"You can't even get good TV here!" argues the realtor, urging her to listen to a certain developer who will carve the Leighs' Tidewater homestead into twenty-nine lots, whose new owners will presumably install satellite dishes.

Reception is haphazard only because the house is down on the inlet.

Great Aunt Eleanora has no time for television. Radio provides her news and good music. She listens as she paints — currently, murals. She started on murals when she had to stay within earshot of Great Uncle Ramsey, and after thirty years no longer could hide out in the chicken coop, which Ben helped her convert to her studio. There, she painted what she wanted, and the days when Ramsey was in court, shipped the cardboard cylinders of canvases off to a gallery in New York. Ben, and later I, transported the bigger paintings in the farm truck. Her works sold slowly over the years, but we quietly invested the proceeds in a fund which now pays the taxes on the farm. So no need to sell it.

I'm one of the few people who knows this. She assigned me power-of-attorney.

Though now from the rafters a family of black vultures would observe every stroke of her brush, she talks of working in the chicken house again, "once the weather warms and these murals are finished."

Today she shows me the half-painted wall. "Still some baf-
fling blanks, and the moats look empty. Ramsey suggested lotus
and Ben urged lilies—but it's old-ladyish to paint flowers. Last
week a stag walked through the snowy yard, then obliged me by
standing still—downright posing—under the English walnut
while I sketched him onto that panel between the windows. But
horses I need to study live again. . . ."

The murals are medieval scenes of knights and their ladies
galloping or strolling around various picturesque European hill-
sides. Frankly, they aren't particularly well-executed, proportions
are off, not half as good as her earlier impressionistic paysages,
seascapes and passionate abstracts.

But Great Uncle Ramsey Leigh hates abstracts. A retired
judge, he likes historic scenes and would wheel his chair, with
Ben wheeling along in his wake, into whatever room she was
painting. The fact that her eyesight and her hands are no longer
as sure didn't matter to them: their own eyesight and coordina-
tion were failing. That didn't stop them from advising.

Increasingly Great Aunt Eleanora cared for both men, one
black, one white. Ben's grandson Jefferson and I shoved the
table against the wall and moved their beds into the dining room,
so they would be easier to feed and keep an eye on while she
was in the kitchen. With windows on three sides, on bright winter days the dining room heats up, and the fireplace keeps it
warm at night. In summer they preferred the veranda, so she
continued her murals there.

Then, even with Jeff's help bathing and lifting them, home
nursing got too much for Great Aunt Eleanora. Or so the county
social worker insisted: "Judge Leigh and that old Ben are two
big heavy men, and here you are, a little wren, trying to care for
them day and night!"

A private room came available for Great Uncle Ramsey at the
Home, and for Ben a bed in the ward.

I thought we'd have a time persuading them to move. But
they consulted each other, just as they used to consult over the
no-till way to sow soybeans while harvesting winter wheat, and

did the barn need a new roof, the mare a new shoe. Finally they agreed to visit the Home: each had cronies living there already, hadn't seen them for ages. They let us sign them in.

"For one week," Uncle Ramsey said. "But just have young Jefferson shove us both into the same room: that'll be cheaper, and we smoke the same brand of tobacco."

The Admissions Secretary blinked, but Aunt Eleanora and I okayed it so the matter was arranged.

Turns out, Uncle Ramsey and Ben rather like being sweet-talked by those pretty nurses, the large-screen color television beats the black-and-white set at the farm, and though old ladies complain, in the Common Room they can smoke without Aunt Eleanora coughing. Still, away from familiar surroundings, they've grown increasingly confused.

At home, though her eyesight is blurring, Aunt Eleanora continues to extend her murals throughout the downstairs. Cats brush against wet paint, leaving her pictures fuzzy and their tails purple and green. I wash the cats and her hair with tirpolene and baby shampoo, just as she used to wash mine when I was a child. While it was drying in the sun, she would teach me to read from a tiny maroon-covered primer, and how to sculpt and fire the statuettes which remain aligned on an upstairs shelf like ungainly anchors for my soul. While we shelled peas, baked cakes or washed dishes together, she would tell me stories, usually about the great dead artists.

Now I tell some of those stories to a few thousand people, at least in a way, when I write catalogues for the Richmond and other museums. And she tells them aloud to herself as she cooks what she needs to feed herself and twenty-six (at last count) cats.

Jefferson, who bought the old tenant house, cuts fallen branches into logs small enough for her to put in the old stove. He also ploughs her road after snows, when he is around, and some Wednesdays his wife Alethea Mae brings groceries. I come by most weekends with a cake or casserole to last several days. Since her washing machine rusted through, I do her laundry in town. I lug my computer to manage her bills and the correspondence

which still comes in from galleries and other artists. I also bring
new brushes and paints, and sometimes, friends for a picnic.
She prefers young people. And anyone who wants to take home
a kitten or two, Great Aunt Eleanora will offer them their
choice.

At her request, every visit I check on the farm, attempt to
patch whatever needs patching. During my childhood summers
here, Ben used to let Jeff and me tag along to "help" and soon
taught us to work with wrench and saw, tractor and scythe. So
last week Jeff and I shored up the sun porch, but another board's
always rotten somewhere. The roof leaks into the upstairs bedrooms, though since she's had trouble with steps, Great Aunt
Eleanora now sleeps off the kitchen, where Ben lived until his
legs gave out. In winter the furnace tends to die, or the chimney
gets blocked as when thirteen bricks fell into the flue, and the
sweep also removed thirteen buckets of soot. The electricity fails
in storms, the circulating pump breaks, the septic tank—

More than one midnight I've driven from Richmond at 65
m.p.h. to cope. And some night, it will be that Aunt Eleanora has
tripped over a cat and broken a hip, or wandered to the beach
and waded in too far. So of course I'm concerned about her, out
here all alone now, fields on three sides, the inlet on the fourth.

"Just sell the place," people urge, "move her into the Home,
and you won't have any more worries."

Since I am her closest relative, everyone is pressuring me.
Sometimes I'm tempted. A terrible decision, to wrest her from
her beloved farm. Today I bring up the move.

"I am perfectly fine here, thank you."

January's wind methodically flaps the shed roof, beats crepe
myrtle branches against the house, rattles windows—three
panes slipped from their sashes as the putty crumbled, and the
glazier is always coming *next* week. Cats meowl to enter or exit,
I suspect some other animal in the cellar, the forgotten tea kettle
shrills, even the chicken soup I'm cooking makes unearthly
burbles.

"But don't all the odd noises bother you at night?"

"At night," she shrugs, "of course there are sounds. Mostly, I identify: from the woods, the hoot owl. From the cove, loons. Scratchings, shrills, chirps in the roof, wind spiralling down all three chimneys—each has a singular moan. And when I pry rot from a window frame, the squeal that freezes against the pane is explainable."

Since Aunt Eleanora is much alone, whenever she has company, she really talks.

"But—" she pauses to pour hot water into the pot, not noticing it splash on the worn Oriental rug, "it's the voices the farm has absorbed across three hundred years—just imagine, from Indian plaints to colonial cries of love! Then this morning when I looked out the kitchen door to see if you had arrived, I noticed among the spindly figs and runaway vines covering the foundations of that first plantation house here (you remember the one that burned in the Civil War, and nowhere in the archives could Ramsey ever discover which side lighted the torch)—I noticed a child in a dark pink pinafore."

"What child?" The nearest house is a mile away, no children there. No picnickers land on her beach in January.

"A child . . . plump, about three. She was crying, her nose was running, she had a cold, or was cold. Then, she was gone. . . . Or, was never there."

"Perhaps not. . . ."

"But every spring when the garden is ploughed, in a furrow near—remember that broken pipe which leads to the barn?— always I find one tattered rag doll. You might check in the pony cart."

Except for Ramsey's ancient Packard and the farmer's tractor, the barn has stood empty for years. But the wood is good, and the stalls still bear the names of horses I learned to ride on: SMOKEY, STORM KING, OLD JESS.

Could raise horses again, someday. . . .

Absently cradling an orange kitten named Titian, Aunt Eleanora stares toward the river. Can she see two black vultures in the moribund oak?

I pour tea into chipped china cups. "But aren't you ever afraid here?"

"Afraid? Of—ghosts? Nonsense. I early learned to settle in with presences. As with the woodchucks in the cellar, raccoons in the roof, cats in the barn their ancestors guard. In time," she sighs, "my voices too will merge with the farm."

"Voices? Did you discuss this with the doctor?"

She looks puzzled. "The—voices? Whatever for? And it's not always voices. Mostly, it's like your computer pinging even if the power's off, or high-tension lines humming across the fields in a blizzard."

"Ringing in the ears can mean something's wrong."

"I meant to mention it to the doctor last year. Happens whenever I close my eyes. A hive in the brain." Her blue eyes focus on me. "You must hear them too. As in town, there's always an ambulance down the avenue, fire engines across the park, jackhammers, traffic, that school yard six blocks away, hooves striking cobblestones."

"Except the cobblestones were asphalted over years ago, and there aren't horses in town anymore."

"Sounds pile up, you know, are stored. Volcanoes exploding decades ago remain in the air. Cathedral chimes, troubadours' plaints, street cries. High-pitched notes that set dogs howling. That's what I hear, when I wake in the night or try to nap after lunch. A music box under my pillow, roosters behind the drapes. I wonder, has my skull become one vast receptor. . . ."

Suddenly she looks concerned. "Do I also transmit?"

"Transmit?" The social worker may well be correct: incipient senility.

"I certainly don't generate. I nap in the armchair—no creaky rocker for me—radio off, phone off the hook. My necklaces which used to tinkle and jangle—I moved like a belled goat— have been stolen. Or sold?"

"You gave them all to me, Aunt Eleanora, don't you remember, one every birthday for the last twenty years. But I'll return them, you obviously miss them, I don't need more than one."

Once she goes into the Home, any jewelry will disappear.

"Oh, don't worry about returning those baubles, dear. I can still hear their symphonies on my bare neck. Lovely. . . . Yes, the doctor suggested tests my next check-up, next year. Today,"— she looks radiant—"Today, I'm tuned to a fishmonger's serenade. . . . Now it's whistling swans. . . . And sometimes, from farther waters, choirs of whales."

She settles back in her armchair. Leonardo, the piebald tomcat, jumps onto her lap. She is content with her voices, her cats. And glad for my company once every week or so.

Then she jumps up, spilling Leonardo and her untouched tea, gathers her splattered smock from its hook, her palette and paints from the kitchen.

"Swans—that's what I need for the moats. And a whale for the bay beyond. It's gotten so overcast outside, would you mind shining that light there—just bend its neck—so I can see what I'm doing. Almost out of white paint—could I trouble you to bring me a tube next week?"

I jot "White Paint" in my notebook. I'm forgetful of late, if I don't write down. . . .

"Now, child, I don't want to detain you. You have a long drive to Richmond, and you had better be on your way before it snows again. Take those cookies for the road. There, in the Louis Sherry tin."

I look in the pantry. Among shoe boxes marked: BRUSHES, CHARCOAL, MARINE FOSSILS (SCALLOPS), MARINE FOSSILS (ANCIENT CLAMS), SHEEP SKULLS, ARROW HEADS, the tin is empty. I write "Fig Newtons" on my list. When I was six, she taught me to arrange them into castles and battlements, as if they were dominos.

Given how the cats are scratching, I add "Flea Powder."

Knowing I might be visiting, the social worker phones. "Good news! Your aunt finally leads the waiting list for the Home. Could be a matter of only a week, at worst two, until. . . ."

Until another resident dies and frees up a bed. Until we—I— must face packing her up. Just the essentials that might survive institutional laundering. The rest will be locked up here until the fate of the place is settled. What of her half-finished canvases stacked in the chicken house? And the cats?

"Is that big ol' house warm enough?" the social worker asks cheerily. "How's your aunt doing?"

"Great," I answer. "And she likes it cool. Let's let her stay here a bit longer. Someone else in more desperate need for a bed can take her place. If necessary, I can get leave from work for a few weeks."

Even years. . . . Since I'm supposed to inherit this farm, I'd better get used to staying here in season and out. Until one morning they discover me collapsed in the barn, or drowned in the inlet, or shrivelled and stiff in this wildly painted parlor, even with brushes dried in my hands. That's the way to go, Aunt Eleanora has said.

I thank the social worker, hang up.

"Next weekend," I promise Aunt Eleanora, "rain or shine, I'll drive you around to see horses. And if the weather should be warm—it will be spring soon—I'll walk you down to the cove, and we'll feed some crusts to the ducks. I could even push you in a wheelchair all the way up the path to the lighthouse."

Preoccupied with outlining her swans, she seems not to pay attention.

I tape another sheet of plastic over a broken pane, then bank the fire, raise the thermostat, go outside with a broomstick to check the level of heating oil. Will that be enough to last until April? She has enough food in the fridge to last the week, a cupboard of cans, as well as the cauldron of chicken I've got simmering on her old iron stove. Afraid she'll forget it, I cut the flame: she doesn't mind lukewarm soup, and the house is always cold enough so it won't spoil. I wash and refill bowls with food for the anxious cats.

What would happen to them?

In a corner of the kitchen counter I notice a bag of crusts and stale bread. Although the weather has been too cold for her to venture outside, she still intends to walk down to the inlet to feed the wild ducks. Despite all her cats, there is evidence the mice from the walls are taking their share of crumbs along the way. She won't let anyone buy traps or poison.

The first flurries of snow. I run to the inlet with the bag of crusts, past the broken skiff caught in the ice rimming the shore. Can still see some red and blue paint where Jeff and I painted the hull, then added a squiggly blue waterline, like waves, which Great Uncle Ramsey warned was ridiculous, but we were twelve or thirteen.

Two mallards are paddling among the waves beyond the ice. I fling the crusts. The ducks skid across to retrieve them.

"More crusts next week, I promise you."

Suddenly I freeze as twenty whistling swans fly in line. They fracture the sun, then veer so low the tips of their wings skim the water like skipping stones. One swan breaks formation, swerves from the others, lands in the cove. At last the rest follow. They reach their long necks underwater to forage for seaweed and softshell clams, until the water is tufted by triangles of upended swans.

When I stop in the house to gather up my computer and Aunt Eleanora's laundry, and to say good-bye, I hear her humming. A whale is swimming into life among the galleons in the sea between the tall clock and the fireplace.

I tiptoe out, load the car, give it a few minutes to warm up.

The whole drive to town, the humming persists.

Inner Haven

The search may begin with a restless feeling, as if one were being watched. One turns in all directions and sees nothing. Yet one senses that there is a source for this deep restlessness; and the path that leads there is not a path to a strange place, but the path home. . . . The journey is hard, for the secret place where we have always been *is overgrown with thorns and thickets of "ideas," of fears and defenses, prejudices and repressions.*

PETER MATTHIESSEN

The whole life of the individual is nothing but the process of giving birth to himself; indeed, we should be fully born when we die.

ERICH FROMM

SUE BENDER

An excerpt from

Plain and Simple

The next spring I went back East to the house on Red Dirt Road in Long Island that my husband had designed twenty-five years before. I was coming back in the quiet season, before the on-slaught of summer traffic jams, beautiful people, and lines at the supermarket. . . .

Unexpectedly, I started cleaning. After twenty-four years and long winters unattended, the house felt neglected. I wrote and cleaned and cleaned and wrote, and somehow the two were connected. I got into corners, emptied cabinets, scrubbed walls, washed windows, polished floors, and loved every minute of it. Far from being a diversion, the housework supported me as I wrote. What do I really need? And out went more and more things. Simpler and simpler.

Stripped down, pared down, the house came alive. Nothing changed and everything changed. Nothing special and every-thing special.

Taking care of my home was no longer a chore. Like a Zen monk, raking the white pebbles at the temple, I spent seven min-utes each morning sweeping the black floor. A meditation.

A friend was horrified. "What are you becoming? An ordi-nary housewife?"

Could I explain it to her?

I had always devalued Hestia, the peaceful goddess of the hearth. I thought poor, dull Hestia, the ugly duckling goddess, was stuck by the hearth, while my favorites, Athena and Artemis, were out there in the world, slaying dragons.

But when I learned that the Latin word for hearth is focus, something clicked.

Sweeping the floor or doing the dishes is the outer form, the thing to which I attached myself in order to learn. What I had been looking for was the calm and focus I felt when I was with the Amish doing the dishes. It was a state of mind I was after.

. . . My addiction to activity had diverted me from looking inside, fearing the emptiness I would find. Yet, beneath all the frenzy was the very thing, that inner calm I was seeking. . . .

. . . The Amish taught me something about the human costs when old values are cast aside, sacrificed for "success." Now I am ready to ask: "Am I a successful human being, not only a success?" . . .

. . . I had hoped that if I could learn the secret of the Amish life of "no frills," it would help me make great art. But their secret is there aren't any secrets. They know there is nothing "out there," just the "timeless present. . . ."

"Before I went to the Amish, I thought that the more choices I had, the luckier I'd be. But there is a big difference between having many choices and making a choice. Making a choice — declaring what is essential — creates a framework that eliminates many choices but gives meaning to the things that remain. Satisfaction comes from giving up wishing I was somewhere else or doing something else."

HARRY CREWS

An excerpt from

Blood and Grits

For many and complicated reasons, circumstances had collabo-
rated to make me ashamed that I was a tenant farmer's son. As
weak and warped as it is, and as difficult as it is even now to
admit it, I was so humiliated by the fact that I was from the edge
of the Okefenokee Swamp in the worst hookworm and rickets
part of Georgia I could not bear to think of it, and worse to
believe it. Everything I had written had been out of a fear and
loathing for what I was and who I was. It was all out of an
effort to pretend otherwise. I believe to this day, and will always
believe, that in that moment I literally saved my life, because the
next thought—and it was more than a thought, it was dead-
solid conviction—was that all I had going for me in the world or
would ever have was that swamp, all those goddamn mules, all
those screwworms that I'd dug out of pigs and all the other beautiful and dreadful and sorry circumstances that had made me the
Grit I am and will always be. Once I realized that the way I saw
the world and man's condition in it would always be exactly and
inevitably shaped by everything which up to that moment had
only shamed me, once I realized that, I was home free.

The Soul's Harbor

Continue for a while thinking of the Minnesota prairies as a natural cathedral with night services. By day money changers occupy the temple, and to them, there is no sacred place. The world is only real estate, and can be filed at the court house. The divine is entirely abstract. . . . since the divine has no body, it needs no place to live, need be fed nothing. In the cathedrals of England . . . God is fed the dead. Their bones line the walls, are everywhere underfoot. . . . it is a sound idea to hallow a place by putting bones inside it. . . .

. . . I think we want a world without dead in it, so that it can be more easily bought, sold, and used up. . . . If we imagine the corpses of a thousand people we loved making a skin on that ground, we would tend it better.

To have a sense of the sacredness of a place involves becoming aware of life that inhabits and dead who sanctify it.

BILL HOLM

SUSAN M. GAINES

Grieving Rights

For a long time I believed, would proclaim with a certain pride
even, that I was rootless. I thought this to be a particularly
American trait, or Western American, or, really, a Californian
trait. I have been leaving since I was twenty and, of course, coming back just as often as I left. To see the family, I'd say, returning after a few months, a year, two at most, from Chile or
Indonesia or Spain, from wherever I had got to. To earn some
money to leave again, or to study for a while—never simply to
live because it was my home. The last time I came back, from
Japan, I said it was because I didn't like where I had got to, that
I was coming back to get away. I didn't realize that I'd come
home in search of you—though even before the letter came, I'd
been planning to visit you, go birding in the Sierras near that
lake you'd salvaged. But then, I'd been planning that for over
a decade.

I see now what an obvious lie it was, the freedom from place
that I professed: like a duck on some odd migratory path, I will
always come back. I left the lover I couldn't live without, to come
back. Another time I left the perfect job, to come back and look
for another. I have left cultures that intrigued and warmed me
with their depth and history, to come back to where we all know
there is no culture: to come back to California and touch the
ground—feel the scratching shift of sand around my toes, the
hard thump of granite beneath my boots, the soft give of redwood
humus—thinking all the while that it is impossible, ridiculous, to
love an arbitrary strip of land. Southerners and Easterners might

have "roots," and Asians and Europeans—origins, I thought, having something to do with people and culture and history, a particular lilt to the language, or character of town. But there is no lilt to my language, no history to my people, no town that draws me back; I'd never heard, didn't want to know, of roots like mine, tucked so literally into the soil and sprawled across a thousand miles of diverse terrain. Even now I shy away from believing, from accepting what you accepted so many years ago: the pain and devotion, responsibility and commitment that loving an arbitrary strip of land—a doomed and dying strip—entails. You, I think, truly believed that you could save it—conceiving your children, you must have believed—for you were older than I, born when hope might yet have seemed reasonable.

I would start at the beginning, and yet I fear that the beginning is not enough: I need some of our prehistory as well, if I am to claim now my right to grieve.

You were born first, the oldest cousin, and then I was born a decade later, the youngest. I was gregarious and affectionate, the easygoing baby girl; and you, according to the grown-ups, were cold, aloof, and inaccessible, even as a boy. Perhaps, then, it was the challenge of your coolness that drew me to you. I don't know what drew you to me—my warmth?—but we drifted past all the brothers and sisters and cousins in between and united.

At first I only saw you when our families gathered, one Sunday a month and all the Jewish holidays—which the grown-ups claimed not to believe in, but celebrated anyway—plus Christmas and, of course, Thanksgiving. I've never been sure how Christmas got in there, surrounded as it was by a vague sort of guilt— perhaps they did it for my mother, though she was no more Christian than the rest were Jewish. When I ask now, they blame it on us kids, saying we clamored for presents and Christmas trees, but I can't remember a time without Christmas and you were indifferent to presents and the like—it must have been the middle kids who clamored.

Your mother was the only aunt who didn't work, your house

the largest and most comfortable, so that was where we gathered. It was in a part of Los Angeles with hills and golf courses and a sea breeze, where each sturdy house was distinct from its neighbors, rather than cloned from a single flimsy master like ours in the Valley. I loved going there, not just because of you, but for the house itself. I liked the carpet: the deep pile, aristocratic white, the large, clean expanse of it. I liked the big windows and the low-lying, deceptively simple modern furniture of some light polished wood. I heard that your family was wealthy, but not rich, and decided that "wealthy" meant classier, more cultured, than "rich." I liked the stone women that your mother sculpted, arranged on the mantel, the pictures your sister painted hanging on the walls, the floor-to-ceiling bookcase, the stereo my father called "high fidelity." There was a piano, always in tune, and I loved how you played, so perfectly and nonchalantly—the same way you played guitar and, later, mandolin and fiddle—as if your talent were just a natural part of your family's wealth, something passed down, something I knew from the first that you disdained.

The gin rummy game started when I was about six. You'd take me to the room off the service porch that you'd chosen for your bedroom—the smallest, coldest room in the house, probably meant for a maid—and we would play cards for hours, entire days. That room was your haven, our card game your escape, and I was happy hiding out with you, the boisterous family hubbub but a distant squall, I was content not to be part of whatever you were escaping. You had a huge pickle jar full of pennies, and whenever I won we dumped it on the floor and picked out the old ones, a penny for every point I was ahead. You played in earnest, I think, winning as often as I, though you didn't award yourself pennies. Thinking back now, it was a strange pursuit for a young man whom the grown-ups called a genius, playing gin rummy with a six-year-old. I heard them call you that often, that word, "genius," passed between them in puzzled whispers; you had been tested in the schools, I suppose, and that's what they'd been told.

You went away to college, and for the two years you spent studying physics, I saw you only at Christmas. Years later, when I was in college myself, I wished that I had questioned you about those studies: I wanted to know what had drawn you into the theoretical marrow of science, what then allowed you to reject it so swiftly, so confidently. But by the time I thought to discuss such things with you, it was too late: you had, unequivocally, moved on, and I was afraid of what you might tell me, afraid of your contempt for what I myself was doing.

The family mythology has it that the only reason you changed your major to German literature was to torment your father, who'd been in Europe during the war. In any event, after you switched you started coming home more often, bringing with you a wild array of friends—a few you studied German with, but mostly they were biologists and geologists and ecologists of one sort or another, so perhaps you did know all along what you were destined for. It does seem incongruous that a naturalist as prominent as you eventually became should have a degree in German literature. Maybe it really was a scheme to abuse your poor father, and you only came home to flaunt it. But in spite of this—in spite of the assortment of drugs, the doubtful hygiene and dubious liaisons of your friends (this was the mid-sixties, after all)—your parents invariably made you and anyone you brought home welcome: meals for whoever showed up, bakery cookies and bagels, clean towels, a double bed for whoever wanted one, the comfortable carpet for sleeping bags.

I don't know where our parents were off to, all those times we found ourselves, you, and your sister perhaps, and all the friends, and me left in your care, with full run of the house. I must have been eleven when I smoked my first joint with you, and my second and third, each of those first joints a grand experience. Lying on the floor in the middle of the living room, on that carpet, with all the lights out and Mahler turned up full blast, smoking joints and learning to listen to music. Oh, I know I sound nostalgic, but I need to be sure that you remember, that they all remember, how far back it goes, how all these firsts of my early adolescence were marked by your presence. For you see, I don't know if you too might have forgotten that you loved me, and that I idolized you—quietly of course, holding always to the cool, rational standards you set for us.

You went away to Germany for a year, and when you came back there was money waiting for you, when you turned twenty-one I suppose it was. An inheritance from your grandfather. I heard murmurs of it rippling through the family—the money from the rich side, your mother's side, the murmurs from the other side, our fathers'. Oh how you hated all that money falling into your hands, unearned, money you didn't need, didn't want! You gave it away. Not all at once, but bit by bit you gave it to various friends who needed, or simply wanted, some money. No ceremony about it, not a loan or investment, no explanation required, you'd just take out a check and fill it out, hand it over. I never knew the details, who got what or why—though I doubt that you required reasons, you gave the money so readily; all I heard were the murmurs of disapproval, words like "spoiled," as if you were a child still, and "cruel"—to your father, I think they meant—as if you were an adult and a stranger. Until the money was gone, and years had passed and it was forgotten, a thing you'd done in your youth.

You spoke German a lot when you returned, and I was learning; you'd talk to your friends and I would listen, and then you'd speak to me and I would answer you in German. Never mind that it wasn't the most lyrical of languages, it was the first foreign language I'd attempted and I loved the magic way it came to me, the sounds and their meanings all at once, intertwined. You, of course, acted as if it were a normal thing to learn with such ease the language it had taken you years of study to master, so it wasn't until much later, when I started traveling, that I realized I had a talent—that I, who had no ear for music or eye for art, had an ear for language. People told me then, they'd say that I should have been a linguist, that I could have been some sort of foreign diplomat—just as they used to say that you could have been a famous musician.

Around this time, not long after you returned from Germany, you began to show me birds, and this is where our prehistory—longer in years and simpler, as one might expect, than the history it builds to—ends, and history begins. Where, or when, or how you learned to identify every bird that might possibly be found in western North America—their markings and habits, calls and songs, even their personalities—I still don't know. It was as if you'd waited until you knew everything, before you started showing me. Our fathers' aunt—who wouldn't know a house finch from a sparrow—told me recently that she was the one who got you interested in birds; you were a difficult child, she said, so she decided you needed a hobby and took you on an Audubon Society outing. Could be true, I suppose, that the birds started as a hobby for a difficult child. It would have been in Los Angeles then, that you first became interested in bird-watching. The golf course—they tell me you used to go birding at the golf course, though you never took me there. You took me to much better places.

I am twelve years old, and we are on vacation, your family and mine, in the desert. It was your idea to come here with the family, but now you've left them to themselves in the campground; all but me, I'm with you and your two friends who met us here, hiking amongst Joshua trees and rabbit brush and various small cacti one of the friends knows the names of, lizards and snakes being what the other one knows. The soil is sandy, not brown but pale gray, supporting not a forest but an expanse of well-spaced individual trees, all standing very erect with gay comic book arms reaching off towards the sides or up towards the heavens, crowned by an occasional white flower spike—evidence, I imagine, of nocturnal pollination rites. Mostly, what we're doing is looking for birds, walking slowly and quietly, stopping now and then to listen, or to wait.

I don't have my own binoculars yet, but every time we see a bird you hand me yours—powerful, heavy, serious binoculars—though I don't yet have the hang of lifting them directly to my

*eyes on the bird the way you've told me. I'm too slow. A bird flies
in close, alights on the side of a Joshua tree, and I know, even before I see the obvious bill or the way that it hugs the side of the
tree, you've already taught me to recognize the undulating flight
as a woodpecker's. You look for a moment through your binoculars, and then hand them to me. Oh—, I say, focusing. Oh, it's—
But it's neither of the two you've already taught me, not an acorn
woodpecker—the one you call the clown because of its funny
face and raucous laugh—and certainly it's not a flicker. What do
you see? you ask me. What I see first, of course, the brightest,
most exciting part of the bird, is the little red yarmelke on its
head. And, I say, it has a zebra back. The female flies into a neighboring tree and you tell me to look, look at the wings in flight;
I see the white wing patches, which, you say, I would need to see
if the male weren't there with his little red cap. Then, finally, you
tell me the name: gila woodpecker. Usually hangs out more to
the east, you add, in the low desert.*

What else would we have seen then? Nighthawks, certainly,
and gnatcatchers and wrens and any number of migrating warblers at the oases, thrashers and hawks and prairie falcons, perhaps a Gampbel's quail and, yes, of course I remember my first
roadrunner. Everything for me a "life bird," the first time for
everything.

In my thirteenth year my father was transferred and we
moved north, out of the flat Los Angeles suburbs. There were
hills and trees where we moved to, oaks and redwoods, and you
were nearby. Weekends and vacations you drove down to take
me to the coast, the mountains, a Grateful Dead concert and an
antiwar demonstration, to chaparral, rivers, forest, up and down
and across the state. What were you doing then, finishing your
degree? And after that, wasn't there a fellowship, a grant? You
didn't have a job, but hadn't you given away all your money, or
had you, after all, saved enough to live on for a while? I do remember a grant, it was for some ecological study in the Sierras—
but how did you get that? How did a young man with a degree
in German literature convince a granting agency that he was

amongst the most accomplished naturalists in the state? How is it that I don't remember these things, all these facts about you that are now common knowledge? Could it be that I never knew, that we were only cousins, after all, with peripheral cousins' lives, is that why I don't know? Or have I just forgotten—knowing that others will remember those things, and there is plenty, too much, for me to remember.

We are up to our knees in mud, in one of the salt marshes that surrounds—that used to surround—the bay. There's just enough predawn light to make our way, and it's cold, late fall, and my feet and legs are wet. I'm shivering, wishing that the sun would come up and warm me, and then wishing that it wouldn't because then the mosquitoes will be out. Freezing cold and not saying anything about being cold or worrying about mosquitoes or looking forward to a cup of hot chocolate in a heated coffee shop later, not saying anything because I'm tough, I'm being tough, I would never say these things to you—and besides, no one is saying anything, we are being quiet, moving slowly, stealthily through the mud. We are looking for rails, hoping to see a yellow rail, so shy and elusive, so hard to spot amongst the reeds in the predawn light, and more than wishing for warmth or hot chocolate or mosquito-proof skin I am wishing to see a yellow rail.

We are walking down the Matole River, headed west towards the mouth, walking on river rock and moving fast because the sun is going down. We're carrying sleeping bags and someone has a knapsack with some food and lots of wine. Mitchell, who I have a crush on, is with us and T.D., who talks to owls. This is not a park or reserve or anything, it's just a beautiful wild place, which means it probably belongs to some rancher—but there is no one to see or hear us, and you taught me early on how to hold apart the wires and duck through a barbed wire fence without getting snagged. I don't know why—if it's from not eating or I've been in the sun too much—but I have the worst headache

I have ever had, will ever have, in my life, and my vision is fuzzy, making the rocks difficult to negotiate quickly without twisting an ankle. I wouldn't think of complaining, but Mitch notices that I'm having a hard time keeping up, and when he asks I have to say, because there are tears sitting in the corners of my eyes from the pain, that I have a headache, though I do manage to shrug and smile when I say it. Mitch calls out to you and you wait for me and say we're almost there, wherever there is, and you take my sleeping bag to carry for me. We have to cross the river, which is pretty deep and Mitch asks if I want him to carry me. I am no longer small, and though I'm skinny, I'm big-boned and know I might be heavy, but the headache and my crush make me say yes. He picks me up and wades into the water, which comes to his hips, and I can tell that he would like to keep on carrying me. You wait for us on the other side and though you don't say anything, you put the sleeping bags down for Mitch to carry and take me onto your back, where I ride until we get to the spot where we will camp. You set me down on the rocks, and I lie where you set me, with the rocks pounding into my head and my eyes open, while you build a fire. The man who talks to owls takes a jug of red wine from his knapsack and offers it up for my headache, and I take a sip and throw up, so he takes his wine and goes with Mitch down to the edge of the water. When he comes back to say they've seen two river otters, you pause before following him, and I know you're looking at me because you know I'll want to see this—and I do, I want to see the river otters so much that I ignore my pounding head and walk down to the water and crouch there on a low flat boulder between you and Mitch watching them play, sliding over and under and between the rocks, and there is a dipper upstream that keeps disappearing and reappearing, and we stay there and the otters stay there and the dipper comes and goes until it is too dark to see.

When I fall asleep in my sleeping bag on the rocks with no pad, my head is still hurting and I dream it has come loose and is being tumbled over the rocks by the river, ground smooth and

*round by river rock, pounded and polished by water—but in the
morning my head is back on my neck and the headache is gone.
It is the only time I will ever, until now, show you any weakness,
but I am not sorry, for it is the first moment, the only moment,
when I know for certain that you love me and will always, in
your unobtrusive way, take care of me—and, though I am fourteen and won't allow anyone else to take care of me, I am elated
that you have, that you will.*

*We have been hiking for five days and not seen anyone but each
other and your three friends, who have lagged behind now so
that it's just you and me. This is my first backpacking trip. My
feet are covered with blisters, and the backpack I'm using is old
and makeshift, sliding off the rack whenever I lean over to tie
my boots. I'm not oblivious to these discomforts, nor to the
mosquitoes, or the cramps in my shoulders, but they only add to
the glory, to this joy that fills me like the water I lap from the
streams with my hungry tongue. We are hiking cross-country,
following the wide track of some ancient glacier, far from people
or roads. I've been camping every summer since I can remember,
but this is different, more quiet and alone and beautiful, more
wild and strange: here I can see clearly how this world, these
mountains, exist without me, existed long before you or me or
our parents or grandparents. I see how small I am and how big
it is, and I'm thrilled, thrilled to be so small, so inconsequential.
We are just below the treeline, the granite more and more
exposed as we climb, great sloping expanses of granite with
wildflowers one of the friends knows the names of poking up
through cracks—and I am in love, absolutely and forever in love
with this clean, warm, glacier-kissed stone, the ubiquitous granite of the Sierras.*

*We've skirted the edge of a lake, nearing the meadow that
rises from one end, and you've stooped to turn over a stone in
search of some rare salamander, when there is a loud rustle and
a cacophony of raucous, nasal, to you unmistakable, voices.
Your hand goes to your binoculars and you move swiftly to the*

edge of the lake. I follow you, keeping my eyes glued to the small group of geese rising from the meadow. We both lower our binoculars when the geese draw near, and you glance at me briefly with a smile hidden in your beard, your always subdued excitement, and I know it's a life bird for me. I even know the name, which you mumble, sounding surprised because they are not to be expected here. Snow geese. And then I'm bouncing on my toes, the backpack throwing me off balance, and pointing, nothing subdued about my excitement but my voice, as I exclaim softly and point, proud to have spotted the golden eagle flying high above the geese. We are both watching and I hear you suck in your breath when the eagle drops with a sort of squeal onto a goose at the rear of the flock. There is a midair flurry of white feathers and screams free-falling towards the lake as the flock moves on; then, suddenly, the eagle gives up and rises away from the goose, which falls another foot before recovering and limping off after the rest of the flock.

Who saw it first and who called whom, no one knows now, but someone has sighted a California condor off Highway 101, in the hills between San Jose and San Francisco. I am at your house for the weekend when the call comes, and we dive into your Volkswagen and drive to where the condor was last seen. For the first half hour it strikes me as ridiculous to be searching for this single bird that could have gone anywhere, but then your mood infects me and I watch closely out my window while you drive slowly along the shoulder, leaning forward on the steering wheel and peering up through the windshield.

The condor is sitting on top of a telephone pole: huge and forlorn and incredibly, deliciously ugly. With my binoculars I can make out all the details of the misshapen orange head, the sad droop to his shoulders, just a large, glorified vulture after all, and I wonder how it would be if turkey vultures were to go extinct—would that make seeing them as exciting as seeing this condor is, or is it just that he's so huge? He's old, you tell me, an *old bird, and I think perhaps that's why he looks so sad, so huge, so sad.*

We stand there for a long time and the condor doesn't do anything; another birder arrives, and you talk for a while, wondering why this condor is here, so far north. I want desperately to see him fly, but I'm growing impatient and don't dare frighten him off. Finally, bored, I wander up the hill towards a cluster of oaks to see if anything else is about—not realizing that I will never see another California condor, that this could be the last— and by the time I notice that he's flown, he's just a large spot fading into the haze over the hills.

All you did, really, was teach me about birds—patiently, until I too knew their names and habits, could identify even the most mottled immature gull—but with each species you handed me some small piece of habitat, a piece of land, of earth, of California. Of God perhaps. Like an extended honeymoon, those years were, an abandoned, innocent time of loving the land without pain or shame or worry, without thinking of the future, and foolishly, I let it into the very core of my being, accepting your gifts without question. Five years, was that all there was to our history, five years in my current thirty, in your forty?

I was the one who changed, I think, who fell out of step with you: suddenly I was eighteen and too old to receive your knowledge, your gifts, to walk at your pace. There were men, of course, too many men—I remember feeling embarrassed of them and of you, not wanting you to know them, or them to know you—perhaps that's where I first broke our connection, with my men. I didn't think about it then, that our history was over, that we had fallen into cousinhood, leading our separate lives and hearing news of each other through the family grapevines—and later, when I realized, I thought it was only temporary, that we were bound sometime to reconnect.

Did you hear—or did I tell you?—that when I went off to college I wanted to be a naturalist? It wasn't long before I learned, however, that what I thought of as a naturalist—that magical mix of science and spiritualism that I identified with you, with your silence and patience, the very set and sparkle to your eyes above your beard—was a thing of the past, of the nineteenth century. My classes were boring and two-dimensional, the science not good enough, the romance completely absent—indeed, the very object of study was fast becoming absent, the land we were supposed to be studying fading and crumbling before our eyes, dwindling, destined for a painful, inevitable death: we were being trained as stewards of the surviving bits, the pitifully cornered parks and preserves, humiliated parodies of the land they'd been excised from. This, then, was the reality I couldn't bear, yet couldn't not see, calling for an optimism I couldn't summon: I turned away, made my first escape.

I didn't exactly choose to become a theoretical chemist. Rather, I fell—like falling in love on the rebound, a bit out of control like that—into a course of study that lifted me soaring above—no, beyond—the world you'd given me, the visible natural world, which anyone but a child could see was history. Who would choose, after all, if one could choose (I thought I could) to love the dying, to fight the inevitable?

For a couple of years all I did was study. I couldn't seem to stop asking questions; as if addicted, I moved from one to the next, with a skepticism that seemed inbred—as if I already knew that the answer to one could only lead to another, that I would never have to deal with a real answer. The college I'd chosen in northern California was on the edge of some of the best marshlands, the wildest coast and mountains in the state, but I rarely found time for hiking or birding. Every day, on my bike ride to school, I skirted the edge of a large expanse of salt marsh, too jealous of my time, too impatient, to stop, yet always feeling oddly guilty for my failure to do so—for not wading out in the icy mud to see what was living there—the simple proximity of the marsh like the persistent whine of a mosquito in my ear. Did you hear, during those years, how intensely I studied, how brilliant they all thought I was, did you disapprove? I never knew

you to judge me, of course, your disapproval is my imagining—
perhaps I prefer it to indifference, which I can also imagine.

I listened, more closely than I intended, to the family accounts
of you, your news, like the marsh I lived near, a small torment,
an itch to do what I was not doing, to be part of what I wasn't
part of. The family had lost its disapproving tone in speaking
of you; they were proud, of course, and they liked the woman
you lived with—an amiable, round-faced woman, who, unlike
you, sent thank-you notes for presents and participated happily
in family events. There was a baby, the first of two, and suddenly you were a conscientious father, warm and loving and tol-
erant—not what one would have expected from listening to the
grown-ups talk all those years. I only saw your children in photographs on your parents' refrigerator, never saw the father in
action, but I believed what they said.

The impressive part of your news, of course, the part that
made the family proud, was the public part, which everyone in
California now knows. There was, is still, a fishless, shrimpfull,
terminal lake at the base of the Sierras, a dwindling alkaline lake,
once fed by mountain streams that for years had been diverted
to the notoriously thirsty city of Los Angeles. On the shores of
this besieged lake you settled, made home and family, as if you
would stand guard, protecting the lake with its novel chemistry
and homely brine shrimp—its great flocks of migrating grebes
and phalarope, its nesting plovers and gulls—from the demon
city of your birth. Not least amongst your concerns was the survival of the California gull, which nested on an island in the
lake. The water level had dropped so far that a land bridge to
the island formed and coyotes crossed over, demolishing entire
generations of gulls. But, of course, no one was going to care
about some trashy, annoying gulls, California or otherwise. You
knew it was the lake itself you had to sell, something simple that
you could point to and take impressive pictures of.

Most of the citizens of Los Angeles had, until you came along,
never seen or heard of this lake three hundred miles to the north,
didn't know they were drinking it dry, wouldn't have cared had

they known. You created a committee and raised funds, took photographs, made a film, wrote a guidebook and led tours to show off the lake's bizarre, spectacular beauty—the sort of beauty that even the most insensitive to nature might appreciate. You made the lake famous, and then you spread word of its impending demise, you simplified and described its complex ecology, you made speeches in Los Angeles, talked to the press, and played diplomat with the Department of Water and Power. In short, you devoted all your time and energy to saving that lake.

When I first heard all this I wondered briefly how you'd chosen: why, of all the beautiful dying places in need of your attention, why this lake? Had it reached out a salty hand and grabbed your wrist, pulled you to your knees on its shore? Then I remembered being there with you one fall, watching the myriad grebes and phalarope that stopped to rest and fatten up for their annual sojourns about the world; I remembered breathlessly identifying species after species on the water, in the dry lake bed and surrounding meadows, along the streams that fed the lake. I'd never been there in spring, but I remembered something you said to me once, when we were backpacking in the Sierras. We saw a California gull soaring above a glacier at eleven thousand feet and I, surprised to see the gull there, exclaimed that it looked so dignified and majestic I couldn't believe it was the same species that hovered about city dumps and raided picnics at the beach. You told me then that tens of thousands of California gulls nested on an island in a saline lake at six thousand feet, far from any city or dump or seashore, that they feasted there on brine shrimp, not garbage. So remembering, I understood—in spite of the relative lack of press the birds got—I did understand the significance of the battle you were fighting. And yet to me, even then before I'd traveled, it seemed too small, too late, too hopeless.

There's no explaining how or why I left that first time, how I, without much thought, dropped the studies I had pursued so feverishly for three years, took the money from tutoring math that I'd saved for next semester, and set out for South America

with a couple of college friends. There was the usual lure of adventure, of firsthand knowledge; and I do remember thinking
I would reclaim some part of myself that science denied, not
bothering to wonder why I headed for another continent to do
so. I packed my binoculars and, because the only book of South
American birds I could find was too big to carry, I took along a
bound notebook in which I planned to write careful descriptions
of the birds I saw. These would be many, I thought, for I would
look for birds everywhere we went, moving slowly and patiently,
and they would all be new, birds of another hemisphere. Preparing to leave, I was imagining my return and the visit I would pay
you: how you would listen, fascinated, to my descriptions of the
foreign birds, birds you'd never seen, how our history would be
resumed.

I thought southern Chile was the most beautiful place I had
ever been, more beautiful by far than California. Perhaps it was
only the largeness that won me, the wildness of the alps as they
dropped off the edge of the continent into the southern seas,
unobserved, it seemed, as yet uncoveted. Surely it was my ignorance of this foreign landscape where I knew no history and
couldn't see the future pressing so relentlessly into my lifetime,
couldn't see the cities and parks, the designated place battles for
survival, that I felt looming in the sky above even the remotest
corner of California. We spent a lot of time in small villages,
learned Spanish, made friends, but, though we did a lot of hiking
and wandering, no one had enough patience for bird-watching. I
had imagined that every bird I saw would be a life bird, and such
was the case—except the only birds I saw were those that came
to me. I didn't take time to follow the elusive ones, or identify
the drab little ones, in short, to look the way you'd taught me to
look. What I saw, then, were the large and spectacular birds,
rheas and South American condors and frigate birds, the ones
anyone would notice and be thrilled by.

*In the distance it's just a crooked white line painted into the sky
of a grocery store landscape. But I know immediately that this*

is no landscape gull, and I watch with mounting excitement as he glides closer, rigid wings tilting almost imperceptibly to arc his flight towards our boat. I'm waiting for him to flap—surely he can't glide forever—waiting and waiting, until slowly, nonchalantly, he pushes the sky down beneath his wings and then, in the same fluid slow motion, lifts them above it. Once. I would reach out and grab your arm in excitement, I would point and cry out—but of course you're thousands of miles away, and I'm alone on deck, everyone gone below to escape the frigid southern wind.

Wandering albatross. I'd hoped, I'd wondered if I'd see one. He's close enough now for me to comprehend his size: wings that encompass the width of our boat, a small cargo ship, a body almost as large as my own. Gliding in wide circles about the boat, he dips and rises effortlessly above the water, tilts his big head to look at me indifferently, around and around, until it becomes clear that he wants to land nearby. Coming low over the water like an airplane checking conditions, he tips away at the last minute, rises, and circles back to try again. When he finally touches the water, it's as if some spell has been broken: he ploughs through the waves in a harrowing crash landing, suddenly clumsy and ungainly, splashing and tripping over awkward wings and feet and head. Then the albatross is bobbing on the surface, looking like some sort of humiliated, oversized gull, with a drop of water hanging from its homely pink bill, and I have to laugh—it's such a pitiful sight.

He bobs alongside the boat for a while, gradually falling behind, until I have to move to the stern to see him. Then he tries to take off, but he's even clumsier than he was landing. Unfolding his mighty wings, he attempts to gain momentum by running on the water like a duck—but his feet go punching through the surface and his wings are too long and stiff to flutter, they get tangled in the waves and he nosedives to a halt. Righting himself, he bobs for a moment, bill dripping, as if he didn't really want to take off after all. Then he tries again, with the same result. I'm laughing aloud now, willing him success on his third try, thinking *what a grand joke nature has made, or perhaps it's a mistake, a giant gaff. But then the wandering albatross is airborne, graceful and apt, and I am not laughing, but envious, thinking: Oh, if I could only choose, I would be an albatross, so aloof, so invulnerable, airbound, let me be clumsy on land and sea, if only I could wander with such freedom and ease, tied to no place.*

We had planned to travel for a couple of months and then go back to work, saving enough money to resume our studies the following semester. My friends returned, but I found a job in a Chilean resort and stayed away a year—eventually returning to California with my Argentinean lover, only to work and save and leave again. Without visiting you, or the lake, or your babies (you had two now), without visiting the nesting ground of the California gull or telling you the story of the wandering albatross.

I am in the mountains of Nepal, where the forest has been gone for centuries, hiking for a month with my lover, climbing until we're so high we can hardly breathe, until we are camping in the snow, perched on the edge of a spectacular skyline. I don't realize until later, until we are back in the lowlands, dropping into India, that I haven't seen any birds, in all those mountains, even below what would have been the timberline, I can't remember seeing or hearing a single bird. Have they gone as well, the birds, gone with the trees? I think not, and I panic, thinking I forgot to look, to listen, perhaps I am forgetting how, and that is the reason I saw no birds.

And now we are in India and I am watching out for birds because of what happened in the mountains of Nepal. I see some flamingos and some kind of ibis, and the flashy but common birds of Asia like the Indian roller; I see them from the road— we're cycling, you see, riding bicycles around the world, did you hear that I was doing that?—but I am much too shy of poor people's stares to stop and take my binoculars out of my panniers. We pass within a few miles of a wildlife preserve, a marshy

*area that must be loaded with incredible birds, all strange and
fantastic and brilliantly colored, but my lover is not interested,
and I am embarrassed of being interested, for it seems a deca-
dence, a wildlife preserve in a country as troubled and poor as
this one. Later, when we are back in Europe, I will think a lot
about this place, I will think what you would have to say about
it, and I'll be sorry we didn't stop, that I couldn't have seen at
least some tiny piece of that country without its people and their
culture, without its poverty and despair.*

We wandered for a couple of years, during which I learned three
languages and didn't see many birds. We ended up in Spain,
where my lover wanted to stay, settle down. I needed to go home,
to see my parents, I told him—though they would happily have
spent their summer vacation with us in Spain. Alone, I returned
to California where I visited my parents and my friends and
your parents and my sister and brother and the other aunt and
uncle and two of our cousins—and then I was restless again, and
I missed my lover. Though I was broke and unemployed, I still
had my return ticket to Spain, which I used. I got a job at a
small university, translating scientific papers for the academic
community, an interesting enough job in a lovely Mediterranean
town—but I wasn't content. I told my lover that I wanted to go
back to college; I was a scientist at heart, I said, and I needed to
go home to study. It wasn't so easy, coming back to stay that
time, for the man I'd traveled with all those years remained in
Spain—but then that's another story, a love story, which I don't
think you'd be interested in.

Though I wonder if you're interested in any of this. If you
ever listened to news of me the way I listened to news of you, if
you wondered, if you cared, how I'd grown up. If it were the
other way around, cousin, if it were I who'd stopped in mid-
flight to hover like a rough-legged hawk above your head,
would you watch me the way I watch you? Would you tell me
your story, the way I tell you mine, tell me my story, the way

I tell you yours, would you miss me the way I miss you? I think not, though it helps to imagine otherwise.

I ended up in graduate school—that much you must have heard, for you saw your uncle, my father, and he would have mentioned it. In California, stuck for five years in California, in the south no less, the city. At least I was near the ocean—not that it mattered much, for I spent all my daylight hours in the lab, my evenings in the library.

I only saw you once in all those years, not long after I'd started grad school, when everyone was proud of me, for I was to be the first Ph.D. in the family's history, the first real scientist. It was the day after Thanksgiving and our families were all scrambled up, your parents at my parents' house, me there visiting. You stopped for dinner, alone, on your way down to Los Angeles for a meeting about the lake. I was so overjoyed, opening the door to you, my hug of greeting burst upon you, briefly unself-conscious, until you returned it with that funny, awkward embrace I had forgotten, a stiff arm crooked loosely around one's back, like hugging a cardboard cutout of a man. We were surrounded by relatives just like when I was small, and you were as reclusive as ever, as cold and impolite, communicative only on your own terms. Except now I couldn't remember what those were and wasn't sure I wanted to take the time to find out—indeed there wasn't time, for you only stayed a few hours. I separated myself, briefly, from the rest of the family, found you over by the piano leafing through some music—but I didn't know what to say to you. You were busy trying to save an entire species from extinction, while I was puzzling over plastic Tinkertoy models of organic molecules, imagining clouds of electrons that were neither here nor there . . . What could I say? So we exchanged a few words, I don't remember exactly what, and I shrank back into the hubbub of the family, embarrassed that they should see me wooing you the way I'd done when I was small. But when I saw you preparing to leave after dinner, I was seized with panic. Frantic, I wound my way back to your side, to say goodbye, at least, before you were surrounded by parents and aunts and uncles, to have a moment of you to myself—only as you were leaving did I realize how much I wanted that.

I remember so clearly, now, when you finally looked at me: standing in the entryway pushing your arms into a frayed down jacket, you looked directly at me and I realized that you were actually seeing me with something like sadness in your eyes, that it wasn't indifference the way I'd thought. You said: Come up and spend some time with us—I'll show you the lake. We'll go out birding. You paused, fine-focusing your gaze, and added, You can help out with the fund-raising. Sure, I said. I will, I'll come up and see you, soon as I get some time. And then we had another of your cardboard-man hugs, and you were gone.

I heard about the big victory, your magnificent accomplishment: there was finally a decision in the courts and you won, you stopped a huge monster of a city, temporarily at least, from sucking dry a weird but pretty lake where a bunch of gulls nobody cared about nested. There was a celebration in L.A.—an hour's drive, I could have gone—speeches and music and more fund-raising. I heard about it afterwards. My brother came down from the Central Valley, my parents from San Jose. Several of our cousins showed up. All the old bird friends I hadn't seen in years were there. And, of course, hundreds of strangers, because by now the lake really was famous, it was a Cause and you were an Environmentalist.

I was too busy to spend that day in L.A. What would I have done there, anyway? I hardly knew the details of your battle. And what difference would it all make in the long term, in the earth's time, on the time scales science uses? I thought a lot that week, between excuses for not joining you, about what you were doing with your life and why: that you, being one man, had chosen your one place, knowing it was one in many, as were you, and that the many together, the very land and all that it encompassed must continue to exist—not for our love of it, but for its own sake—it had to survive. It was something like trying to protect God from technology, what you were trying to do, and of course I understood, with an excruciating empathy—for hadn't you taught me to see the way you see?—but I was too utterly faithless. It was all too hopeless for me to invest my time, my soul, my life the way you did—and anything less, I knew, would be more pointless still. The week after the celebration that I didn't attend I understood, for the first time I admitted, that it was not my busy life that kept me away from you, but guilt.

There was a moment then—a brief, glaring, fluorescent moment—when I thought that I truly needn't care. It was so simple I could scream, not caring was, and so appropriate, in 1984, the release from guilt immediate and absolute. But of course I couldn't do it, couldn't make use of that solution—you'd made sure of that when I was young—and so the guilt lived on.

I was in a land of no emotion when the letter came, so innocent and light with its American stamp, my Japanese address so carefully printed in my mother's hand. What perverse twist of fate had landed me in Japan, I don't know—there'd been a job as an "environmental consultant" that I was overeducated for, but I thought that by accepting it I would be doing something small about the guilt and, more importantly, about my restlessness, for I'd been in southern California for five years. The job turned out to be a joke, a parody of my illusions—a helpless thankless bureaucratic construct of no meaning—which is why, no doubt, it was given to a female, American at that, chemist. At least there was a new language to learn, and culture in plenty, layers and layers of culture to fascinate and perplex me. Culture that, my older Japanese acquaintances bemoaned, was disappearing so quickly it would be gone before they realized they should do something to hold on. What impressed me about Japan, however, more than the perversion of its culture—for I came from a younger people, with little culture to be lost—was what had happened to the land itself. Never had I seen a landscape so tethered by man, so absolutely tame, so tainted by technology. It had happened so fast, on top of centuries of such gradual, but absolute, domestication, that no one even recognized this other loss to be bemoaned, no one saw, no one knew what it was that had been lost. Ironically, I found myself trying to explain to my Japanese friends what I meant when I spoke of "nature," trying to explain about places out of control, about unowned, undesignated space. They'd nod and tell me to go visit this or that park or garden—all, but for the trash on the ground, of exquisite beauty—and I'd shake my head and try again to explain. Once I was sitting on the rocks of a rugged coastline with my closest friend in Japan, the surf pounding and foaming about us, the Inland Sea opening out before us. I took a deep breath and felt refreshed and at peace, as if my soul were stretching its cramped limbs. Turning to my friend, I gestured widely with my arm. I said: *This is what I mean when I talk of nature, this space, this air, the openness.* She smiled at me and nodded vigorously. *Ah,* she said. *You are homesick.*

She was right, my friend was right: for the first time in my life I was truly, admittedly homesick. The size, the shape, the latitudinal drift of that island all taunted me, as if the island would laugh at me for hating it, for hating what my own home, what California, was so swiftly becoming, a home estranged and bound to vanish before I even understood that I had loved it. To this, then, the latest exile I'd discovered for myself, came my mother's letter. The one with the news, and then the others that followed, hoping from afar to soften the blow.

One doesn't quit one's job, one isn't given leave, one doesn't buy thousand-dollar airplane tickets, because a cousin has died. They didn't tell me until after the funeral anyway. Which is okay. What rights would I have at a funeral? What right to sob, to shake, to rage, to cry, what right have I to miss you so, when it's been fifteen years since I knew you? No, a cousin should have tears sitting sadly in the corners of her eyes, she should comfort and console the parents and brothers and sisters, help organize and keep the family functioning, that's what a cousin should do at a funeral.

I know, though there is no one here to counsel me, that it is called grief, this ocean of despair with no bottom. There are the letters, telling me how everyone is doing, how they're coping. They send me newspaper articles full of praise for you and what you accomplished—even the L.A. Department of Water and Power now speaks well of its fallen enemy—eulogies and honors tossed out like life rafts, all of us expected to grab hold and climb in: I can see them bobbing irrelevantly on the surface, miles above my head, as I sink, knowing there's no room for me in those life rafts, that I gave up my place years ago.

I tuck the newspaper clippings, still folded and unread, into a manila envelope and stash it at the bottom of an empty suitcase. I don't need to read, I know only too well, what a hero you are: what I don't know, can't understand, cousin, is why you haven't died a hero's death. Why not a free fall from the edge of a ravine, why not cross-country skiing, an avalanche perhaps, or the strike of a giant rattlesnake—though I know, because it happened to you once, that one needn't die from that. To be honest, I don't know what kind of death a hero nowadays should die. An old man's death, that would be the one for a naturalist: your wisdom finally filled with age, your beard grown white and grizzled, your cool shrug frozen in arthritic shoulders. Not this. This mundane death to crown your fortieth year—how could you die in an automobile, of all places, wrapped in the twisted metal of California's curse, why, for you, this asphalt death so lacking in grace, so outrageously out of sync with your life? I can see you at the very moment, hovering there above your own exploded body, wincing at the mess, this moment frozen and unyielding behind my clenched eyelids. I see from the bitter flutter of your wings, which you taught me how to read, I can see that even you feel something of my cynicism—though in the end I know, I wait, for you to hold true to yourself, to arc your wings in that shrug that's not indifference but a kind of acceptance, and soar off. I'm waiting, cousin.

When I arrive home they are surprised, and it's my turn to shrug. You died six months ago, so that's not the first thing they think

of. I hated Japan, I say. I've never said anything so absolutely
negative about anywhere I've been, so some eyebrows go up and
I am questioned further. I'm thinking about moving to Colorado,
I say, or Montana, or Wyoming, somewhere with lots of space.

First, I go to see your parents. I behave properly—as properly
as I know how, for who knows what to do, to say. It's been six
months now, they are somewhat in control. They talk about you
some; I've heard that's good, that's what they need to do, though
it is hard to listen. They talk about you to your cousin, as if we
had no history of our own, you and I: they've forgotten, that's
all, and who am I to remind them now. I don't know what brings
it up, what makes him think it in his grief, but my uncle says—
your father says—to his wife, and to me, Well, he says, she was
always his favorite cousin, you know. I wince, and smile a little
to hide it, then shrug to hide the smile. It's something, I think,
though I know, and I believe you know now as well, that it's not
enough. But then your mother argues the point—with her husband, not with me, I suppose she thinks I'd be indifferent. Oh
I don't know, says my aunt to my uncle, he was fond of all of
them . . . and she names some cousins from her side of the family you played with when you were small. I look down at the
food she has prepared for me and squint back the tears: I take
what she's said and swallow it and hold it down inside.

I don't go to Colorado or Montana or Wyoming. Instead,
I spend the summer backpacking in the Sierras. I go to see the
lake. I finally build up enough courage to visit your widow and
your children—but I don't stay long, I don't feel I have much
claim to know your kids, and I never knew your wife very well.
I don't have a job, and I suppose I'll run out of money soon, but
I bought a new pair of binoculars anyway. I had to buy a new
field guide as well—my old one had molded shut in my parents'
attic, and I certainly can't bird without one now. Though they
all look and sound familiar, the birds I see. A warbler's white,
not yellow, throat. A certain wren's musical song. The white
patches on a swallow's rump. A silhouette perched upright on a
dead tree branch, its bill slightly heavier than light. The flight

pattern of a hawk, the long rounded, not square, tail . . . I know them all at first sight, in that first intuitive moment I remember, I *know—Oh it's a—*but the names elude me, the birds have the forms of dreams in my memory, a language forgotten through long disuse. When I look more closely, through the binoculars, I wonder if I ever really knew, if the birds only seem familiar because of my talent—all languages seem familiar, as if I *ought* to understand them all. In reality, I can't even place the genus of the birds I see now: I confuse a warbler with a vireo, a wren with a thrush, a peewee with a kingbird, an accipiter with a buteo.

I don't have to search: everywhere I go I find your ghost. Watching me and waiting, patient as always. Waiting to see if I will regain my linguist's tongue and spend these frigid predawn hours calling in the owls to chat in their various languages. If I will strain my back until I know what kinds of warblers are flitting about at the top of that fir. If I will sit down at the edge of this meadow to watch the flycatchers dance into dusk. Waiting for me to decide what it is I need to do next. To earn my right to grieve, and have done with it, so you can be off.

I weave haphazardly about the Sierras, half-lost, surprised to find myself always reconnecting with the John Muir. The trails are full of people. Well-meaning people, who want to enjoy nature, see this beautiful place, get away from their cars. But there are too many. We must be careful where we step. Stay on the trails. Carry plastic shovels as proof that we bury our shit. I'm told not to drink the water now without treating it first with iodine—the way I used to do in Asia, where there have been too many people for centuries. I head north to Lassen, which isn't yet so popular. I camp by a lake, all alone for a week, watching a pair of bald eagles fish and thinking by what a narrow margin they had escaped. The eagles make me cry all week; I head out to the coast, thinking to watch the osprey fish instead, maybe find a marsh to muck around in.

There aren't too many marshes left, and I'm afraid to walk out into the few there are. They look so fragile. I'm afraid of the damage my boots might do. What if everyone waded out, I think, the marsh would be ruined. Then I see the signs saying as much, your ghost perched on top, looking at me with eyebrows raised, shoulders raised in a half shrug. A marsh keeps its secrets to itself unless one mucks around in it.

Are you learning this with me, cousin, your ghost and I side by side as grown-ups, learning what our fathers never taught us in their flight from Judaism? We know now, don't we, we've learned that there is, can be, no death like the one they taught us; you haven't died, have you, the death they thought you died. Oh, but of course you knew all along, you were a naturalist, not a scientist. I'm the only one still learning, and here I've finally talked myself into a hole, haven't I, and you perched on its edge, still waiting for me to come to the only conclusion we both know is possible.

I'll have to learn, the way you did, all that diplomacy and politics—maybe being a chemist will help, my Ph.D. of some use after all, if only for show. Science and technology have always been confused: perhaps when I speak people will think of technology and listen, believing I speak of a future, instead of the past. Here I go now—don't stop watching yet—I, who would have been a wandering albatross could I have chosen, searching within the confines of my home for that place, that one doomed place in so many, where I will come clumsily to rest.

HOMELESSNESS

The Loss of Childhood

As winter grew deeper and we waited for hog-killing time, at home the center was not holding. . . . daddy had grown progressively crazier, more violent. He was gone from home for longer and longer periods of time, and during those brief intervals when he was home, the crashing noise of breaking things was everywhere about us. Daddy had also taken to picking up the shotgun and screaming threats while he waved it about, but at that time he had not as yet fired it.

While that was going on, it occurred to me for the first time that being alive was like being awake in a nightmare.

I remember saying aloud to myself: "Scary as a nightmare. Jest like being awake in a nightmare."

HARRY CREWS

SHERMAN ALEXIE

Father Coming Home

THEN   Father coming home from work. Me, waiting on the front steps, watching him walk slowly and carefully, like half of a real Indian. The other half stumbling, carrying the black metal lunch box with maybe half a sandwich, maybe the last drink of good coffee out of the thermos, maybe the last bite of a dream.

SPOKANE   Father coming home from work five days a week. Me, waiting every day until the day he doesn't come walking home, because he cut his knee in half with a chainsaw. Me, visiting my father laying in bed in the hospital in Spokane. Both of us, watching the color television until my mother comes from shopping at Goodwill or Salvation Army, until the nurses come in telling us we have to go.

CEREMONIES   Father coming home from the hospital in a wheel-chair. Me, waiting for him to stand up and teach me how to shoot free throws. Me, running up to him one day and jumping hard into his lap, forgetting about his knee. Father holding me tight against his chest, dark and muddy, squeezing his pain into my thin ribs, his eyes staying clear.

AFTER   Father coming home from the mailbox, exercising his knee again and again. Me, looking up from the floor as he's shaking his head because there is no check, no tiny miracles coming in the mail. Father bouncing the basketball, shooting lay-in after lay-in, working the knee until it bleeds along the scars.

Father crying from the pain late at night, watching television. Me, pretending to be asleep. All of us listening to canned laughter.

INSOMNIA   Father coming home from another job interview, limping only a little but more than enough to keep hearing no, no, no. Me, eating potatoes again in the kitchen, my mother's face growing darker and darker by halves. One half still mostly beautiful, still mostly Indian, the other half something all-crazy and all-hungry. Me, waking her up in the middle of the night, telling her my stomach is empty. Her throwing me outside in my underwear and locking the door. Me, trying anything to get back in.

HOMECOMING   Father coming home from drinking, after being gone for weeks. Me, following him around all the time. Him, never leaving my sight, going into the bathroom. Me, sitting outside the door, waiting, knocking on the wood every few seconds, asking him *Are you there? Are you still there?*

NOW   Father coming home finally from a part-time job. Driving a water truck for the BIA. Me, waiting on the front steps, watching him come home early every day. Him, telling my mother when they think I can't hear, he doesn't know if he's strong enough. Father telling mother he was driving the truck down Little Falls Hill, trying to downshift but his knee not strong enough to keep holding the clutch in. Me, holding my breath. Him, driving around the corner on two wheels, tons and tons of water, half-insane. Me, closing my eyes. Him, balancing, always ready to fall. Me, holding onto father with all my strength.

ELIZABETH GRAVER

Have You Seen Me?

Willa stood in the patch of light from the open freezer door and watched as the mist climbed in tendrils, swirled and rose. The milk carton in her hands was heavy, its surface smeared with yellowish cream—her mother had made more potato soup. Already the two tall freezers in the basement housed cartons and cartons of soup, enough to last them almost forever—carrot and broccoli soup, soup made of summer and acorn squash, rows of green and yellow frozen rectangles inside the cartons that had once held milk. And on the outsides of the cartons, rows of children— frozen too, their features stiff, their faces etched with frost. *Have You Seen Me? Do You Know Where I Am?* Each time Willa put the cartons in the freezers, she set up the children in pairs so they could have staring contests when she shut the door.

Go on, she thought to Kimberly Rachelle and David Michael, to Kristy-Ann and Tyrone. Stare each other down. She put them boy girl, boy girl, catalogued them by age. Some of the missing children were babies, and these she put on the shelf closest to the bottom. The ones who were eleven, her age, she gave special treatment, tracing their names in the wax coating of the milk cartons with her finger, dusting the frost from their eyes. She could recite their DOBs, their SEXS, HTS, WTS, and EYES, the color of their hair. Willa's mother didn't know about Willa's ordering of the cartons; she was upstairs cooking or painting child after child lined up like soldiers, serious kids in uniforms carrying weapons or naked, puzzled kids looking up at the sky.

Willa's mother expected the end of the world. She donated

her paintings to three friends in the town twenty miles down the highway, and they turned them into posters which they hung in the public library and in the windows of the real estate agency that doubled as an art gallery. "You Can't Hug Your Child," they printed in fake child scrawl, "With Nuclear Arms."

Willa thought everyone was overreacting. Sure, there might be silos under the ground and blinking lights that could go off, and escape systems that would lead to nowhere, and broccoli and cauliflower that would grow big as trees afterwards, like in the paintings her mother made. There might be all that, but still what did they know about the end, for she was sure something would survive, making it really not the end at all—maybe only an insect or two, a shiny blind beetle or an ant like the ones in the ant farm her father had given her—some sort of creature, hard, black and shelled, rolling from the rubble like a bead.

She would not go with her mother to the rallies in Chicago and St. Louis, would not wear the buttons and T-shirts or lend her handwriting to the posters. In her room she hung photographs of animals instead of her mother's art work—slow sea turtles and emus with backs like the school janitor's dirty, wide broom. They came from the Bronx Zoo in New York City, the animals on the postcards. Willa's father sent them now and then.

Once a girl in one of her mother's paintings had looked just like Willa, small and dark and suspicious, with the same mess of curly hair. Then Willa had screamed and kicked.

"Take me out of your fucking painting, who said you could paint me? Just take me out!"

"Okay, now stop!" her mother had said, catching Willa by the shoulders. "Just stop screaming and don't go crazy on me. Listen to yourself—listen to yourself, would you just calm down?"

And she had squeezed a big wad of beige paint onto her palette, speared it with a paintbrush, and spread it over the painted Willa's face.

"It wasn't even you," she had said, but Willa had known it was, that her mother had put her there in that lineup of children with puzzled looks, had painted her empty-handed, naked, and puzzled next to an orange boy with wide shoulders and a bow and arrow in his hand.

"Just because I say 'fucking' doesn't mean you should," her mother had told her, but then she had kissed Willa's forehead and taken her far down the highway to McDonald's, where Willa ate two hamburgers and drank a thick chocolate shake while her mother drank water and tried not to look at the food.

Underneath their farmhouse was dirt, and underneath the dirt—if not directly underneath, then near enough, her mother seemed sure of it—were silos which were not really silos at all, but this was not Willa's problem. In a movie she saw once, a man drowned in the wheat of a silo, was smothered as the golden grain poured over him like sand, filling up his nostrils and his mouth. She told her mother about it afterwards, the danger of this silo filled with wheat. With *wheat*, Willa had said, which was what silos were supposed to hold.

"Actually silage," her mother had answered. "They're supposed to hold silage—fodder for cows and horses. It must have been a grain elevator."

No, said Willa. It was a silo. She saw it.

"I guess they could do what they wanted—it was only a movie," her mother had said, and then, more thoughtfully, "Hmmm, I suppose it probably happens now and then."

School was one thing, and home alone with her mother was another, and in between were her mother's three friends, who were thin and pretty like her mother and drove out to the house on weekends with bags full of magic markers, envelopes, and petitions that few people in the little town would sign. Sasha was a real estate agent and divorced, and Karen was married and taught kindergarten at Willa's school, and Willa didn't know what Melissa did, except stare sadly at her mother's paintings and say, "Hello, Willa," as if Willa's name were a password or something deserving of the utmost seriousness. Willa's mother gave her three friends homemade bread and sketched their faces on napkins. Sometimes they drank vodka and orange juice and stayed up talking late into the night. When Willa came downstairs in the morning she would find the women sleeping on the couch and floor, still dressed, still wearing rings and necklaces and sometimes even shoes.

At night when no visitors shared the house, Willa's mother told her stories. This had been going on a long time. First it had been her father and mother together. He would say a sentence: "Once there was a truck who lived alone in the Sahara Desert," and her mother would add a sentence: "And he had no glass in his windows and at night the sand came blowing through, and he had no wheels," and her father would add on, and then her mother, each of them perched on Willa's bed, always touching part of her—her knee or her foot, her hand or the small of her back.

Then, when she was seven, her father went to live with a woman he said he had loved in high school, and Willa only saw him twice a year when he left his new family, she left her mother, and they stayed in a hotel in New York and went to museums and the zoo. She always got blisters on those trips from so much walking. After her father left, her mother came home with a whole stack of glossy children's books. Willa couldn't stand the pictures of fat, dimpled children and pets, the stories about going to the dentist, getting a pony, or cleaning up your room.

"*Tell* me one," she would say to her mother, and her mother would try, but she never knew how to start, and the stories stumbled along for a while until Willa grew bored and fell asleep. But over the years her mother improved, or else Willa just grew used to her way of telling. She gave her mother rules: no stories about zoo animals, vampires, or kids named Willa who lived on defunct farms. No stories about the end of the world. Instead, her mother told her more stories about objects—superballs looking for somewhere to bounce, a barn which threw up because of the smelly animals inside it, a snowflake in search of a twin. Sometimes her mother sat at the end of Willa's bed and leaned against the wooden railing. Other times she cupped herself against her daughter and talked right into her ear. Sometimes she slept there all night, squeezed onto the edge of the twin bed.

Willa didn't like this, found it sad and embarrassing, though she couldn't say why, but she wouldn't kick her mother out. In winter they stayed warm that way, like pioneers, for the farmhouse was big and drafty in the middle of its field, and the wind came howling round.

After Willa filled the freezer with several loads of soup, she took her book on ants to the kitchen and settled by the wood stove. When the doorbell rang, she didn't look up, too busy with a glossy color photograph of a magnified ant with legs like shaggy black trees. But then her mother came back to the kitchen followed by a girl, or maybe a woman—to Willa the stranger looked young, though she carried a child who hid its face in her coat. Willa's mother showed the girl and baby to the living room, and then she returned to the kitchen and whispered to her daughter that this was a new friend, her name was Melody. They had met at a demonstration in St. Louis; Melody had worked in a nuclear power plant for four years, but now she had quit and was waitressing. She had come to the house for a lesson because she wanted to learn how to draw. Her son was blind and had just turned three.

"It should be fun for you," said her mother after she had called Melody and the child back in. "Isn't he awfully cute? Would you do us a big favor and watch him while we draw?"

Willa had watched the tiny, silent granddaughter of the farmer down the road while the farmer rode his tractor, but she had never babysat for a blind child, had never met anyone who was blind.

"I don't, I mean—" she said. "I don't really know—"

"Oh listen to you, you're just being modest," said her mother. She turned to Melody. "She's terrific with kids. Already she's babysitting at her age."

"He's pretty much like any other kid, aren't you, Tiger?" said Melody, readjusting the child buried in her arms. "Better, even—he's good as can be. If he wants anything, you can just give a holler. We'll be right upstairs. Or, if you want, we can take him with us."

"I'll watch him," said Willa, for her mother was giving her that look.

When they went up to the studio, her mother and Melody left the child sitting on Willa's baby quilt on the kitchen floor, his back to Willa. For a while she hunched over her book and ignored the boy at her feet, but when she finished the section on carpenter ants, she lifted her head and stared at the child, who had settled on his stomach on the red and yellow quilt. As she stood and leaned over him, she saw that not only was he blind, but he had no eyes, just skin and a row of pale blond lashes where the eyes should have been.

Willa gasped and brought her hands up to her face, then stood for a moment peering into the darkness of her palms, trying to make herself look again. When she lowered her hands, she saw that the boy was sucking his thumb and using the end of his index finger to trace circles on his face. She stared. Did he have eyes under there, so that he wasn't actually blind at all, just confined to a view of his own pale skin? She moved closer to see if she could make out a bulge of eyeball above the fringe of lashes. The skin was smooth and flat like part of a back or stomach—as if nothing were missing, as if eyes had never been invented. Then the boy wrinkled his brow, seemed to be looking at her: Could he see through those eyeless eyes?

He could have been born that way, thought Willa. Not because his mother worked in a nuclear plant, but just because he was born that way. Paula, a fifth grader at school, claimed she had gone to a fair in Florida where they had people like this— Siamese twins joined at the head, children with flippers like dolphins and claws like lobsters, or as hairy as apes. Paula said she had seen the lobster family, three kids and two parents. They were ugly as anything, she said, but they loved each other, that family. They just stood there smiling like goons and holding claws.

As Willa leaned over the child, he reached a hand into the air. "Ma?" he said.

And she said, "No."

"Can you talk?" she asked, kneeling by him. "What's your name?"

He was perhaps the palest, blondest boy she had ever seen, his hair like milkweed puffs standing straight up on his head, his skin so white you could see veins running underneath it, could see how his blood was blue. He wore a red turtleneck and pink flowered overalls that should have been for a girl. From the way he clenched his fingers to his palms, it seemed he must be angry, or else cold. He did not answer her. As she leaned closer, he reached up and grabbed a fistful of her hair.

"No," she said, starting to unclench his fist with her fingers, but he opened his palm and batted at her curls, swinging them back and forth.

"Girl," he said, and she nodded yes.

He lowered his hand, and she rocked on her heels and looked at him. She could stare and stare, tilt her head to examine him, and it wouldn't matter, for this boy had skin in the place of eyes. He reached out again.

"What?" she asked, backing up. His face grew red as if he might begin to cry, though she couldn't imagine where the tears would go.

"What?" repeated Willa, and the boy lifted his arms toward her, so she bent down and scooped him up. He was awkward in her arms, his legs dangling down, but surprisingly light. Willa was used to the house, wore four layers in winter, but this boy's whole body was shaking. With his arms tight around her neck as if he might pull her down, he began, quietly, to sob.

"Oh don't," she said, wanting to drop him and run. "Please don't cry. Don't cry—"

A thread of spittle ran down his chin; perhaps, she thought, his tears flowed like a waterfall down inside his head and out his mouth. She began to circle with him to warm him up, boosting him a little higher each time he threatened to fall.

"This is the kitchen," she told him, and he stopped crying as she went to a bag of onions on the counter and had him touch the brittle skins. She held an onion under his nose, and he batted her hand away. She went to the fridge and pressed his cheek against the side. "Listen," she told him, so he would hear it purr. She took him to the dining room where the table was covered with petitions, posters, and books.

"We don't eat here," she told him. "Usually we eat in the kitchen."

He touched the tabletop and ran his fingers over a copy of a drawing that a Japanese war child had made of its mother. The mother had bright swollen lips; the skin on her hands hung loose like rubber gloves. Willa hated those pictures, had seen that one before and read the caption: HIGASHI YAMAMOTO, MY MOTHER 53 YEARS OLD. Willa's mother had promised to keep them hidden, but sometimes she forgot and left one lying around the house.

"Not for you," said Willa, though she knew he couldn't see it, and she backed up.

She brought him to the front room where she used to sit with her mother and father counting trucks in the night, the lights coming toward them on the highway out of nowhere, the rush of sound, then everything growing smaller and smaller, less and less noisy, until it was quiet and they were just sitting there again. In summer they had watched from the porch, and then they could feel the wind of the passing trucks, like feeling the waves the motorboats made when she swam in Lake Michigan on vacations—more ripples than waves, really—and with the trucks it was not quite wind, but more a slight, brief wall of air. Her parents didn't argue when they sat there watching trucks. Her father didn't talk about his office, and her mother didn't talk about the rallies. It was the quietest time they had.

What a baby she'd been in her father's arms, thinking that under the ground was more ground, that in the silos was wheat, that her father would sit there forever in the green stuffed chair. She sat the boy down beside her in the creaking chair and told him to listen for trucks.

"Car," he said, and she said, "A truck is a big car."

"Plane," he said, and she thought of the ones she took to New York to visit her father. The flight attendants always gave her coloring books full of drawings of pilots and suitcases—books meant for much younger kids. Willa knew she should save them for her father's little children, but since he always took her to the hotel, never home, she left the books and crayons on the plane with a wonderful feeling of spite.

He had two children with his new wife, one who was just hers and one who was both of theirs. This meant that Willa had a half-sister and a step-brother, which should have added up to something whole, but though she knew their names were Katherine and William, which was so close to Willa, she had never seen them, not even pictures, and part of her was not convinced they existed. The boy squirmed in her arms, so she put him down and took his hand, but he stumbled, groping at the air, so she picked him up and carried him again, making her way unsteadily to the ant farm in her room.

She couldn't show him, really. She could press his fingers to the glass, but that wouldn't tell him anything, so instead Willa read to him from a library book about army ants, though her ants were simple garden ants. Army ants always moved in columns five ants wide, she told him, marching and marching for seventeen days; then they stopped and laid eggs until they were ready to march again. They had jaws like ice tongs and could eat a leopard, and almost all of them were female. The boy sat in her lap with a mild, interested expression on his face, so she told him about the replete ants who filled their abdomens with nectar until they swelled like grapes, then hung suspended from the ceiling of the nest. When the other ants were hungry, Willa said, they tapped on the mouth of the replete ant, and it spat out a drop of honeydew.

The boy looked a little bored, and he was still shivering, so she lugged him down to the basement where they could be close to the furnace's warmth. As he sat on the floor by the furnace, she kneeled beside him and lightly touched his hair, so like milkweed. How did he get to be so blond, she wondered; his mother had hair as dark as Willa's.

"Stand up, would you," she told him, and when he did she took both his hands and led him slowly across the room. "See, you're not a baby, you're a big boy. You walk fine."

"Fridge," said the boy when they stood before it, for he must have heard it humming, and he reached out and placed his palms flat against the large white door.

"Did you know some children don't live with their parents?" Willa told him. "Either the kids get taken away, kidnapped when they're still young and cute, or else they run away when they're a little older and no one wants them."

Holding the door ajar with her foot, she hoisted him up and guided his hand to the middle shelf of milk cartons. This was the shelf of two to five year olds: Jason McCaffrey with blue eyes and brown hair, Crystal Anne Sandors, DOB July 22, 1979, who was three and a half now, pouting like a brat and wearing tiny hoop earrings and pearls. Some of the children had been computer-aged, so that Billy, who was two when he disappeared from his aunt's shopping cart in Normal, Illinois, appeared three years later on the carton as a five year old, his face grainy and stretched-out, coated with wax.

To call those children missing, Willa knew, only meant they were missing for somebody, even though maybe they were found for someone else. Just because they were not at home did not mean they were wandering the earth alone. There were too many of them, just look at all those cartons. First Crystal probably ran into Jeffrey, and then Crystal and Jeffrey ran into Vicki, and soon there were masses of them, whole underground networks. When she went to the supermarket with her mother she spotted them sometimes, kids poking holes in the bags of chocolate in the candy aisle or thumbing through a comic book—kids in matted gray parkas that once were white. They had large pupils and pale skin from living inside the earth.

They knew how to meet underground, these groups of children, knew how to tell a field with a hidden silo from a field of snow, how to comb through the stubble of old corn to find the way down, then slide behind the men in uniforms who guarded the silo like an enormous jewel. They could pass by the waiting dogs, for they were scentless from being frozen for so long. They were thin and coated with wax and could slide quite effortlessly through cracks. Underground they formed squads by age: the blue squad for the nine to eleven year olds, the brown squad for the babies who couldn't walk yet and were covered with mud and dirt. In the underground silos they found piles of wheat and hay left over from the days when the silos had been used on farms. They slept on the hay, woke in the morning with straw stuck in their hair. For breakfast they ground the wheat with stones, formed it into patties, cooked it into small round cakes.

The children knew Willa only as a sort of looming presence. They couldn't see her, but they could feel a shift in the atmosphere when she picked up their cartons, as if a cloud had cast its shadow or a truck swept by the house. They didn't understand how much she made them do; they thought they had their staring contests when they were bored, when really it was Willa pairing them up so they would stare into each other's eyes. Some of them she liked more than others, and these children received favors. The ones who had been there the longest got to sit at the front of the shelf. So far none of them had had to leave. This soup was not for eating. Her mother called it soup for a rainy day.

Someday Willa might have to join them. She did not know how to get there, exactly, but she knew she would figure out a way. Her mother would not be with her, or her father. The larger you were, the harder it was to survive; she could tell that from watching her ants. At eleven, Willa was still quite runty for her age, though her mother made her drink glass after glass of milk. She put the boy down, and then she took out the missing children and told him about each one, placing them in a large ring around him on the concrete floor, as if it were a birthday party and time for Duck Duck Goose. When she got to Craig Allen Denton, REPORTED MISSING FROM THE HOSPITAL ON THE

DAY OF BIRTH, 9/11/80, she stopped and stared at him, then wiped the frost from his face with her cuff.

Craig Allen Denton had a shriveled face as white as milk and eyes screwed into slits. His mouth was open in a howl, his fist clenched in a tight ball by his cheek. Willa looked at him again, held him under the light, then turned and stared at the child in her basement. The baby in the picture, she saw, was the toddler on the floor. Melody must have stolen him, or maybe Melody's baby had been switched with him. Before, Willa had thought the baby in the photo had closed his eyes because he was crying. Now she saw that he had no eyes.

Somewhere, to somebody, this eyeless boy was missing. Melody had a son, and the boy had a mother, but still something was wrong. Something was always wrong, no matter how right things seemed. Willa had known this for a while, but still it gave her a headache to think of it. She pulled the boy onto her lap and rubbed her forehead against his hair.

"What's your name?" she asked, but he only sneezed.

When she heard a creaking on the stairs, Willa assumed it was a cat. She was showing the boy how to run his fingernail along the side of a carton and gather tiny flakes of wax. She was telling him about Gail May Joliet, DOB 3/12/71, EYES hazel, Gail May who had been computer-aged so that the edges of her face were visible now as a series of small black dots like poppy seeds. "Computer-aged," said the print beneath, and in the wavery lines of her cheeks you could see how they had taken away Gail May's baby fat. Now she looked like a five year old whose cheeks had been carved away.

"She lives in the underground village," Willa told the boy. "She's a gymnast, you should see—she does back flips and balance beam and horse, and I think parallel bars. She's the head of the blue squad. Also she carves tunnels. She's two-and-a-half months older than me."

And she took his hand and placed it over Gail May's face.

Her mother must have been standing there watching from

the stairs. She must have been staring at the ring Willa had made of all the soup, of all the milk cartons, arranged not by flavor but by child. She must have been looking at Willa and the boy sitting in the center of the ring. As Willa's eyes lighted on her mother and Melody two steps behind, she tightened her hold on the child.

"What on earth are you doing?" said her mother from the stairs.

Willa shrugged and touched the child's staticky hair. Her mother came toward them, kneeled outside the circle, let out a strained laugh.

"What are you doing with all the soup? It's melting, Willa. Will you just look at that? All my good soup is turning to mush."

She was right. Tiny puddles of water were collecting underneath each carton as the soup began to sweat. Her mother started to pick up a carton, but Willa leaned over the boy and swatted at her hand.

"Leave it, Mom, okay? I'll clean it up."

"I thought you were reading in your room," said her mother. "We heard you reading to him."

She stepped over the cartons, scooped the boy up, handed him up to Melody, and whispered something. Then Melody and the boy disappeared up the stairs. Outside the ring of cartons, Willa's mother crouched.

"Were you building a city?" she said. "There are blocks in the attic if you want to build with him. Why did you have to defrost all my soup?"

If she had felt like it, she could have explained things logically to her mother, how in an Emergency Situation the radiation would seep into the basement, inside the furnace, inside the canned goods, stacks of magazines, bottles of wine. How it would go right through the thick white insulation of the fridge, through the wax and cardboard of the milk cartons, through all those dotted faces to the soup.

Bur her mother knew that, and still she kept making soup.

Willa sighed. "I wasn't defrosting."

"What were you doing then?"

Her mother stepped over the cartons and kneeled by her side.

"Just playing."

"Well then," said her mother. "I'll put them away. I can't have all that soup melting. You can't refreeze, it doesn't work."

"I'll do it," said Willa, and as her mother sat cross-legged in the middle of the circle, she began collecting the cartons by age, by group, starting with the babies and moving up.

"Melody has potential as an artist," said her mother. She handed her daughter a carton, out of order.

"I'll do it. Let me do it." Willa peered at the carton— G. Phillip Stull, red squad—then put it back on the floor.

"Oh—oh I see," her mother said. "You were talking to him about these pictures, weren't you? You were telling Melody's baby about the children on the cartons."

Willa continued her ordering.

"I think a lot of it is media panic, honey," her mother said. "I mean, from what I've heard. A lot of these kids are with their divorced parents, or there's a custody problem, or they ran away. You'd be surprised. Most of them aren't actually missing at all."

Willa turned and began to collect the two to four year olds.

Upstairs, she went to Melody, who was cutting an apple into pieces in the kitchen, and stood by her side. In the living room she could hear her mother murmuring to the child.

"Hi there," said Melody, and Willa said hi.

"Your Mom said I could cut Jo-Jo an apple. Thanks for playing with him. Did he give you any trouble?"

Willa shook her head. Melody popped a slice of apple into her mouth and chewed.

"He's a good kid. All his babysitters love him, once they get used to him."

"Did he, I mean, was he—"

"He was born like that."

Willa nodded, and Melody squinted at her. "Has your mother been telling you stuff? About where I worked and all?"

Willa shook her head.

"Oh, okay. It's just that I've had a bunch of jobs, worked all over the place, but my last job was at that power plant down by Acton, and it's hard to say, about his eyes. You can never say for sure, but if your mother told you I shouldn't take any more chances with that place, I can't argue. Too many funny things."

"What'd you think when he was born?"

Melody shook her head. "I had a C-section—you know, when they cut you open?" She traced a line down her stomach. "I was out cold."

"So you didn't see him."

"Oh sure, I saw him. They bring them in. I was real happy, seeing him there. I was—I guess I was so drugged out or something, but I just kept waiting for him to open up his eyes, you know?"

"He's got such blond hair," said Willa.

"His daddy's a towhead." Melody leaned toward Willa and whispered confidentially. "I'm blond, too, really," she said, lifting a lock of her dark hair, "but not white blond like him, more washed out, kind of dirty blond. Now you've got a real pretty color. That's all natural, huh?"

Willa nodded, and Melody smiled a crooked smile which almost looked sad. Then she touched the tip of Willa's nose with an outstretched finger.

"Lucky you. Hang onto that hair, okay?"

She scooped the rest of the cut apple into her hand, tossed the core into the garbage can, and walked away.

When Willa went to the living room, she saw Melody on the floor with the boy. They were playing the game where his mouth was a tunnel, the apple a chugging train. Jo-Jo was laughing and had his fingers splayed across his mother's face. Willa stood in the doorway, a sour feeling in her gut.

"I hate to say it, but we've got to get going," Melody said to her mother.

And her mother answered, her voice quick and concerned. "So soon, but you just got here. You hardly drew at all."

"They say the weather won't hold out." Melody looked up at the ceiling as if it were the sky. "We have a drive."

Willa's mother came and stood with her while Melody lay Jo-Jo on his back and zipped him into a snowsuit. Then she and her mother moved to the front door and watched Melody pick her way down the slippery stairs with the boy on one hip, a knapsack on her back, her drawings in a roll under her arm.

"You two take care now, okay?" said Melody, turning when she reached the bottom step, and Willa smiled a quavering, forced smile. Melody strapped Jo-Jo into a car seat that looked like an elaborate plastic bubble, slid into the driver's seat, and sat there a moment warming up. The car was blue and rusty, coughing as if the air were too much for it, but after a minute Melody waved. Then she and Jo-Jo drove away.

"Why couldn't they have stayed longer?" Willa asked after the car and then the sound of the car had disappeared. "I have nobody to play with."

"I don't know, honey," said her mother, and her voice sounded tired and disappointed. "People have things to do."

Willa went to her room and lifted the cardboard shield which tricked her ants into thinking they were underground. They froze for an instant, then saw it was just Willa and continued on. Their paths were so easy to follow; she could see through the glass on both sides and watch their every move. She would let them go, she decided. Not now, when the ground was frozen, but in spring when the earth grew soft and they could burrow down. She would take the farm outdoors, crack open its sides, and let the ants spill out like beads.

But then Willa remembered the Queen ant, the one who had broken off her own wings when she settled in the farm to lay her eggs, who lived off the energy of her useless flight muscles, leaving the broken wings in a corner of the farm. Auto-amputation was what they called it in *The Wonder World of Ants*. Willa had wanted to get rid of those wings, hated looking at them, but she couldn't reach them without dismantling the farm. The Queen couldn't fly, and she was too fat to walk. Out in the world, abandoned by her guards and workers, she would die.

Willa wished her ants were leafcutter ants, the kind who dragged bits of plants and caterpillar droppings to their underground nests and grew fungus on them, like farmers. Then they ate the fungus and fed it to their kids. That was practical—the leafcutters could live through almost anything, but Willa's ants were used to bread and honey and being fed by her. The missing children, the way she saw them, were more like leafcutter ants. Somehow they knew how to get by.

Ants had survived on this earth for more than a hundred million years. It didn't surprise her. The smaller you were, the better your chances. Her mother made her drink milk so she would grow big and strong and so there would be cartons for the soup. But big and strong was the wrong thing; small was what you had to be. She would not drink milk anymore. In the end, if it came to that, she would find a friend like Jo-Jo. Underground he would shine in his paleness like the fireflies in summer in the field out back. Blind, Jo-Jo would be able to sense corners, the twisted workings of the paths, and if she took his hand, he would guide her far from the silos, deep into the insulated center of the earth.

LINDA KANTNER

A Shelter Is Not a Home

A shelter is not a home. It's a place to go when there is no place else. It's a place to be, not a place to live. A shelter for children is a place to wait. Wait until somebody decides you can live in a home again. Your home, a foster home, a group home. Wait until your family is fit or you're able to fit into someone else's home. Wait until you or your family recognize that how you have been living is not what everyone else thinks is normal. Wait until everyone changes. Wait and wait and wait.

Wait because your mother drinks too much and forgets to come home. Or she takes you to the bar and makes you wait in the car. It gets cold and your fingers freeze. She forgets to buy food or send you to school. She forgets that she is smoking and burns long black scars into the couch and the kitchen table and her sheets. You watch her and put out the fires just in time. Sometimes you watch her all night. Now that you're in the shelter who will watch her? Who will put out the fires? Who will remind her that you exist?

Wait because your dad put his hands in your underpants every Friday night while your mom was at work. You learned at school that this was not okay. You told your mom about it and she said don't make up such nasty things about your dad. So you told your teacher even though your dad told you not to. Now everyone is mad at you and you can't go home.

Wait because your mom goes crazy sometimes. She sees the walls bleed. She needs you to stay at home and mop up the blood. She forgets to take her medicine or decides not to take it because it's poison. Then she thinks you are the devil and she hangs you out of the apartment window by your feet. You live on the third floor and she hopes to scare the devil out of you. You think maybe she has.

Wait because your dad believes in hitting. He believes in respect and fear. He believes in the wooden spoon and wire hangers and black leather belts. He believes in his fist. He wouldn't hit you if you weren't so bad. He wishes to God he didn't have to. So do you.

You wait in the shelter with kids who are so mean. They say "fuck" all the time and hit for no reason. They say, "Your mamma is a whore and a bitch and a slut." If you ever get anything new, like tennis shoes from the social worker, they steal 'em or rip 'em or throw 'em on the roof.

If the kids aren't mad, then they're crazy. They giggle for no reason or pull down their pants in the lunchroom or shit on the floor. If the staff asks them why they did that, they just laugh or twirl or bump their heads against the wall. They make you nervous and sometimes they make you laugh. Most of the time you just hope you don't turn out to be like them.

The worst kids are the criers. They cry when they come in and they never quit. If you touch 'em they cry, if you look at 'em they cry. If you don't look at 'em they cry too. All they say is, "I want to go home. Please, let me go home." It reminds you that you're not home and you want to hit 'em. But if you punch 'em the staff says, "You better not do that. No family is going to want a kid who hits."

That list goes on forever. No family wants a kid who swears, who wets the bed, who won't pick up his clothes, who picks her nose, who is fat, who doesn't do her homework, who is afraid of the dark, who hides food in his room, who lights fires, who runs away from school, who is dumb, who's black, who's Indian, whose dad stuck his hands in her underpants.

No family wants the kind of kid who waits in the shelter. Waits behind walls made of concrete blocks painted the color of snot. Walls carved with initials, dirty words, and "Mom." That word is crossed out, painted over, put in a heart, burnt with matches. Rooms lit by a flash of fluorescent light that makes kids look like raw plucked chicken. The rooms smell like the given-up, given-away, hand-me-down stench of the Goodwill store. Beds are bolted to the wall. The mattresses are made of loud cold plastic that cracks when you lie on it, giving away every secret bedtime move that could comfort you. "Don't touch yourself." The staff yells from the front desk, giving away what you are doing. "No one wants a kid who does that."

Then one day the social worker calls out your name. He says, "Get your stuff, they have found a family for you." You fall onto the mud-colored carpet like you have been shot. You throw your arms and legs around the social worker's steel desk and scream, "No, I don't want to go. Please don't make me go. I want to stay here. I'll do anything."

Suddenly you love the green Jell-o filled with peas and red pimiento that they serve every Tuesday. Your room with no doorknob and ten boxes of Froot Loops hidden under the bed is the coziest place you have ever stayed. The kid who smashed the ceramic owl you were making for your mom is your best friend. The staff lady who embarrasses you, tucks you in every night. She says, "Sleep well, pleasant dreams." She's there when you wake up screaming and she'll let you listen to the all-night gospel review on the radio until it's safe enough to go back to bed.

The social worker says, "You can't stay here. This is no place for a kid to grow up."

But it's too late. You already have grown up. You were grown up before you came. It's safe here. If you were to run away this is where you would go. This is home for a kid who hits and steals and swears too much. This is home to a kid who picks her nose and wets the bed and is afraid to go to school. The shelter is home for an Indian kid and a black kid and a white kid whose father put his hands in her underpants every Friday night.

The shelter is home.

Rebecca Eagle

The Baby
and the Bathwater

Here's me in black 'n' white—fourth of August, 1976, Riverside
playground, Jefferson, Maryland—standing rigid on a swing,
my elbows crooked around link chains. I cut my hair uneven;
my bangs stick straight out. You can see my nipples through my
shirt. Eyes squinted, face scrunched, I'm scowling like I can't
stand whoever took my snapshot.

I watch Nat undress. He's grown much taller than me. I'll inherit
the worn cutoffs and white tank top he drops to the floor. Nat
rips a tag off the back pocket of the stiff Levi's, size 23, and pulls
on a new blue T-shirt with folds pressed across it. He's so handsome. Girls at school just call me *Nat's sister* and ask, *What's he
like?* I collapse on his cast-off clothes heap.

   I cut Nat's hair same as mine: jagged bangs across the forehead. His hair is shaggy and black, like mine.

Mum's hair is yellow now. She looks like a movie star.
   "Mum, you're different, you changed to yellow!" I say. Her
hair's cut blunt.
   "*Blond*, Sylvia," she corrects me. She talks like a movie star,
tips her head back, her voice like honey, cigarette smoke veiling
her. I always wanna touch her, crawl on her belly, press *her* into

me, so that everyone would know she's mine. Mum lets Derek, but she won't let me.

She lies; she's yellow, like Derek's car.

It's my mum's twenty-sixth birthday, and we speed to the seashore with the convertible top rolled down. Me 'n' Nat press spines against the back-seat upholstery. I stretch my hands up far overhead, catch the wind like on a roller coaster.

Mum turns around from the front seat. "Git down, Sylvia." Her hair's a yellow line above her sunglasses. Her silky white scarf takes the breeze, and I lean toward her so it flipflops over my face. I trail a hand out the window, touch the cool smooth yellow of Derek's car.

Mum reclines against the passenger door, slips off white sandals, and slides bare feet under Derek's leg. He reaches to her; one hand strokes her neck, the other lazes on the steering wheel. He brushes his thumb over her lips, then pushes it into her mouth and she sucks.

Me 'n' Nat laugh till it hurts. We're racing over one hundred miles per hour, nobody else on the road, it's so sunny and I'm giddy. The countryside spins past like spilt paint: a blurry mailbox, a firehouse, three dogs.

I roll onto Nat and laugh with my eyes teary. Then Mum spins around.

"What's so funny? Monkeys!" She reaches one arm back to separate me 'n' Nat. A sparkly bracelet sways on her wrist; her hand flails in mid air like a fish slapping rock, and we cackle harder.

"Jesus, Derek! My own kids mock me! The Lord gave me chimps insteada kids."

Suddenly, I feel carsick. I lean elbows over the front seat.

"Can I sit up front?"

"Hush."

"Mum. I'm hot. Where's my sun hat?"

"It's wherever you left it."

I rummage in the back seat but can't find my hat.

"I need my hat. I'm too hot."

"Where'd you leave it?" Mum sighs.

"Dunno."

Nat shades my face with both hands. Then I squeeze my head under his T-shirt and fall asleep against his stomach.

High noon at Ocean City, Mum spreads a blanket over sand and we plop down, munch fried chicken and barbecued potato chips. I flip chicken bones to a flock of seagulls, and the birds squabble over them.

"Cann-abulls," Mum declares. She spreads Coppertone over Derek's broad, naked back, rubs it in, then hands me the bottle. I wear a red daisy-covered bikini. Mum ties the ribbons of her straw hat under my chin, and the brim falls into my eyes.

"I gotta pee," I announce, and head across the sand.

"Don't touch the seat!" Mum yells, her voice blending with the cries of the gulls.

In a bathroom stall, I hang my bikini bottoms over a hook. I lift up on tiptoes, but the seat's too high, and my butt grazes the hard, sticky plastic. Pee dribbles down my sandy legs, and I rub the trails with toilet paper.

Later, Derek takes me out far, beyond where the waves break. He can't even touch the seafloor, and treads water with me on his shoulders. "Hurng arn tigh-rt," he gargles, and clasps my calves against his chest. A big wave crashes over us, and I tumble away from him. I float on my belly like a jellyfish and taste the frothy saltwater.

Then we rove along the surf, feet crunching seashells, shifting on wet sand. Derek carves a heart in the sand with his big toe, writes DEREK N SYLV, then an arrow through the middle. A wave splashes, erases the point of the heart, and my name. *Write it back.*

He dawdles across the hot sand to the blanket, and I follow. Derek opens a beer, spraying fizz over our cooler. He gives me a sip. Mum snaps open one green eye. "She's too young for that."

So Nat 'n' me droop lazy arms over an inner tube, float in the surf.

"D'you really like Derek?" he asks.

172

"Sometimes." I can't recall my real dad, but Nat remembers. When I ask, "What was he like?" he says "He's okay," like Nat still knows him.

I thought Will was my dad, since he stayed the longest time. His eyes were black. Once at breakfast, years ago, Mum heated milk for me and added one spoonful of coffee. She drank her coffee black, and read the funnies.

"You look fabulous," Will told her. Mum wore a baby-blue minidress and white stockings; her hair was red and curly back then, and golden seashells hung from her earlobes. Morning sunlight brushed her face; her painted lips shone like rubies, and her eyes were slanted green emeralds.

"Can I stay here? I don' wanna go to school," I said.

"You gonna get educated," Mum said.

Will winked. "But Sylv's a gypsy baby. We'll float ya down the river in a basket."

"Don't give her no notions, William." Mum crinkled the newspaper. "Please."

I keep a snapshot of Will in my diary. He's behind smoke, flipping hamburgers in our backyard. He wears Mum's Yellow Submarine T-shirt, and he's looking at her like he's sorry. Mum would burn my picture if she found it.

I walk beside Mum, on the way to the A&P. Her thongs slap the hot sidewalk. I sneak two fingers into her closed hand. It's cold and damp, like a sweaty can of soda. Mum shakes my hand away.

"I hate you!" I cry and run off, hoping she'll race after me. She continues, *slap, slap, slap, slap, slap.*

I wait in the shady front yard.

Slap, slap, slap, I hear her approach.

"Lookit what I gotchya, Sylv." A box of Popsicles crowns her brown-paper sack.

We lie on the back porch, sucking and slurping Popsicle after Popsicle. They're lime. Mum doesn't mind that green sticky syrup globs all over my face and shirt. Together, we devour the whole box. The sun's hot, but I feel shivery inside.

I'm so thirsty, I can't sleep. I tread to the bathroom for water. My bare feet feel strong, spanking the hall's hardwood floor. I hear Mum and Derek in the dark living room.

"I shoulda seen trouble coming after twenty-three hours of labor. She didn't wanna come out and I daresay she'd go back in me, if she could. Ya know, s'a good thing they tied up my tubes, if any soul can say good. Not that the doctors gave me much say. I sure seen better days, my man." Mum drags deep on a cigarette, and turns her head to exhale. Derek kisses her hair. "Then she acts hateful as a weasel, like she'll tear up this whole town. She needs so much and I just don' have it to give. Not even sure what is it she needs."

"She'll be heartache," Derek says.

I see their silhouettes. Derek runs his hand up Mum's leg, under her dress, and her head falls to his shoulder. She lifts her bottom and he slides off panty-hose one leg at a time.

Whatcha doing?

Derek kneels on the floor and rests his head and folded arms in her lap. Then Mum jostles him, lifts her dress over his head, and clasps both hands behind his neck. He nestles between her open legs. It sounds like kissing, but wetter, and Mum scoots herself to the sofa's edge.

I forget I was thirsty and lie on the hard floor.

Mum stretches, twists, and makes sounds just like a cat.

The next morning, I leave my lunch sack in the fridge and don't ask for milk money. In the school cafeteria, I sit with other kids who munch peanut butter and jelly, baloney, Oreos, carrot sticks.

My friend Polly offers me half her salami sandwich.

I shake my head. "I'm not hungry."

I tell Mum, "I need thirty cents milk money." She's by the bathroom mirror, smoothing on lipstick.

"Why donchya ask Derek? He's got plenty money."

I can hear change clinking in his pockets when he dances with me.

"Hang on." Mum dabs lipstick on my mouth. "What're you gonna ask, Sylvia?"

"Can I have thirty cents?"

"Put your mouth like so." She squeezes my cheeks together, so my lips pucker. "Now, ask."

"C'n I huv thurdy cends?"

"Make yourself like so." She thrusts out her chest, and places one hand on her hip. Her bathrobe falls open and I see the soft edges of her breasts. "Money, please," Mum murmurs thru parted lips that hardly budge. Then she laughs and pats my butt.

I sneak into her bedroom and steal two quarters from a night table. They're fancy, fresh-minted for the *Bi-sin-tenn-yul*.

"Let's play cats," I say to Nat.

"That's just for babies."

"Is not, lots of grown-ups do it."

"How would *you* know?"

"I know."

"You don't even know how to play."

"I do so."

I pour milk into a saucer and set it on the floor. Then I crawl to Nat, where he sits on the sofa, and rub against his leg, purring. I nibble his jeans.

"Come on." I miaow. "C'mon."

"You don't know how to do it right."

"And you do?"

"I know more than you."

"So?"

"I'll only play if we can really play, not just pretend."

I catch his shoelaces between my teeth.

"Okay, Sylv?" he asks.

"Mum's coming home soon."

"Do you wanna do it or not?"

"Sure."

"You sure?"

"Sure."

"Real cats don't wear clothes, didjya notice that?"

"Mum's coming home."

"You *said* yes." He's right. I pull off my T-shirt, then unzip and wriggle off jeans. I leave on my underpants and socks. I watch Nat undress. He takes off everything. His body looks much stronger than mine. There's some hair down below.

"Cats don't wear socks, Sylvia. Or underpants."

"Sometimes they do," I protest.

"You're just a baby."

I take off my socks, then underpants, and toss them in the pile of our clothes. Then I crouch over the saucer and lap milk. It trickles down my chin.

"Lick me off," I tell Nat.

"That's gross."

"You *said* we would." I drink more milk. "You do it, too."

Nat braces forearms against the floor, and pushes his face in the saucer. Milk covers his nose and chin.

"You don't do it right," I say. With just my tongue, I sip from the saucer. *"You're* not a real cat, smarty pants." Nat watches me. His eyes are troubled, electric, black like mine.

"C'mere," I call. "Here, kitty, kitty, kitty." He approaches on hands and knees. I lick milk from his cheeks, nose, lips, neck. There's fine black hairs on his upper lip.

I hear Mum scream thru the wall. Then it's dead quiet, then a scream again. Each shrill cry makes my heart thud faster. I creep to Nat's bed, crawl under the covers, and snuggle, toasty-warm, against him. He smells like chlorine and sweat.

The next day, I help Mum cut onions for tuna salad.

"Does he hurt you, Mum?" I ask.

"Who?" She sounds dreamy. She slices celery with a sharp knife.

"Derek!"

"Sometimes." Her face looks funny and sad.

I'll kill him if he hurts you, I'm gonna say. But Mum clamps the tuna can to an electric can opener and it buzzes too loud for her to hear me.

The radio blares a new song. Me 'n' Nat dance and sing along. Nat swings his hips, twists backward and yells, *"Ya just slip out the back, Jack."* I shimmy over and screech, *"Make a new plan, Stan."* Then it's Nat's turn, *"Ya don' need ta be coy, Roy."* We patter our feet and spin around and around. *"Jus' set yourself free."*

Then we leap up, press our cheeks together, and chirrup at the top of our lungs, *"There mus' be . . . fifty ways ta leave your lover! FIF-TY WAYS TA LEAVE YUR LOV-ER!"*

Mum marches in and snaps off the radio. "That's enough." Her face looks pinched. "Don't you guys have homework?" She's serious, so we scram.

Nat 'n' me sneak out the window to meet Weston at night. We're not supposed to play with him, since Derek called Weston a problem child. Weston fights at school and smokes cigarettes.

But Mum says, "Weston is so handsome." I don't think he is at all. He always smiles, like he's the happiest boy on Planet Earth. Mum just likes him cuz he's filthy rich. Her green eyes sparkle when she says, "Derek's right. Stay away from *Wes-ton.*"

Nat climbs out the window first, hangs from his hands, drops down atop a bush. He locks his fingers together for me to step, as I scramble over the window ledge.

"Get your shoes," he tells me, and hoists me back. I rummage in the closet, then jam on yellow rubber rainboots and buckle 'em up.

The moon casts shifting black 'n' white shadows as we walk down the middle of the street, to Riverside. Weston waits on a curb, his heavy black boots glinting like panthers' eyes. He lights a cigarette when we walk up, and he coughs. Nobody speaks.

We are ramblers. The boys trample flower gardens, topple snoozing cows, karate-kick mailboxes and fences. We walk through a rocky ravine. I can't balance in my boots; my heels keep flapping up. I trip and fall on rocks. Blood spreads over my leg, but I won't cry. I can't sit up. Nat tugs off his shirt, wraps it around my leg, and ties the sleeve together.

"*Go away,*" he hisses at Weston, who's fumbling with a rock pile. "She's *my* sister. She's *mine.*" He hoists me over his shoulders and we piggy-back homeward.

"You better not tell," Nat says before we clamber in our bedroom window. Moonbeams light his creased forehead, his black hair, but his face is swallowed by shadow. I can't really see my brother.

Smells of pork chops sizzling and steamy-hot cherry pie waft through my open door, and I can't concentrate on long-division homework. The phone rings, and I scurry to answer. "Hullo?"

"Hiya sweetheart. Lemme have your mum." The man's voice sounds oily, like someone selling cars on TV.

"Who're you?"

"M' Freddy Block." *Like he's somebody.*

"Mum's not here."

Before I hang up, I hear his liquid voice drop from the dangling receiver, "When's she com . . ."

Mum walks in, wiping hands on her apron. "Who was that, Sylvia?"

"Wrong number." I stare her straight in the eye, until she looks away.

I pour bubble bath in rushing bath water and hop in the tub. I watch Nat undress. Nobody told us *don't,* but still I lock the door. Nat steps gingerly into hot water. I turn my back and he shampoos me. "Behind the ears, too," I say.

He lathers me with a fat blue soap bar. "Soap me here,"

I instruct him, and part my legs, and bend knees from the water.
I sink backward, luxuriate, dip my head underwater. Then
I straighten my spine, and scrunch Nat against the tap. He re-
leases the soap and it bobs on the surface.

Derek left my mum. All day long, she drinks vodka and white
lightnin' and smokes Salem mentholated cigarettes. She only quits
her room to empty ashtrays or line depleted bottles and jam jars
along the kitchen floor. I hear her crying like she'll never stop.

I wait all day, then I tap at her door.

"Who is it?" She puts on her polite voice saved for company.

"It's *me*. It's Sylvia."

"What do you want?"

"Can I come in?"

I flick off the hall light, since Mum hates bright. But she won't
open. I pound her door with my fists.

"Let me in, please, let me come in!" My knees bump to the
floor, and I sob. I can hear Mum inside; she's crying harder than
me. *I'm gonna die.*

Today is my birthday party. "Yur-a-whole decade," Mum slurs,
and I feel like I did something wrong.

I clean up the living room, stack dishes in the kitchen, shove
clothes in the hall closet. Me and Mum blow up balloons and
hang streamers.

I wear a dress Mum sewed from an old one of hers; it's
crinkly pink, with a bow at the waist and dangling ribbons over
the arms. Mum bought me a slip so boys can't see my underpants. Polly, Daisy, Alyssa, Steven, Ralph, Nicky, and Junior
come over.

I'm spinning between radio stations when Nat jumps through
the living-room doorway in a Darth Vader mask. All the girls
shriek but me, since I know it's just Nat. Mum tosses her head
back and har-har-hars. "Take that thing off, buddy. You be good
to your sister, she's the onliest you got."

Mum baked a double chocolate cake and an angel food cake with almond icing, and we hover lustily over them, waiting to dig in.

"Waita sec!" Mum smushes a Polaroid against half her face. "Smile bright," she urges. We all lookit the birdy, and smile. But the shutter won't snap, won't snap, will not snap, till she groans and hurls the camera against a wall. Then it snaps.

Ten insta-magic candles relight no matter how hard I blow. Three times I make a wish, then take it back when the flames flicker. I drown each candle in ginger ale and cut humongous slabs of the white cake for everybody but Nat, who refuses. We drink fruit punch, but Mum mixes hers with Chartreuse. Jolly as Santy Claus, she hands everyone ribbon-tied baggies of nuts and plastic toys. "I luv yuh all, so lemme me tell you guys a thing. It ain't a bowl a cherries. Life. Don't let 'em tell yuh wrong."

Then my favorite song comes on the radio. "Turn it up-up-UP!"

Nicky asks, "Ya wanna dance the cha-cha-cha?" I *do*, and scramble to him. He swivels his hips and squeals, *"Ya c'n tell by the way I use mah walk, ahm a woman's man, no time ta talk . . ."* He spins on his toes, shoots one arm above his head, shifts weight, shoots up the other arm, while I pitter-patter and circle one-finger-pointed fists. We lock hands and swing till I'm dizzy. But not too woozy for the chorus, *"Ah-ah-ah-ah'm stayin' alive, ah'm stayin' alive . . ."*

"Not too close, kids," Mum warns halfheartedly. "Whyn't-chyous have some lemunade?" Our song's over, but I still wanna dance.

We stomp balloons, sing songs, chomp more cake, then tack up a paper donkey.

"Blindfold me, too. I wanna play. I'm the birthday girl's mom, after all." All my friends titter. Alyssa ties a sock around Mum's eyes and spins her. Mum grips the tail and, ankles wobbling, stumbles toward the donkey. She falls, and everybody can see she's not wearing anything under her dress.

Soon afterward, I feel a shiver down my back. A chilly draft blows through the open front door: Polly's dad's here early. He's tall; he wears fuzzy brushed-suede shoes. Mum purrs "How ya doin'?" and undoes the top two buttons of her dress.

"*Really*, Mrs. Robbins. There're children here." He talks deep, like a newscaster. *Really.* He surveys spilt punch and over-turned chairs. "Let's go, kids." He hustles my friends into his station wagon and drives them all home.

The room is empty.

"Well, I declare," Mum says. She locks herself behind her bedroom door. Nat runs away; I watch him fly down the street, beneath dark clouds that threaten rain. My big brother looks so little, with his skinny arms and legs pumping.

I listen to rolls of thunder, and my thumping heart. Sudden rain breaks and pounds the roof. Lightning cracks the air over our front porch. Then another bolt, hot and friendly, jags into the living room. "Go away," I say, then wish it would return.

After a while, I hear a click and Mum emerges. Her high heeled shoes poke from under the thickly folded cuffs of Derek's camouflage pants. They're way too big; she's got them belted tight, the hems in several rolls. Derek's army cap balances on her head. I watch Mum weave down the driveway, ease into her Dodge, slam the door, and back out. She bumps a tree near the sidewalk, stops the car, inches forward, and speeds away.

Well after dark, Nat returns. He's soaking wet; his face, arms, and clothes are muddy.

"Where'd you go?" I ask.

"None of your beeswax." Nat glares at me. *Fire.* Dirt cakes his skin; he looks like a monster. "Take off that dress," he says. "Your party's over." He rips the ribbons from my sleeves.

"It's not over till *I* say it is."

He grabs my shoulders, shakes me, then pins me hard against the wall.

"You're crazy, Sylvia. You're a loon." Calm, he pronounces each word distinctly. "You're going to end up just like grandma."

"I know that I will not." My grandma Sylvia's locked in the loony bin.

Nat's strong hands have me trapped against the wall. Its hard surface crushes my bones, and I can't move.

I see myself reflected in Nat's eyeballs, then he ferociously pushes his face so close that both his eyes become one black blur. "You dunno whatch'ya do," Nat says. *To me, to Mum, to Derek, to Dad.*

I will not cry.

That night, I sleep in Mum's bed, in my party dress. I wear it to school the next day. Still she's not home, so I don't have to bathe or brush my hair.

In the fridge, there's half a chocolate cake and a jar of mustard. I peel frosting off the top, sides, and middle of the cake and dissolve it in my mouth. Its sweetness makes my head spin, lifting me to scrumptious dreams, where each 'n' every one of us grins and whispers *cheese* from a Fourth of July picnic blanket.

Again I sleep in the dress Mum made. There's ashes and cigarette stubs under the covers. Next day, I wear my dress to school.

On the third evening, Mum comes home. She looks shrunken inside Derek's camouflage pants. The cuffs unrolled, and reach to the middle of her shoes, so that her gait's unsteady.

"You're filthy, Sylvia," she says, and marches me to the bathroom. She runs the water hot, and billowy steam rises.

She jerks my dress off over my head.

"Get in." I peel off underpants and step through steam, over the bathtub brim. The water burns my skin. Mums scrubs me fiercely with a hard-bristle brush, until I cry.

Mum cries too. Her spirit seems to melt; she collapses with her cheek against the tiled floor. "I'm so sorry, baby," she says, her eyes closed.

I guess she's talking to me.

"S'okay." I climb out of the tub and press my soapy face to

her hair. "Derek's coming back." Mum just wails and sobs, her small body trembling against the floor.

Later, she lies beside me in her bed. I'm wrapped in a big plush towel, with my hair twirled in another. My head's propped on two pillows. The window shades are pulled tight; it's dark and quiet as a tomb.

Mother? I wanna say. *Feel my head. Fever: There's a crack straight through it, where ten years' memories escaped. Nobody's here inside me no more, just a terribly high blue sky, empty but for you 'n' me reclined on this bed.*

"Mother? Where'd you go?"

I wonder if she heard me; silence surrounds us for minutes. The air feels holy—if I twitch it'll shatter like a smashed windshield. Then my mother says, "I was walking."

For three days. "I don't believe you."

Deepest silence. Then, "Believe me.

"I . . . yes, I used to walk all over this state. When I was young, y'know. I was just another farm girl in coveralls. I lived outside, you couldn't get me under a roof, and I was happy. Honey, I had clover for my pillow, wheat fields for my shoes. It was different back then, more farms, pastures, nobody'd mess with you. It's just gonna worsen too, you listen to your mom. Yeah, I know I changed since then, you watch yourself, 'cuz that's what this masquerade party'll do to a body.

"Tough times, I get so cooped up here; gotta keep things going for one man or another, for you and Nat. I can't think of me. Gotta keep you guys fed and dressed decent. It's not a piece'a cake for a ditz like me, never even graduated ninth grade. Life costs money, and it's the men who make the bucks. Men . . ." She sighs, then lights a burning-mint cigarette, inhales deeply, shakes out the match.

"Now there's a loaded gun, whichever way I figure. Take you from your own kids, from your own self, then they turn around and don't even know ya. They want you like they want you. And you want it too. You dunno what that's like . . ."

A circle of tobacco crackles in the dark. "Whattabout my dad?"

"Your dad. Your pa was a gypsy. He happens into town. You know I was crazy in love with him. But he was too much for me, too *real*. Fire and water, somebody's gotta back out. You look just like him, y'know." She's mumbling so I can barely hear. I think she might be sleep-talking.

I nudge Mum gently, cup my hand under hers in case her cigarette falls. "What happened to my dad?"

"Mmm . . . so, the whole story's what happened, big as could be. We lived together like a coupla young roosters. Mother couldn't stand . . . we wouldn't tie the knot. She thought we was evil incarnate, thought your dad was a bum 'cuz he was always broke and we never really set up house nowhere, no two cars in the driveway like I keep it for you, no way. I dunno if that's what drove Mother to the nuthouse. Too much religion, could be what did her in. Yeah, she kinda changed her tune, I figured, when Nat came along; she realized we was serious. But I was just fourteen years and three-'n'-a-half months old. Well, I couldn't stay with your father forever, and he couldn't stay with me. That's the only man where I did the walking . . .

"But really I don't regret a thing. See, there's a long universe out there, ya can't see it from where you're put, but it sure goes by quick. You gotta stay in school, hon, there's a lot to learn that your mom don't know nothing about, I *know* there is. An' lemme tell ya one more thing, while I gotchya up here in the sky. You stay away from the boys as long as you're able. They don't mean no harm, that's just the way that melody plays these days. What else can this body give ya. Whaddo I say. Forget it, I'm sleep-talking. Donch'you regret *nothing*. The rest's just . . ." My mother drifts asleep.

I hear her mumble and tip my ear toward her. "Wha' more I need, I got the beautifulest babies in this world." Her voice fades to a breathy snore, easy as a lullaby.

Mum's singing *"Mah baby-luv, yur luv is precious as a summer's day, that's wha' I gotta say mah baby-luv . . ."* I perch on the bathtub rim, in fresh pajamas. She stretches an eyelid, applies mascara. I peek up her tight red minidress. Lower, she wears zigzag pink stockings and black 'n' white flats. Her hair's fluffy, yellow with a black stripe at the part. She hairsprays the tendrils on her neck. She's going disco dancing with Freddy Block.

I can tell by how she's dressed that he don't love my mum.

"He *will*." She glances at me. "Cheer up, bluebird."

But I have to meet Freddy. "Just say howdy," Mum tells me. "And hon, don't lookit your feet, okay?"

Then easy and sure, she comes to me, folds me in her arms. My head falls heavy against her stomach. Her dress is soft, her hands tender. I feel her heartbeat, and its slow rhythm matches mine. Mum pulls away, and I lookit her feet.

Black 'n' white, then white 'n' black, Mummy's shoes are panda shoes. She doesn't know.

The Self in Exile

The I *without the* Thou *lives a lonely existence.*

BRUNO BETTELHEIM

There is no ache more
Deadly than the striving to be oneself.

YEVGENY VINOKUROV

SHARON OARD WARNER

Learning to Dance

I have a brand new stainless steel mixing bowl, big enough for
a baby to swim in. I'm glorying in the shiny professionalism of
it, thinking how much easier it will be to mix one large batch
rather than several small ones. The hunks of cream cheese warm
on the counter; in July it doesn't take long for them to soften.
I drop egg after egg into my big, beautiful bowl. The yolks drift
in the bottom like lily pads on a pond, and as I stand watching
them, I begin to sweat. It's only been half an hour since I got out
of the shower, but already I feel like climbing back in. Why didn't
Momma put in central air conditioning, I ask myself for the first
time today. Instead, she bought these damn window units that
I can't afford to run. They're stuffed into the windows, like faces
that grin at me. Evenings, I break down and turn on the one in
the TV room, but mostly I go naked and work on changing my
attitude. Sweating is healthy, I tell myself, recognizing Momma
in this strategy. She didn't believe in disappointment; she just
convinced herself that she wanted whatever she got.

The cuckoo clock in the hall begins its hourly racket, and
though I try, I can't stop myself from counting the cuckoos in
my head—one, two, three, four, five, six, seven, eight—as I have
done all my life. Just as the cuckoo jerks back inside and the little doors slam, a loud buzzing fills the house. I don't recognize
the sound at first, and when I realize someone's at the door, I decide not to answer it. I'm naked, and by the time I put on clothes,
whoever's there will be gone. I twirl the eggs with a spoon so
that they spin in slow circles around the shiny bowl.

The door bell keeps ringing, a punctual buzz-buzz, as though the person on the porch is sending Morse code. I begin to feel a little guilty, although I'm sure it's only some salesman or, worse yet, a Jehovah's Witness. After Mother died, I might as well have had "vulnerable" stamped on my forehead and a sign in the yard that said RELIGIOUS FANATICS STOP HERE. I collected a whole stack of *Watchtowers* on the coffee table, and once in a while I was even tempted to read them.

The buzzing stops, and a loud knocking begins. I give up, drop my spoon in the sea of yolks, and run to put on a T-shirt. The T-shirt's not really long enough to be decent, but I'm only planning on opening the door wide enough to say no.

When I peek out the little window in my front door, I see it's no salesman or Jehovah's Witness. She has no briefcase, no Bible, no pamphlets. Ready to leave, she hesitates on the edge of the porch. Her bare feet hang half-off, half-on, so that her balance is thrown back on her heels. She's wearing bright yellow shorts and a matching shirt—the kind of outfit you expect to see on a little girl—and she has arms and legs so long and lean that I clutch my own meaty thighs in dismay. Perched there, she stares out at the house across the street and the cars roaring by, as though the whole world is brand new to her.

And then the little boy who lives next door comes out and begins his daily routine. For an hour or more each morning, he rides his Big Wheel up and down the sidewalk. I bake my cheese-cakes to the sound of plastic being ground away by concrete. He rounds the corner of his driveway and peddles past the woman on my porch, but she goes on staring across the street. I try to think what she's seeing—just an ordinary house, I know that— but what color is it? How many windows in the front? I keep failing these little quizzes. Yesterday I couldn't remember my mother's middle name. Eventually, it came back to me: Eileen. Helen Eileen Hobbs. Even so, I felt funny and disconnected. It's my mother's house I live in; her cheesecake recipe I bake every day; her wild cat who comes to the porch most evenings for scraps. My life is so closely connected to hers that I can't even think of my father except as her husband. Still, I can forget her middle name.

The woman on my porch leans forward, throwing herself off-balance so that she has to hop down the steps one after another. She smiles to herself, as though she's discovered a fun game, and I almost expect her to climb the stairs and start again. That's what I want her to do, but she keeps walking down the sidewalk. She's nearly to the street when I notice the coin purse and a section of the newspaper in the chair.

"Hey," I call out, opening the door, because I don't want her to leave. But she doesn't hear me. The little boy is on his way back now, his short legs pedaling faster and faster, the roar of his wheels drowning out my voice.

My T-shirt doesn't cover me, so all I can do is lean out a little farther and yell louder. But she doesn't turn around. She stops at the curb and looks up and down the street, for the bus maybe. Then she must remember her coin purse because she turns and catches me hanging out the door.

"Hello," I call out, feeling silly. Smiling, she walks toward me; her hands lift as though they're birds about to take flight; then, abruptly, she pulls them back to her sides.

"Did you knock?" I ask.

She nods and holds out the paper with the ad circled in purple marker. I reach out to take it, and the door swings open, exposing me. First, I crouch and yank at the shirt; then, slam the door and run for my pants. I expect she'll be gone by the time I return, but I find her squatting in the flower beds, examining the petals of the petunias and pansies. When she sees me, she stands and hands me the paper. It's my ad, but it's been running so long I've almost forgotten about it. Evidently, people don't rent rooms anymore. But putting the ad in the paper was only a gesture; I didn't expect anyone to answer it, and until now, no one has.

"Come in," I say, holding the door open. "You're welcome to see the room." The room I plan to rent is my old room. For the last year I've been living in Mother's room.

As I lead her down the long airless hall, I call out a warning. "It'll be hot and dusty." She doesn't answer, but when I glance over my shoulder, she gives me another smile.

Even the cut-glass doorknob is warm. "It'll be hot," I try again. This time she nods. I push open the door and feel her fingers graze my back. It means nothing, I know, but I can't help being startled. No one has touched me in over a year.

We gasp as hot, dry air hits our faces. I spend several minutes trying to unstick the windows, and, while I grunt and heave, I imagine her leaving, those long legs carrying her down the hall, those bare feet coming down softly on the hardwood floors. Even after the windows are open, I go on standing with my back to her, giving her every chance.

But leaving is my idea, not hers. When I turn around, she's standing in the doorway, an anxious look on her face. Suddenly, I recognize it all: the alertness of her eyes, the way her head tilts slightly forward, her hands and fingers never quite still. She's afraid I've been talking, and she hasn't been able to read my lips. Does she just assume people will figure it out, I wonder. And then I remember the ones I've met in grocery store parking lots who have little cards and trinkets to sell. One way or the other. Either you pretend that you're like everyone else, or you announce that you're different. And she is one who pretends.

She moves about the room, running her fingers over the furniture, testing the mattress, but it's the two prints on the wall that hold her attention. They're by Degas, paintings of filmy ballerinas with pink flowers in their hair. Momma gave them to me on the morning of my seventh birthday, and they've been hanging in this same spot ever since.

She looks at them for some time, and when she turns away, there's a yearning, a restlessness about her. She points first to the pictures then to herself. Sounds come from her throat; I know they're words, but I can't make them out. She reminds me of a little girl trying to speak with the voice of her father. Not until I make sense of her gestures do I understand the words.

"Dancer, Libby's a dancer," she keeps saying.

"You're a dancer," I answer quietly, looking at Degas's ballerinas for the first time in years. Their bodies are indistinct, as though they're dancing in a dream.

I line up boxes in front of the closet. Then, before I can reconsider, I begin pulling things from hangers, one after another, and tossing them into the box behind me. Occasionally, I stop to examine a shirt or a sweater I can't remember wearing. Momma bought a lot of clothes. She bought them on credit, or she put them on layaway and paid for them piecemeal. She said she didn't notice it much that way. I'd come home from school and find these carefully arranged clothes on my bed. Momma would bend a sleeve on the shirt or ruffle the skirt so that it looked like some invisible girl was wearing them. I hated trying them on because it seemed to me that they looked better on the invisible girl than they ever would on me. When I modeled whatever it was—usually a skirt or a sweater—she always gave me the same smile, her big mouth turning up on each end so that she looked a little clownish. "Yes, very nice," she'd say, and after I retreated down the hall, she'd call out, "You'd better take care of that now."

They all look good as new. When the closet's empty, I tape the boxes closed and haul them out to the garage. Every time I go to the grocery store parking lot, I see that big box for the Salvation Army. That's where these clothes belong, but for the life of me, I can't bring myself to take them. Instead, I cover the boxes with a tarp because the roof leaks. Everything in the garage smells of mildew and rot. I suppose, eventually, the clothes will smell of it, too.

I'm expecting Libby; in fact, I've been waiting for her all morning. Still, she surprises me with her loud knock. When I open the door, she hurries in and I watch while she drops a big suitcase in the middle of the floor and gives it a kick. I know immediately what she's feeling. She reminds me of mimes I've seen on TV, only I think that maybe she's even more expressive.

"Did you take a taxi?" I ask.

She shakes her head, says "bus," and pretends to be riding one, jerking her head and shoulders before reaching out for the imaginary seat in front of her.

I smile because I don't know what to say. I'd like to compliment her, but I'm afraid she'll take offense.

Libby's wearing a leotard and cutoffs, and in the bedroom, where the light is better, I can see she's been sweating. Her hair's wet and combed straight back from her face, accentuating a widow's peak. I've never seen hair or eyebrows as black as hers; she looks stark. Nothing about her blends in—she's all motion and expression. Catching me studying her, she smiles and makes some signs I don't understand. Her hands are quick and fluid, and I think again of birds, how they can be sitting so still one instant then rise into the air the next.

I go over to the dresser and begin opening drawers to show her they're all empty. The drawers make hollow banging noises as I close them, and I feel strange, knowing I'm the only one who hears them. A small panic begins in me, and it grows as I open the closet. Although I want to look at Libby, I can't bring myself to turn around. I stare into the darkness of the closet and wonder how long before something happens. And then I decide to talk to her. It's a relief to think she can't hear me.

"I hope you won't think I'm crazy," I begin, my voice quiet, my eyes on the back wall of the closet. "It's just that my mother is the only person I've ever lived with. Since she died I've been here by myself. I hardly ever see anyone. Never had a real job." I reach up and rattle the empty hangers on the pole. "I guess I'm not your normal person, but I do want you here. Not just for the money either. I really want you here."

When I turn around Libby's sitting on the bed watching me. She has her shoes off and her feet tucked under her. Her back is straight, but she looks pale and very tired.

"You've been dancing?" I ask. I form the words slowly and exaggerate the movements of my lips and tongue.

She nods and motions for me to sit beside her. When I do, she puts her hand on my knee, looks into my eyes, and makes sounds I can't understand. Her attempts at speech take obvious effort, but the results are still flat, guttural, and often undecipherable. I stare at her blankly, and she tries again, then once again, those same sounds in that same loud, toneless voice. Finally, I shake my head.

Jumping up, she opens her suitcase and rifles through it until she finds a pencil and a pad.

I CAN TEACH YOU SIGNS FOR THE LETTERS OF THE ALPHABET, she writes, covering the page with big, unruly letters.

I grab the pencil and write WOULD YOU? Realizing what I've done, we both laugh.

"I forgot I can talk," I explain.

Libby smiles and nods, and then, almost as an afterthought, she touches my cheek with the tips of her fingers.

By ten o'clock at night the sky is so full of stars that even the darkness seems to shine. It's the best time of the day for watering; at least that's what my mother always said. She watered after dark to cut down on evaporation, but I water at night because it feels good. The yard is full of sounds—crickets, locusts, the occasional frog—but underneath the noise there's this stillness I feel I can rely on.

As I sit on the porch waiting to move the sprinkler, I think of going to bed with my windows open. While I sleep, the trees and grass will be soaking up moisture. It's a pleasant thought, and I stay with it for quite a while.

Somewhere down the alley a party is going on. Every now and then, laughter wafts down between the houses. And when I'm moving the sprinkler for the last time, a band begins warming up. Spurts of guitar, drums, and electric piano overwhelm my quiet backyard sounds. After positioning the sprinkler so it will spray the branches of the weeping willow, I walk across the damp grass to the back fence. In a minute, the band launches into an old song by the Rolling Stones. It's "I Can't Get No Satisfaction." The words are distorted, but the beat travels well, so I stand against the fence and listen. Truthfully, I'm not anxious to go inside. Even having Libby asleep in there does not kill the sensation I sometimes have that the house is more alive than I am, that it pulses with an awareness I mistake as my own.

Libby goes to bed early. She spends all her mornings and most of her afternoons dancing at the university. It's called The Summer Institute for Deaf Dancers, the first of its kind. Over and over she's told me how proud she is to be here, how this experience is a "great dream" come true. Yesterday afternoon, she showed me the sign for "dream." Her face was still flushed, and as she stretched out on the recliner, she arched her feet and tightened the muscles in her legs one last time before drifting off to sleep. I watched her sleep for several minutes and practiced the other signs she has shown me: "dance," "flower," "practice," "fast," "slow," "yes," "no." They're fun to do. Every day I learn a few more.

As I lean against the fence, I think about how hard she works and how utterly it absorbs her. But when summer's over, she'll go back to her typing job in New Jersey, back to being Libby Duncan, the girl who-would-have-been-a-beautiful-dancer. I wonder if this dead end bothers her as much as it bothers me.

The breeze picks up, and drops from the sprinkler spray across my back and down my legs. I turn to wipe them away and see Libby standing on the top step of the porch in her underwear. For a moment, all I see is the white of her bra and panties; then I can make out her arms moving slowly, like the shadows of tree limbs. I think her fingers are moving too. Is she talking to herself, I wonder. The music gets louder, and Libby hops down the steps, her body swaying in time to the beat. She must hear after all, I think, but then I remember what she has told me about music: she doesn't hear it, but she can feel it, like pulses, through the ground and in the air.

She doesn't see me, so I sidle over into the shadow of the

garage and crouch close to the ground to watch. She's stamping her feet, raising her knees higher and higher, like some Indian lost in a war dance. Then, she reaches the center of the yard, and the tautness of her body goes suddenly slack. She seems about to fall before she breaks suddenly into a twirl. Her arms reach out and up; her body twists, twists; then, she hurls herself into the air. Once, she passes so close to me I can hear a soft rattle in her lungs as she pants. Even after the music dies away, and the crickets and frogs hold sway again, she goes on weaving in and out of the trees. I hear an occasional splat-splat when the spray from the sprinkler hits her, and a little later I watch her leap and fall forward, slowly, as though she had control for that moment even over gravity.

In the morning, I find grass in the bottom of the tub, and as I bend to rinse it out I realize it's been days since I've thought of Momma.

The manager of The Garden Cafe asks if I can make a chocolate cheesecake. "I don't know," I answer.

"People come in and ask for it," he says. "Must be someone here in town making them."

"I'll try," I say. "When do you want it?"

"Soon," he tells me and turns away.

Pulling out of the parking lot, I wonder whether I can alter Momma's recipe. What would some melted chocolate do to the consistency? I feel a sudden unreasonable anger toward this man, and when I stop at a light, I realize I've gone half a mile in the wrong direction. I'm headed toward the university and away from my house. After the light turns green, I take the first right, but instead of going home, I turn again and come in behind the university. I'm going to watch Libby practice, but I don't admit this to myself until I begin circling the streets in search of a parking place.

It's been two years since I was last on campus. Momma was still alive then. I've taken a couple of classes over the years—

Spanish, biology, English. Once I even enrolled in a ballet class, or maybe I only thought of enrolling. Either way, I'm sure I never went. The only class I ever finished was biology. It seems to me now that somebody else must have gone to those classes and told me about them, but I can't think who it would be.

Only lucky people park close to campus. I find a space six blocks away and go through the agony of parallel parking Momma's old '71 Continental. I've walked three blocks when I realize I don't know which building Libby is in. Not knowing which building is a good reason to go home. Any reason, no matter how flimsy, has been good enough in the past. I stop in the middle of the sidewalk, my heart pounding, that weightless feeling in my head. A ginger-colored cat watches me from the banister of the house across the street. The cat narrows his eyes and lengthens his body along the banister, stretching like an enormous furry caterpillar. The sun is directly overhead. I glance up at it, and when I look back at the cat, he's covered with green spots. The heat is a simple but convincing reason to keep walking.

Finding Libby is not as hard as I thought it would be. The dance building is new; I remember reading an article last year about the opening and dedication. I walk in what I think is the right direction and ignore all the older structures. The new buildings are clustered together, and by the time I ask a woman sitting in the grass, the building is in view. As she points it out, I thank her, and the world around me seems to brighten and sharpen by degrees.

The sound of drums takes me to her. I follow the noise up the stairs and down a long hallway to a door with a little window. When I look through, I see the practice room, all windows along one wall and all mirrors along the others. The polished floor reflects the bright colors the dancers wear: green, yellow, pink, red, blue. Degas should be alive to paint this, I think. The dancers are taking a break. About a dozen of them mill about, stretching their legs and waving their arms. One man jumps up and down, up and down. I expect him to stop, but he doesn't.

Libby stands at the bar, one leg propped up, the other lean and straight as a flamingo's. She bends forward until her face touches the bar then raises up again. Her red leotard sticks to her back, and the bandana tied around her head is dark with sweat. After a few minutes, another woman comes over and touches her shoulder. They're beautiful together, Libby with her black hair and pale skin, and this other woman with her blonde hair tied up in a ponytail and a midsummer tan.

The woman begins signing, her hands a blur in the air. Libby smiles at first and nods repeatedly; emotions cross her face in quick succession: pleasure, anxiety, and finally tenderness. When the choreographer calls them back to practice, Libby gives her friend a quick hug, and as she does, her eyes stray to the door and seem to look directly into mine. Suddenly sick, I back away.

Momma always told me there's nothing worse than a spy, and she was talking about me. When I was a little girl, I used to hide in her closet. Sitting among her shoes in the dark was my way of being close to her. But she didn't want me to be close to her that way. Over and over, she dragged me out, both of us screaming. For a second, I expect Libby to burst through the door and drag me down the halls. But it doesn't happen. The dancers form a line, Libby on one end, and I find my way home.

By late afternoon it's so steamy outside that I retreat to the TV room, turn on the air conditioner, and watch reruns. Twice this week I've seen episodes I remember watching as a young girl. Now that the jokes are somewhat familiar, the shows are actully funnier. I feel a tenderness for Jethro and Lucy and Topper, faces from my past. I sit smiling at their antics until I doze off.

Usually, Libby takes a shower and eats something before coming in to talk with me, but today she knocks on the door first thing, waking me so that I look all dazed and silly when she opens the door. Her face is damp with sweat, but she smiles brightly, clearly glad to see me. Relieved, I wave her in.

She sighs, then plops down on the footstool in front of my chair and pulls the bandana from her head. I smell sweat and deodorant and something else I can't identify. Libby smoothes the bandana on her knee, folds it neatly, and turns her gaze to me. She's smiling, as though I've just given her the answer to a question. What is it? I wish Libby could hear, or else I wish for deafness, too. It occurs to me now that deafness might have helped with Momma. Maybe she wouldn't have expected so much. Maybe we would have gotten along. These thoughts surprise me. Not so long ago I told a pushy Pentecostal woman that Mother and I were uncommonly close. I remember holding up two fingers, one curled around the other, and seeing the pity on the woman's face, I burst into tears.

I am wondering what the truth might be when Libby begins finger spelling. She goes so fast I miss the first few words. My blank expression tells her to begin again, slower this time. When I concentrate, I catch most of what she tells me.

She's describing another dancer, a friend from the South who has wonderful golden hair. She spells out "shy," then cowers, a gesture so unlike her that it looks comical. She's bold and proud, expecting great things of the world and herself. I'd give my hearing in an instant to be like her.

"In trouble," she spells. Then she frowns, puzzled over how to go on.

Of course, it's the girl I saw her with today. I try to call her face to mind but all I see is the flashing of her fingers against the green leotard and the pale shine of her hair.

Libby tells me the story of Anna and her boyfriend in Georgia, a "hearie" who rides a motorcycle and works at a discount store. They've been going together for a year, but he's never learned to sign. That's how Anna knows that she can't keep the baby.

"Has she told him she's pregnant?" I ask, and Libby shakes her head.

Evidently, Anna wasn't sure until a few weeks before the

Institute. She hoped that all the dancing would take care of it. Now she worries that soon it may be too late.

"What do you mean, too late?" I ask.

Libby's face softens. "Before," she signs, then she presses her fingers against her belly and makes a delicate movement.

I nod and try to think what it would be like to feel something moving inside me. Babies are what I see other women pushing in strollers. So far as I can remember, I've never even held one.

"She wants an abortion?" The clinic on Duvall is about a mile from a restaurant that buys my cheesecakes. I pass it every day. Sometimes people are picketing, carrying signs that say things like GOD DOESN'T BELIEVE IN ABORTION. Once, I passed a young girl sitting on the curb crying. Her purse lay open beside her; the contents were rolling into the street.

Libby makes the nod with her fist that means "yes" then spells out "help."

It's the question she wants me to answer.

I stare at the television screen. A commercial is on, and I pretend interest to give myself more time. I feel sick to my stomach now, and my throat's beginning to close as I answer.

"I'll try, Libby."

Anna lives in a small apartment complex within walking distance of the university. The outside doors are only a couple of steps apart, and I can imagine the tiny dark studios built for students who only come home to sleep. Restless, frenetic people, I tell myself. I wouldn't want to be like them. One comes home as I wait—a lean young man, shirtless and carrying a tennis racket. I watch as he disappears behind his orange door.

The parking lot is shady, and I don't mind waiting. Libby explained that all she really needs is transportation. Anna will be weak afterwards. It didn't seem like much to ask. Cars swish past; heat flies off the wheels and into my open window. I turn my face away and am not surprised when the young man emerges, wearing a shirt and carrying a notebook. It's ten in the morning, and we've just delivered my cheesecakes. As I sit listening to the car radio, a dense pleasure catches me off-guard. All Libby's doing. This morning she helped me mix the cream cheese and eggs. Later, she admired the neatly staggered pans through the window in the oven door. I'm thinking about how I'll miss her when she emerges with Anna from one of the second story doors. They stand on the landing, smiling and waving at me. I start the motor.

We don't go to the clinic I pass every day. This one is hidden away in the same building with an optometrist and a dentist. Outside, a lone protester stands like a sentry; inside, the walls are painted cool pastels and the hallway is strewn with rag rugs. Someone has struggled to give this place a homey feel.

Anna has a 10:45 appointment, but around 11:00 I realize that her appointment does nothing more than assure her a place in line. The room overflows with women, but since we arrived, only one name has been called. A woman beside me keeps sighing and checking her watch.

Anna holds a magazine in her lap. She tries to read, but now and then I catch her studying the women around her. One is visibly pregnant, and Anna's eyes fix on her. Even after the woman notices and shifts in her seat, Anna keeps staring.

"What are you looking at?" the woman finally asks. Her voice isn't loud, but the room is so quiet that everyone looks up.

I wonder if Anna has read her lips and how she will respond. I expect her to look away, but she doesn't. She goes on staring, her gaze stiff, almost befuddled.

"She's deaf," I say, and everyone in the room turns to me.

"What?" the woman asks. She's older than the others, and I'd bet this isn't her first unwanted pregnancy. Waiting for her at home are more children she didn't really want.

"She doesn't hear what you're saying," I explain, pointing to my own ear. "It's nothing personal. She's scared, that's all."

Several of the other women nod, keeping their eyes on me

and away from Anna. Libby signs "thank you"—the same sign that means "good"—and takes Anna's hand.

In a few minutes the nurse calls the woman's name. She rises slowly, but instead of following the nurse, she comes over to Anna. The blouse she's wearing is snug around the belly, and she tugs at it before she speaks.

"I'm sorry," she says. Her hand reaches out, as though she wants to touch Anna's hair. "It's just that I knew what you were thinking."

Anna nods and makes several signs I don't understand. The woman seems satisfied because she turns and walks away with the nurse. When the door closes behind them, Anna picks up her purse and motions for us to follow.

Out in the hall, she leans against the pale blue wall. She's panting, and her eyes are squeezed shut. She signs, "too late, too late."

Libby shakes her until she opens her eyes, then asks if she felt the baby move. Anna shakes her head. She looks at both of us, then down at the floor.

"I feel *her* baby," she finally signs. Libby and I stand stupidly, not sure how to respond.

"Okay," Libby signs at last. "Let's go."

An old movie is on. Libby and Anna sit on the couch and stare politely at the screen. I wonder if they'd watch it if it weren't for me? At least it's cool, but the window unit rumbles so loudly it sometimes drowns out the actors' voices: then, I, too, am watching a movie without sound. Surely they're bored. I get up and go into the kitchen to cut thick slices of cheesecake. This one is experimental. I mixed melted Hershey bars in the batter, and I'm looking for reactions. It cuts easily and holds its shape on the plate. So far, so good.

When I return with the tray, Libby and Anna stand in front of the television, and the room is alive with music. Notes swell and beat around my ears. My heart pounds. The melody's familiar—

Tchaikovsky I think. Libby has her hand on the volume knob, and she's turned it up as loud as it will go. Anna touches her arm and they move apart. Then, I can see the screen. It's classical ballet; a whole corps of dancers cover the stage. Their movements suggest the music: I can predict every leap and twirl, but not the grace or energy, not the beauty. As the music slows, the principal dancers slide into an effortless arabesque, and while I watch, Libby and Anna slide with them. Both lean forward at precisely the same instant and hold the stance until the dancers on the screen move out of it.

Afterwards, I turn the volume down and go get them some water. In the minute or two it takes me, they eat halfway through the cheesecake.

"How do you like it?" I'm looking for honest feedback.

They go on eating then hold out their plates for more.

"Could you hear the music?" I ask when they're finished.

They shake their heads. I'm surprised. I assumed they must have heard at least a whisper of it.

"What was it like?" Anna asks.

I shrug. How can you describe a particular piece of music to someone who's never heard music at all?

"Different as it went along," I say. When I can, I use signs, sometimes making them up to get my point across, but mostly they have to read my lips. "At first, the music was smooth and deep, like a lake you can't see the bottom of. Then it got stronger and more turbulent, the way a storm blows in and makes waves on the lake. Have you ever stood at the window and watched a wild storm?" They both nod, and Libby reaches for Anna's hand. "You know how you start to feel wild yourself, like the storm's becoming part of you? And then later when it passes, the birds start to sing, and you know exactly how the birds feel, too? That's kind of like the music."

I wait for their response, but they go on holding hands and looking at me, as though they think I'm not finished.

"I guess I can't explain it," I say.

Libby leans over and squeezes my knee, hard. "Thank you," she signs, and then "beautiful."

I wake when the clock in the hallway strikes three. My eyes open as the last chime dies away, and I lie listening to the silence then get up and walk the length of the house to the bathroom.

Libby usually sleeps with her door closed, but tonight, perhaps because Anna's visiting, she's left the door ajar. I stop outside the room and look in at them. It's a hot night, so they aren't using the sheet. Anna wears a T-shirt, Libby nothing at all. Moonlight shines in the window, highlighting the nape of a neck, stretches of leg. How lovely they look, tangled together like a pair of exhausted lovers. My breath catches in my throat, and I remember Libby's hand searching for Anna's, the grace and urgency of her fingers. Then I think of this afternoon when Anna stood outside the clinic and told us she'd felt another woman's baby. Drawn to their bedside, I peer down at Anna's flat stomach. I look for some sign, but the baby is still a secret. Anna shifts and tucks her chin close under Libby's arm. I step back, though what I want is to lie down beside them.

The light from the window shines on Degas's dancers. I can make out one frothy skirt then a pale arm and hand reaching upward. Even as Momma hammered the nails and hung the heavy frames on my wall, I knew somehow we'd both be disappointed. But tonight she has her wish: beautiful dancers are sleeping in my bed.

The crowd is larger than I expected. The seats are full. I twist in my seat, surrounded by a sea of faces. An usher hurries past, searching for singles. Who are all these people, I wonder, and how did they end up at a recital for deaf dancers? My hands lie quietly in my lap, and I wear one of Momma's best dresses. As I strain to hear the comments of those around me, I begin to feel important. I know two of the performers. One is my best friend.

Finally, the lights dim, and then go out. We sit in the darkness, suddenly hushed, and listen as the heavy swish of drapery brushes against wood. After the curtain opens, the thud of the dancers' feet punctuates the silence. Like the rest of the audience, I lean forward and peer through the darkness to see them. In a minute, the lights come up, and the dancers start to move. Still no music. Just when I've decided this will be a silent performance, the drums boom, and we jump in our seats.

Libby stretches and curls, but the stiff way she holds her head tells me she's scared. Anna's dancing is more practiced, less instinctual than Libby's. While I watch Anna moving in and out of a row of motionless dancers, I imagine a life for her—a golden-haired little girl and a new man, someone who'll be captivated by them. It's not hard to imagine.

Libby's the last in a line of frozen dancers, and when the others have all begun to move again, she still stands alone at the end of the stage. I wait for her to move, and when she doesn't, I tap my heels on the concrete floor. Move, Libby, I command her, sure that nerves are keeping her rooted. But she's only waiting for her moment, and when it comes she's off running, circling the stage in long leaps, a bird learning to fly.

Tonight it's so cool I don't need the air conditioner in the TV room. A wonderful breeze brushes against my skin. I sit naked in the armchair and watch two movies and part of another one. I've been watching lots of TV since Libby left; that's one way I know I miss her. The other way I know is that yesterday I packed up the two prints by Degas—frames and all—and shipped them to her. It cost an arm and a leg, and still they couldn't assure me that the glass wouldn't get broken. But like the guy said, they have glass in New Jersey.

It's nearly eleven by the time I go out to move the sprinkler. The crickets and cicadas are quieter tonight. They must be waning, like the moon. It's just a chip of light in the sky, and I have to wait on the porch until my eyes adjust to what at first seems like painted darkness. In a while, I can trace the branches of the willow undulating in the cool night air; later, I recognize the dull gleam of the metal fence and catch occasional flashes of light on the garage windows. It's enough to set me at ease, and as I step off the porch and onto the wet grass, I feel a sense of belonging I've never felt before. It begins as a vague contentment, an enjoyment of the wet, tickling sensation on the soles of my feet, but as I move the sprinkler and stand listening to the spray beating lightly on the leaves of the willow, it grows inside me until I must rise up on the balls of my feet and stretch my arms skyward.

MARK SPENCER

Home

In early July, the summer Pete Rose will break Ty Cobb's record for most career hits, Lon Petersen returns home after being gone six years. His daddy has died and left him the family farm. When he reaches Adams County, in the hills of Southcentral Ohio, sixty-five miles east of Cincinnati, Lon visits his daddy's lawyer in the county seat, West Union, before he goes to the farm. As Lon drives into town, he reads the sign saying the population of West Union is 3658. The town is shrinking. Pete Rose has more hits than West Union has people, Lon notes. He sees that the front windows of Williams' Hardware, Ed's Diner, and Debbie's Beauty Salon are empty and cloudy with dirt; they've all shut down. Main Street is full of potholes. Farmers are committing suicide. But Lon's daddy just died of a wrecked heart. On the phone long-distance, the lawyer said he fell over in the kitchen.

When he finishes with the lawyer, Lon takes a roundabout route to the farm so that he passes the mobile home park outside of town. The road the farm is on has never been paved, is still gravel. The neighbors and their place look essentially unchanged. They have only nine acres on the side of a hill and live on their tobacco patch and county welfare. Most of the paint has peeled off their little house. Five rusty car corpses sit in the front yard. On the porch in straight-back wooden chairs, two obese women in sleeveless dresses sit with their hands resting on their thighs, their tanned upper arms looking like hams. Standing by the chair of one of the fat women is a pregnant girl about eighteen. As Lon drives by, she brushes her lank hair out of her

face with her hand and tucks it behind an ear and yells something at a little boy playing on the hood of an old car. The child
is naked except for a tee-shirt with Pete Rose's face on it. Lon
waves, and they all wave back.

The farm that is now Lon's has eighty acres. His daddy
always planted soy beans, alfalfa, corn, and a patch of tobacco.
The house needs paint and some roof work but looks a lot better
than the tall, narrow barn, which leans way to the east and
won't be standing much longer. When he was a kid, Lon would
throw a baseball against the side of the barn and catch it on the
rebound. The barn is huge, and when it falls, there should be
quite a crash.

Lon never liked life on this farm much, mainly because of the
work, but looking around at all the weeds and peeling paint and
rusty barbed wire, he feels sad. All this couldn't have happened
in the six weeks it took the lawyer to locate him in Oregon,
where he was selling encyclopedias door to door. He realizes
now that this deterioration probably started the summer he left
home to play minor-league ball for the Raleigh, North Carolina,
Rebels—the same summer his mama died of a stroke. His wife,
Pamela, came home for the funeral but couldn't persuade Lon to
come. He was afraid of the crying people and his mama's dead
body. Now he wishes he'd been there. The day of the funeral he
played in a game against Macon and went 0 for 4.

He remembers his daddy constantly sneaking up on his
mama (while she washed dishes or threw feed to the chickens—
any time) and grabbing her big breasts and saying, "I just love
melons."

She'd push him away and point at Lon, who would be
watching and smiling. "The boy, Frank. The boy," she'd say.

Daddy was probably broken up more than Lon ever figured.
Lon didn't see his daddy again after he went to Raleigh the day
after high-school graduation, and after Raleigh released him,
Lon never wrote and called only on Christmas each year from
wherever he was, static filling up the gaps in the conversation.

Before he goes inside the house, Lon walks out behind the

208

barn and looks off at the woods and thinks of growing marijuana. A lot of guys in the minors smoked it (you could afford
cocaine only if you made it to the majors). When he walks back
toward the house, he looks at his car, a '74 Pinto, half rust and
half orange. It has bald tires and a cracked rear windshield.

He unlocks the backdoor and enters the kitchen. On the table
there are stale crackers and an open jar of peanut butter. In the
refrigerator are three eggs, sour milk, and an empty ketchup
bottle. In the living room there are cracker crumbs on the sofa.
The flowery wallpaper is faded, everything is covered with dust,
and the whole house smells like puke.

Lon turns on the old black-and-white TV. The picture's snowy
but good enough. He has watched a lot of TV in the last six years
and sits down on the sofa to watch a game show he's familiar
with. Then he remembers the beer he bought before crossing
the county line—Adams County is dry. He gets it out of the car
and drinks it warm in front of the TV. He drinks one can after
another. He figures he'll keep drinking until he feels ready.

But he never feels quite ready and passes out sometime during a
rerun of *Miami Vice*. When he wakes up, Wile E. Coyote is falling off a cliff, and The Roadrunner is saying "beep beep."

He rubs his eyes and goes to the kitchen sink where rusty water
comes out of the faucet. When it clears up, he puts his mouth to
the faucet and drinks. Then he slides the plastic checkered curtains apart and looks at a field that's a mess of grass and weeds.

He remembers he dreamed about Pamela, who now lives outside West Union in the mobile home park with her new husband.
He can't recall the details of the dream. It was she he was trying
to get ready for last night. Distance has always helped him not
to think about her much, but since he started the drive across
the country from Oregon, she's been on his mind a lot. Now
that she's so close it seems his destiny to see her. He hasn't seen
her for over five years, not since a few weeks after Raleigh gave
him his release.

A lot of Vietnam vets have flashbacks, Lon has heard, and

nightmares, and that's why they can't live normal lives. Lon told a counselor at the junior college he attended one semester in California that he knew how those vets felt. They'd failed; he'd failed. The counselor smiled. Lon had gone to him because he never felt like studying. The counselor said that baseball and Vietnam weren't at all alike. One was war, the other a game. Just a game. It wasn't really a very significant thing, a person would realize if he thought about it. The world could get along fine—in fact, a lot of people in the world *did* get along fine without baseball, he said, still smiling, his fingers twined together on top of his big desk.

When he was in elementary school, Lon read biographies of Babe Ruth and Lou Gehrig. The books said they were great men, beloved national heroes. He also read biographies of Lincoln and Washington, and he saw no difference between them and Ruth and Gehrig. The books all sounded the same. In the seventies, when the Reds won six divisional titles, they were front-page news in Cincinnati: REDS WIN EIGHTH IN ROW. At the bottom of the page, below a picture of Pete Rose or Joe Morgan or Johnny Bench, below the picture's caption or pushed to page two, would be a headline like EARTHQUAKE KILLS THOUSANDS IN SOUTH AMERICA.

Lon looked at the counselor, smiled, and said the world could get along without war, too, couldn't it?

He doesn't eat breakfast. He takes a walk behind the leaning barn. The lawyer sold all the chickens and hogs, so the farm is quiet. Lon walks to the edge of the woods but doesn't enter it. He decides he won't grow marijuana hidden in the woods. He's been in jail for fighting in bars and didn't like it. But he's pretty certain too that he doesn't want to be a farmer.

He walks back to the house and turns on the TV. Later, in the middle of the Reds game, the real-estate agent Lon has been expecting drives up in a Ford LTD. The agent is a fat man in a lime-green leisure suit. He and Lon stand outside between the house and barn, both looking around, and the agent jokes about how the value of Lon's property would shoot way up if some-body killed the neighbors and burned their house. He tells Lon that he ought to try to fix up his own place a bit and that it could bring thirty thousand if they find some city people looking for a rural retreat and a tax break. Those kinds of buyers have been keeping the real-estate business going pretty well in this area, he says. They'll list it for thirty-five.

As he's about to leave, opening the door of his LTD, the real-estate agent says, "By the way, I remember when you were playin' ball for the high school."

Lon shrugs and grins, nods his head.

"You were the best damn player anybody'd ever seen around here. I remember that."

Lon looks up at the sun and says, "Thank you."

Lon drives to Brown County and buys two six-packs of beer. He's ecstatic. With thirty thousand dollars he can buy a new car and some nice clothes, and he's gotten the idea of becoming a real-estate agent in this area. A lot of local people will remember him from his high-school playing days, and the city people from Cincinnati looking for rural retreats will take to him fast because everybody from Cincinnati is a baseball nut.

Like the Reds, Lon was once front-page news—at least in Adams County in the *West Union Gazette*. He hit .536 his senior year, was county MVP three years. Jesus, he thinks, if he could go back and freeze his life at that time, just be in high school for eternity . . . For Christ's sake, he screwed three of the school's five cheerleaders.

He drives around, drinking, looking at houses and farm land. He could have an office in West Union. It amazes him now that for all these years he's been afraid to come home. What was he afraid of? What a fool. But no more! He feels higher than he's felt for years, and he heads out to the mobile home park.

The trailers are beat up and old. Lon drives slow, looking at the names on the mailboxes. He vaguely remembers the guy Pamela's married to. Lon and he were in high school at the same time, but the guy didn't play any sports. When Lon finds Pamela's mobile home, he sits in his car for a minute and looks at it while he finishes a beer. The trailer is a two-tone aqua and white sixties model with an air conditioner sticking out a front window, chugging and dripping. He remembers a picture Pamela drew one time of the big house she and he were going to live in after he made it to the majors.

He climbs the wooden steps to the door a bit unsteadily—his head is starting to spin—knocks and waits. Her husband opens the inside door and looks at Lon through the screen door.

"Hey, Bobby," Lon says.

"Lon."

"How you been?"

"I ain't had no work in a year. But Pam's workin' at the McDonald's over in Peebles." Behind Bobby, the inside of the trailer is dark, the curtains drawn, the lights off. The air conditioner continues to chug.

"I figured Pamela would be home. My daddy died, you know. Left me his farm. I just wanted to say hi to her."

"She's workin' right now."

"My real-estate agent says I might get nearly forty thousand for the place. Daddy didn't owe on it."

Bobby nods.

Lon looks at the neighbors' trailer, then up at the cloudless sky, then at Bobby standing on the other side of the screen door in a white tee-shirt and baggy blue jeans slung low on his skinny hips. Suddenly, Lon puts his arm through the screen and grabs Bobby's shirt and says, "I can tell you exactly how she sounds when she's about to come."

Bobby gets away and backs into the darkness of the trailer's interior and says, "Don't you come in this house."

For some reason, Lon doesn't want to go inside. "House?" Lon laughs. "Shit."

"She told me you was crazy." Lon squints at the darkness inside but can't see him. "She told me how you used to bust up your apartment after you messed up in games, makin' her think you was gonna kill her, and then tellin' your old man you was doin' great when he phoned you."

"I never once hit Pamela," Lon says and hits the frame of the screen door with the heel of his hand.

"Said you threw things and punched walls."

"I never hit her, God knows."

"It was in the paper here about you battin' one-fifty. Everybody was talkin' about what a disappointment you was. And nobody was real surprised when Pam come back home."

"She has a big mole right next to her pussy."

"I know all about it."

"You goddamn hick. You never done anything or been anybody."

For a minute the only sound is the chugging of the air conditioner. Bobby's neighbors, an old couple, have come outside and stand squinting at Lon as if they can't figure out what he is. Lon doesn't know what he wants to do now. Then out of the darkness comes Bobby's voice: "Lon."

"What?"

"She's growed a new mole. Right on the other side of her pussy."

He wakes up Sunday morning in his old room, which still has posters of baseball superstars on all four walls. Lon opens the closet door and touches the sleeve of his high-school uniform. He thinks about buying light-weight, colorful clothes and going to Miami to live and maybe become a vice cop. It seems like a worthy job—he likes *Miami Vice*.

He drinks a New Coke for breakfast and turns off the TV when he finds only religious programs. Pamela comes to mind, and he says out loud, "Screw her." He sits down and starts reading volume six of the *New World Encyclopedia*. He got into the habit of reading volumes of the encyclopedia when he was selling them in Oregon. Sometimes, when he didn't feel like bothering people, he would find a park or playground or shopping center and sit down on a bench and read his samples. He started by looking up famous baseball players. Pete Rose was in there. Then he started reading articles at random. He doesn't care what the subject is. He opens the book to any page. He wonders why he couldn't study when he was going to college.

Before he sold encyclopedias, he was in Minnesota, driving an ice-cream truck. Before that he was in New Mexico, Arkansas, Colorado, California.

After working on it a full day, he gets the tractor started. For the next couple of weeks, he mows fields, repairs fences, and slaps paint on anything that needs it. He drinks beer, reads the encyclopedia, and watches TV. He's found an old bat and ball and keeps them by the backdoor. Occasionally, he swings the bat at an imaginary fast ball down the middle or tosses the ball high over his head and makes basket catches, Willie Mays style.

Sometimes the Reds games are on TV on channel 3 out of Huntington, West Virginia. Pete Rose gets closer to Ty Cobb's record. "Go, Pete!" Lon shouts at the TV, the way he did when he was a kid. Rose was gone from the Reds for five seasons, but now he's back as player-manager. Pete is home where he belongs, Lon thinks.

Once, while he's watching a game, he reminisces about his summer in Raleigh. He usually tries never to think about it, but today he remembers one good moment, the time he hits his only homerun as a professional baseball player. The score was tied, and he hit the ball to the right field corner, where it took a funny bounce off the wall. The outfielder slipped, trying to get to it. As Lon ran toward third, the third-base coach pointed to home plate and yelled, "Home, Lon! Home!"

The Rebels later lost the game, partly because Lon dropped a fly ball hit to him in center field, but Lon replays in his mind only his inside-the-park homerun. Bobby said he hit one-fifty. It wasn't true. He hit .205.

One day when it's raining and Lon has been drinking beer all morning and watching game shows, yelling the answers at the

TV (he's learned a lot from reading the encyclopedia), he drives to the McDonald's in Peebles. It's lunch time, and long lines are at all four registers. Pamela is scrambling. After she notices Lon, she starts to get people's orders fouled up. "Girl, I didn't ask for no fish," says a woman. "I hate fish."

When Lon gets to the counter, she won't look at his face, but says, "Welcome to McDonald's. May I take your order?"

Lon looks her over. The blue uniform doesn't flatter her, but he smiles—he can tell she still has her figure. "I just wanted to say hi, honey." His head feels light, and his stomach is a little nauseated. He belches.

"Your order, sir."

"My daddy left me his farm."

Pamela looks behind her. The other girls are buzzing around, shouting orders. The lines are still long. The restaurant is noisy with all these people.

"You gotta order something."

"So how are you?"

A man in the kitchen yells, "Hey, what's going' on on number two?"

"I been thinkin' about us."

"You want a hamburger, okay?" She whirls around, grabs a hamburger wrapped in paper off a slide, and shoves it into his hand. "Fifty-five cents, please."

Everything is confusing and noisy and happening too fast. "Don't you want me?" he whines.

"You're drunk."

"But . . ."

"Fifty-five cents."

Lon hands her a dollar but doesn't wait for his change; he's started to shake all over and knows he's going to puke any second.

One night in August a storm blows the barn over. Lon hears nails and boards screaming. The house shakes.

In the morning he calls the real-estate agent, but he's out of his office. Lon hasn't heard from him in seven weeks. He's almost out of money and is trying to decide what he can sell. The money from the chickens and hogs went to the lawyer and for property taxes.

The next day Lon sells some rusty parts of old farm machinery to an antique dealer in West Union, who says city people will hang the stuff on their walls. Lon calls the real-estate agent again, gets hold of him this time, asks what's going on, and tells him about the barn. The agent says he's going to put "make offer" in the paper and the real-estate catalogue.

After it's dark, Lon drives to the trailer park and sits outside Pamela's mobile home. One window is dimly lit. Finally, he gets out of his car but doesn't know what he'll do. He stands under the lit window. Then without warning, it goes black. In a minute he backs up, charges, and kicks the side of the trailer below the window. The noise echoes through the park like a scream, and dogs start barking. Lon leans against the trailer, feeling the vibration of the metal. The window stays black.

Having driven the thirty miles to Portsmouth, Lon stops on an empty street just a few yards from the Ohio River and walks to the low wall at the river's edge. He looks across the river and up and down it. A barge floats slowly upstream towards Pittsburgh. After a while, Lon pees into the river, then drives home.

Sitting on the edge of the sofa, leaning toward the TV, Lon sees Pete Rose line a single to left field to pass Ty Cobb. As soon as the ball drops, fireworks go off, and Lon wishes he had a color TV. Now he sees Pete's mom and his young wife, who's holding her and Pete's baby, Tyler. The Reds players surround Rose. The older players who have known him a long time slap him on the back. The younger players shake his hand. Marge Schott, the team owner, shuffles out to first base and hugs him. The TV announcer says Pete's dad is probably looking down from somewhere above and smiling on his little son Petey.

Lon sits back as he watches Schott present Rose with a new Corvette, the excitement suddenly draining from him as it hits him that what Pete Rose has done does him, Lon, not a bit of good. He wonders why anybody cares what a baseball player does. But fifty thousand people in Riverfront Stadium in Cincinnati are still cheering their heads off.

He leaves the TV on but he goes outside, picking up the old bat and ball by the door. It's only a few minutes after eight, and there's still some light. Lon stands sideways and tosses the ball as high as his eyes and swings the bat. There's a satisfying crack, and for a moment he sees himself in a filled stadium—his mama and daddy and Pamela sitting in boxseats behind home plate. And the ball sails over the collapsed barn.

Melinda Johns

Leaving the South

You were born in the same year as the first controlled, self-sustaining nuclear chain reaction. The key words are controlled and self-sustaining.

You are getting too old to keep moving. It will have to be the last time you jettison goods, pack the car and take off with the cat. The cat and the car are not young either; both have been around since the Christmas bombing of Cambodia. You have little money and your collision insurance has lapsed.

This time you will go to the Northwest where the sun is not threatening. You were there once as a child but you remember little. You are leaving the South, a place you never felt you really understood.

The South

Gretchen's Oyster Bar. Gretchen placed second in a recent oyster shucking contest and has gained considerable fame. I would not have thought of patronizing her oyster bar without a companion because it looks rundown and authentic. The TV over the bar is tuned to Hee-Haw. The jukebox is playing "I'm So Lonesome I Could Cry." Gretchen can barely keep up with the demand for oysters.

I am with a man who, I am beginning to notice, drinks more than usual, at least when he is with me. It is an hour after the Seminole-Gator game and everyone has drunk more than usual. The women tilt slightly like canoes in a swell; their eyes placid and unfocused. The men are exuberant and confiding. They flash V for victory signs to new arrivals, slap each other's shoulders. They assume we are all glad the Seminoles won. My companion, who claims to hate football, is flushed with victory and waves his cowboy hat, which is really, he tells me, a Louisiana sharecropper's hat. Rebel yells. Rounds of drinks. Common ground.

Most everyone present is willing to fight with fists for the right to catch blue crabs in the state preserve, for the reputation of their women or men, for room on the dance floor, for the glory of the Seminoles. Violence is always possible. It is predictable and serious.

I am pleased to be taken as one of them.

I am happy the Seminoles won.

THE RADIO

Once past Pensacola, you begin twisting the car radio dial. An Irish patriot/terrorist is in the sixty-third day of his fast. The disc jockey who reports the news calls him a spoiled boy trying to get his own way. He laughs his slightly hysterical disc jockey laugh. The Oak Ridge Boys sing "Elvira" with numbing monotony. Your cat sits between your feet next to the accelerator and looks at you.

You ease north, avoiding the highway that you drove a decade ago through Mobile to New Orleans.

You only feel safe when you are on your way to someplace else.

THE BUS STOP

I remember my cities by their street people. Long after I forget other details—the city's layout, my dentist, cash and carry franchise names, fellow workers—I remember the restless ones who cry at coffee counters and can be seen wandering before dawn, who brush their hands nervously over bald heads, who cover their coats with many buttons that say, "I support the Guardian

Angels" or "Let's do it in the road" or "If you're so smart, why ain't you rich," the talkers who corner me in hamburger booths and relate vivid narratives that I believe for awhile.

Every workday morning, in the dark, I take the same seat on the empty bus, across the aisle from a thin black man wearing a stocking cap, high-top sneakers, layers of cut-off shirts and pants saved from military duty. He is of the age to have seen service in Vietnam; the tilt of his head and a tight jaw proclaim his disinheritance. We do not recognize each other, but it bothers me if he misses a day. We know we are in this together and hold tight secret smiles for each other.

A young man with patches of sparse hair on his face lives three seasons in the westbound bus shelter on Main Street. He appears to spend his day watching the ebb and flow from his nest of ragged blankets, his hands like wet leaves on his lap. If I walk down Main at night, I see his profile through the shelter window against a headlight and wonder where he washes, what he eats. One spring morning he is not there.

Across the street, at the eastbound shelter, another one, a mutterer and pacer, spends his daytime hours. His belly hangs over a rope belt and a porkpie hat lies forward on his head. I dislike him because he is actively crazy. I don't dislike the flaccid crazy one across the street. They are conspicuous, these two white men, in the shelters crowded with black women.

I remember Paul, another vet, a Grateful Dead drummer, who makes pot pipes out of deer horns and hawks them in the school cafeteria. Scrambled and generous, he offers me a dusting of cocaine from the stump of what once was a thumb. He is courtly with me and I with him, as if we shared a difficult history.

And Darlene, who works with me in the student health clinic and is careless of the consequences of reading medical records or smoking pot in the bathroom. On a slow day, she puts my long straight hair in curlers, then pinches me when it refuses to curl. She leaves without notice for Houston. I miss seeing her run a comb through her limp, straw-colored hair, hearing her threaten to rip out the eyes and feed to the hogs any woman who comes near her husband, a man she left a year ago for someone else's husband. Not a thought went by unuttered.

THE FEELING

Pure, rich and sorrowful, it comes with no warning and remains only the brief time it takes for me to become restless and frightened. It whispers relinquishment and regret. It has many names. I call it homesickness.

YOUR HOROSCOPE

You pick up the *Missouri Star* to read over morning coffee in a motel in Columbus. Your horoscope tells you to Focus on Travel and to Open Lines of Communication.

You have never been very good at opening Lines of Communication. It is because you are intense. Lines of C are probably dangerous for a female alone in any event. Oklahoma farmers are not apt to talk crops with you over a fence, Arkansas mechanics unwilling to estimate the merits of shock absorbers while sharing a soda and a bag of sunflower seeds.

These L of C's are not likely.

And if they were, the subject would travel to politics or religion or Women's Lib and you do not want to hear opinions anymore. You prefer a few illusions.

You carry your cat from the motel room to the car, check to see if you have everything and climb in. Your gears slip and you back into the truck behind you. The noise is very loud. Three men appear on the balcony, vault the rails and leap to the ground. You edge out of the car so the cat won't escape and all four of you collect around the bumpers.

One of the men is missing part of an earlobe, the other, an arm. The third owns a waxed mustache and one earring. They look like boarding pirates and you are afraid.

The blow has popped the hood of their truck. It will not close. The man with one arm uses it to push down the hood. He assures that no harm is done although it is obvious that harm *is* done. "Go ahead" says the ragged-eared man. "It's okay." They scratch your car window with their blunt fingers and say "pretty kitty" to your cat. You get in and drive away. When you reach the corner, you wave.

HOME IS

Home is Lena, the sunbather, who spends many hours by the pool in my apartment complex. Platinum and pleasant, she is industriously making a perfect tan more perfect. Home is Pasha, my neighbor's Labrador, who waits at the entrance to the laundry room greeting visitors.

. . . the waitress who remembers me and brings my coffee without asking. The arrival of the blooms on the dogwood and the mockingbird that sings through the night. Afternoon thunder, cats on the porch.

Home is something that can be relied upon to continue once I'm gone.

Fire hydrants standing on Main Street are cast in my hometown in upstate New York. They appear on Main Streets all over the country. I always check.

THE RADIO

Outside Starkeville, a road sign warns "Beware of Hitchhikers." You need no warning. Airwaves announce serial murder, random mutilation. The Irish patriot/terrorist weakens, loses his sight. Johnny Paycheck tells you to lay your troubles on his shoulder and put your worries in his pocket. An investigation of the candidate for US Attorney General has revealed financial misdealings, but is expected to be confirmed anyway. Loretta Lynn has collapsed in Memphis. Schoolchildren send her a card with signatures that measure 140 feet.

Three turtles, their heads and feet pulled into their shells, dot the center of the shimmering highway in spaced intervals like some cosmic shellgame. The Mississippi Delta is so hot you imagine your radiator overheating. Your cat drips saliva from a pink tongue. She refuses to drink and you dip her paws in water—a gesture she interprets as abuse.

Coming into the South the First Time on Your Way West the First Time

You were younger and the trip was an eager one, although even then you were leaving something behind rather than going toward it. You intended to camp in the Great Smokies, visit New Orleans and see the Painted Desert before you settled someplace in California. You pull into Eufala, Alabama, and call a friend of a friend who, you have been promised, will put you up. She is "just thrilled" to hear from you but her house has recently burnt down and there's no room at her mother's. She wants to meet you though, can you come to the Eufala Memorial Hospital? Her son has an ear infection. You spend the next three nights in a motel and three days in the hospital lobby with her mother, her aunt, sister and cousin. They are soft, gentle women who do not question why you are here although your presence confuses them. "How do you like the South?" "I like it fine." They are pleased. This is the first time you hear the archetypal story. "We moved to Oregon. It rained everyday for three months. We couldn't wait to come home." It is the rain Southerners remember. This story is repeated with satisfaction to a widening group of relatives. "We moved to Oregon . . ." "How do you like the South?" "I like it fine." "We moved to Oregon once."

Your hostess is distracted. She sleeps with her son on a cot by his bed. You cannot, under any circumstances, leave until her son is better. When he is, finally, you find it hard to leave this lobby, this large pleasant family. You promise to return when she gets another house.

Road Euphoria

You expect nothing when you travel. No one knows where you are. You are free of expectations. Despite worry over the car, the cat, the reliability of your map and vividly imagined catastrophe, you feel a guilty exultation and you sing snatches of songs that make your cat raise her ears and stretch nervously. "My funny valentine, sweet comic valentine. . . ." You do not travel to meet the real people, to see the authentic places, to know yourself better. You don't know why you travel. It seems to give you time to remember what you don't remember.

WHAT YOU DON'T REMEMBER

... previous routes through the country, the name of your nephew, the significance of relativity, the identity of the people in the snapshots you still pack and carry with you, precisely why you ran away from home, why you never returned, the steps leading to our involvement in Vietnam, the names of the men you slept with or why you stopped, the streets of your hometown where the fire hydrants are cast, the locations of the schools you attended, the place where John Brown's body lies a mouldering in the grave. . . .

The high plains winds bring a crisp earth smell. Your cat seeks the slipstream through the vents under the dash. The South is fading to sepia like some of the pictures you carry. You must hurry to make connections and shape the memories before you no longer remember.

THE SOUTH

I return to work after a week of the flu. I feel queasy and notice the smell of perfume. Fellow workers waft clouds of vanilla and gardenia, rose, jasmine, musk. Scents clash for attention. A passing canoeist on the Wakulla lays a wake of Fabergé. Honeysuckle and magnolias are in blossom. The air is torpid with a fragrance which is close to decay. Everything is a minute past its peak.

Palmetto bugs, big as a silver dollar, sprout wings during their mating season and dive at people waiting for a bus. Once a morning, while the season lasts, one or the other of us will turn into a pumping dervish, flap at our heads and subside again into a waiting pose when the bug retires.

The public I serve look Tupelo-blonde and honey-bronzed. Swimmers and divers, tennis champs, they wear white cotton, ruffles, curls and gold. Flesh is firm on the thigh. All gestures languid. Although they are students, few carry books, some have no pens. When two Cuban women enter the office, I am startled by their hoop earrings, red lips and vivid, energetic speech.

I have stayed too long.

THE ROAD

You drive through Guthrie, Oklahoma. The only monument to Woody is the Senior Citizen Home. When you return to the car after coffee, you discover that the springs have given out. The body of your car has subsided to its absent hubcaps. It is not a big problem and not worth fixing says the mechanic whose car this isn't. But, you must negotiate every pothole at ten miles per hour. You drive as if you were atop an elephant.

You barely miss a runaway mule on the highway outside Midlothian. He gallops against the traffic, his neck lathery, his eyes wide and fixed high.

A black van with impenetrable windows hugs the lane next to yours. The word KILLER is painted on its side; underneath, a dagger drips vermilion blood. You keep your eyes on the highway and Killer finally pulls ahead and away.

Your stomach roils from the last meal and the one before that. There are few menus that announce a crisp tossed salad, no egg that doesn't arrive slippery with grease. Patrons in roadside cafes swivel in their seats like sten guns to assess your advance. Waitresses slop refills for Hank or Sam but ignore your cup until you wave it with menace. You buy skimpy pale sandwiches to gnaw as you drive.

THE LAST FAIRY TALE

I remember his long slender fingers resting on my knee. He never uses them to caress. He tells me that his wife and a subsequent girlfriend left him with no explanation and I know that this is how it will happen to us. There is always an explanation. I allow myself to feel indignant on his behalf anyway.

We wear each other's shirts and go fishing and visit Gretchen's Oyster Bar. He says "Hia" to anyone he meets on the street and is courteous to drunks. He swims every day in a pool on campus. From my office I can watch him do laps—twenty, thirty— I lose count. When I am distracted for a moment, he is gone.

He is from Kentucky which he denies is part of the South; therefore he does not know he has that heels-in-the-dirt resistance with which Southerners have dealt with carpetbaggers for a century. Give them hospitality and tell them nothing. His assumption is that things are understood without talking about them. I sense this allegiance to secretiveness in Darlene or Paul, in many I meet. It says back off.

They take pleasure in talk but not in words with any substance or commitment. They use words to divert, entertain, obscure. Things are left out, secrets I think I could discover should I find the key.

His silence obviously indicates a past too painful to talk about and I interpret this as a test. If I show good faith, I will win his confidence and he will tell me about the scar he hides, the sister he won't mention, the nightmares, ambitions, the explanations.

Perhaps, he will then ask about mine.

I do not remember why I loved him. Perhaps it was because he "loved me but was not in love with me." This is not anything I haven't heard before.

He is looking for the grand passion: crisis, obsession, action, pain. I am at a disadvantage with my earnest talk and good manners. I cannot be thought of as painful.

I have given some thought to what men want and I concoct a profile for him. She must have the sensibility of Madame Bovary, the heedless passion of Catherine in *Wuthering Heights,* the ruthlessness of Ward Nurse Ratchett. She should be as devoted as Anna Karenina, careless as Fitzgerald's Daisy and demure as Little Nell. High cheekbones help as does a knack for handicapping horses, playing the flute, baking bread and a fondness for dogs and baseball. One would hope she were of childbearing age.

This is the wrong thing to present as a joke because it isn't and he knows it.

I wait for a response that never comes. A history dies with him. We part with no explanation.

THE SOUTH

The US Bureau of News and Weather Report in the South does not factor wind chill for obvious reasons. It does not state humidity levels for less obvious ones. I am told the levels are the same as the temperature announced on every bank—100. I go through many yellow traffic lights because I will sweat profusely while waiting for the green.

Spanish moss hangs in limpid strands from standing oaks. On roadsides, kudzu silently strangles entire strips of green. The tomato plants on my deck grow but do not produce a crop.

There is no definition, nothing clipped, little clarity under the sun.

PAST TIME

I planted a juniper, a cedar and a pine in the front yard of a rented house in Ohio. The roots took. After the landlord evicted me because his daughter wanted the house, I continued to return to see my trees. Years later, I wrote and asked a friend to look at them for me. He could not find them. Even the house, he wrote, seemed to be missing, maybe the entire block. It was, he confessed, confusing. Was I sure of the address?

THE ROAD

You are closer to the sky now. Clouds boil up and fly over. Twisted stands of cottonwood lean in the wind.

Dodge City, with its stinking feedlots, is so hot the road tar bubbles. Bawling, dry-nosed cattle are hauled here to the meatpacking plants to be rendered into saran wrapped packages. You are paranoid for no good reason. You are, you tell yourself, clearly recognizable as human and in no immediate danger of going through the assembly line.

A vet in Kansas confirms that your cat is constipated. He gives you an enema packet that contains a syringe and instructions. He does not volunteer to do it for you.

You haven't the courage to inflict it upon her. But you feel you must and you do it in the weeds behind a motel in Longmont, Colorado. She does not scratch nor does she respond. Although it is not a success, she will nevertheless leak a thin gruel for the rest of the trip. Each night you haul in the kitty litter she will not use and open a fresh can of cat food she will not eat. You swab her face and tail with damp motel washcloths, poke vitamins down her throat and make a nest on the bed for her. She believes you are trying to kill her and you sense her reproach and sadness from the corner of the floor where she chooses to sleep.

PAST TIME

Tilled gardens in back of houses, chocolate brown furrows topped with waving tufts of green filigree—radishes maybe, or carrots. I had a garden once. It was a flat garden. I forgot to plant my seeds in the humpy high furrows. I planted corn. The San Diego soil was dusty and, I'm guessing, alkaline. The crop failed.

Not since I belonged somewhere, have I had a fresh picked ear of corn. When my mother was young and drove with bare feet, we went to the foothills of the Adirondacks where a taciturn farmer sold corn. There was no CORN FOR SALE sign. She just somehow knew. While we squatted in his front yard listening to the whine of katydids high in the trees, he husked two dozen. Sugar turns to starch in three hours. Within two, we were eating ears dripping with butter.

Maybe once a year I'll buy a few ears from a supermarket and graze the starchy things in neat rows, careful to wipe my mouth like Chaucer's nun. Even in Iowa, where discrete towns can be lost among cornfields, where corn grows in plots at gas stations, in between railroad ties on straight tracks, "fresh picked" was not a possibility. It was shipped to Kansas for the cattle, to New York City, to Russia.

228

THE ROAD

From the flats of Eastern Colorado, you see, in the distance, an extravagant and absurd heap that looks like the Emerald City of Oz. You are no longer the biggest thing on the landscape. With the Rockies comes proportion.

Boulder has bookstores, alternative newspapers, café au lait and food coops, counterculture backpackers with faces red from hard traveling.

You could stay here if there wasn't more land ahead to travel across.

In a newspaper, you read that the Irish patriot/terrorist has died. Bombs explode in Belfast.

It is now high and cold. Your car is not prepared for the tablelands of Wyoming and climbs every incline reluctantly. Under the Grand Tetons, you stop to watch the bold, flashy magpies. A moose feeds on willows downstream. Rumors of snow. You do not stop in Yellowstone to await Old Faithful. It is all forward movement now—get there.

The cat sits on the dashboard. When she shifts, her smell hits you like a sandbag. You talk to her, tell her that you love her, that she must pull through because you will soon find a modest home with a perch by the window for her, perhaps a plot of earth in which to grow small blue flowers. You will purchase a rocking chair and she will sit on your lap and watch the sun set over the Pacific. You promise you will stick to this home like a barnacle.

THE SOUTH

. . . is a line of florid men shaped like Tweedle Dee and Dum, loose jowls, genial, senatorial smiles, oracular tones. The South is silent cedar swamps, cormorants drying their wings on docks in the Gulf, civil servants with umbrellas, water moccasins wrapped around the limbs of stunted trees, daily radio messages from Paul Harvey, sinkholes, the busdriver on a distant run who declares over the transit radio that he is lonely,

alligators in drainage ditches, laps in the pool, quicksand, flail-
ing, entropy.

Past Time

I consigned a goldfish to an ornamental pond in a park in
Tallahassee. I had named him Ping Pong because I won him by
tossing a ping pong ball into a cup at the county fair. It was
moving time and he could not be expected to weather the trip.
He was large and exuberant, if fish can be thought as such, and
I hoped that he could live to fertilize many fish eggs. I think of
him when I see ponds in other city parks and imagine that he is
noticed by park visitors for his fierce beauty.

You stop to hear a street musician in Missoula. With her
blind eyes raised to the sun she sings "Desperado":

> *It seems to me some fine things have been laid upon your
> table,*
> *But you only want the ones that you can't get.*

You brood about the trek you have yet to make on semi-bald
tires through the Bitterroots and Cascades. As you begin, you
drive by a lilac bush hanging over a white fence.

> *Let somebody love you before it's too late.*

Home Is

A juniper, a cedar and a pine, the 6:45 bus, a hospital lobby in
Eufala, Alabama, your goldfish in a public pond, freshpicked
corn on the cob, fire hydrants made by Rensselaer Pump and
Valve, Gretchen's Oyster Bar, a street musician singing a song
you remember.

The drive becomes a long roller coaster of dramatic beauty.
Snow on the mountains. My foot seldom leaves the brake. The
cat curls up on the seat next to me and sleeps profoundly.

230

I know what I must do when I get to the new blue town: find a place that will accept cats, find a job, make it new. I wish for a moment to turn and sail like a hawk across clear cold winds above Wyoming.

I stroke the cat, my hand following the curves of her body. She wakes, yawns, climbs onto my lap and curls up to sleep again. I try not to shift and brake too often so that she will stay.

Out There

*The night is beautiful as the frost begins to set, but my pace feels
pushed. I feel nettled and tangled like those berry vines. Earlier,
I had listened to "All Things Considered," as I do most evenings.
President Bush was saying again, "There are people really hurting out there." It's the "out there" that bothers me.*

*Where is "out there"? I ask myself as I crunch along the
gravel shoulder and stop. The sky is full of light. The handle of
the Big Dipper tips deeper into the West. Tonight I feel like I am
"out there," and I remember a line from a Solzhenitsyn novel,
"When you are cold, do not expect sympathy from someone
who is warm."*

*"Has it come to this?" I ask the night. Are we unable to see
that what's happening to one of us is happening to all of us? Are
we unwilling to see and feel that "out there" is here? Here among
our neighbors? Our families? Nearer than we are able to imagine
or bear?*

BARBARAJENE WILLIAMS

ANN NIETZKE

An excerpt from

Natalie

INTRODUCTION

There is no simple way, no easy or uncomplicated way, to look
into the face of a filthy old woman on the street. We are frightened or saddened or repelled, feel guilty if not resentful, and
then we avert our eyes. In a society that disdains old women
even in the best of circumstances, we are naturally overwhelmed
by those who belong to no person or place, those who in the
very state of their existence violate every conventional notion of
"femininity" and force us to remember death. If the old gal is
crazy as well—and so many of them are—we hurry past, cross
the street, avoid her altogether.

What follows here is a brief excerpt from *Natalie,* a book-
length account of my relationship with an elderly, schizo-
phrenic "bag lady" who lived for a time on the streets of my
central Los Angeles neighborhood. When she first appeared
with her shopping cart and miscellany of plastic bags, she drew
particular attention because she chose to navigate the sidewalks
of narrow residential streets rather than sticking to Vermont
or Western Avenue, Santa Monica or Olympic Boulevard.
Jogging past her on my daily morning route I would take to
the gutter, relinquishing the entire walkway to Natalie as she
inched her cart along. If she looked my way at all it was with
anger and suspicion, though I greeted her consistently with a
neighborly "Good morning." Sometimes she'd respond with
a stiff, childlike wave (from the elbow down), not smiling,

demanding loudly of the space between us, "What's *her* hurry-hurry-hurry?"

From incidental references, I guessed that she had been in the city for many years, having lived variously on the streets, in hotels downtown, and in board-and-care or nursing homes. Homeless and unmedicated during the two-month period I knew her, Natalie was progressively at the mercy of her paranoid delusions, hearing voices and plagued by an invisible male dictator who prevented her from seeking or accepting the help she so desperately needed.

Natalie would have been in her mid-forties when deinstitutionalization began and may very well have been among the patients released from state mental hospitals in the late 1950s or early 1960s. With stubborn persistence (and Natalie's eventual consent), I was able to arrange her short-term admission to a county hospital, from which she was discharged to a board-and-care home.

DAYBOOK
November 5

Rain on and off for several days, and more is predicted. Natalie keeps her cart against the base of the palm tree, though the fronds afford her little protection. She has a thick sheet of clear plastic spread out to cover all her bags, and makes her bed down the middle of this display, where she lies flat on the sidewalk, covered head to toe herself except between showers, when she folds back the plastic to breathe. She seems to be lying down most of the time, to the point where I am relieved whenever I see her standing up or moving around a bit. Natalie is often sleeping when I approach and may be groggy but is not usually irritable at being awakened. I think she tries to stay alert and vigilant at night and lets herself doze during the day. She claims that the plastic keeps her dry enough, which I guess it does, but the lack of air underneath it is creating a thick, sour odor among her bags and her clothing. The stench rises up and sometimes forces me back a step or two for air before I can give her the food I've brought. Her face and fingertips are blackened with grime, and I hate to consider her hair, which is mostly tucked beneath a blue cap.

So far I have taken her eggs, soup, chicken and tomatoes, blackeyed peas and cornbread, pudding, crackers, V-8 juice, bananas and oranges, a bran muffin and doughnuts. I have never actually seen her eat anything, but I can understand her wanting privacy. She is self-conscious about having no teeth, and sometimes she'll cover her mouth to smile or laugh.

"You look like Martha Washington today!" Natalie says. I think this is a response to my wearing a skirt instead of the usual sweatpants or jeans, but still I don't know what she means by it. There is no use asking, although I try.

"You know," she says. "Don't you know Martha Washington? I had almost given up on you today. I thought maybe you had to go to court."

"No, I was just a little late getting home from work," I say.

"Well, I knew you were in court. I didn't know when they'd let you out if they ever would."

Sometimes when I approach I hear her talking softly, even pleasantly, to herself. "What's happening?" I'll say.

"Oh, I'm reminiscing," she'll whisper. She is always asking me if I remember people or places or events—certain drunken men and pimps, certain hotels and streets, certain stabbings and explosions. She is sure I must have been there, that she knew me "back then," and she is always surprised anew when I say I don't remember. Today I hand her a plastic bag from Von's Market, and she mentions that it closed, which is true.

"Ann, you remember old Von's down there at First and Western. Don't you, Ann?"

"Yes!" I say. "Yes, I do! And you're right, it did close. Now it's a Korean store."

"Well, I'm glad you remember something," Natalie says, more exasperated than pleased, since this reminds her of how much I seem to have forgotten.

She is using my name a lot these days. Maybe she knows it pleases me.

November 6

It's an ordeal to get Natalie to distinguish between what is her daily garbage and what is part of her permanent collection. Because she is staying in one place now, excrement is becoming a very real concern, and I'm starting to approach her only with plastic bag in hand, in case she consents to let me carry the mess away.

Today she is sitting up between showers, keeping her legs stretched out beneath the plastic. I wonder at how she can stand the hardness of concrete for such long periods, with only the furry coat lining between her and the dampness of the sidewalk. Beside her, on the grassy strip near the curb, is a bright pink box of thin cardboard, the kind birthday cakes come in. Maybe someone brought her leftover cake, but that's not what's in the box now—there is brown seepage around the bottom edges of pink. I coax her into lifting up the box and depositing it into the grocery bag I've brought, though she is reluctant for me to use a brand new plastic bag for this purpose. The stench is so bad I have to tie up the bag and carry it to the garbage bin behind my building before I can bear to stand and talk to her.

"I can control it most of the time," she says when I return. "But I don't get quite enough food, really, you know, and that makes it hard to do. And then if somebody's talking at you all the time about whether he's getting more food or you're getting more food, that can make you somewhat nervous. That doesn't help to control things either. See what I mean?"

"Maybe you can walk somewhere else to go," I say. "Find some hidden bushes or grass, so you don't mess up right where you're living here."

"You mean just walk away and leave everything?" Natalie looks at me as if this is perhaps the most absurd idea she has ever heard in her life. She promptly agitates herself into a violent paranoid fantasy about what will happen if she takes her eyes off the cart, even for a moment (to hear her tell it, the neighborhood is brimming with people who not only covet her possessions but are just watching and waiting to see her destroyed, preferably blown to bits).

"INTO THIN AIR," she shouts. "CAN'T YOU UNDERSTAND ANYTHING?"

"So, Natalie," I say quietly. "Natalie."

"What?" Her tone descends to the usual pseudo-whisper.

"I have to go," I say. "What can I get you? Do you have any water?" This is always a complicated issue. Natalie often claims to have water, but I don't believe she does, and if she does, I don't think she drinks it.

"They don't understand how thirsty I get," she says. "I get so thirsty."

"I know why you get thirsty," I tell her.

"Why is it?" she asks, genuinely curious to know.

"Because you don't drink enough water."

"Well, what goes in must come out, you know."

"I know," I say. "And what goes up must come down. What goes around comes around." We laugh. I know she avoids drinking water in order to avoid urinating.

She digs deep into one of the bags underneath her cart and pulls out a pint-size glass bottle that I gave her water in days ago. I am surprised she's remembered and kept track of it all this time, but she seems quite taken with the name "Socco," printed in black on the silver lid.

"Socco, Socco, Socco," she says gaily. "What on earth would you expect it to mean?" She studies my blank expression. "Soc-Soc-Socco. Just like a Socco. They all have their favorites, don't they?"

"So sock it to me," I say. "I'll fill it up for you."

"I don't know. Maybe so. Do you think so? Do you think it would work? I don't think so." She hugs the container with both hands, close to her heart. "He said not to give Ann that Socco bottle back," she whispers. "No telling. You say it's fine, but I'm the one he's gonna beat up. I hate to be hit like that, just beat to a pulp."

"Well," I say, "the hell with him." I have no idea how Natalie might respond to this. I feel as if I've taken a big risk, but she actually looks pleased, as if I've been a naughty, naughty girl, but she is pleased with me anyway. "Just give me the bottle, and I'll bring you some water and the hell with him," I say again. "You'll have a nice fresh drink and he'll stay out of the way for awhile."

Natalie lets out a rather mischievous, snorting laugh and hands over the jar, and when I bring it back, scrubbed clean and filled with cold water from the fridge, she unscrews the cap and drinks about half of it right away, one of the best things I've ever seen her do.

"There," she says, wiping her lips and chin on the back of her glove. "What about it?"

November 7

Finally a sunny day with no more rain predicted. Last week I asked Natalie if she would wash if I brought her a bucket of water and soap, and she said yes, she believed she would. I am hoping she (or "they" or "he") hasn't changed her mind. I decide to get her her own bar of soap and think Ivory will be good since it will float in the bucket.

"Do you like Ivory?" I ask.

"Yes, Ivory's all right," Natalie says, not looking at me. There is a *but* here, slow in coming. "I prefer Caress," she says. "Really. Palmolive Gold is good. But Caress is the best. It makes your skin so soft."

I've never heard of "Caress," but the wizardry of American advertising reaches far and wide and deep—brand loyalty even on the streets. After I get past my initial "beggars can't be choosers" reaction, I have to laugh. Why can't beggars be choosers? Sure enough, the little Mexican market on the corner carries Caress, and when I bring Natalie the metal bucket full of warm water, she latches right onto the soap, very pleased and excited.

"Boy, I can use that. Can I use it? But how much was it? I can't run my bill way up. They tell me not to keep money, you know. They say not to show that money. I have to keep it. . . ." Natalie rolls her eyes at me in such a way as to indicate that she must keep her money inside the front of her zipped-up coat. "They'll steal everything you let them. Hide it here, hide it there. You can't be careful enough, really. How much was it? If my bill gets too high, let me know. They don't like it when my bill gets way up."

"Seventy-nine cents," I say. "Let's not worry about it now." I'm afraid she's about to talk herself out of bathing after I've so consciously talked myself into it: I have on old clothes and shoes and have vowed not to flinch.

When she is finally convinced that the soap is hers to use, that her bill is not too high, and that she doesn't have to pay me, which would involve showing me her secret money, Natalie consents to open the box of Caress and accepts the washcloth I've brought. It takes some coaxing to overcome her inhibitions about doing this cleansing in broad daylight. "He" and "They" seem to be lurking about, threatening and scolding and bossing her, which she tends to verbalize or respond to by muttering under her breath.

"Who do you think you are?" She keeps fussing with the box of soap. "Just who in the hell do you think you are, anyway?"

"Get up and let's do it," I say. "Let's do it right now. It'll make you feel good."

Natalie gets to her feet, and I am surprised at her strength when she suddenly lifts the bucket by herself. She takes a misstep with it and is nearly pulled over but manages to set it right, close to the palm tree for privacy from one direction. I stand in front of her on the street side. Behind her, across a small yard, is a one-family house with no sign of activity, and on the other side the cart and bags lend at least the illusion of protection. Natalie takes her grimy gloves off, folds them neatly and lays them on the sidewalk.

"They told me not to take these gloves off today," she says, testing me, I think, for reassurance.

"It doesn't matter," I say. "You have to take them off so you can wash. It's not going to be a problem."

She drops the washcloth into the bucket and then hesitates, unsure of what this procedure is going to involve.

"Step out of those shoes," I tell her. "And then give me your hose. I'm going to bring you another pair." Natalie is wearing black knee-high hose which at this point are nothing more than several giant holes held together by a strip of elastic and a strand of nylon here and there from top to toe. She looks at me as if I'm being naughty again, but complies anyway. Her toenails are a revolting sight, yellow and ill formed and so long and thickened I don't think I own anything that would cut them. I open up a plastic bag and Natalie deposits the hose with an air of proud finality.

"Now the underpants," I say.

She chortles as if I've made some impossibly obscene request.

"What's funny?" I say. "Aren't you wearing any underpants?"

"What does *she* have in *her* mind?" Natalie turns to inquire this of the palm tree.

"Come on," I say, all business. "I'm going to bring you clean ones."

Natalie gives me a salacious wink and a silly, toothless grin as she bends over and, forsaking all modesty, hikes up her skirt and pulls down the panties, which are brownish-gray from the waist-band down and soaked with what has to be fairly recent diarrhea. I manage to act as if I'm not giving this a second thought, hardly a thought at all, really, as they splat into the bag on top of the hose. I close the plastic tight, double-knot it, and set it in the gutter several feet away, toward the corner. With her skirt still up in back, Natalie reaches for a stray piece of napkin that lies on the sidewalk beneath her cart.

"Excuse me," she says politely. "I have to wipe my a-hole," which she proceeds to do while I keep my back to her, grateful for the momentary absence of passing cars.

I get the Caress out of its box and hand it to her when she turns around. "Wash your hands in the bucket first," I tell her, and I wring out the washcloth while she accomplishes this. "Now your face. Do your face before anything else."

I stay long enough to make sure she's doing this before I hurry off to the garbage bin and then upstairs for clean things. I find some pale yellow knee-highs of sturdy texture and some pale green, stretchy cotton panties that I'm sure won't be too small. I wish I had a suitable skirt to replace the long woolen one Natalie has worn since her arrival. It is filthy now, as is her jacket, as is the jersey top beneath. I settle for an old burgundy sweatshirt with several pockets.

When Natalie sees what I've brought she declares, "You've worked hard, and I've worked hard. I don't want you to do too much. It's too much trouble. Isn't it?"

"I'm in the mood today," I say. "Catch me on the fly. Let's do it."

"Well, okay then," Natalie says. She acts as if she's finished washing, and her face does look a lot better, though there are still small areas of caked black dirt on one cheek. The water in the bucket is murky brown, with bits of grass floating on top. Natalie balances herself against the tree and sticks each foot in to soak for awhile.

"Feels so good," she says. "Dance with a dolly with a hole in her stocking. Don't you think so, Ann?"

I hand her the old dishtowel I've brought for her to dry on, and I leave both it and the washcloth in the bottom of the bucket to throw away, once I've poured the water down the storm drain at the corner.

"What did you say I owed you for the soap?" Natalie starts to obsess again about the Caress, but she certainly confiscated it while I was gone: it's nowhere in sight. I just hope she's keeping it in the box.

She is pleased by the bit of lace on the waistband of the panties. "My, my, my," she says, and pulls them up fast. Then leaning against her cart she somehow manages to get the hose on standing up and, miraculously, avoids causing runs with those monstrous toenails. She slips into her black flats and

242

walks around with a spring in her step, showing me how good she feels.

"You look great," I tell her. I think I feel happier than she does, actually. Having achieved this much I wish I could get her really clean and into clean clothes, but she shows no interest even in the sweatshirt I've brought. She accepts it politely while rejecting the notion that she'll ever be able to change her clothes.

"They'll think I'm crazy," she whispers. "I have to be careful about wearing a man's clothes, honey." I reassure her that it's a woman's sweatshirt, but she's not buying this, I can tell.

"Promise me you'll at least try it on after dark," I say. "You need to have a clean shirt on now that you're so clean. We need to get rid of the one you're wearing. Promise?"

"Well, I promise," she says, straightening her furry bed on the sidewalk and settling down into her usual niche. "But nobody seems to get a certain point. He'll be up in my bowel before you can blink that eye, see. He doesn't like these gloves all over the ground like that."

I come home exhausted. Oddly it is not the odor of feces or stale sweat that clings to my clothing and hair but the smell of the stuff that Natalie has collected, a palpable odor from all those bags that have been under the plastic cover with her for days in the rain. After a bath and shampoo, I carry my own clothes down to the garbage bin knotted in plastic, too.

TIM SCHMAND

Crossing Rampart

The bus's rear doors spilled Harley out onto a noon-bright, hot and humid Rampart Street. A shoeless winehead, fringed in black rags, trying to beat the driver for a fare, ducked past Harley and sat down on the steps just inside the doors. He winked at Harley, held a finger to his lips. The doors closed. Diesel exhaust sputtered from the bus, enveloping Harley in a black haze.

Shadeless trees along Rampart's edge twisted up out of grass patches, littered with bottle caps, broken glass and lead wheel weights. A drug dealer hissed at Harley from an alley bordered by a burnt-out liquor store and a shuttered alternator repair shop. Dressed in a purple muscle shirt and a black head wrap, he stepped from between the buildings. "Got your rock," he sang in a falsetto. "Got your powder. Got the ticket that makes you feel right."

Harley shook his head.

The dealer fell back between the buildings.

Traffic broke; Harley jogged across Rampart to the Crescent City Plasma Center. A group of men lounged on the building's steps beneath the No Loitering sign. A bottle of cheap wine made the rounds on the bottom step. Higher up, men sipped beer from sweating tall-boy cans.

As Harley climbed past the beer drinkers, the center's double doors burst open, with an explosion of slamming chain and grating metal. A thin man in a bright orange beret charged down the steps. He pushed off Harley's left shoulder, vaulted a black pipe railing, and raced down the street.

The doors exploded again. A muscular man bounded out onto the steps; plastic tubes ran from his left arm to a half-full bag of blood hung on a wheeled aluminum tree. Two nurses followed, fussing over the tubes, the blood, and the tree.

"Where'd he go?" the man shouted.

One of the loungers pointed in the runner's direction.

The smaller of the two nurses screamed at the man, "Jasper, you can't do this here. Jasper?" The other adjusted the tubes and the needle poking into Jasper's arm.

Jasper shouted, "Richmond, you motherfucker. I'm going to kick your ass next time. Kick your ass. You hear me, Richmond?"

A laugh cackled up from the steps.

"What's so damned funny? Huh? What's so goddamned funny?" Jasper stuck a finger in Harley's face. "You think it's funny?"

Harley relaxed every muscle in his face. He shook his head. "No. I don't think it's funny."

"Well, which one of you pussy-whipped, meat-beating motherfuckers thinks it's funny?"

No one answered.

"Figures," Jasper said. He hawked twice and spat a gob down on the sidewalk. "There, in case any of you motherfuckers get hungry."

Jasper turned back through the center's doors.

The men on the steps were silent for a moment. Then a voice piped up from the beer section. "I got a straw, me, if anyone wants a sip of Jasper's spit."

The men laughed, gagged and cried.

Someone shouted from the bottom, "Aw, Roy, you got to be one of the sleaziest motherfuckers I ever saw."

Roy shouted back. "If it's mothers I be fucking, Benny, you know I started with yours. You know that's right."

The men hooted.

Benny cursed.

The bottoms of beer cans, and the wine bottle's green glass, flashed in the sun.

Harley stood on the steps, waiting for Jasper to make his way back to wherever he had come from. He knew the Jaspers and Richmonds and all the men lounging on the steps. He had grown to hate and fear them all, because he could feel himself being sucked deeper and deeper into their world.

Harley had been a roustabout on an oil rig in the Gulf of Mexico. Fourteen days on, seven days off; money flowed in and out of his pockets like oil at the wellhead. When the barrel price of oil fell below thirty dollars, Harley dropped a lot further.

Claude Richard had warned him. On what turned out to be their last night together on the rig, standing landside so Claude could smell the wind blowing off the bayous, he had asked, "Harley, boy, do you smell it?"

Harley was leaning against the railing, just barely conscious of the pumps thrumming beneath his feet. "Smell what?"

"Trouble. Hard times."

"I smell what I smell every time we been out here. I smell the gulf, some diesel fuel."

"Harley, boy," Claude said. "I hope you saved your ass some a' that money. I hope you did."

Harley only laughed. "Wait, you know what I smell?" He took a deep breath. "I smell good food and fine whores in New Orleans. I smell . . . I smell a round of drinks at the Absinthe House and dinner at Paschal Manale's. That's what I smell."

Claude sighed, "Harley, boy," and shook his head.

During the first months after the rigs shut down and Harley found himself on the street, the only sure thing in his life was that tomorrow he would get back. But after more than a year, he felt as if a wall had been built to prevent his return: a wall known only to those on the wrong side of it. He knew what made the wall. It was made of the way the Jaspers and the Richmonds incited each other to violence over the slightest offense; the way the wineheads sat, passed judgment, made plans; the way they wore their clothes, the way they talked—in rambling pronouncements about the state of the world, with the maudlin flavor of cheap wine and the salvation of Jesus Christ, the one and only true god, thrown in.

But, now, Harley was getting out. He wiggled the toes in his right boot and could feel the two twenties pressing against what was left of his sock. He repeated the arithmetic that had become his prayer for the last four days. Forty dollars plus eighteen for selling blood, plus, if I can get it, two days of day labor, equal one hundred and twenty-two dollars. One hundred and twenty-two dollars could get him off the street, get him on a bus, and get him up to his sister's house, with money left over to begin again. Harley didn't think he was getting off the street tomorrow anymore, but maybe the day after tomorrow.

A gray-haired, small-eyed male nurse sat in a security booth in the small vestibule just past the plasma center's front door. He looked up at Harley through a wired glass window and shook his head. "I told them and I told them, keep the music playing I says. Music. It's the only thing that keeps them calm. But they don't listen. They've never listened." He shuffled some papers on the counter and picked up a pen. "Donor number?"

"I don't have one," Harley said.

"Okay," the nurse said. "Name?"

"Harley Ives," he said.

"Harley? That your real name?"

"Yes," he said.

"Ives spelled I V E S.

"Yes."

"Do you know what we do here?"

"You take my blood and give me eighteen dollars."

"You're close. We don't take whole blood, Harley. We only want your platelets. We take two pints. Spin out the platelets and put the two pints back. Do you understand?"

Harley nodded. "Sure."

The nurse smiled. "Okay, now, if you answer yes to any of the following questions your blood will be ineligible. Do you understand?"

"If I say yes, you say no, right?"

"Right." The nurse laughed.

"Since 1979 have you had sex with another man?"

"No," Harley said.

"Too bad." The nurse smiled at him. "Have you had sex with a prostitute?"

"No." He lied.

"Had sex in exchange for drugs?"

"No."

"Visited any countries in West Africa or had sex with anyone from West Africa?"

"No."

"In the last twelve months have you gotten any tattoos or pierced anything?"

"No."

"Traveled outside of the United States or Canada?"

"No.

"Are you an intravenous drug user or have you had sex with anyone who is?"

"No."

"Let's see your arms."

Harley held his arms up to the glass.

"Turn them sideways," the nurse said. "How do you feel today?"

"I feel okay."

"Congratulations, you pass." The nurse pushed an identification card and a pen through the slot in the bottom of the wired window. "Sign it next to the X," he said. "This is your donor card. Any time you want to complete a transaction you must have this card." The nurse leaned forward on his seat and pointed toward another door. "After I buzz you through, knock on the first door on your right. Another nurse, there, will test your blood."

The door buzzed open. The air smelled of blood, old clothes, and antiseptic. Small rust-colored splashes dotted the lime green walls. Down the hall, Harley could see into a room where gurneys were set up in rows. A forest of aluminum trees stood next to the tables. Bags of blood, like ripe fruit, hung dripping platelet-free blood back into various bodies.

Small voices mumbled together in the waiting room. Nurses and aides, dressed in whites, moved noiselessly across the linoleum floor.

Harley knocked on the first door.

"Come," said a voice.

Harley stepped into a room that reminded him of a doctor's office: white walls, clean counters, deep sinks. "Hi," he said to a black woman nurse who was sitting behind a desk, paging through a *People* magazine. "They told me to come here next."

The nurse held out her hand. "ID card," she said, without looking up.

Harley handed her his card. She copied his number onto an adhesive label, peeled off its backing, and attached it to a small plastic vial. "Stand over there in the corner," she said. "Face the wall and drop your pants."

"Huh?" Harley asked.

She looked up at him for the first time. "Go stand in that corner." She pointed. "Face the wall and drop your pants."

"I don't have any underwear on," Harley said.

"Good for you," she said.

Harley stepped into the corner and slid his jeans down past his buttocks.

"All the way, honey. I need to see the back of your knees."

Harley pushed his pants to the ground.

"Okay, turn around."

Harley turned in small steps, his ankles bound by his trousers. When he faced her, the nurse was looking back down at her magazine. "Okay," Harley said.

"Cup your testicles and lift them, so I can see the inside of your thighs." She squinted. "Get dressed," she said. "And sit down here."

Harley pulled up his jeans, tucked in his shirt, and sat down in a chair alongside the desk.

She pushed the magazine aside and took his arm firmly, turning it sideways, running her index finger over his veins. "Oh, we won't have no problem tapping into you," she said. She tied a rubber tube around his bicep, flicked a vein with her finger, swabbed it with a rust-colored liquid, and plunged a needle into his arm.

Harley's blood sprayed into the vial on the needle's end. He felt queasy and looked away.

The nurse held the full vial up for Harley to see. "Is this your ID number?" she asked.

Harley compared it to his ID card. "Yes."

The nurse dropped the vial into a tiny wire crate holding four others. "Go sit in the waiting room. They'll get you when the tests are done." She looked back down to her magazine.

A soundless television, suspended from the waiting room's ceiling, glared the image of a televangelist walking through his assembly. He stopped, touched someone, and reached skyward. The camera pulled in tight on his face: tiny beads of sweat and freckles dotted the bridge of his nose.

Harley looked from the television to the people filling the molded fiberglass seats bolted to the floor. The room looked like so many other places where he was forced to sit and wait: in the early morning at the day labor office, at night at the Rescue Mission, outside the hotels for occasional work.

Harley glanced quickly around the room. He made no eye contact, searching out those who were safe and those who were not. An old black man and woman, dressed as if for church, sat stiffly in the far corner, eyes glued to the television. A white wine-head sat next to the door, his nose like an exploded strawberry. A thin white woman, wearing a green straw hat and a strange print dress, sat next to the room's only empty seat, nervously bouncing an infant on her lap. Harley had been avoiding women of late. He knew he smelled. He knew no woman wanted to be near him, and he was afraid one might actually tell him so.

Harley grabbed a shredded copy of the *Times Picayune* from the floor and walked over to the seat. The area around the mother and child stank of piss and baby shit. Harley breathed in short soft breaths, trying not to gag. He sat down and saw the baby's face for the first time: blue veins criss-crossed its forehead, its eyes bulged out from a skeletal face, its skin was drawn tight around its head.

The woman said, "Hey."

Harley nodded and unfolded the paper; compared to the baby his smell wasn't at all bad.

"I'm so glad it's a white man sitting next to me," she whispered. "Better anytime than some of those toads who think that a white woman caught a little short would do anything."

"What toads?" Harley asked.

"Niggers," she hissed.

Harley winced and glanced around the waiting room to see if anyone else had heard what she said.

"God, Jesus," she continued. "I hate them toads. Back in Mississippi ain't none of them as uppity as they is here. We wouldn't stand for it."

Harley flipped through the business pages looking for the barrel price of American Light Crude.

"That's what I'm doing here. I sell me some blood for cash money, and get a ticket back up to Machias, Mississippi," she said.

A nurse came into the room and called a number. The old black woman raised her hand. Her husband helped her to her feet and she followed the nurse out the door.

"Now that old auntie, we got them like that up in Machias. Nice, you know what I mean?"

A six-foot-six black man, dressed in work clothes, shouted from the entrance to the waiting room, "We got a bus leaving, in ten minutes, for a pipeline camp in Morgan City. Meals, board, and good wages for a good day's work. Who wants to work?"

Harley looked around the room. He raised his hand slowly. "Me," he said. "I'll work."

"Okay. That's one. Who else? Who else wants to work?" He looked around the room. "Okay, buddy," he said to Harley.

"Let me check one more thing; I'll pick you up on my way back through."

Harley said, "Great."

The man left the room.

A young black guy in the corner, said, "Hey."

Harley looked up. "Me?"

"Yeah, don't be going out to Morgan City with that man. You work all day and end up owing him money. Don't do it. I'm telling you."

"Come on," Harley said.

"For true," the guy said.

The big guy stuck his head in the door. "Let's go," he said.

"I changed my mind," Harley said.

"You did what?" The guy's eyebrows went up, his hands curled into fists.

The woman next to him spoke up. "I ain't letting my husband run off when we got ourselves a new baby."

The man looked from Harley to the woman. "She your old lady?"

Harley nodded.

A short white guy, dressed in cowboy clothes, stepped into the doorway. "Cleatus, you get anybody?" he asked.

"No," he said.

"Then let's get the fuck out of this hellhole."

Harley turned to the woman. "Thanks," he said.

"Hell, we got to stick together against the toads," she said. "I'm Sue Ann Riley. And this is Charles Robert." She propped the baby up and said, "Say hello to the nice man, Charles Robert."

"My name's Harley," Harley said.

"Is that your real name?"

Harley nodded. "Yeah."

"What do you think of the Big Easy?" she asked.

"It ain't so easy," Harley said. "I ain't had a real job in . . . I can't even remember now."

"Well, me, I'm going home. I get my blood money here and

I'm gone. Goodbye, New Orleans. Hello, Machias. My daddy's still got his farm. I swore I'd never go back. But now?"

"That's nice," Harley said. "You got a place. That's nice."

"You got no place?" she asked.

"I got a sister, but I ain't sure she'd have me."

"I'll tell you what," she said. "Why don't you come up home with me?"

Harley laughed. "That's funny."

"Don't laugh at me," she said. "I'd be helping you and you'd be helping me."

"How would I be helping you?"

"Help me explain this." She bounced Charles Robert in the air.

Harley smiled and shook his head. "I got to tell you, I'd love to get out of this town."

"Well, let's do it then. You wouldn't have to stick around forever. Just long enough to make it look right. You know?"

"Let me think about it," he said.

"Great," she said.

"I'm just thinking about it."

"I know," she said.

Harley and she sat there trading smiles and laughing. Harley did kind of like the way she smiled. The missing teeth weren't bad, really. He was missing two himself. He liked the thought of a farm. He'd never been on a farm, but he liked the horses that pulled people through the French Quarter. And he liked milk that came from cows that lived on farms. He knew people ate a lot on farms. He knew they had porches and barns and hay and chickens and pigs. He knew farms were quiet at night, and you could sleep.

Harley turned and smiled at Sue Ann Riley. "Do you really mean it?" he asked.

"Yeah." She nodded.

"Okay," he said. "I'll do it."

A nurse came into the room and called a number.

"That's me," Sue Ann Riley said. "Here, hold Charles Robert."

Before Harley could answer she dropped the baby into his arms. Charles Robert felt as delicate as a pillowcase full of wine glasses. The child began to squirm.

"Don't worry, he just needs to get used to you," Sue Ann said. "If he really fusses or anything, here." She reached into a dirty pink cloth satchel hanging from her shoulder and handed Harley a dusty pacifier.

Harley nodded, but as soon as his mother left the room the baby let out a howl that woke those dozing in the molded fiberglass seats. That was followed, as impossible as it seemed to Harley, by an even louder shriek. The child's wails vibrated walls, affected television reception, brought the center's security guard hustling into the room.

Harley cooed pleadingly, trying to force the pacifier between Charles Robert's quivering lips. The baby's frustration brought tears to Harley's eyes. "I know how you feel," he said. "But I don't know what I can do for you."

Charles Robert's cries weakened and he settled down to occasional moans and trembles. Harley tried to sit as still as possible. The baby's urine passed through the blanket and soaked his jeans; his right arm tingled. Harley began to feel that the entire world would smell forever of sour milk and dirty babies.

As the afternoon crept toward evening, the waiting room emptied. Two wineheads began laughing in the corner. Harley shushed them and jerked his head toward the baby.

They raised their hands, palms out, and nodded.

A nurse, about Harley's age, stood in the doorway and adjusted her dress. She called out a number. Harley fished his ID card from his pocket. He waved his hand and stood up. The baby cried out and was quiet.

"Here, could you hold him?" Harley asked. "His mother should be out of there any second."

The nurse backed off. "I'm sorry, sir, but we aren't responsible for your," she paused as if searching for the word, "ah . . . belongings."

"This ain't mine. I was just holding him for his mother. She's in there now, giving blood."

The nurse looked at the child and shook her head. "This baby's mother ain't in there."

"Sure she is," Harley said. "About this tall. Green straw hat. Missing these two teeth." Harley tapped his teeth with his free hand.

"Her? She got her money and been gone about an hour."

Harley opened his mouth to speak; nothing came out. He shook his head. "What the hell am I supposed to do with this?" Charles Robert began to fuss again.

The nurse looked at the child. "You could start by changing its diaper."

"Lady, this ain't my kid. His mother asked me to hold him for a while. I don't have any diapers or pins or any of that stuff. And it ain't my baby."

The nurse stood looking at him for a moment. She cocked her head to the side.

"This is not my kid," Harley said. "Ask any of these people." He gestured around the waiting room, looking for a face that had been there as long as he had. He saw no one.

"Sorry," the nurse said. "We can't take him. Insurance . . . liability."

"Well, I can't. I sleep at the mission." Harley swayed back and forth trying to soothe the child.

The nurse shook her head. "About all I can do is call the cops."

"Do it," he said.

The nurse took Harley back to the blood room. He lay down on a gurney with the baby cradled in his arm. The nurse who had screamed at Jasper on the front steps came to his side, carrying an empty blood bag and tendrils of clear plastic tubing. She leaned over Charles Robert and studied his face.

"This baby needs some serious vitamins," she said.

"He ain't mine," Harley said.

"So, do that mean that you starve him to death?" The nurse

tied off his bicep and swabbed his arm. "This is gonna pinch," she said. She pushed a needle into Harley.

"Ow, shit," he said.

"Watch your language, mister," the nurse barked. "Just because you treat your son like that, don't mean you can go through the world treating everyone that way." She attached plastic tubes to the end of the needle, bent over, and hooked an empty bag to a balanced lever near the floor.

Harley knew that nothing he said would change the nurse's mind; he stared straight up at the ceiling tiles. Charles Robert's weight grew comfortable in the crotch of his left arm. The baby cooed once and a snoring sound crept from its mouth. Harley leaned up and pulled the nipple from the child's mouth. Charles Robert's lips continued to move up and down.

A bell jingled beneath Harley's bed. The nurse hustled over and grabbed the full bag of blood. "Don't go nowhere," she said. When she looked up, it seemed that she suddenly remembered she didn't like Harley and scowled at him.

Harley closed his eyes and listened to the sounds around him: Charles Robert's tiny snores, nurses and sellers padding across the floor, mumbles and laughter, a hoot, a curse, the whine of the centrifuge.

After a while, the nurse came back and hung Harley's bag from the tree alongside his gurney. The blood began dripping back into his body. He could feel the first drops reaching his veins: cold, purple blood, flowing up his arm to his shoulder. He envisioned the blood coursing through his body, washing through empty veins, splashing against the walls of his heart.

Charles Robert screamed. Harley opened his eyes with a start. The clean white ceiling was brilliant overhead; the nurse hovered just above his gurney. The bag, drained of blood, hung limp on the tree. Charles Robert squirmed. The nurse jerked the needle out, swabbed the crook of his arm with a small washpad and stretched a Band-Aid over his wound. She handed him a slip of paper. "You give them this up front for your money."

Harley sat up and swung his legs over the side of the gurney. He felt woozy; when he stepped down, his knees buckled.

The young nurse was leaning back against the cool green walls, talking to a uniformed cop, when Harley stepped into the hallway. She had her arms crossed under her breasts and pushed them up, smiling, as she spoke. She jerked her thumb toward Harley as he approached.

"All right," the cop said, nodding. His name tag read Forche. He had been cleaning his nails with a Buck knife as he spoke to the nurse. He clicked the blade shut and slid it into the black sheath on his belt.

Harley said, "All right."

"I hear the stork left you a little gift," the cop said, and laughed. The nurse giggled.

Harley nodded and smiled. When a New Orleans cop laughed, he knew enough to smile.

Officer Forche asked the nurse if there was a more private spot. She took Harley and the cop back to the room where Harley had his blood tested. The room was empty, but the *People* magazine still lay on the desk.

Harley sat in the chair alongside the desk. The cop opened a report folder and began asking him questions. The nurse stood behind Harley. Officer Forche smiled at her and winked frequently through the entire interview.

"Well, that's it," Forche said. He flipped the folder closed and stood up. Harley stood, too. "I guess I can go, now," he said. He tried to hand Forche the baby.

Forche waved Harley away. "I ain't touching that thing," he said. "Some social worker from Charity will be here directly. You just sit down in that chair like a good boy."

Forche and the nurse talked quietly behind Harley's back. He heard a scuffle and glanced over his shoulder. Forche's fingers ran back and forth across the nurse's uniformed breasts. She had her eyes closed and was smiling. Forche scowled at him. Harley snapped his head forward and began rocking Charles Robert from side to side.

Charles Robert stared up into Harley's face, his big eyes liquid, cool. Harley blinked away tears. Fabric rustled behind him. Forche and the nurse's whispers turned breathless. It ain't my fault, Harley thought. It ain't my fault. There's nothing I can do to help you. I'm having a hard enough time on me. On me.

Forche was sitting behind the desk with his feet up flipping through the *People* magazine when the social worker came into the office. She took the baby from Harley and handed her card to Forche. "Send me a copy of your report," she said, and left the room with Charles Robert.

"Can I go now?" Harley asked.

"All right," Forche said.

On his way out, Harley pushed his slip through the hole in the bottom of the window. The small-eyed nurse slid eighteen dollars out to him and leered. "Can I ride you somewhere?" the nurse asked.

Harley shook his head and pushed through the double doors back out onto Rampart. The wineheads on the steps glanced up at him, then turned back to the traffic. Across the street, the dealer came out from between the two buildings, wearing a green straw hat and singing in a falsetto. "Got your tickets out of here. Got what makes you feel right."

Harley stopped at Rampart's edge and thought forty dollars plus eighteen for selling blood, plus, if I can get it, two days of day labor, equal one hundred and twenty-two dollars. He ran his thumb over the crisp edge of the bills he had in his pocket and wondered how long it would take Charles Robert's smell to disappear from his nostrils.

DIANE LEFER

Strange Physical Sensations in the Heartland

Jaclyn went spinning off the road one night in a borrowed (from the minister's wife) car. It was a country road; the Buick flew across the snowy open fields like an old-fashioned sleigh and then into an apple orchard. Jaclyn didn't remember anything, of course, but the tire tracks remained on the fresh snow to show where she'd been. It must have been like a miraculous dance at first, a childhood game, in and out the windows; she must have dodged the trees and circled and spun and probably thought she'd got off scot-free. What she hit was the rusted hulk of an old Chevy truck, abandoned back of the orchard, saved for parts.

Barbara went to see her in the hospital. On the way over, she felt the same faint nausea she remembered from when she'd just started on birth control pills and her boyfriend took her to dinner to meet his parents; she'd wanted to make a good impression, but her stomach was so queasy she couldn't eat. It was the same feeling all over again. Faced with Jaclyn rigged up in the hospital bed and the visiting church lady with her disapproving eyes, Barbara knew the encounter was important and feared that she would blow it, her throat so tight, her voice almost too constricted to speak. She said, "Loving women won't kill you but the drinking will."

This happened almost twenty years ago, when alcoholics were colorful and homelessness was still an aberration, when Abbott Center had a small shelter for winos and other human flotsam—male. After the occasional insurance arson in the cheap houses

259

by the river, a few welfare mothers and their kids would be accommodated at taxpayer expense out on the highway in the motel. In those more innocent days, individuals suffered—lost souls—but society itself was not considered lost.

It was still a criminal offense then to "transport a pauper into town," but Abbott Center looked out for its own, and if Jaclyn—who was often homeless—didn't quite fit into the scheme of things, she was still a native daughter and in some ways fit in very well, as comic and familiar as the ever-startled woman behind the counter in the drugstore or the gentleman who appeared on the town sidewalks dressed in shorts even in sub-zero weather, pushing his lawn mower in an apparent attempt to mow concrete. Barbara did not fit in at all.

She'd fled her wildly erratic boyfriend in Chicago and headed for the heartland, expecting to see nothing but grasses on the plains, so she was charmed by Abbott Center, a rural county seat with shady tree-lined avenues and a row of old houses by the courthouse square. She found a job, an apartment, and stayed. She expected to make friends easily with happy, well-adjusted people, to feel safe. But as there was no apparent good reason for outsiders to move to Abbott Center, local wisdom had it that transplants were running away from something; there was no point in making such fugitives feel welcome. As Barbara was shunned, she began to believe she would never have found her way to the town if there hadn't been something terribly wrong with her life to begin with; that conviction made it hard to leave. She was depressed and lonely and only twenty-two.

She developed an eccentricity: staying up all night baking when she was too miserable to sleep.

In the days before she met Jaclyn, when she woke up in the morning and headed down the hill to work (where, as a legal secretary, Barbara had the dirt on most of the families in the county, but as an outsider was unlikely to gossip or even to care), she believed she was the only flesh-and-blood being in town. In her better moods, everyone else was a wind-up toy and, therefore, at least given the dignity of three dimensions. More often, she saw them as Potemkin people, and the town as a counterfeit stamped from plastic—little facades of houses, a collocation of white faces, trees placed where a child's whim might desire—all flat, eminently movable, without roots. When she drove, she imagined herself in one of those drivers' training simulators; the other cars, the road itself were nothing but illusions of light, and she sometimes wondered—would there be an impact if she drove head-on into one of those shallow jolly little trucks.

The town had advantages: her furnished room was cheap; there was no crime. Barbara rarely remembered to lock her door.

One Saturday night, she came home alone from the movies, batted at the air to find the cord for the kitchen light. The fluorescent halo buzzed and glowed, and she stopped short of the open bedroom door. There was a man sleeping on top of her bed, one muddy boot on, the other fallen on the rag rug—the first person to visit her apartment since she'd arrived. He didn't move when she turned on the light and stood looking at him. The air seemed to vibrate. It was like the forcefield that used to surround her with the crazy boyfriend: a swift, almost sickening sense of connection. (Sometimes she'd thought it was only because they drank so much coffee when they were together; she confused emotional excitement with caffeine.) In this case it wasn't coffee, but alcohol—she could smell it and even imagined she could see the molecules breaking down and rising from the stranger's pores. He was short and stocky and slept in a red-and-black checked lumberjacket, his arms over his chest and hands tucked in the armpits. A few blemishes and bristles broke through the surface of a weathered chin.

"Hello?" she said, "Who are you?" Her voice came out a whisper, because as she spoke, she realized the stranger was a woman. It was Jaclyn—this was how they first met—and Barbara turned instantly protective. Even when she'd thought the person on her bed was a man, it had never occurred to her that he might hurt her. Now she worried over what might have happened to this woman—why she'd come seeking refuge—and was unwilling to disturb the poor thing's sleep. An outcast herself, she looked on the unexpected guest as a comrade, feeling a rush of pity and self-pity in a pleasant mix. "You're in a safe place," she whispered, then tiptoed away, lay a big bath towel down on the kitchen linoleum and stretched out.

When she woke in the morning, Jaclyn's hands were on her shoulders. As Barbara started to struggle, they both screamed.

"Thank God, thank God," Jaclyn muttered, and let go. She squatted, hands clasped on knees, and rocked back and forth a moment with eyes closed. Then she started to laugh, looking to Barbara like a dwarfed Santa Claus, endearing and trustworthy somehow even though a mess, her breath foul with tranquilizers, her body with the raw onion pungency of metabolizing alcohol. She stumbled to her feet and opened the refrigerator, reached inside before turning a perplexed face. "The beer?"

"I'm sorry. I don't have any," Barbara said.

"You? Isn't this . . . ? Oh, shit. Excuse me." Jaclyn leaned back against the refrigerator, then slid till she landed, sitting, on the floor. "This is *your* apartment. Shit. Excuse me." She touched the edge of the towel and shook her head, acknowledging that Barbara had spent an uncomfortable night. "I lived here," she said. "Till the landlady—*your* landlady now—threw me out. . . . I guess I've been on a toot. . . . God. . . . They just let me out of the State Hospital." Then she told about a woman named Suzanne who got her so mad and jealous, she'd wanted to kill her, but ended up hurting herself instead. A mixture of booze and pills. "That's why I was so scared when I saw you lying there . . . I'm capable of hurting someone," she said. "Usually the wrong person."

Barbara couldn't help herself; she started to laugh. But the stranger didn't mind. She seemed to think it was pretty funny, too.

"Well, back to the Men's Shelter."

Men's? Barbara stared, uncertain again, and watched the lumberjacketed shoulders rise, not so much in a shrug as a half-hearted attempt to straighten up.

"Stay," said Barbara, both surprised at herself for making her loneliness so apparent, and pleased with herself for not being a snob. "For a cup of coffee," she added.

"Naw. Don't bother. Coffee's the one thing they *do* give you there."

"Then take a loaf of bread. Homemade." Her visitor accepted one foil-wrapped loaf, then a second at her urging, "I've got plenty." She held back a moment, but for her hospitality felt entitled to have her curiosity satisfied. ". . . the Men's Shelter . . . ?"

"It's the only game in town. Till maybe someday they build a place for women, which they're not going to do just for me. But really I don't mind. The guys all know me." Then the woman introduced herself at last, saying, "Everyone in Abbott Center knows Jaclyn Boehm."

"What were they thinking of, releasing you on a Saturday afternoon with no place to go?"

Jaclyn sprawled in the chair by Alice McDonough's desk, picked at her cuticles, grinned, and shrugged.

"Where did you spend the weekend?"

"The heat vent behind the bakery," she lied.

"Have you had anything to eat?" Alice McDonough was like that: asking concerned questions, clucking her tongue and acting like it was a damn shame, a human being deserved better, even though she wouldn't or couldn't do anything about it. Jaclyn, who trusted no one but thought the best of everyone, liked her a lot.

"Someone gave me some bread," she said.

Alice McDonough had been her State caseworker on and off for years, and they had the kind of relationship that clients and social workers were likely to have, back in the good old days. Jaclyn usually didn't qualify for a State check, but every now and then, she turned eligible: after the nervous breakdown and once the bout with pneumonia that ended up complicated with empyema—from the drinking, they said; they tried to make it a case of wilful disability, but in the end they started paying her just about the time she got better.

"There's nothing wrong with you this time, Jaclyn Boehm," said Alice. "Nothing that'll keep you from holding a job, that is. You know if you need temporary emergency help you don't come here. You've got to go to Marcus."

"After what he did the last time?" Marcus was the town Overseer of the Poor; he was the one who could write out a slip to get you into the shelter. Jaclyn had told Alice he'd once asked her to have sex with him on top of his desk in exchange for a grocery order. It wasn't really lying because it was obvious Alice hadn't believed her; the story had made her laugh. Jaclyn thought Alice deserved a laugh or two—it was a depressing job, Welfare. "You get a kick out of me, don't you?" she asked.

"I'll phone him," said Alice, "and tell him what you need and no funny business."

"Could you help me," asked Jaclyn, "with something else?" They both sighed, Alice because she knew what was coming, Jaclyn with pain. "When can I see Myra?"

"You know that . . ."

But Jaclyn wasn't listening. She went through her speech. It wasn't that she'd memorized it, but when she thought about Myra, her thoughts went into the same tracks and so it was no wonder her words came out the same. "There's a woman with a stroke, and she can't even take care of her baby. The State sends in people to help her. No one took her baby away. And look who I lived with. My father. Forget my father. And my mother. Blind as a bat. She gave me away once or twice when things were very hard, but she always took me back when she wanted. *Do you want a little girl? She ain't pretty to look at, but she can work.* Blind as a bat. I used to have to lead her around, and each time she left me at some farmhouse I'd hope she'd lose her way without me and freeze, and then I'd cry when I thought she was dead. I'm Myra's mother. She's crying for *me.*"

"I'm Income Maintenance," said Alice, "not Child Welfare."

"While I'm here, can I see the Child Welfare?" She liked Alice so much; when she looked into her eyes like she did now, Alice didn't look away.

"I'd get settled first," said Alice. "You're filthy from sleeping out. You need a bath. Among other things. You're not looking your best today, Jaclyn."

"I don't make a good first impression. But you've known me a long time. You know I'm all right. Better than the woman with the stroke. She can't even take care . . ." Jaclyn closed her eyes. She was about to go off again. Even she recognized the repetition and the telltale monotone. "Do you think I should go to night school?" People usually spent a few more minutes talking to her when she mentioned night school.

"There's a new term in January," said Alice.

"So you think I should start in January?"

"Jaclyn, there's clients waiting. I'm calling Marcus right now."

"Marcus Keller. He's something other than human." She had heard the mayor say that once about Marcus; it was meant in praise but hadn't come out quite right, and she enjoyed repeating it. "But I was talking about Myra. You think I'll just forget her. You think I have the attention span of a child. She's my daughter . . ." But Alice had already started to dial. "Did I tell you," she asked, a last attempt, "did I tell you how I almost killed Suzanne?"

"You what?" Alice looked at her again, shaking her head, but Jaclyn was sure there was a little smile turning at her mouth. She liked it so much when Alice seemed curious about her and amused.

"You know *me*," she said. "I can't help it. Sometimes I'm just *wild*!"

"Are you drinking again, Jack?" asked Alice.

"I'm no alcoholic," said Jaclyn. "I can stop any time I run out."

At Town Hall, Jaclyn wished the mayor happy birthday; there was no one in this town she did not know. Marcus met her in the corridor with her shelter slip already signed. Since she'd started telling people about sex on his desk, he was afraid to let her into his office. Their transactions were quick and painless now; she no longer had to sit politely and listen to his lectures about proper living, his good advice.

She headed for the shelter, actually the gymnasium of the old high school, all that was left standing after a tornado tore off the classroom wings. No, she'd never had sex with Marcus, but in the damn shelter it was another story. It had happened to her there, all right. At least she thought so. A counselor once asked her about her blackouts—didn't it frighten her to come to and not remember where she'd been or what she'd done? But Jaclyn considered her blackouts a stroke of good fortune, the only evidence she had of a benevolent God. When—as happened all too often—she was in a situation she didn't like and couldn't avoid, at least she knew if she got drunk, she wouldn't remember a thing. As if it had never ever happened.

At the shelter, you checked your belongings, if any, in the locker room where dozens of cots got stacked until night. During the day, you were not encouraged to hang around, but a few guys always managed to stay by playing sick or making themselves useful—sweeping, running errands, cleaning the coffeepot. This time, Jaclyn found Andy Bornholt crying on the bleachers and telling his shoes how diabetes had made him impotent, Wally Judd pushing a mop around, and some privileged character still stretched out on a cot at the far end under the basketball hoop.

Jaclyn could play at being one of the boys, but men scared her. For some reason, she never tried to defend herself against them, even though she knew how to fight. That was her reputation, but she only fought when she lost control, and the only thing that made her lose control was passion. Sometimes she thought that's why she ended up in the shelter whenever she broke up with someone. After an outburst, being with men was the only way to cool off. Among them, she felt numb.

And Wally could be a problem. His eyes lit up when she walked in. "You're back. Just in time! Oh, it's good to see you!" He was at her side, half a step behind her, a hand at her elbow, the way she used to guide her mother. Wally urged her forward to the cot to see James E. Boone who'd died during the night— that was why no one had made him get up and leave. None of his relatives would claim the body. "Mr. Owens and I have been phoning all day," said Wally. "As soon as they hear *James E. Boone,* they just hang up."

Jaclyn pulled the sheet back over the man's head, as a courtesy. It didn't bother her to look. But . . . Jaclyn usually divided the world into two kinds of drinkers: gregarious drunks like herself, and antisocial drunks like James E. Boone. What bothered her was the suspicion that James E. Boone was what gregarious drunks turned into when they grew up.

"Terrible, isn't it?" asked Wally. And then, what she feared: "Jack, you know you're the only one I can talk to."

Wally had a terrible secret in his past, or so he said, and apparently he'd once confided in her. Now, whenever their paths crossed, he looked at her meaningfully and said, "You're the only one in the world who knows." She supposed he really had told her something, but whatever it was, she'd been drunk. Another case in which her blackouts had stood her in good stead. Something had Wally feeling very guilty, and she really didn't want to know what it was. She tried to stay away from him when she was sober, in case he'd try to tell again.

"I know where we can get a bottle," he said.

She rewarded him: "I like you anyway, Wally," she said. "In spite of what you done."

These days, you can hardly imagine a homeless woman paying social calls, but back then, outcasts weren't so entirely cast out. Jaclyn didn't hesitate to show up again at Barbara's door. Admittedly, she was a little nervous: she had a favor to ask and wasn't sure of the best way to be ingratiating. She liked to think she could handle anyone, but Barbara—a stranger from Chicago— might be unpredictable.

"There's a six-pack in the refrigerator," said Barbara.

That was interesting: she was expected, and Barbara had apparently even looked forward to seeing her again.

Jaclyn peeked inside the refrigerator, but instead of taking a bottle, she paced the perimeter of the kitchen. She was thirty years old and felt like a teenager; she remembered the first time they sent her in to see a counselor, how she was supposed to sit in front of the woman's desk and talk about herself, but she'd stalked around the office. By now, she'd learned—from going to Welfare—how to act at an interview, but she felt like a kid again, afraid to sit still.

"Could I use your shower?" she asked at last. "There's just the big open one in the locker room. I won't go in there with the men. And I want to look for a job tomorrow." People always liked to hear she was looking for a job.

Barbara gave her towels, and Jaclyn used one on her shampooed hair and had the other wrapped around her—but not quite—when she emerged from the bathroom. She displayed herself, watching for Barbara's reaction (after all, why else would she be so nice?), but Barbara didn't even look. She was like Alice McDonough that way; she seemed interested, but you just couldn't tell. Barbara sat in the kitchen rocking chair sucking on one of the longneck beers, staring (or pretending to stare) into space.

Jaclyn did get a job—working in the State Hospital laundry— and a small furnished room down by the river. She and Barbara became friends. They got together on weekend afternoons, drank and talked. Barbara talked about Chicago and how much she hated Abbott Center. Jaclyn told of her scandalous escapades, lowered her voice to hint at affairs with teachers, nurses, the mayor's wife. But what they most liked to talk about were strange physical sensations.

Sometimes, Jaclyn said, when she was lying in bed, just before she fell asleep, she felt as if a screwdriver or steel plate were prying off her kneecap, just enough, like lifting a scab. That part never hurt but then, suddenly, it was like a blade slipped in and electric pain would radiate down through her legs. Barbara agreed she had felt the same thing, and had never heard anyone describe it. How about, asked Barbara, have you ever felt raindrops hitting the back of your hand, but you're indoors? They had many things in common: both of them, when hearing about an accident or surgical operation or anything involving blood, felt a cold and fiery tingling running between their knuckles and fingertips.

Barbara believed that these conversations kept her sane. Jaclyn was teaching her the trick of surviving smalltown life. She was used to urban noise and constant stimulation. No wonder she found Abbott Center deadening. Someone had to teach her to pay attention to her own perceptions; then, her mind came alive, alert. What she never mentioned, however, was the sensation that interested her most: the sizzle right down to her bones. She'd felt it when she first started getting close to that crazy boyfriend and she felt it sometimes talking to Jaclyn, synapses flashing in a frenzy of empathy.

They had these conversations in the kitchen. Jaclyn usually claimed the rocker and often put her feet up on the table. Barbara would sit cross-legged on a straightbacked kitchen chair. It was wintertime and the sun went down by four; the air would grow dense with gray, and near the windows, freezing tongues of air insinuated themselves through the cracks, but the room itself was warm—overheated, really. The landlady's 100-year-old great-uncle lived on the ground floor; for his sake, she never skimped on oil. Scarves, sweaters, heavy socks would end up in a pile, and Barbara and Jaclyn would sit at the table, barefoot, in T-shirts. They'd play cards. Sometimes Barbara imagined they were far from Abbott Center, wasting their lives in some end-of-the-road boardinghouse in Africa or on the Amazon. She liked the idea: somehow, a hot climate made being a loser more interesting.

When the room grew so dark that they couldn't tell hearts from clubs, once their silhouettes at the table had turned black, Barbara would be on her feet, the hum of the overhead light, and the refrigerator door opening, and Jaclyn would laugh and ask, "What's the Salvation Army serving tonight?" or "What's new from Julia Child?"

Once, there was no bread with dinner. Barbara had run out of flour during a late-night baking bout, after all the stores were closed. She'd gone down to the pizza joint and tried to convince the girl behind the counter to sell her some flour, but the girl asked the man there—her husband or her father—and he'd said no.

"I bet I could get it from her," Jaclyn said.

Here's another one: Barbara can be made to feel dizzy and drained, like after giving blood. She goes into a state of suspended animation. It happened when her boyfriend showed up one night babbling his plans to hold up his uncle's jewelry store. She had known she should reason with him, but she felt cut open with a knife; blood, spirit, will all evaporated in the indifferent air. It turned out to be OK: he soon forgot his brainstorm, and they avoided a fight. She was just as silent and helpless when Jaclyn came banging on her door in the middle of the night, went straight to the refrigerator as if Barbara weren't even there, acknowledging her only when she turned to accuse her: "No beer." Jaclyn jabbed at the refrigerator door with her fist. "We've got to toast her. We've got to toast my daughter. It's her birthday."

Barbara said nothing; Jaclyn left.

And weeks later, when Barbara finally asked about this daughter, Jaclyn was threatening, stepping close to Barbara's face. "What do you know about her? What are you? Another goddamn busybody like the State?" But she calmed down quick enough, claimed the rocker, picked at her cuticles and plunged into her monologue: the woman with the stroke who got to keep her child, her own blind mother taking her from door-to-door.

When their silhouettes were black and Barbara stood and reached to turn on the light, Jaclyn said, "I'm not hungry. I don't want to eat," and Barbara sat down again and Jaclyn went on talking in the dark, about Myra, seven years old and in foster care. She'd seen her three times in six years. She even stopped drinking for a while, started going to A.A., which was interesting, socializing with doctors and lawyers and all. But it was no use. The State said it wasn't enough. She still wasn't "straightened

out." And she would do it. She would do it, she would do anything, if she could. But there was just no way to straighten
some things out.

"You've got to go to Chicago," Barbara said. She talked
about the city, where people and the courts and the social workers were more open-minded. It wouldn't be easy, but at least
there would be a chance. The city was the place to be. She said
nothing, however, about how she'd seen Chicago police beat
protestors. Or about her recurrent dream: every day she thought
about going home, but at night, she would find herself walking
down dark city streets alone, footsteps gaining. She would hurry
to catch up with the people talking and laughing just up ahead,
a crowd in stylish winter coats and hats. Her heart would pound
and finally, believing herself safe, she would join the happy
people. Then they would turn around and show their faces, monstrous in grease paint. They'd laugh and stick out their tongues
and thin sharp knives until her heart would stop and their blades
would slide in beneath her kneecaps and she'd wake with a
painful jolt. Barbara's eyes filled with tears, for Jaclyn and for
herself. She knew she was becoming like the people of Abbott
Center; the very thought of places that were not narrow and
constrained filled her with fear.

She said, "You don't have to live this sort of life."

"Are you going back to Chicago?"

"Yes." Barbara lied. "Soon."

Jaclyn rocked a moment in the dark. "Are you asking me to
go with you?"

"Well, uh, I mean I could help you get settled if you . . ."

"You know what *I* mean," Jaclyn said. "And the answer to
my question is *no*, isn't it?"

"You're the only friend I've got in this whole damn town . . ."
But Barbara had to admit, "It's *no.*"

Barbara thought she knew why weeks went by after that conversation and Jaclyn didn't return, but she was wrong. Jaclyn
had fallen in love, and for weeks she had time for no one but

Sheraldeen. Sheraldeen left the pizza joint and her husband and went to work at the Chinese restaurant out on the highway, where a plastic basket of white bread came with each meal and the menu included navy bean soup. They found a nice apartment in a decent neighborhood. They spent long nights in bed, or sometimes sitting up with the newspaper—Sheraldeen making Jaclyn read, so it would be easier for her if she really did go back to high school. They talked about the home they would make for Myra.

Finally, they stood in Barbara's doorway, and Jaclyn announced, "There's someone I want you to meet."

The lovers giggled and blushed, embarrassed and proud. They handed over a six-pack of ginger ale. They nudged each other with their elbows, happy and shy over so much happiness, shuffling and looking at the floor and darting quick glances at Barbara, waiting for her reaction. They shoved each other lightly, palms against shoulders. Barbara laughed along with them and something hardened and scratchy came dislodged, though there was still a twinge of pain, a raw scrape somewhere inside where the block had been.

"We're so respectable," giggled Sheraldeen. "We're even going to church."

Jaclyn nodded her head and spoke in that familiar, lowered tone of voice. "The minister's wife," she said.

"Oh, come on," said Barbara. "Her, too?"

"Is she ever! At least, she sure used to be!"

People like Jaclyn. You couldn't help it. She was like a puppy in need of housebreaking, such a shameless mess, so eager to please. At church, not just the minister's wife but also Mrs. Davis of the Youth Committee took an interest in her. (Jaclyn was thirty, but the way the church saw it, an unmarried woman not yet elderly required the same sort of guidance as any teen.) Mrs. Davis was well-versed in hellfire and abominations, about Sodom and Gomorrah and unnatural practices, about who was fit to be a mother and who was not. About what sorts of influences a little girl named Myra most certainly did not need. It was only a matter of time, then, till Sheraldeen, thrown over, showed up alone and crying at Barbara's door. Until Jaclyn, on a binge, spun the minister's wife's Buick through the orchard where the trees were all bare of forbidden fruit.

I hate this place, thought Barbara. She visited Jaclyn in the hospital. She said what she had to say and didn't care who heard her. I hate this place. She passed the pizza joint and saw Sheraldeen, back behind the counter. Her husband glared. Barbara saw her black eye and bruised face before she turned away. I hate this place.

The phone calls started, at home and at work. (Once she screamed into the receiver, "I like men! I like *men*! I just think that . . . ," and she was embarrassed for saying it, then relieved that the caller had already hung up.) Cars swerved at her intentionally when she crossed the street. Someone put sugar in the gas tank of her car. Rocks came through her windows so often, the landlady asked her to go.

Barbara packed. Before she loaded the car, she phoned Jaclyn. "I've hated this place all along," she said. "Thank God for the bigots. If they hadn't forced me out, I might never have made up my mind to leave."

"You don't belong here," said Jaclyn.

"Neither do you. They'll destroy you."

"No," said Jaclyn. "I was born here. This is the one place where no one can tell me to go back where I come from."

"No one will say that in Chicago."

Jaclyn said, "How can I go to Chicago? . . . Myra's here."

Barbara did go home. A lawyer now, married twice—this time sensibly and, she hopes, for good—she hasn't baked bread in twenty years. But one night when she stops for gas, she thinks of Abbott Center. Maybe it's the cold and desolation, the man who comes at her, coat torn and hair matted, or the cashier, safe in his glass booth, who looks away. All he wants, the ragged man, is to fill her gas tank for a tip. She knows that, still she's frightened. "I don't need help," she says. "But I do," he tells her. His hands are red and bare. What she fears is revival of a certain openness, her weakness; her fingers throb, susceptible to empathy. Barbara fights it these days, the old tug towards people in trouble. She doesn't want that enlivening pain. She seizes the hose; she pumps her own gas. It was never, she tells herself, love.

In Abbott Center, Jaclyn has discovered a strange new physical sensation: she often stumbles and falls not because she's drunk but because the nerves in her feet no longer send signals— *here's the sidewalk*—to her brain. There's a shelter for women now, but Jaclyn doesn't like it. The place is crowded with mothers and their children, screaming brats. Jaclyn begs at the Men's Shelter to be let back in. "I can't stand babies and children," she argues. "Never could."

Displaced in the World

To emigrate is always to dismantle the center of the world,
and so to move into a lost, disoriented one of fragments.

JOHN BERGER

S. Afzal Haider

Brooklyn to Karachi via Amsterdam

My cousin Azra who lives in a basement apartment in Manhattan gave me a contraption for catching mice. It was a cardboard box that, when folded in the prescribed method, assembled into a miniature igloo with a single entrance. The inside bottom was covered with a thick, sticky, gluelike substance that shone like glossy polyurethane on a dark oak floor, rather like the one in the dining room of my own house.

I used the trap one time. I found the mouse still alive, anchored to the shiny floor just out of reach of the bit of bread I'd used for bait. It made desperate chirping noises as it craned its neck forward trying to reach the bread. I didn't like this method of entrapment, alive and stuck, nourishment just out of reach.

I put the igloo in a white plastic bag from Lucky's Grocery Store, tied it with a green wire twist, and dropped it into the garbage can outside my house. I wondered how long it took a mouse to suffocate. They don't collect the garbage until Thursday on my block, and it was only Monday.

It is Thursday evening, just before dinner. The six o'clock news flickers without sound as I learn from my brother through international telecommunication that Baba's ill health has taken a turn for the worse. Asif is a doctor, a professor of pathology.

"His mind is fine," Asif tells me in his clinical voice, "but he is refusing to listen, he doesn't want to eat or drink and he won't take his medication. He's going to slip into a coma anytime now." Baba has been dying for over three years now. There is a tumor on his bladder that bleeds through a sore on his back.

Three years ago while visiting me in Brooklyn—his last visit—
he saw a doctor at my insistence. He refused to have the recom-
mended surgery. He did not like, he explained to me, the idea
of the blood transfusion, his own blood mingled with that of
strangers who might drink alcohol or eat pork.

I couldn't look him in the eyes. I growled, "People are having
heart transplants these days and you're worrying about a blood
transfusion."

He smiled and asked me to sit beside him on the bed. He
kissed my forehead and rubbed his silver beard against my cheek
and said, "I would consider a brain transplant if necessary, but
no thanks, I want to die with my own blood pumping through
my own heart."

Later in Karachi he refused the surgical treatment again,
telling Asif that he couldn't bear the idea of being chemically put
to sleep. "What if the surgeon is having a bad day and performs
a lobotomy by mistake while I'm out?" He added, "A man dies
only once. I want to die wide awake, with my eyes open."

"If you want to see him," says Asif, "you ought to come
immediately."

I don't know what to say. I ask to speak to Baba.

"You should," says Asif. "He likes you better and he listens
to you." I want to protest but I know it's not the right time and
besides, we both know it's true. There is a long wait while the
phone is brought to Baba, a wait filled with clicks and chirps of
transcontinental communication. They are lonely sounds, unan-
swered in the vast impersonal distance that lies between the two
telephones. I wonder if Baba really is going to die this time.

"How are you?" I ask when Baba comes on the line.

"Pretty bad," he says. What I admire most in my old man is
his courage, even when he is afraid.

"I hear you're not eating or drinking anything," I tell him.

"Yes," he answers, "I cannot."

"Why not?" I demand.

"My gums have shrunk and my dentures don't hold. I can't

chew anything, I can't get up and go to the bathroom. I've been sick long enough. It's time to go."

"Baba—" Against my own rational good sense, I am becoming angry.

"I can no longer paint," Baba continues in the same soft voice, full of the calm of reason. "I am tired of thinking about things I can do nothing about. All men die," he says. "All men die."

"I'm going to leave tonight. I'll be there on Saturday morning," I tell him with my voice breaking. "I want to see you."

"I want to see you too, dear boy, but I don't like being trapped in my own body, unable to move." I remember the mouse. I plead with him. "Please eat and take your medication. I still have a lot to talk to you about." I always tell him that. "I don't want to find you in a coma when I arrive."

"I can't promise, but please come." His soft voice is weak.

I hate overseas phone calls. They are always about bad news. When I return to the dinner table the six o'clock news is over and my food has gone cold.

"Did Baba die?" asks Sean as I carry my plate to the microwave.

I have been speaking in Urdu so the entire conversation has been lost to them—them being my Forest Park, Illinois-born Oriental wife, Virginia, our four-year-old son, Sean, and our infant daughter, Sarina.

Last year alone I traveled twice from Brooklyn to Karachi to visit my ailing father. At the end of each visit I wondered if I'd ever see him again, where I'd be when he died. My mother used to be big on weddings and funerals. "Parents should arrange weddings for their children," she said, "and children should bury their parents." I married a woman of my own choosing and missed my mother's funeral—the fate of the transplanted person. The least I can do is bury my father.

"Did Baba die?" Sean asks again.

"No," I answer, "but he may die any day."

"What if Baba dies on my birthday?"

"Then we can celebrate a birth and mourn a death on the same day." I sit down at the table again and look at Virginia. She is burping Sarina on her shoulder and she looks back at me, waiting.

"I am going to leave tonight," I say. "If I make the right connections, I can be there in twenty-four hours."

"What if your plane crashes?" Sean asks.

I begin to put food in my mouth. I have no idea what I'm eating. My wife's excellent cooking is as devoid of taste as Styrofoam. I reach over to tousle my son's hair. "What if it doesn't?" I laugh.

"What if it does?" Sean insists. "Planes do crash. I don't want you to die."

"When I die, I shall be extraordinarily ancient with a long white beard down to here. You will be grown up with a family of your own and you won't need your old man anymore." I look my son straight in the eye when I tell him this. I hope I'm right.

That night I leave for Karachi via Amsterdam. I am due to arrive in Karachi on Saturday morning. As I try to fall asleep on the plane, exhausted and wired, I think of Baba and how as a little boy I always hoped that he could come home at night before I fell asleep; that I would be up in the morning before he was gone for the day.

Before my family migrated to Pakistan, we lived in a small town in India, on the banks of the River Jumna. In the summertime, early on Sunday mornings, Baba woke me with kisses on my forehead and a rub of his unshaven beard on my cheeks. Before sunrise, my mother, who prayed faithfully five times a day, went to *Fajr*—morning prayers—but Baba and I set out on our fish hunt. His gun in its case across his shoulder, his hunting bag secured to the rear carrier of his bicycle, dark hair combed neatly back, dressed in a loose white shirt and trousers, he sat me on the crossbar and urgently pedaled the long uphill route.

We always arrived at the bank of the Jumna just as the sun rose. Baba parked the bike carefully on its stand and began the

ritual that never varied: the gun was removed from its case, the
single barrel, ball and muzzle loader cleaned with a ramrod.
Then black powder, a homemade lead bullet, and a piece of rag
were packed in. I would stand at the edge of the river, watching
him aim at bubbles bouncing like pearls to the surface of the
water. Baba would cock the gun, put a cap on the nipple, aim,
and fire. Then he would lay the gun aside, place his glasses carefully next to it, kick off his sandals, and jump into the water. For
a few moments it was as though the river swallowed him up.
I would search the surface with my eyes, knowing he would appear again but anxious nonetheless. Suddenly he would split the
water with a great splash and climb the bank with a fish in his
hands, the river streaming from his body, his brown face shining
in the sun. My father was a sure shot. He thought there was
nothing in life that couldn't be undone. With our fish filleted
and packed in the hunting bag, we would sail downhill toward
home, Baba smoothly pedaling the bike, a strong forearm on
either side of me, his cool wet white shirt flapping against my
head, to Mama's Sunday-morning breakfast.

Baba was an art master at Sarsuti Part Shalla, the local Hindu
high school. He made his living painting portraits of famous
people and common folk. A Gandhi for a Mohan Das, a Jinnah
for a Mohammed Ali, and someone's deceased mother when
commissioned. He wore eyeglasses that he needed to take off to
see what was directly in front of him. I would watch him for
hours as, in slow motion, he observed his subject through his
spectacles. When he was ready to paint, he took them off. "People
wear their lives on their faces," Baba used to say. "To see what a
person has lived, you have only to read his face." I saw a bit of
his face in each portrait he painted. Sometimes I look into a mirror and see my father looking back.

Baba gave me the most he could. Unlike my mother, he hardly
ever prayed, not even on high holidays, but he read the Koran
every day. Upon my departure for higher education in America,
he gave me his Holy Koran. "Read it for peace of the soul," he

admonished. It sits on a bookshelf now, unread. Baba was a generous man, but he wouldn't permit me to wear his shoes, not even his house slippers. He was a complicated man. My mother would tell him about mischief I had accomplished during the day and he would reply that it was too late, I'd already done it. Knowing the pattern of my daily difficulties, Mama would inform him what I was about to do. He replied, "It's premature, he's done nothing yet."

During the British Raj, Baba shaved daily with a 7 O'Clock brand blade. He wore gabardine suits, silk ties, and a gray felt hat. He smoked Passing Show cigarettes. On the package was a picture of a man with a brown face wearing a gray felt hat. Folks around us called him *Sahib*. His friends called him *Kala* (black) *Sahib*. *Kala Sahib* enjoyed good food and dressed well, and I, having read his *Kama Sutra*, could guess what he did for good sex. "The art of loving is in knowing your own state of arousal," he said. "The cuckoo should not call before it is the hour."

Flying against time, I arrive on Saturday morning at 11:05. When I step off the plane I collide with heat so intense it feels like violent physical assault. I have an instant of panic as I realize that my years in northern latitudes have finally robbed me of the ability to tolerate my native climate. A large delegation of relatives meets me at the gate. Even before we speak, I can see from the faces of Asif and my sister, Rashida, that I am too late.

I ride with Asif in his almond-green Morris Minor, listening to Urdu songs on the radio. We proceed directly to the graveyard and Asif finds a bit of shade to park in near the entrance. As another car full of relatives pulls up next to us, I look around, stiff from travel and lack of sleep, enervated by the heat, and feel the smallest tugging lift of spirit.

I love graveyards in this part of the world. They are like a carnival or a baseball park during a game, alive and full of people. Vendors by the gates sell flowers, rose water, incense, Coca Cola. Inside, people are resting, reading the Koran, burning

incense, chanting prayers aloud or praying silently. Asif buys a
large bottle of rose water, a package of incense, and a clear plastic bag full of red rose petals. My cousin Farook buys seeds to
feed the birds. The three of us, along with Rashida and her children, Adnan and Naheed, and Asif's son, Habib, named after
our father, make our way toward the family plot. Farook rubs
his eyes with his fists and says that Baba was more like a father
to him than his own father.

At our feet is the new grave: my father, the brown face in the
gray felt hat, *Kala Sahib*. Someone begins the prayers for the
dead. I sit down between the graves of my parents, one smoothed
and benign, the other fresh, raw, a ragged wound that has not
yet scabbed over. I'm wearing Levi's, a western shirt, and Adidas
and I'm soaked with sweat. I listen to Farook chant *Sura Al
Fatiha: Praise be to Allah, Lord of the creation . . . King of Judgment Day."* I pick at tiny clumps of dirt, crushing them with my
fingers. My mother once expressed her fear that some day
I would be unable to recite even a silent prayer for her. She was
right: both my heart and my mouth are dumb.

Rashida sits next to me, holding my hand, sobbing openly.
I want to cry but I can't, or perhaps my whole body weeps as
the salt of my perspiration pours out, drenching my clothes and
hair so that I cannot tell the difference between my sister's tears
and my own sweat.

"Tell me about Baba," I say.

Rashida turns her face away from me and stares out at where
her children are moving among the graves. She says, "He was
sitting up in bed when you spoke with him. He looked very gray.
I wrung out a towel in cool water and bathed his face. Then
I helped him to lie flat. He was shivering. That frightened me
more than anything else, his shivering. The heat was really bad,
worse than today. The floors were so hot I was afraid the children's feet would blister. And Baba lay there shivering."

My sister closes her eyes and presses the end of her veil over
her mouth. I look down at her hand lying in mine, the familiar
structure of bone and tendon under rich brown skin, a delicate,

fragile-looking hand, a lie of a hand, because it contains the strength to have done those things for Baba all alone when I was far away.

"I covered him up with a cotton quilt—the one printed with gray leaves and white flowers that you gave him the first time he visited you in America. He lay there quietly with his eyes open on the single bed, next to the bed where our mother slept. I'd been sleeping in it for the past week. I wondered what people think about when they are dying. I picked up his Koran and sat down next to him. I read aloud, you know, *Sura Al Rahman,* he always liked that."

It is The Merciful who has taught the Koran. He created man and taught him articulate speech . . . which of your Lord's blessings would you deny? I remembered it well.

"Then," Rashida goes on, "he asked for *Sura Ya Sin.* His voice was very strong. Do you remember, *Ya Sin, I swear by the wise Koran that you are sent upon a straight path? . . .*"

I nod.

"I started to cry, but I wouldn't let myself. I finished: *'Glory be to Him Who has control of all things. To Him you shall return.'* When I stopped reading, his eyes were closed. I knew then he was dying. He opened his eyes and looked up at me. 'All men should be blessed with a daughter,' he said."

I squeeze her hand. "A daughter like you," I tell her.

She says, "A tear rolled down my cheek and dropped onto his beard. I don't think he noticed. He was frowning as if he were trying to remember something, then his face relaxed and he smiled. At that moment, oh, I wished you could have seen him— he might have passed for his old self."

Yes, I think, the man in the gray felt hat. In my mind's eye I see my sister's tear sink into Baba's beard like an uncut diamond into the fine ash of a spent fire.

"He said then, 'Go now, please. I am ready to sleep.' I kissed him and left the room." There are a few moments of silence as Rashida labors for control. Finally she says, "At dawn on Friday as you were somewhere over the Atlantic, I heard the muezzin call out from the mosque, 'Prayer is better than sleep.' Baba did not waken for *Fajr.*"

I close my eyes and continue to hold Rashida's hand. Baba died on *Al-Jumma,* the day of congregation, under the portrait of our mother he painted when she was a young woman. He had been bathed, groomed, and wrapped in a white cotton shroud. After Friday congregation in the mosque, funeral prayers were offered. In one hundred and seventeen degrees, he was buried the same afternoon.

Rashida gets up to join her children. I sit in silence as Asif scatters a handful of rose petals on Baba's grave. He, Rashida and Farook, my nieces and nephews move on to the other graves in the family plot, chanting prayers for the dead. Habib sprinkles rose water; Adnan and Naheed cast rose petals. I turn to my mother's grave, thinking of Camus's Monsieur Meursault and his vigil beside his mother's coffin. I too do not feel any sadder today than any other day.

My mother has been here long enough to have a name plate. I gather a handful of the rose petals scattered by the children. They are already curled and fading. Dust blows in my face and I close my eyes. Even this hot breeze, a draft from some circle of hell where the rootless and homeless wander, feels good against my wetness. I see my mother's face, red in the sun, smiling at me. There is the mole on her cheek that I had forgotten. Silently I repeat the prayers for the dead. My brother lights a few sticks of incense. I stand up, easing the stiffness from my legs, rubbing the rose petals between my palms. I open my hands; the crushed petals and their wisp of fragrance fly away with the blowing heat.

As we drive through the noisy, crowded streets toward Baba's house, Asif tells me that one reason he never went abroad was to spare our mother the shock of losing both her sons. That was kind of him, I think; noble, even. "Are you happy?" I ask.

"Am I happy?" Asif repeats. "I am well accomplished. Daughters are happy when they become mothers. Sons always have to fight the battle of their fathers."

I ran from my father's battles when I was eighteen, never to return to live with him, not even for high holidays.

The next morning is cloudy and dark, blanketed with heat and humidity. Perhaps it will rain, I think with hope, but by noon the wind picks up and blows away the clouds. The temperature climbs to one hundred twelve in the shade. I spend all that day and the next in Baba's room, cleaning out his closet, looking at his papers. There are awards and certificates (Drawing Master of Merit, Artist of Distinction), his membership in the Royal Drawing Society of London, yellowed invitations to high teas with dukes, banquets with shahs. I feel a swelling of pride and admiration: this was a grand man, my old man—my dead old man. Among his letters are a ribbon-tied bundle from an internationally renowned artist who lives in Lancaster, England. He had sought out Baba during his travels to India. There are also letters from Faye Dincin of San Antonio, Texas, a woman Baba befriended during his travels to the States after my mother's death.

Rashida wanders in now and then to bring me a cup of tea or merely to stare, as if to convince herself that Baba has not come back, as though he'd gone on a business trip to Delhi and might reappear at any moment. "I knew he was going to die," she says, not to me especially. "I thought I was ready, but now that he is gone I still can't believe it." The end of her shawl is wet from dabbing at her eyes.

The spare bed is covered with paintbrushes, palette knives, tubes of paint, sketch pads, boxes of charcoal and pastels. The walls are lined with ranks of unfinished paintings. The fragrance of turpentine and linseed oil, a smell that in my childhood always meant Baba, hangs over everything.

I lie down exhausted on Baba's bed. I stare up at the blades of the ceiling fan. Despite the heat I do not dare to turn it on for fear of disordering the carefully sorted personal memorabilia and papers of no consequence to a dead man. Holy Jesus, I think.

Rashida comes in to sit next to me on the bed. She fans me gently with a paper fan. "Before I went to the States," I tell her, "I had an emptiness, a certain loneliness that I thought would pass with time." I shift my weight and slip into the mold that Baba left in the polyfoam mattress. "I thought it would be easy to leave it all behind."

Rashida stares at me. "You can never leave it all behind," she says. "A son is like a tree: the more branches it sprouts, the deeper grow the roots."

I smile at her. "And a daughter?"

She smiles back, a smile full of deliberate mystery and mischief, the smile of the child sister I left when I went to America. "A daughter is like a river. Miles and miles it flows to merge with the sea, yet its banks remain unchanged."

On Thursday, Mamon Majid, Uncle Majid, my mother's brother, dies unexpectedly of heart failure. It is as though the gods have repented making me miss my father's funeral and have kindly provided another in its place. After *Zuhr*—afternoon prayer—at the graveside, I see Mamon Majid's face for the last time. He lies in the coffin he brought back from his pilgrimage to Mecca, wound in a black sheet, only his face exposed. His head is bent slightly to the right, as though he died in the act of an ironic shrug. I bend over him and the pungent odor of camphor stings the back of my throat. He is pale, motionless, so very still, the way Baba must have looked. A big drop of perspiration slides off my nose onto Mamon Majid's eyelid and rolls down his cheek. He looks as though he is crying.

The morning after Mamon Majid's funeral, Friday, the one-week anniversary of Baba's death, the sky remains dark with gusting winds blowing at near-hurricane force. Trees and utility poles are bent and uprooted, TV antennas blow like tumbleweed, and billboards fly like pages of yesterday's newspaper. Half of Karachi loses electricity. Hail falls, giant frozen teardrops on the yellow grass. At last the rain comes in a great drowning torrent and the streets turn to rivers. Three members of a cricket team are electrocuted when their bus is stranded under a bridge and they walk on live power lines buried in the floodwater.

As the lightning and thunder crash and the winds howl around the house, I pack for the return trip. Into my carry-on bag I put Baba's portrait of my mother and an unfinished self-portrait. I also take two of his books, a biography of Mohammed and the poetry of Ghalib, his silver betel tin, the letters of the renowned British artist, and Baba's diary from 1930 to 1937. It is a thick black leather-bound notebook, with his name engraved in fading gold capital letters.

That evening, the weather calm once more, I leave on a non-stop flight to Amsterdam. At the gate, Rashida takes me in her arms and holds me for a long time. I feel her strength flowing into me, as though she is trying to transfuse me with it for the ordeal of my journey home. She tells me in a fierce whisper that she is afraid she will never see me again. I tease her, reassure her, make Asif promise to bring her when he visits me in New York next year. I think of what Baba used to say upon my frequent departures, "Why leave if you are planning to come back?"

A bright sun shines over the clouds all the way from Amsterdam to New York. Virginia meets me at the airport, leaving Sean and Sarina with my cousin Azra, the one who gave me the mousetrap. Virginia kisses me gently, holds me close. "I missed you," she whispers. "I'm glad you're home." On the drive from Queens to Brooklyn, I watch a sunset dramatic enough for Hollywood: red sky, banks of purple clouds, radical oranges and violets dimming and drowning in the blackness that creeps from the east. On the car radio, Springsteen sings "My Father's House."

During the night, lying next to Virginia in the darkness that comes with sleep, everything becomes more real than waking life. It is sunrise and I am at the house on the banks of the River Jumna. Every door in the house is open, Asif's tricycle stands in the courtyard, the teakettle on the stove has just stopped boiling.

I walk from room to room. The beds are made up, covered with red, yellow, and green quilts; Rashida's dolls sit on her bedroom shelf. I can sense them all there, the members of my family. As though they have just left each room as I enter it, I smell my mother's fragrance, the smoke of Baba's Passing Show cigarettes. I call out, but no one answers. I rush back into the courtyard and cross over to Baba's studio. The door stands wide and I find myself on the threshold of my own Brooklyn dining room. On the far side, across the gleaming expanse of dark oak floor, stands Baba, his back to me, working on a canvas. I feel a rush of indescribable joy. "Baba!" I shout and start across the room to embrace him. He turns to me, and there is on his face a smile of such ineffable love and sadness that I freeze midstep. I call out again, but my feet are stuck, immobile on that fatal shiny expanse that stands between me and my father. It is only then that I see what he is painting: a self-portrait in a hall of mirrors, and the faces looking back at me from the canvas are Baba's, my own, and my son's.

Leaving the stranger who is my wife alone in bed, I sit in the living room of the unfamiliar house where my American children are growing up in a city as alien to me as the deserts of the moon. I drink coffee and chain-smoke, something I haven't done in years. I watch dawn come up over Brooklyn. One day soon, I tell myself, I shall write to the renowned artist in Lancaster, England, to Faye Dincin in San Antonio, Texas, and tell them that Baba is dead.

K. C. Frederick

Patria

I buried N yesterday. Recently I saw my father's face. I'm the last
of our group.

It seems necessary that someone speak for us, but to whom?
I can't pretend that what I write is our farewell note to those in
the Host Country who've been able to ignore us completely all
these years.

Better to imagine that I'm addressing History. A doddering
old crone in a nursing home, N once called History, clutching
the arms of her wheelchair with claw-like hands, a dazed smile
on her face, mouth drooling as she recalls—no doubt inaccu-
rately—something from long ago, so rapt in her musings that
she can ignore the moans and screams of those around her.

History. Does she remember any of our demonstrations and
protests, our disruptive actions, the letters, the statements
and the manifestoes? Can she spell the name painted on walls
and bridges, recall the sacred dates?

"The folk art of our lost country," N called those slogans,
lifting our spirits as always. And when, so many years ago, we
exploded the bomb on the pier so that the visiting representative
of the Occupying Power had to disembark elsewhere, X laughed
and said it was nothing more than a cough in a hurricane.
"But," he insisted, "we dare not stop coughing."

We were all younger then.

N, X. Although there's no longer a need to hide anything,
long habit makes me more comfortable not using real names. To
me these initials are our true identities.

Still, I insist on stating that we were real enough, we had corporeal forms, were figments of no one's imagination. I, for example, am a man of medium size, no longer young, sitting here in a shabbily furnished room in a middle-sized industrial city of the Host Country. Outside it's raining heavily, a spring rain whose very smell, I can't forget, is filled with hope.

On the wall beside my table is a map of another region of the world, warmer, drier than this place. Those who drew it chose, unsurprisingly, to ratify the greed of the Occupying Power that swallowed our country generations ago. My map is corrected though: the bold red lines of my crayon trace the hidden shape, corrective surgery performed on the Occupying Power, whose thick, reptilian language has been eliminated from the places beside the dots marking our towns and cities, the alien words carefully blacked out and the historic names restored. I pause as I write and listen to the rain, looking at the outlines.

As a child I remember a map of my father's: it was large, printed on good heavy paper, strong as cloth. Our nation was colored a pale rose, with splotches of deep blue in my father's province of high northern lakes. In the northeast corner of our landlocked country was the wrinkled shape of the river that for so long separated us from the Occupying Power, though there are few today who'd recognize our name for it. The short, sturdy words of our own language indicated that the map had been printed in what had been our national capital and I can still recall the wonderful musty tang of the old paper, like the smell of dried mushrooms. Even now I can feel the strong fibrous material between my fingers.

Our land had already been stolen from us before my father left his native village but here in the Host Country so far away clubs and groups were formed, there were gatherings in public rooms where the walls were covered with flags and the portraits of mustached rulers of earlier times. I remember my father and some of his friends playing a game from the homeland, slamming the pictured cards to the table with shouted words in the old language. I remember small glasses of amber liquid that were refilled from a bottle with a picture of a fierce warrior on the label. Late in the evening songs were sung, eyes were wet with tears.

Hearing this rain and looking at my spotted hands I realize just how long ago that was. I see my own map, improvised, inelegant, and I can become frightened. I can understand N, I can understand how one's faith can be tried, how terrible it can be to wake up on Wednesday, then Thursday, then Friday, knowing each time that all you hope and dream for has receded so much further from you while you've slept. Oh, I know. I listen to this cold, relentless spring rain and I keep telling myself that soon things will be blossoming.

But my father. To be candid, my father was a traitor. Not the kind who stands shivering with terror in the stone-paved square of the village, a beefy soldier of the Occupying Power jamming a rifle into his ribs, so that he fears for his life, for the safety of his wife and children, his hands trembling, his heart pounding as he imagines all too vividly what they'd be willing to do to a simple man like himself; and he at last blurts out the name and hiding place of a comrade, regretting it the moment he's done it, feeling only shame and horror like the acidic smell of the urine that runs warmly down his legs. Not that kind of betrayal, not that surrender before an overwhelming passion like fear; but rather the insidious gradual corruption of the ordinary, the daily, that changed him, hair by hair, into a citizen of this Host Country of ours, with a nickname in their language, an interest in their sports, a taste for their food, their cigarettes.

I remember asking him about the old map. He told me to forget all that. I was born in this country, he said, I had more of a chance for a future than he had. All this silliness, as he called it, was appropriate for the national holidays we still celebrated, drinking the amber liquor and singing the songs; but all that was like a game, which shouldn't be taken seriously.

He was a small man with the quickness and strength of a fox. He had red-rimmed eyes with heavy pouches, a drooping dirty-grey mustache and a nose that seemed always to be running. He touched me softly on the shoulder that time, something he rarely did. "I'm serious," he said, speaking my name. A traitor.

I was young then, with a young man's need to believe in something. All around me I saw strangers. I walked for a long time before I realized I'd come to another neighborhood, only slightly better than our own. Dogs were barking lazily, an airplane droned in the distance. I saw a man washing his brand new car, a dark blue sedan. I stopped to wonder, seeing how ardently he was working to make the metal shine. He paused for a moment to look at the wet car, smiling. Water ran down the curb, the sun shone, my stomach quivered. This was the real world. There must be more, I thought desperately. It was immediately after that that I joined our group, I met N.

Cackle, old crone, laugh your toothless laugh, your head and hands moving to a din that no one, hearing it, would mistake for music. Yes, so many years ago I joined our group.

I remember the plan we once debated for taking over a local television station in the early morning when few people would be around to protect it. We were going to place a card bearing the silhouette of our country before the camera. Who, I wondered even then, would have seen it at that hour? Lovers concerned only with their own passion, insomniacs kept awake by worry over their health. Confronting that strange shape on the screen, the puzzling name, they'd think of obscure diseases and shudder. I confessed this to N and he laughed. "Yes," he said, "our cause is an affliction." I was uneasy. He smiled. "To be people like ourselves," he said, "requires a sense of the absurd." I felt better then and remembering it, I feel better now.

Yes, those in this Host Country who surround me: smug, comfortable, suspicious and concerned, what would they have seen in that dark shape and the strange name? One could hardly expect them to have been able to imagine the pale rose beneath the opaque mass, how could they have recognized the twisting shape of our great river in the northeast, they'd have no sense of the deep cold northern lakes from which for centuries our fishermen pulled out the wriggling silver creatures with hard clear eyes. No, for them it would only have been a shape, as meaning-less as a stain on the tablecloth.

A disease. Yes, I'd agree, a disease. But they might at least have acknowledged us.

In the early days of our activity when, frankly, there were more of us, when we had a visible cause and we could persuade ourselves that the citizens of the Host Country could be inter-ested to some slight degree, we tried to win popular support. In those days it was the fashion to be reasonable, to seek out alli-ances. The well-known rivalry between the Host Country and the Occupying Power could be used to our advantage, we told ourselves. We associated with other groups then. Their blue-jawed spokesmen would lean forward over the tables of work-men's cafes, their shirtsleeves carefully rolled to the elbow, and tell us that reasonably speaking our little nation, our peripheral language, were destined to disappear, had well nigh disappeared already; but that this shouldn't dismay us since we could all struggle together for a larger cause. We looked into our beers and were silent.

How reasonable! Our allies, our fellow conspirators. Yet as ignorant as the well-fed masses of the Host Country of the soft shapes of our southern mountains, the names of our poets, our children's games.

"Fools," X called them. "Their nation is an idea. Let them be buried there." X was a small man, prematurely bald. He spat when he talked, he was always wiping his mouth. His eyes were large and his words came quickly, he sometimes stammered. "Yes," he'd shout above the noise of the tavern, "of course we're insane. Who else but the mad would spend their lives fighting for the liberation of a land they'd never seen, living in a country where nobody ever heard of the place for which we deny our-selves the pleasures that this wasteful nation strews around us?" He'd shake his head. "Remember," he'd say, using my name, "our allies are the mad."

He was killed in a political argument years ago, stabbed to death by the partisan of a group even more obscure than our own. Surrounded by strangers, I had to travel by bus to the distant city where he died and where a small memorial service was held for him. The bus broke down and for a time the passengers stood around, smoking, looking at their watches. From someone's radio came the popular music of this alien country where I've lived my life. It was warm, we were far from anywhere. Brown treeless mountains stood on one horizon; the other, in the direction we were going, was flat and empty.

Standing there alone and apart from the others, outside some obscure cafe in an obscure part of what I'd learned to think of as my Host Country, beside a road I'd never travelled before, I looked into that empty landscape, so far from the piece of this earth we'd spent our lives fighting for. As a truck's whine began to obliterate the dim music in the background I heard a cough from one of my fellow passengers on the other side of the bus, a curt, strangled bark. All at once I felt such an appalling sense of estrangement that I wanted to walk to the person nearest me, to touch him and tell him who I was, tell him about my father and his card games, the rose-colored shape on the map, our commitment, the patient poring over history books, the countless articles, memoranda, leaflets, the meetings in unheated rooms, the incidents, arguments, confrontations, the bomb at the pier. I wanted it known. Facing that blankness I wanted it known.

I have to stop here. Even at this distance I can feel the force of an emotion that might well have unhinged me. How I wish there were something soothing in this relentless rain.

Facing that memory, I have to remind myself that there were other times, I have to turn my mind deliberately toward another incident that, though its practical results were ambiguous, I can't help thinking of now with fondness.

We were relatively active then, strong, it seemed to us at the time, though now it's comically clear how little weight we carried. None of us, of course, had seen our country but we were fiercely proud of our regional differences. When we managed to persuade an old woman to make one of the soups of our people, for instance, N would no sooner put the spoon to his lips than he'd begin shaking his head and proclaiming that though it was good, in the southern province from which his family had come different spices were used. When we spoke the language whose literary works we'd painstakingly studied we tried hard to preserve the regional dialects. Still the sad fact was that, separated from the land by so many miles and generations, we spoke our language not as natives but as exiles.

One night N and X and I drove in X's untrustworthy old car through the blowing snow to a nearby college where a minor official in the government of the Occupying Power was giving an address on economic matters. The three of us had carefully laid out our plan to stand up in the middle of the speech, to raise a banner and to confront the speaker about his government's continuing scandalous failure to grant self-determination to our people.

The talk was sparsely attended and we'd been able to be seated quite close to the stage. The deputy minister was a stocky bald man with a thick neck and heavy-lidded eyes. As he began his speech about agricultural exports, reading from his text in a bored, slightly contemptuous voice, I heard his accent and realized that, in spite of his name, which had no doubt been changed in order to advance his career, he came from the region of our lost country. My pulse quickened as I looked at someone whose ancestors might well have looked upon my own and for a moment it was as if I were seeing again that rose-colored map of my father's.

We three stood up at the predetermined moment, unfolded our banner, we began to shout all at once in the language of our country, accusing, indicting, pleading. At first the deputy minister looked up from his text like an awakened sleeper, adjusted his glasses and searched us out. Never for a moment did he look threatened, though, and when he saw how few we were his mouth curled into a sneer. We'd been shouting and X, who had (mysteriously to N and me) bought some candy minutes before, began hurling chocolate balls at the speaker. In seconds security men were leading us roughly out of the hall as we sang our national anthem at the top of our voices. The few spectators were wide-eyed with puzzlement and fear but at the podium the speaker leaned forward on his elbows and said into the microphone, not in the language of the Occupying Power but in the one with which we'd accused him: "If these hooligans intend to represent the cause they claim for their own they could at least begin by learning to speak the language correctly." I thought that I heard, under the irony, a genuine sadness.

"And whose fault is it," N asked later, as we drove back through what had now become a blizzard, "that we're separated from the land where our own tongue is spoken? Whose fault is that?"

X, at the wheel, peered into the frost on the windshield and seemed to be listening for the echo of the one chocolate ball that had managed to strike the podium. "I'd love to see their faces," he suddenly said, "in the capital of the Occupying Power when this is reported back to them."

Meanwhile over the ticking of the windshield wipers I kept hearing the voice of the deputy minister, remembering how thrilling it had been to listen to the sound of our ancient language, spoken with elegance, precision and force, coming over the microphone and entering the ears of those uncomprehending sheep from the Host Country who'd never heard it before.

"His kind will be the first to be hanged," X declared.

"Only," N laughed, "after we've allowed them to teach us to speak the language correctly." How I miss his cheerfulness.

When I think of the three of us, dedicated, united, oblivious to the treacherous snows outside the car as we speculated passionately about our lost country, I can believe that that battered car of X's was our true homeland.

Really, all this happened so long ago. Occasionally I realize: my life has passed. Where has it gone? Who in this country knows of our cause anymore, when so many others crowd the news? Who remembers that minor nuisance in the sleepy college town? Better, one might agree with our former "allies," that we should simply forget, simply allow this peripheral people to fade away. Where are the Babylonians?

Let me tell you, old crone: there was once a people, not richer and more powerful than the Babylonians, certainly, or those of the Host Country. And no better, either, I'll admit. The land had its share of scoundrels, frauds and monsters. Our early barbarian kings, some of them little more than gangsters, the warriors who fought bravely and those who fled, our saints, our peasant women, our glamorous actresses, our political thinkers—ours was the common fate: to struggle, to suffer, to try to lift ourselves, to confess our sins or to forget them, to celebrate our glories, real and invented, and—hardest of all to accept—to disappear.

Soon we'll all be gone: the barbarian kings, the poets, N, X, myself. Unremembered. Having written this, I find that I can contemplate it with tranquility. I'm grateful for the peace.

Still, I don't intend to mislead by giving the impression of heroic fidelity. Like my father I too could have surrendered. Once, for instance, there was a woman in my life whom I'll call Sister and, without going into details let me say that the relationship was much like others of its kind.

Neither of us was in our first youth, there were things we'd already given up forever and though we were sensible we were no stronger than other people. Marrying her wasn't out of the question. But I can point, as if to a place on a map, to the moment when everything became clear in that regard. Things had arrived at a certain point between us and we took a vacation together at a lake in the mountains. We rented a cabin, we swam, at night we listened to the pine branches moving against the roof, we were lulled. How far away now was that pier, that college lecture hall. In truth what pathetic failures they seemed beside that quiet lake, and how blessedly distant. In the little country store as I carried a bag of groceries in my arms, smelling the freshly ground coffee, the tang of cheese, watching the light play across a mound of bright lemons, I felt what seems at this distance a swooning, I realized how easily I could be swayed, how the gentlest breath of breeze could reconcile me to things as they were, how a puff of wind too soft to wrinkle the lake's surface could turn me forever to forgetfulness, to the Wednesdays, the Thursdays and the Fridays; and Sister must have seen it in my eyes because she touched my bare arm and said nothing.

Let me be honest: I wanted that breeze to come, I longed for the full force of a gale.

Yet only a few hours later that same evening, as I rowed the boat and Sister lay back against the seat, her hand trailing in the clear water—she had such lovely skin—listening to the creak of the oarlocks, the splash and pull of the oars, the hiss of the water dropping from the blades to the surface of the lake, I found myself absently studying the contour of the water and land, the dark mass of trees, thin sliver of sand beach, reflected clouds, and I realized that I was thinking about the lakes of my father's province in what was now the land of the Occupying Power: did they look like this? And if, by some fantastic coincidence one of them should exactly resemble this one in every detail; yet how totally different for me the experience of rowing on this lake and not one there, in that other place.

And then, realizing with horror that if I were capable of forgetting, of betraying that land, that rose-pink shape, it was possible everyone might forget, that the land, its people, its language and its history could vanish forever, I felt an actual breeze and I shuddered. Sister was startled, she asked if anything was wrong. Though I said nothing I'm confident there was some recognition and she didn't persist.

We walked back to our cabin in silence. I remember the horror I felt when we encountered the man who owned the cabins. He was washing his car and as we passed he turned briefly from the water-slick metal to wave at us with one hand while the clear liquid poured thickly from the bright green hose he held with the other, making a flat arc that fell with a splash to the earth below. As we walked under the pines I kept hearing the splash of that water.

Listen, old crone, how I wish I could take you by your bony shoulders and shake you. I'd shout into your face to tell you how it frightens me to think I will have lived and died in exile.

I can anticipate certain questions. Why, for example, haven't I ever taken the opportunity to visit the land of my people, to see the village my father left all those years ago? As a matter of fact, when he died there was a little money, a small sum but quite enough. Still, I didn't go there.

I've tried to be honest with myself about all this. Let me admit then that I've imagined that trip a great many times. And could anyone doubt how moving it's been for me to contemplate my actually being there, dipping my fingers into the cold waters of one of those mountain lakes, feeling beneath my feet the steady flow of that great river, walking through the narrow streets of our ancient capital, stepping out of the sun into the deep quiet shade of one of the old places of worship? Do I even have to say that I've dreamed those scenes countless times, only to awaken with my eyes stinging as I see around me the dismal brown walls of this shabby room, knowing that beyond them are only the alien sights of this land that, though I've lived here all my life, I can only think of as my place of exile?

And still I've refrained from going there. In some sense, I've told myself, it's part of the price I've been willing to pay, part of the sacrifice. Maybe my dedication is better maintained by my memory of that old rose-colored shape, maybe to remain pure it's better not to complicate things with a reality that's likely to be more troublesome than the cherished vision.

Let me be blunt: I've never tried to go to our homeland be-cause I've been afraid. Yes, I'm no less immune to fear than the rest of them. And yet the fear I'm talking about isn't that the authorities there would lay their hands on me, because I know very well they dismiss our actions, in spite of what X thought about the consternation we were provoking in the capital of the Occupying Power. No, what I've always feared is that, were I to go there I'd very likely find a population as sheepish and con-tent with the way things are as the likes of my father. Since the

Occupying Power cleverly permits them the celebration of the major ethnic festivals where costumes are worn and songs are sung, bold drunken threats are shouted, an observer might be misled about the rebellious spirit of the people. But when the holidays are over the kings and martyrs of our people will be put away like seasonal toys while the population resumes its pursuit of the rewards the Occupying Power dispenses in return for a mere betrayal of centuries of history.

However else my life might end, such a sentimental visit wouldn't provide an appropriate close to the story. Better to visit that pier where the damage from our bomb has long since been erased, better to think of that pier as the homeland.

How they of the Host Country would laugh if they were to read this, they who live in a country so powerful they can easily delude themselves into believing it's been there since the beginning of time.

Let them laugh, then.

There was only one time when I saw this country transformed, saw it catch its breath in horror like the savage who glances fearfully at the black skies just after the lightning bolt has shattered a nearby tree, leaving him for the moment deaf to everything but the frightening clap of thunder that seemed to have erupted from beneath his feet.

It was when the popular hero who'd seemed invulnerable was brought down.

I saw it in their faces: the smugness and the arrogance were suddenly gone like windows blown out in a violent storm. Now there were naked eyes looking toward others. On buses, on streetcorners they gathered in clumps, saying little, seeking the comforting presence of others. I walked among them as the streets grew dark, the very sound of the traffic itself seeming muffled, the drivers disinclined to use their horns. I saw people huddled in groups before television sets, I saw them reading the newspapers under streetlights, reluctant to go home, disbelieving maybe for the first time in the reality, the primacy, of their private lives.

Maybe for a time they were like me.

I'm not an animal. In a way I was touched by the sight of this nation bemused and fearful, yet maybe what I felt after all was more of an intellectual satisfaction than a turning of the heart. Walking among those whom I'd thought nothing could move, whom I'd seen so often in the past insulated from our quaint importunings by their endless supply of machines that provided comfort, pleasure and distraction, I had a sudden revelation of their vulnerability and for the moment I was heartened, my faith was restored and my sense of purpose fortified.

Though that time has receded, like every other time, into the past, the mere memory strengthens me and enables me to speak directly now of N, the last, the best of my friends.

"Forgive me," he'd written in his suicide note. At the end, regrettably, he'd lost his wonderful, comforting sense of humor.

I would have understood despair over the failure of our cause but it was shocking to learn that what N succumbed to was something more mundane: trying to assure himself of a minimal degree of comfort in the old age he saw advancing on him he grew fearful, he let his small savings be used in certain schemes involving less than honest people. And he told no one, it was his little shameful secret. When these dealings came apart N, who himself had done nothing wrong, nevertheless considered himself dishonored, and he shot himself with the revolver he'd bought years ago in order to be prepared for any action our group might sponsor. "Forgive me," he asked.

There weren't a half dozen people at his funeral, none besides myself had been associated with N in political activities. It was a bright day and the noise of jet planes from the airport near the cemetery kept swallowing the words of the simple service. I spoke a sentence or two of tribute, in the old language, of course, I called him a patriot. I returned to my room alone, thinking of N's being buried so far from the land we both loved, wondering where my body would soon be laid. I inherited his few possessions. I forgive him his lapse. A lifetime spent in such dedication can't be rendered invalid by an isolated weakness.

Yes, I still consider him a patriot, though in all honesty I felt an acute sense of betrayal at first, or should I say more precisely, abandonment. When I think of him—tall, thin with a slight stoop, an ironic smile playing about his lips—what strikes me as curious is that as he grew older he resembled more and more the professor that I jokingly told him he would have become had he lived in the old country. I see N sitting with his students in a cafe in our capital city, sipping the amber liquor while his eager listeners wait to hear him resume the telling of some anecdote from our people's past.

How certain faces haunt us. I saw my father's the other day. I was in the bathroom, I'd just suffered one of my dizzy spells. I almost fainted. I held the cool porcelain of the sink under my trembling hands, hearing my breath, unsure for a few moments where I was, and I saw him looking at me from the mirror. I put it that way because though I recognized within seconds that it was of course my own reflection I was seeing, still in the interval before my reason established control that was exactly how I experienced it. People have, of course, remarked on the resemblance for years but there was something truly frightening about seeing oneself that way, from the outside. The doctor has told me recently how fragile my health has become and it's some consolation to know that such visitations are, after all, only the result of physical weakness.

When I saw that face, though, when I realized that to the outsider I'd become my father, with the same grey hair, drooping mustache, even the running nose, it came to me more sharply than ever before that the final judgments on my life were soon to be rendered.

Let me be frank, let me acknowledge my terror.

Because our nation was small and we were constantly being overrun the legends and folk tales of our people don't celebrate invincibility but rather persistence and determination. We have a story about a small hill in the south of our land where a particular kind of sweet fern grows. One of our legendary rulers is buried there and according to the story when a worthy youth of obscure origin will make from the reeds of the several regions of our land a pipe on which he'll play a certain ancient song the melody will be heard deep within the hill by the sleeping ruler and his knights, who have waited for centuries to be called to restore their land. References to this ruler and his warriors abound in the patriotic songs and literature of our people.

Now, myself facing the shadows, I could try to find some consolation in that story though N, the scholar in our group, used to point out how many conquered peoples had similar tales. When I first heard this I responded by saying "History weeps at these stories." N shook his head. Even as a young man he had an air of worldliness. "History is not sentimental, my friend," he told me. "History smiles at these stories, History is amused."

So, writing for History, I anticipate its response. N was right, of course. I expect nothing from History. Rather, as my dear friend wrote in his farewell to me: "We had our lives. They are ours and no one else's. This was our land, our beloved country."

Let me surrender those cold mountain lakes, that great twisting river, the narrow streets of our capital that I've never seen, give them up once and for all, completely. Now, wearing my father's face, I recognize my country in the rose-colored shape, in small rooms that smelled of cabbage, solitary walks through the chilly streets of this middle-sized city, my friend X, with the rapt expression of an avenging angel, hurling a chocolate ball at a speaker, N shaking his head thoughtfully as we toast each other with the amber liquor on one of our people's holidays, Sister listening with me to the pine branches moving softly against the roof of our cabin. This, all, mine, a world, more than I can contain. My country, my people. Soon to be buried with me.

I wait for no worthy youth's melody to call me back, to restore, to complete what was lived completely. When this fierce rain ends I expect only silence.

I welcome that silence.

The ſoul Adrift

*The choices open to women and men today—even amongst
the underprivileged—may be more numerous than in the past,
but what has been lost irretrievably is the choice of saying:
this is the center of the world.*

JOHN BERGER

Politics

I am thinking of Egyptian babies this morning as I sit here in my daughter Rebecca's Brooklyn kitchen, waiting for a call from Deirdre. We are going to plan next month's Passover Seder. Since college, when they shared a house together, Rebecca and Deirdre have hosted feminist Seders, Third World Seders, poor people's Seders. Maybe it's the richness of its metaphors—the hard-boiled eggs for life, the saltwater for tears—and because it celebrates freedom that Passover lends itself to so many political interpretations. Of course, as Deirdre points out, the Last Supper was a Seder.

For the past two years, since Rebecca is always studying for medical school exams, Deirdre and I have taken on Pesach. We call ours eclectic Seders and invite everyone, the family, of course—my son David, his girl Jenny, my nephew Sam— and any Italians who are visiting Carlo, Rebecca's lover. Last year there was Sam's Japanese girlfriend and her French roommate.

When it comes to tradition, I am a practicing minimalist. Still, at holidays I long for ritual. I want music, flowing robes, cherubs blowing trumpets, and miracles—the parting of the Red Sea, the survival of the Jewish people. At Passover, I feel it's my responsibility as a mother to insist on a core of ceremony. At least I want the Seder plate with its green parsley and roasted shank bone. At least wine, blessings, and matzo.

Last year Rebecca suggested we not celebrate the killing of

the firstborn. "Why take it out on Egyptian babies? What kind of meaning is that?" she asked.

"I feel rootless," I tell Dr. Mutter, my therapist. He looks at me a vast distance across his small Oriental rug. I look at his white jug filled with daisies.

"Rootless?" he asks. "Aren't you a Jew?"

"What kind of question is that for a shrink?" I want to know. "Yes, I'm a Jew but I am talking about my Polish mother, my Austrian father, my American children. I am talking about my two marriages, one ending in divorce, one in my husband's death. My children and I are what's left of our family. We are homeless in some basic, modern way."

"You are talking here about personal history," he tells me. "Not politics."

I ask how he can separate them.

It's being widowed that makes me feel like one of the homeless I see everywhere. Tomorrow, before I go back to Boston, I will join them in the stale-aired waiting room at Penn Station, wrinkled women my age wearing all their clothes, young men like my son talking to the air. Most of the benches have been removed so people with nowhere to go will not loiter there. I feel so powerless standing among them I always have to remind myself I am not really one of them.

I am waiting for a train that I take because it's cheaper than flying and feels less dangerous. I have options.

I have a home, filled with objects from my travels, a ceramic cart from Sicily, a Bedouin wedding mask with strings of coins and amber. Four years ago I bought it from an Arab in Jerusalem's Old City. We sat in his shop on a pile of bright-colored rugs and drank bitter coffee. I thought of him last week when I read in the *New York Times* that Israeli soldiers on the occupied West Bank were breaking the hands of Palestinian rock throwers. As a Jew, I feel ashamed for those soldiers.

I do not want to be a victim or a conqueror. What can I do about it?

I think of the inevitable Sunday leavetaking as I look about Rebecca's kitchen, empty wine bottles on the table, glasses stained with dregs, and on the stove what's left of Rebecca's triumphant eggplant dish. Yesterday I watched her prepare it, marinating the rounds overnight in a pan on her neglected loom. And now this hardened muck.

I am always saying good-bye, always coming and going, on business trips, on holiday journeys, on visits to Rebecca and David. Since Ted's sudden death in a car crash seven years ago, I know that all good-byes have mortal overtones.

As her name suggests, Deirdre is Irish. At least her parents were. Deirdre herself has never been to Ireland, never been outside the United States. Big, blond, and pretty, Deirdre is the youngest of eight children. I think it was getting the last piece of every family pie that's made her such a fervent revolutionary. Which she is, at least philosophically. She supports the Irish Revolutionary Army. She wants the English out of Ireland now. She also supports the Palestine Liberation Organization. I do not think this means she wants the Jews out of Israel, just that she believes the Palestinians should be there, too. I agree with her. However, we do not discuss it often. When we do, we always fight, pushing each other to extreme positions.

Deirdre has only Arab lovers. I've told her it's guilt politics. She loves Arabs because she thinks they're downtrodden. She says if she wants to feel guilty, she'll call her mother. I tell her I'm her mother-substitute.

"Well, Mother, it's not guilt, it's sex. Lots of people are downtrodden. I just like Arabs."

Two years ago, when Deirdre worked for me in my short-lived design business, she flirted outrageously with every Near Eastern delivery man.

"Stop it," I told her. "Keep your love life out of the office." I meant it literally. We were working together in a very small space.

"You're prejudiced," she'd tell me cheerfully, having just made a date with the souvlaki take-out man.

Her last lover, a Lebanese, was in the United States illegally. Her present lover, Rafik, is Palestinian. Rebecca calls him Rafik the Sheik. I wonder how this will affect our Seder.

Thinking how politics affects transportation and vice versa has made me a nervous traveler. All those hijackings, those international suicide squads. It started at the Munich Olympics with the slaughter of Israeli athletes. Ted and I saw part of it on TV in a Barcelona bar. Then there were the random bombings like the Paris café, the planned executions like the Turkish synagogue, the *Achille Lauro* shipjack, an old man in his wheelchair thrown overboard to make a point about Jews and Israel.

The summer of the *Achille Lauro,* as we traveled through Italy, Rebecca and David and I made bad jokes about what we would do if a commando came down the airplane aisle demanding Jewish passports. Underneath the kidding, there was always a well of panic.

"Mom, you could get run over crossing the street," David told me.

"But not because I'm Jewish."

"We'll go to Stonehenge for our Seder," I told David. "Rebecca and I will come to England. We can celebrate anywhere, as long as the three of us are together." It was 1985. David was at the London School of Economics. And I was serious about Stonehenge. It compared in grandeur and mystery with those pyramids the Jews were forced to labor on in Egypt.

Then the Americans bombed Libya. "Let's go KLM," I told Rebecca. "Nobody's mad at the Dutch." She knew I meant on KLM we wouldn't get hijacked.

"It's not safer," she said, "just more expensive."

Here was a sudden role reversal. Usually Rebecca is dauntless and I am a coward. Determined to see my son, I convinced myself to be fearless. "Passover is about freedom," I told Rebecca. "Terrorism is another slavery."

"Phrasemaker," she said.

As we boarded the KLM flight, I worried if, God forbid, something happened to Rebecca, I would have failed as a mother, failed to protect my child. When David was eight and afraid he would be drafted if the Vietnam War went on forever, I told him I would take him to Canada. Now I told myself I could no longer protect my children against life's dangers, that, in fact, it was my job to encourage them to live it bravely. I fastened my seat belt.

In London, David studied Monday to Thursday while the city celebrated the queen's birthday and Rebecca and I played tourist. Streets were roped off in case the IRA tried to interrupt the party. At the British Museum, we were asked politely to open our bags.

"We've learned to live with it," a motherly Traveler's Aide woman told us in Victoria Station, where we stopped for maps.

Friday, en route to Salisbury Plain in our rented car, we discussed politics. I was against the bombing of Libya. David argued for it.

"This is *real politik*, Mom."

"*Real politik* as in Bismarck?"

David said I was a knee-jerk idealist. I thought he was too conservative. Rebecca remained neutral so no one would be outvoted. None of us wanted this argument to ruin our vacation. I wondered how much of our intergenerational squabbling was about Libya.

In a Salisbury department store that reminded me of Macy's, we bought a roasted chicken. At Stonehenge, at dusk when the crowds left, the guard let us through the ropes to roam the circle of huge gray rocks. We sat on the ground in the fading light and talked of the Stonehenge people, what little we knew of them, wondering how they hauled those enormous stones, what spirits they worshipped here.

I remembered the rock face of Machu Picchu, a trip I took with Ted a year before he died. I missed him terribly and decided not to mention it.

Later, at a bed and breakfast where we stopped for the night, in an overcrowded bed/sitting room, among three burled walnut wardrobes and a roomful of Dresden shepherdesses, we made our Seder. From our bags we took our chicken from Salisbury, matzo from a supermarket in Golder's Green, and hard-boiled eggs we'd made at David's apartment in London.

"You ask the four questions," I suggested to David.

"Wherefore is this night different?" he asked.

"Because on this and all such nights we are together," I answered, as Rebecca settled a candle in an ashtray and lit it, as I dipped the eggs in salted tapwater.

"Because our forefathers were slaves in Egypt. Because of our home in each other."

In Jerusalem, after I bought the Bedouin wedding veil, I went to King David's tomb to meet my travel group. I could smell the urine from the public toilets as I climbed the stone steps. On the roof, the rabbi, looking very American in his chino pants, a plain silk yarmulke on his curly ginger hair, handed me a sheaf of papers. I wanted to look at the Judaen hills, take myself back centuries.

"We were talking about Jerusalem," the rabbi told me, swaying as he resumed his chanting:

The Holy One blessed be He who created the World. He created the World as a human being is created. A human being begins with its navel, and develops outwards. So, too, the Holy One began with the navel. And where is the world's navel? It is Jerusalem.

Now I know why standing at the top of King David's tomb I thought of my mother, why the Jews cling to Israel and the Palestinians cannot be torn from their land to be repatriated. Jerusalem is the long tunnel we all came from and through which we will return.

Jerusalem is more than the nation of Israel. It includes the whole world. Its unity symbolized the possible unity of all humanity.

"'E's as bad as them 'ippies," our Stonehenge hostess told us at breakfast, filling our plates with meats I couldn't identify. "They think it's some bloody Woodstock. I'm a landowner 'ere, goin' right up to them stones. Fancy them kids like my 'Arry callin' themselves Druids, protestin' 'cause we won't let them 'ave a summer solstice party on them rocks."

When we left, Harry was in the driveway, a tall skinny boy in black, his long dirty hair pulled back in a ponytail. He posed for us in front of his home, a tin shack on wheels, pointing to his graffiti: "Free Stonehenge."

How would Rebecca describe her politics? She is always protesting something, starting when she was ten right there in our living room, between the Danish sofa and the giant avocado plant.

"I refuse on principle," she told the census taker.

"I don't get it," David said later. "What are you against?"

"Counting," she told him.

In high school, she was against hierarchy and faculty domination. At college, she demonstrated against South Africa, studied Navaho, and spent two summers on an Indian reservation, studying weaving and looking for female shamans. I supported her all the way.

"What kind of job will I get with elementary Spanish, advanced Navaho, and a record of getting arrested at every student demonstration?" she asked when she graduated.

Not many, she discovered.

It stunned me when Rebecca told me she wanted to be a doctor. I thought of her as an artist, a weaver, a musician. I never thought of her as a scientist. I do know Rebecca wants to bind up the world's wounds. Whatever is wrong, she wants to make it right.

When I asked her, "But why be a doctor?" she said, "Doctors have power. If I'm going to do it, I'm going to do it right."

Perhaps Rebecca is the only one in our family who's not conflicted. It scares me how little I know about my children.

The Seder reminds us that the one who questions history learns what it is about. That's what I'm thinking in the taxi on my way to meet David at Junior's for a late breakfast after Deirdre calls and changes our appointment.

"Maybe I can come this afternoon," Deirdre says. She has been fighting with Rafik and needs time to recover. They have been arguing about Passover.

"I don't think he'll make it," she tells me. I think she is talking about lunch this afternoon, but she means the Seder.

"What about you?" I ask.

She hesitates. "I've told him it's a tradition with me and Rebecca. I've told him we're family. Let's talk about it later."

In the taxi, I imagine that we are in the midst of the Seder and Rafik appears at Rebecca's door with three friends and a machine gun. "You have taken our country and we are going to kill you," he says in my fantasy.

I try to reason with him. "History has made us enemies," I say. Even to me that sounds pretentious. I start over. "Rafik," I say, "history can be evil. You and I have nothing against each other. We should work this out together and be friends."

"We are slaves in your country as the Jews were slaves in Egypt," he says, holding the gun before him like a banner. "Slaves and masters cannot be friends."

I tell him it is not my country, meaning I'm an American.

"It's my country," he says, "my father's before me and before that my father's fathers'."

"We should share it. My children and your children." I imagine telling him what the rabbi said about Jerusalem, about the possible unity of all humanity, about the primitive symbolism of the Seder.

"The Seder celebrates many gods," I tell him. "The fish for Leviathan, the egg for life and for Aziz, the ancient god of atonement." I am stuck about what happens next.

Next year in Jerusalem, we chant at every Seder, to remind ourselves as Jews of the longing for our home and the end of exile. I think how one people's hearth is another's graveyard. Whose Jerusalem will we be speaking of at the Seder?

"So what do you think?" David asks, pointing to the menu.

I can't make up my mind. There are too many choices.

David has too many choices, too. But the consequences for him are more important. David is in law school and he's bored. "I'd rather be in government," he says. "I'd rather be in politics."

Most of all he'd rather be an international negotiator, helping everyone resolve their differences. I'm sure that comes from being a child of divorce. He's sure that's nonsense.

What should he do with his life? Should he be a corporate lawyer and make a lot of money? Should he work for the government? What kind of life does he want?

I tell him I'm meeting Deirdre for lunch to plan the Seder.

"Is she bringing her Arab boyfriend?" David asks. "Do you think that's a good idea?"

"Why not? We have to be able to talk to each other."

"Mom," he says, "some of your ideas are ridiculous."

I try not to tell David what I would do with his life. Instead, I give him a check to buy clothes for his law firm interviews. Children are beyond politics. I remember when he was three and I asked, "Where are you?" and he answered, "Here my are."

Deirdre is waiting for me in Rebecca's kitchen. Although Deirdre is always effusive, always hugs, kisses, touches, she is so exceedingly affectionate I know something is wrong. Also, she is early, unheard of for Deirdre.

"You may have to count me out," she tells me.

"What am I counting?"

"It's Rafik," she says. "He likes Rebecca. I know he'd like you. He's just too upset about what's going on in Palestine. I've told him the Seder might be a good place to talk about it. We could have a real dialogue. But he's afraid it would be a fight instead."

For a moment this makes me nervous. At the Seder, do I really want a dialogue? I decide to risk it.

"Anyway it's not a question of his coming," Deirdre is saying. "He won't. And he's making it tough for me. He says I have to make a choice. He says that's what politics is about."

"So what is friendship about? And family. How long have you been friends with Rebecca? That's what the Seder is about."

"No," she says, "it's about politics." She reminds me of all the Seders she and Rebecca have made, all of them about politics.

"You know what Forster says," I answer. "If I ever have the choice to betray my country or my friends, I hope I have the courage to betray my country."

"That was easy for him to say. He wasn't homeless, he wasn't fighting for his life."

"Rafik isn't fighting. He's here in America. So are you. So are Rebecca and David. So am I."

"We chose to be here."

"So did he," I point out. "How will Rebecca feel if you chose not to come because it upsets Rafik?"

"We've talked about it. Rebecca understands."

"What does she understand? That you've been friends for years and now you choose Rafik? Is that your politics?"

"Rebecca says it's my choice."

"Of course it's your choice. It's just the wrong one. It doesn't help history that we choose not to sit down together. It doesn't help politics. Most of all it's not good for friendship, for family. We have to stay together. We have to support each other through life."

"Whatever the cost? What if I lose Rafik over this?"

"You won't lose him over this. And what kind of a man is he if you do? 'Nationalism is the last refuge of scoundrel.'"

"You're big on quotes today," Deirdre responds. "What about 'My country right or wrong'?"

"My family right or wrong," I tell her. "My friends and my family."

"And my lover?" she asks.

I don't have an answer.

A. B. Emrys

Arsenic and Old Tape

I'm loitering in the drama aisle of the Hollywood Palace video franchise. It's a painfully bright place, all lobby and no theater. I'm waiting for Louie to show up, nineteen years of him, so we can rent a video. This is a family-time ritual: first we'll have the instant togetherness of these shiny breakfast cereal boxes, then at my apartment we'll roll the TV cart up to a couple of chairs, instant den.

Of course I'm early and of course I get itchy. *I* rent videos. *Louie* rents videos. Just not together. I'd had the machine a day or two, maybe, before he moved out for college, as if it were a consolation prize for the empty space he left. Lose a son; rent movies. Now we've said jokingly on the phone in the last two weeks, sure, once he's home, we'll watch a tape or two. Now he's home—at his father's. In town three days and we're still voices on the phone, and I get that not-right feeling swelling a few internal organs to bursting. One of my co-workers used to swim every day for stress till she developed an allergy to the chlorine. After twenty years, I've got anaphylactic family shock.

And why did I tell him, "Let's meet there?" I never go to these huge video barns on the strip mall crossroads. Usually I go to my corner store, run by two Korean brothers (their family time, I guess), but for Louie—I don't know—if not the best, the biggest. Who knows what he likes to see now, and besides, he and his college pals probably go to these big emporiums all the time. Probably they take video cornucopia for granted.

I take it on the chin. This store is categorized, unlike my

corner one where Schwarzenegger and Olivier coexist. Here everything is clearly marked off: Drama, Comedy, Family (nondramatic? unfunny?), Horror, Sci-Fi. In back there's War and Westerns. Guns, I think they should call it. This labeling of fictions disturbs me. For one thing it's too much like people labels: yuppie, working-class, fortysomething, son, mother. But mostly it screws up my shopping. I don't know if I want tears, car chases, vampire bites, or what. I can't browse with labels.

I get out of the aisles up by the front counter. New Releases. I try to follow its advice. I breathe in confidence. I breathe out fear. It's good there are choices. I *want* to have choices. It's good.

Louie and I are not such worlds apart, only about ten blocks when he's in town between semesters. But he doesn't stay overnight with me now, too old to shuttle between his father's house and my apartment, and as he says, "Mom, I'm not really anywhere anymore, except at State." He says it all ironically in quotes, "State," "Mom," "anywhere." We see each other now like old friends, we do lunch and brunch: You feel like Mexican? Great, meet you at El Jardin. Over the holidays we were crunching corn chips next to a family, mom, kiddies, grandpa with a video cam. The tots, maybe twins, black-haired boy and girl in blue bow tie and pink hair ribbon, staggered over to Louie's knee. They stared up at him expectantly and then together clapped hands and crowed. Louie was enchanted. By conducting he got them to do it again, and Grandpa captured it on film. I thought of walking up and down library aisles with my mother, choosing books for her to read to me. Once I got old enough to read for myself, we never went world-shopping again.

Maybe I am just doing a "mom" thing here. Maybe Louie's going to humor me. Anything you want to see, Mom.

The longer I'm in Hollywood, the less possible it gets to pick anything. I stagger down this flashy aisle choking on choices. There are just too many possibilities, over three thousand, according to the sign in the front of the store. Things I've seen I spot in passing, like faces in dreams from years ago, and I don't feel like dreaming them again. Things I haven't seen are maybe no good. I know this is stupid. I can feel the stupidity, keen and narrow as if I'm stabbing between my ribs with it, but I can't stop. I refuse to settle for the merely motherly—whatever you want to see, dear—I want something perfect for Louie and me. I want a shazaam video. I might as well be choosing a world for us.

I wish I could, too.

I watch the counter to see how other adults are handling this. Coming past me out of Drama is a tall black woman about my age in a pink sweatsuit. She's taking four or five, just in case. But I can't bring myself to do it. I look just like I did when I came in, a skinny little blond mom with empty hands, nothing to shove into the player. I start snatching new releases off the wall, refusing to say to myself what kind they are. I pick them by scenes on the cover, by color and slap them back on the shelf as soon as another catches my eye.

Beside me on a monitor Rodney Dangerfield disgusts his son by enrolling in the same college. I'd never do that. I remember freshman year only too clearly, praying for my parents to leave me and go home. No, I did the opposite. Louie had ten years of shuttling back and forth between custodies like a commuter prisoner. He's probably relieved to stay in one bed from month to month.

But when I spot Louie outside he's striding confidently. I see he's solved the clothes-labels problem: good leather court shoes, shorts, and "Dead" T-shirt. Louie grins as he pushes in the door. His nose is freckled and pink with sun. He hangs his wrists on my shoulders, still pleased to be taller, and says, "It's okay, Mom." Whatever it is. "Chill, Mom, really." I take a deep, shuddering breath. He sees what I'm holding and says, "You hate Michael Douglas." It's true; I do. I tell him I have video vertigo. "This place is huge," he says, and strolls off bravely into the categories. "We'll find something," he calls back. "Really." I breathe. I gulp trace elements of confidence out of the air.

Louie cruises down Drama into Comedy. In my other hand I'm still holding the *Doonesbury* movie—we've both seen it, we talked about it on the phone, but the tape has a *Far Side* cow cartoon—and a remake of *Arsenic and Old Lace,* now called *Charge!* Louis picks things up and puts them back. Sometimes he reads the back, or just stares at them unfocused, like I do. He does this through three aisles, working his way into Horror and out again.

I shadow his nonchoices. Frowning at the boxes, he looks like me, with his father's serious expression. It gives me another not-right rush, like the day Louie packed his jeans and pulled his CDs off my shelves. Not unlike the one I got when I packed my records and clothes. I think I mean my own going-to-college stuff, but the things I see myself packing include child-size T-shirts and grown woman's running shoes. Then I realize I'm actually holding one of those family movies in which the troublesome mother dies, and I put it down like a snake.

At the moment Louie is still empty-handed. I show him *Charge!* and he's heard of it somewhere. "I never saw the original," he says. I never took him to see any of my classics. I took him to see *Star Wars.* I sat through years of *Miami Vice* gunfire, hoping its bullets would fly over his head. Whatever you wanted to see, Louie. We stand there till I think he can hear my heart thud and boom, exactly like a washer turning over an unbalanced load of clothes. "Okay," he says finally, in the tone of "anything."

We turn to the desk but now it's surrounded, as if a small crowd is pressing against the ropes for the best seats. Louis waves the box of *Charge!* in the air at the clerk but the red-faced man shakes his head no. "All out," he mouths. I thought they always were available if the box was on the shelf, but not in Hollywood. We bait and switch ourselves.

I say, "We should have gone to my neighborhood place," and Louie says, "How far is it? Let's just go." And we leave Hollywood. I feel better instantly, because we both chose this. I let him drive the six or seven blocks out of the strip malls back into my neighborhood. I'm limp in the air-conditioning. Chill, Mom, cool out. Louie tells me at college there's a great little store by campus, lots of art films and a student discount. "Big selection, but depth—you know? Not just blockbusters."

He parks so beautifully that I nearly cry.

We climb out and stroll together into the little doorway of the KC Video Shop. It's dim and quiet, a wine cellar of racked boxes. I see *Charge!* on the shelf and show it to Louie. "Well, shall we take a chance?" Louie says he likes remakes. He says, "It's interesting to see them without having seen the first version. To see if they stand on their own." Then maybe later he'll see the original. The stocky young man behind the counter grins at us from behind his thick glasses and has already pulled the tape off the shelf. We read the box. Mortimer is now Mort, a film critic, and everybody's throwing scripts at him. I wonder if that means Elaine too, and I wonder if they still marry. I wonder if the crazy aunties write scripts too.

As we leave, I say I've got beer at my place. I start to say home and then choke it off. I say "my place," "your dad's place," "college," as if none of us had homes. Pretty soon, "Louie's place," and I don't even know where that'll be. But I don't want to hear him say it: "Your place, Mom." So I say, "We should get some munchies and go home."

We climb two flights of carpeted stairs into my apartment. This place was never big enough for two. I saw that the minute Louie moved out. I remember how big it looked empty when I rented it, the sun pouring on the wood floors like spilled light. I could afford it, and I thought here's a big room for Louie and a big room for me, plenty of closets, bookshelves. Roommate thoughts. I never get it right. I rent us a four-year space and then I forget and want Louie to come back to it, like the lifetime bedroom in the family—vault, I almost said. On the stairs Louie asks me if the guy with the bulldog is still in the apartment below, but he's gone, replaced by a yuppie couple only home after dark, like reverse vampires.

Louie doesn't seem to mind or even notice that his old bedroom's my study now, his bed a couch. He wanders from kitchen to bedroom and back examining things. It's me who sees our time here, though, all Louie's high school years layered under the landslide of the present. I'm waiting for the sofa to scrunch back into a bed, for Louie's possessions to worm their way out of cupboards into action again.

They don't, though. Louie breaks out a couple of brews and a bowl of chips, that's all. He drinks out of his old A&W mug, but I use it too, sometimes. Meanwhile I roll out the VCR cart and plug it in. I haven't been wanting to see the new version. I know the old one so well, even the parts I don't like, that I assume the changes won't be for the better. And there are too many old quotes of mine Louie could redeliver in my teeth about change, about how people sometimes have to rethink choices, how they choose to live differently, separately after all.

But now Louie's excited about seeing the remake "fresh." Something, he points out smugly, I'm not able to do. While I fry up grilled cheese for us Louie leans on the counter and frets at not having the box information to read again. He pumps me about the new version. Arsenic and Miniblinds, I call it. I say we never had program notes for movies in the old days.

Louie won't buy that for a second. "You had previews," he says. He nudges me. "You ought to get one of those fat video books. You ought to, really."

I'm thinking about the plot of the old version. Specially, I think about Cary Grant playing Mortimer, trying to stuff the dark side of his force into the window seat and be normal, normal, normal. All the crazy people in the film looked happy, but Mortimer looked like a corkscrew. He wanted to ignore things — corpses, marriage. I guess he thought it would be all big blue eyes and kisses, and he'd never have to roll over Niagara Falls in a barrel, just gaze at it. I guess everybody thinks that.

I ask Louie if he remembers Star Wars. It seems to segue okay. "Hah!" he says. He stands up and his head tilts at an inhuman angle. His elbows swing out and hover stiffly. "Oh, Master Luke!" He goes up another octave to his old boy-voice.

322

"Master Luke, you're safe!" He swivels his torso backward and down toward the refrigerator. "And no thanks to you, R2."

"Come on 3PO," I say. "Showtime." He shuffles behind me into the living room. "Master Luke, your drink!" It's no immortality. He's certainly not me. It's more amoebalike, as if my nose and chin and long narrow feet oozed off duplicates that became part of somebody else. As if I can fuse lives as well as divide them. Well, there it is, as they say in Action Adventure. Even though he's grown, even though I have a life, even though I split up our old one, I want our worlds still to collide. I want us to love the same videos. Some of them. I want to wake up in the middle of some nights and hear Louie breathing in another room. I just do. I catch him smiling and for a second he lets me have it, blindingly. "It's okay, Mom. Really," Louie pushes in the tape eagerly and waits for the remake to roll.

HOLLIS ROWAN SEAMON

Middle-Aged Martha Anne

> Middle-aged, middle-aged Martha Anne
> Lived alone in a frying pan.
> 'Til the cook threw in grease
> And Martha slid to her release,
> Never to be burned again, again,
> Never to be burned again.

Nonsense rhymes were continually spawned in Martha's brain, fidgeting there until she gave them voice and let them out. The only way to get rid of them, she knew by now, was to supply them with reasonable rhyme and some sort of rhythm, and then they would obligingly take form in the air and be gone.

So middle-aged Martha Anne, cooking bacon in her frying pan, sang her little song and then was free to eat her breakfast in something very like peace. Her kitchen clock ticked earnestly, her tea kettle bubbled brightly. The late summer sun slanted across the table, tickling the edges of the asters in the vase. The air was full of lingering dew. Back, Martha thought, in her olden days, she would have slept past the dew, dressed in alarm, gulped too-hot tea, and spilled herself upon the mercy of bus drivers in her rush to the office, where she could fall halfway back to sleep over the television jingles and magazine ads that she wrote. And rewrote and rewrote until their infantile strains had infected her dreams and impaired her ability to think in straightforward prose.

And who would want to anyway, day after day after day?

Martha wondered, as she washed her dishes in her awfulorange (one word, her own) sink. The house where she now lived, following her flight from her city townhouse and the world of work, was not what one would expect if one dreamt dreams of solitary retreats as rustic cabins upon isolated, flowered-covered hills. There were no darkening pines, nor even crude water pumps to make the house romantic, the proper abode of a hermit or half-mad poet. It was just a small, cheaply built house on the edge of a farm, originally meant to accommodate hired hands, whose hands were no longer needed, as so much of the farm had fallen away, field after field become house lots and developments, and the farmer grown rich on harvests of banker's green. The hired man's house had, in earlier days, been lived in by countless restless workers, coming and going like breezes, each decorating the bits and pieces of the house and leaving a cumulative design in walls of many colors.

Martha often wondered who had chosen the awfulorange sink and stove and refrigerator set and then who had capped them off with the brilliantly speckled magenta linoleum floor. When Martha redecorated the house she left the kitchen quite alone, a masterpiece of a sort, contenting herself with painting the living room walls ivory (in defiance of their previous puce) and her bedroom walls blue. Except for the bathroom, that's all there was to the house, and quite enough.

Martha had removed the plaster elves and lantern-bearing pickaninnies from the yard, but did not destroy them (for the good of humanity, as her son suggested) but allowed them to gambol for all time in the ripe darkness of the abandoned chicken shed, where she believed they spoke on Christmas Eve, although the substance of their conversation with the shades of departed hens was beyond even her imagining. The house, the yard, even the village to which they were attached by dint of postal obligation were, in short, absolutely tacky, and Martha loved them all, for she owed them nothing and they surrounded her with pleasant impersonality, a gift. She did not plan to leave them for a long while yet, despite Justin's constant pleas, calling often,

asking her to come home. A kind man, her son, if a bit blind to
his mother's needs, as who, all told, is not?

Dishes done (sparkling clean, shining like a dream), Martha
donned her old woolen sweater for her walk into town for her
mail and daily dram of groceries. The need of the sweater brought
foreboding of fall and Martha shivered. Last winter the house
had been more than a little cold, frost forming on the inside
walls at night, for she had refused to listen to reason or neighborly advice, and cover the outer window frames with opaque
plastic, which might have kept a bit of winter out, but would
surely have kept Martha in, unable to see outside at all. And she
needed to see the bird feeders, to gauge their fullness and to
watch the birds at their meals. Thirteen different varieties had
come, on one glorious frostbitten morning: first the plain brown
sparrows, then the juncos and chickadees, soon titmice had
come along, bringing with them the nuthatch and the finches,
red, purple and yellow finches all aglow, lit along the sunflower
feeders; the mourning doves squatted on the ground, catching
drops, too placid to annoy the screaming jays, their blue-like
lightening on the snow. The evening grosbeaks joined in, brush-
ing wings kindly with the unpopular starling and blackbird.
Finally, like a benediction, like grace without prayer, came the
cardinals. That day of riches still glowed in Martha's mind,
whittling away winter's sharp edge.

And still, Martha thought as she started down the road, still
it was quite warm yet, September just half over and the sun
trailing summer behind it.

She strode quickly along, exercising her heart and lungs, if
not her soul. At the dusty little post office the woman gave her
her mail with a smile, mostly catalogs, some already full of
Christmas wares (toys and joys for girls and boys). She bought
her supper needs at the grocery store where she chatted with the
clerk, a lovely bald man with glasses and an undaunted ability
to draw pleasure from each day's conversations about weather
and gardens and such. Martha headed home, taking the long
way, her contact with mankind done for this day, a contact small

but satisfying, amply nourished by mutual interest in the commonplace. She looked forward to settling in at home with the catalogs, spying out all sorts of lovely things which she might order, for herself and Justin and Judith.

After lunch Martha would enjoy her nap, a tiny one, upright in the blue chair, a mere touch of sleep to give piquancy to an afternoon of wakefulness. Waking, she would garden, read, listen to the radio and cook, if she felt like it. Late in the afternoon, on fine days, her landlord, the wealthy retired farmer, eighty-odd years old, would often visit and they would sit on the peeling porch and talk, or not, as they pleased. Mr. Bell would most often talk of days far gone and people whom Martha had never known but who had come to interest her, as tales of their lives drifted about her porch and lawn and settled in the window boxes among the impatiens. Nighttime, Martha watched Mystery Theater or Great Performances on PBS, never deigning to flick to other stations, where she might, God forbid, hear one of her own inane ads. She would sleep early, and well.

With this day all stretched before her, Martha walked home. On the final bit of the walk, she passed one of the farmer's last cornfields. The corn was her measure of the passage of time, more accurate than most. In May the field was brown sweet-smelling dirt. In June the new corn reached her knees, in July her waist, in August her shoulders, and now in September waved far above her head. In October it would become a field of stubble, studded with a few missed ears. Today the corn rustled with huge green energy, full of frantic whisperings and signs. Martha quickened her steps just slightly and was bravely hurrying past the looming plants when she heard the cry from within the corn.

She quashed her urge to run away and stood on the edge of the road, her ear bent to the inner green, and listened. The cry came again, high and pitiful. A cat, Martha thought in relief, just a cat. Here, Kitty, she called, bending down at the very first line of stalks, peering into the corn, here kitty, kitty, kitty. (Pussy cat, pussy cat, where have you been? I've been in a field, all green, all green. Pussy cat, pussy cat, what did you do? I trapped old ladies, all blue, all blue.) The cat's cry was momentarily silenced by Martha's voice but soon resumed, higher and more frantic, a plea from somewhere inside the corn.

All right, Martha thought, I'm coming, kitty. I'm coming. Martha was fond of cats and only did not own one because it was such a cliché for a middle-aged lady living alone to keep a cat and tell her friends endless stories of its adorable antics. The cat kept hollering, in hope now, and Martha blundered her way into the tall corn, pushing away the sharp-edged leaves that reached curiously for her face and neck. The light in the corn was completely different from ordinary sunlight—pale green and full of floating specks. Martha felt choked and fought panic as she crashed about, calling, here, kitty. The cat's answer came back to her and she followed it as best she could without foundering among the protruding roots of the corn plants. She really did not wish to fall dead, to nourish the field with her fertile flesh. (I enjoyed the earth, now the earth's enjoying me.) She pleaded with the cat, here kitty, please come here kitty.

The cat just kept on wailing and Martha just kept on blundering about until they found each other at last, clear on the far edge of the cornfield. (Martha, had she known, could have walked quite easily and safely around the field.) The cat's apparent obstinacy in not coming was made clear. Her leg was caught in a fox trap, the grey fur all crushed and bloody. Her yellow eyes made clear the fact that she'd felt herself doomed, but now didn't, quite. Oh, poor kitty, Martha whispered, and then, city-bred Martha Anne, never having seen a fox trap (nor a fox), opened one with her bare hands and set free the cat, who could not walk, and had to be carried quickly, wrapped in Martha's wool sweater. The crushed leg had begun to bleed heavily with the release of the pressure of the trap, and Martha ran home with her, crooning, poor, poor, kitty. She put her straight into the car, which luckily started after months of disuse, and drove to the nearest vet.

Who said he'd better put the cat to sleep and had Martha noticed the cat's pregnancy and what's more, advanced state of starvation? Unlikely to live or to produce quick kittens, at any rate. And Martha, said no. Let's not kill this cat. Let's try to save her. And the vet said, who will pay for the surgery and Martha said, I will, and the cat's yellow eyes closed in anesthetic sleep as the vet removed her useless leg and she awoke in Martha's house in a box lined with baby blankets (25 years old, from Justin's infancy and soft with many washings). The cat slept again and again, then woke to lap cream and then to stand and stretch on three legs as though she'd never had four. The cat obviously intended to live and the kittens within, by their deep underskin movements, showed that they too scorned hunger and fox traps and the tricks of vets and were bound for life.

So Martha came to own a three-legged pregnant cat and was fond of its company in the little house and fed it prodigiously and watched with full joy its belly grow and shift in the sunlit mornings. Martha felt quite unalone and was surprised when Justin called on the phone again in the last week of September, to ask how she was doing up there all by herself.

(Just I myself and me, a jolly noisy three) Martha thought, but said, "I'm fine, Justin, just fine, and how are you and Judith?"

"Fine. Really great," answered Justin. "But I'd like to see you, Mom. I need to talk to you. Can I come up tomorrow?"

"Of course, lovely. Yes, please do Justin. I'll make a cheesecake."

The receiver down, Martha thought, dear, dear, whatever will the man in the grocery think when I buy three packages of cream cheese, and after all the cream lately too. He'll expect to see me grown fat as a balloon soon, she laughed. (Soon a balloon or was it buffoon?) She shrugged away her worry—she knew Justin would ask her to go home again and she would have to turn him down, again, that's all.

In the twittering fall evening, for the earth had now turned away from summer, Martha lay in her bed and remembered Justin, her son. Not that she'd not seen him often, even since her move, but still she liked to remember. Her thoughts fled backward from the tall bearded man he was to the child he'd been and she stroked her memories like a cat. She saw again the awkward, trembly-souled teenager, the golden-haired boy with the baseball bat, the toddler with a rubber ball, the baby in the cradle. She caressed the images no one else would ever carry, his father's memories gone into the grave. Martha rubbed the cat's taut belly as her thoughts wandered, and the cat slept soundly on the quilt beside her.

Oh, kitty, she thought, the tricks the world plays on mothers. Forcing us, beyond our power to resist, to love our children with an intensity we could hardly have dreamed of, before. And then, to take them, by steps away. If they die (as had Justin's infant sister), the loss tears apart our souls, our guts are almost burned away with the pain. If they live, we lose them still—lose the baby flesh whose very smell was precious, lose the toddler curls that brushed our face as the small head rested on our shoulder, lose the sturdy bruised knees as they're forced into school pants, lose eventually, the trust and finally the need. And the great grown son, the good successful man, is no recompense. None at all.

The cat, so full of its own impending children, had no answer and Martha felt comforted by the absolute lack of one. That Justin should care to see her would be enough. That Justin loved her she did not doubt. Her only living child, he had come to her without hesitation when her need was great, when Jack died and the terror of loneliness had battered her. That Jack should die, at fifty, falling flatly, untreatably, irrevocably dead upon the tweed carpet of his office, with Justin grown and gone, and leave Martha alone with nothing but the agency job and her vast and beautiful townhouse, was unthinkable. Martha could not have conceived it. When the flurry of women friends had subsided around her, their wave of support gone back to their living husbands and jobs and gracious homes (the homes requiring such care, these days, such exquisite nurturing care, more even than the children), Martha was left to spin in circles of despair. She could not be, alone, the Martha Anne she knew, the woman of means (her husband's), the woman of grace (her own), the woman of plenty (her son). She was falling, floating, when Justin came home.

330

Justin had come back to their townhouse, putting up, she was certain, although he would never say so, with "Mama's boy" remarks from his fraternity brothers as he left the frat house. He had refilled her house with his presence. The bright rooms had lost their vast echoes and she had, once again, reason to put flowers on the breakfast table, and greens and holly on the mantle at Christmas.

Then, when Justin married Judith, two springs ago, (Justin and Judith and Jack, brought to you today by the letter J) Martha had left. She felt they needed privacy, and she felt, quite suddenly, that she didn't need them any more. And she'd found this lovely-awful house, much to Justin's dismay, and lived in it, in singular unexpected peace. That's all, except for the family fiction, which was that middle-aged Martha Anne, in search of herself, had gone to follow her true talent as a writer, to forsake the ads and to WRITE, in capitals. That she hadn't put pen to paper in over a year, did not dispute the idea, for no one knew it but Martha herself, who had no intention of writing anything, ever. But let them think so, an easy explanation. Martha Anne shifted onto her side in bed, and slept.

At 11:15 the next morning, Justin arrived and Martha held him tightly in her arms, enclosing for a moment the infant and the child and the man as best she could. They sat down to cheesecake and coffee and talk. Or really, Justin talked, seeming to have memorized his little speech on the highway. "Mom, I have great news." His eyes asked her to think it great. "Judith's pregnant. And, Mom, we really want you to come home now. Listen, we've thought it all out, We can fix up the top floor of the house into an apartment. You'll have all the privacy you need. We've already started to put a kitchen up there. A very nice one." He just avoided shuddering at the kitchen in which they sat.

"Judith is going to keep on at school, Mom, right up until the baby comes, studying to pass the bar. And after, well, we know she'll find a place in a good firm and we'll have plenty of money for sitters, and you'll be free to be with the baby, but you'll have time to write too, and . . ."

Justin's breath finally collapsed and he looked at Martha quietly. "We'd like you to come home."

Martha felt betrayed by her instantly filled eyes. She fiddled with the coffee pot before speaking. "Justin, that's wonderful news. A grandchild. How lovely. How grand! But, still, I thought I'd stay here for awhile, you know, finish my book (liar, liar, pants on fire). And I'd hate to move the cat now, and all," she ended limply.

"Oh come on, Mom, the cat? We'll bring the damn cat. Last year it was the birds. Remember? Here it was fifty degrees in this shack and you couldn't leave because the birds would die if you didn't keep filling the feeders. Remember? Honest to God, Mom, birds, cats, babies, are they all the same to you?" Justin's face was dark and pressing.

Martha sighed, acknowledging his point. "No, of course not. It's just that, you know," and here Martha spoke more truthfully than was her wont with Justin, "You know, there is nothing so despised on earth as pregnant cats and middle-aged women. I just think we should stick together, that's all." She tried a smile.

"Mom," Justin's voice was full of compassion hovering just above annoyance, "That's a crock. You're not despised, you're wanted. We really want you, Judith and I. And the baby, think how the baby will want you."

The baby, a baby with a mother in a law firm, a baby with no one to cherish and preserve in memory all the days of its small and singular life. Martha's eyes betrayed her again, but she tried to rally. "Justin, I just don't know. I'm happy here, you know."

Justin stood up, clearly hurt. "Judith and I are happy too. We just thought that maybe we could all be happy together. I respect your work, but I just can't believe you have to be all alone in some godforsaken place to do it."

Her work. Martha had no reply, nothing at all to answer her son.

Justin bent, then, and kissed the top of her head. "I'll call soon. You think about it, O.K.?"

Martha, looking at her magnificent magenta floor, asked,

"Give me a month, all right? One month to decide." She felt Justin's smile, and knew he was quite sure of her now.

"Sure, Mom, a month is fine. The baby's not due until after Christmas anyway." He laughed and said shyly, "We'd like you to help us with names—with your imagination I know you'll come up with something great."

When he left, he walked with the long strides of his father in the past and his child in the future. He carries it all within him, Martha thought, watching through a cracked pane. She was hardly necessary to all that now, was she?

In about a month, Martha thought, the corn would be chopped and the leaves gone from the trees. She hadn't yet begun to feed the birds.

Deep in the night, the cat gave birth. Martha awoke to a pained mewing and arose to watch as the cat labored in the box. She shivered in her flannel nightgown beside the small drama and watched each kitten arrive, wet and smelling deeply of blood and birth. There were eventually four, all the same undistinguished grey as their mother. They mewled about, then found the cat's nipples and gave suck, strong and healthy. The cat purred and licked.

Martha finally found the courage to dislodge one of the tiny beasts from its mother's breast, and she held it against her cheek, breathing in its odor of life. It struggled and cried, and alarm sprang into the cat's yellow eyes, so Martha returned it, safe, to the soft nest of Justin's baby blankets.

Pussy cat, pussy cat, where have you been?
I've been to London. I've been a queen.
Pussy cat, pussy cat, that is not true.
I've been a queen, I say. Have you?

PAUL GRUCHOW

Thinking of Home

I live in the watershed of the Cannon River. There, as it happens, grows the only plant endemic to Minnesota, the dwarf trout lily. It is a humble plant: it grows two simple, sometimes faintly mottled leaves four or five inches high, and for a week or two in the springtime on wooded slopes in Rice, Goodhue, and Steele Counties—and only there in all the world—it produces blossoms of the palest pink, each no bigger than a dime and supported on a stem about the thickness of a sewing thread.

Grant that the dwarf trout lily is exceedingly rare. Still it is tiny, unspectacular, hard to spot, only briefly in bloom, and impossible to identify when it is not blooming. Suppose it were extinct. What would we be missing? Why should anybody care? This question was put to me rather aggressively one evening by a member of a dinner party who was less than enthralled by my account of a day spent in the field hunting (successfully) for new populations of the plant.

I had to admit that it is unlikely that we will be materially ahead by saving dwarf trout lilies. It may be that they harbor some chemical that will prove valuable as a medicine in the future. Perhaps they preserve the key to some critical mystery of genetics. Perhaps they will be understood eventually to play some vital role in the ecology of the maple-basswood forest. But it would be disingenuous to argue for their preservation on these grounds. It is much more likely, in fact, that they will produce no medicine, hold no great genetic secrets, and play no essential ecological role in the forest community of which they are a part.

Life, in all probability, would persist quite satisfactorily without dwarf trout lilies.

Neither is there any compelling aesthetic argument to be made for them, I was obliged to tell my dinner partner. True, they are lovely on their own terms, their diminutiveness and rarity being no small part of their charm. But the great beauty of the Cannon River forests would be infinitesimally diminished by their absence, and then only for the few people who have actually seen one. Almost everyone who finds beauty in the Cannon River watershed would find quite as much of it there even if it harbored not a single dwarf trout lily.

Well, a guest who was on my side offered, wouldn't it be true nevertheless that the extermination of dwarf trout lilies would render the Cannon River watershed one degree less natural? Wouldn't this human alteration in the character of the place, however slight, make it in some respect less complete and therefore less wholesome? This is, I suppose, true, I had to say, but only very marginally so. For one thing, extinctions are also a natural phenomenon, and, for another, there is certainly not any place in the Cannon River watershed that has not in a thousand other ways already been altered by ten thousand years of human habitation. This additional minor alteration would not in any fundamental way change the nature of the place.

So why should we save dwarf trout lilies? Why ought their existence matter to us even for a moment?

This is my answer.

Dwarf trout lilies persist only because the forests of the Cannon River watershed exist. If they are destroyed, it will be because their habitat, which is a kind of organism, has been destroyed. Dwarf trout lilies represent the health of that organism; they are one of its rarest and most sensitive points of pressure.

Think of that organism as a home. A home, of course, is not just a house. Habitation makes a house a home. The well-being of a home, therefore, depends upon the welfare of its residents. It is the responsibility of the keepers of the house, if they would make it a home, to tend to the prosperity of those who live there.

Every householder who withers or dies as a result of the neglect of the keepers of the house not only diminishes the potential of that house to become a home, but also represents a judgment upon its keepers.

The Cannon River watershed is one of our many houses. If we would make it a home, we are obliged to care for its members, even the least of them, even the dwarf trout lilies. We cannot escape this duty because we are human and as humans are endowed with powers and resources unavailable to the other members of the household. The householders are inescapably dependent upon us to be good keepers. We, in turn, are dependent upon them for the possibility of rich and fulfilling lives, because it is their lives as much as ours that make our house a home.

To think of this watershed—to think of any place—as a home is to see it in a radically new light. It requires us, for one thing, to expand our horizons in an ecologically appropriate way. If we perceive that we are at home not just in a house or an apartment or on a farm, but in a watershed, as we are, then our loyalties will reach far beyond our families to the human communities in which we necessarily and intimately live, and beyond them to the biological community that binds together and supports our human communities.

As the visionary geneticist Wes Jackson has said, to see ourselves as at home in this way is to recognize our own history. We were hunters and gatherers long before we became agriculturalists. Through most of our existence as a species, ever since we came down from the trees—for all but the last eight or ten thousand years—we have been foragers. And the basic unit of organization among the foragers was not the nuclear family, but the tribe. The technology of farming did not allow us to transcend this heritage, as we sometimes mistakenly think, but only to scale it up. The community—the neighborhood, the city, the congregation—is simply a bigger kind of tribe. We still live, as we always have, in groups. Our species could not long survive outside of the group; we are, by our nature, communal. So to

336

understand that the home in which we live is the community, that the fealty we owe is to the community, is only to acknowledge our evolutionary heritage. Indeed, this understanding is encapsulated in the word *home* itself, which derives from the ancient Goth word *haimes,* meaning "village."

Nor have we transcended our lives as hunters and gatherers. We may think so. We may imagine that farming is an extranatural process, but the fact is that for all of our machines, for all of our genetic management, for all of our chemicals, the success of our enterprise is in the long run still tied to the health of the earth, to the fertility and structure of its soils, to the rains that fall, to the sun that shines, to the integrity of the layer of ozone high above us that shields plants as well as sunbathers from ultraviolet radiation. We may gather now from tended fields and farmers' markets, and we may hunt these days in feedlots and butcher shops, but we still hunt and gather, and it is still the bounty of the earth that we reap.

This is why no plan for making a secure home upon earth can long succeed unless we are mindful of the way in which we farm. It is no more possible in the long run to mine the earth, as we now do, and to make a home here than it would be for us to heat a house by burning its shingles and its siding. Our farming has to be sustainable—it has to honor, to preserve, and to protect the biological house in which we live—or it cannot possibly sustain us in the years to come. And what is true for our farms is true for our lives. This, too, is a truth embedded in our language. When we say these days that something haunts us, we are using a word that comes from the same lineage as *home,* but is older; what haunts us, in the ancient language of the hunt, is whatever calls us homeward.

It is no coincidence that the basic unit of organization in nature is the same as among humans. We are, after all, however much we rebel against it, natural. Nature, too, is organized into communities. We would not say that we had made a satisfactory human community if in the community there were only a random chance for the survival of any one of its members, or if we regarded some of its members as worthless and therefore expendable. Our whole system of ethics is founded upon the realization that in exercising such restraints as will secure life for the least among us, we strengthen the prospects that all of us will endure. We need to come to the same terms with the biological community. If we realize that we are citizens of it and dependent upon it, then we will extend to its other members the same protections that we offer to ourselves, on the same principle, that it is ethical, and for the same practical reason, that to do so enhances the prospects for our own survival. It is in precisely this sense that dwarf trout lilies are important. To the extent that we are able to restrain ourselves from destroying them, we will have demonstrated the capacity for a moral behavior large enough to preserve and protect ourselves.

Unfortunately, this capacity has not always, or even usually, been one of the end products of modern education. David Orr, who directs the environmental studies program at Oberlin College, is fond of noting—and he is right—that the only humans in all our history who have lived sustainably were illiterate. The advantage people living in some preliterate cultures had was that they had not yet imagined themselves as independent from nature. They still lived within the great kinship of the living earth. This kinship exacted a rigorous—some would say terrible—discipline. Perhaps none of us would ever volunteer to live in such a way again. But it had one virtue that tantalizes us in the end days of the twentieth century: it was a way of life that did not threaten the prospects for the survival of the human species.

We, in our modernity, on the other hand, have managed to devise duplicate strategies for destroying ourselves. We can now bomb ourselves into oblivion. By puncturing holes in our atmosphere, we can heat or irradiate ourselves to death. By exhausting the vitality of our soils, we can starve ourselves to death. By ignoring the biological carrying capacity of our planet, we can copulate ourselves to death. All of these are recent achievements. If this is progress, it is hard to see how it will do us much good to have more of it. The record has prompted Allan Savory, the director of the Center for Holistic Resource Management, to re-mark that the only real threat to learning is too much knowledge.

The great faith of our epoch has been in progress. Progress is a triune god: change is its truth, science and technology are its ways, and material comfort is its life. But that faith is dwindling. Octavio Paz, the great Mexican writer, suggests that we now live in the twilight of the future. "For our grandparents and our parents," he said in accepting the Nobel Prize in Literature,

> the ruins of history—the spectacle of corpses, desolate battlefields, devastated cities—did not invalidate the underlying goodness of the historical process. The scaf-folds and tyrannies, the conflicts and savage civil wars were the price to be paid for progress, the blood money to be offered to the god of history. A god? Yes, reason itself was deified and was prodigal in cruel acts of cunning, ac-cording to Hegel. And in the very order, regularity, and coherence (in pure sciences like physics), the old notions of accidents and catastrophe have reappeared. This disturbing resurrection reminds me of the terrors that marked the advent of the millennium, of the anguish of the Aztecs at the end of each cosmic cycle.

And, Paz adds, "Pollution affects not only the air, the rivers, and the forests, it also affects our souls. A society possessed by the frantic need to produce more in order to consume more tends to reduce ideas, feelings, art, love, friendship, and people them-selves to consumer products. Everything becomes a thing to be bought, used, and thrown on the rubbish heap. No other society has produced so much waste, material and moral, as ours."

The twilight of the future, Paz says, "heralds the advent of the now." He does not have in mind a passive, a devil-may-care now, but rather one in which there is a revival of what he calls "critical vision."

As I imagine it, at least four qualities will characterize this critical vision, one of them practical and the other three moral.

The practical quality is simply stated, but immensely complicated in its execution. We must learn to take nature again as a model—a template, a standard—rather than as an obstacle to be overwhelmed. The plainest example of our departure from this principle, it seems to me, is modern industrial agriculture, which substitutes systems of annuals growing in monocultures for the natural pattern of perennials growing in polycultures, and then polices the departure from the natural pattern with an ever-escalating arsenal of bioengineered plants and animals and chemical weapons. To make peace with nature in this endeavor, as in others, will require of us a new way of thinking about work.

In a sense, the world in which I grew up caved in after the Second World War. The postwar years were boom times in farming country; we had Europe to feed as well as ourselves; we had, for the first time, both the machinery and the chemicals to accelerate exponentially the pace of production in the countryside; and the gospel of "scientific" farming had been planted for long enough to have taken root. Farmers had learned to let go of their conservative land wisdom and to follow the more adventurous, not to say reckless, advice of their bankers—debt being the first article in the new faith—and of the university extension agents, whose lack of practical experience in farming was seen not as a handicap but as a recommendation: they had, after all, risen above the menial, the backbreaking, the filthy labor of farming, as it was ever more fervently described; they wore white shirts and ties, and were never in danger of soiling them.

The bubble of the late 1940s quickly burst; by the Eisenhower years, we were suffocating in surplus grain, prices had collapsed, the government was bribing farmers not to grow crops, and farmers were dumping milk to protest their plight and turning upon each other; some shots were fired. These were people who had defeated the Great Depression and survived the battlefields of Europe and Asia, but many of them would not endure industrial farming. In the 1950s some ten million farm people left the

land, broken by what is still—sometimes despicably—hailed as
the great triumph of modern agriculture.

My father managed, despite the odds, to hang on, largely,
I think, because he was by nature a contrarian. He kept his farm
small, practiced diversity, eschewed machines and chemicals when
the labor of his own hands was a suitable alternative, avoided
debt. He was, by today's standards, now that the environmental
and social costs of industrial farming have become obvious,
a virtuous farmer: careful of his land, as respectful of its wild
edges as of its tilled acres, conservative in the use of expendable
resources, attentive to the requirements of scale, and motivated
by the already novel conviction that farming was primarily a
moral rather than an economic endeavor, that its purpose was
not chiefly to accumulate capital but to feed the hungry.

We were poor and we worked hard, although not so hard, in
fact, as our more modern neighbors. We toiled when the sun
was up, rested when it was not, and took Sundays off, as our religion required, while all around us at planting and harvest times
the machines rumbled late into the night and Sundays were on
their way to becoming ordinary days in the relentless turning of
the weeks. As elsewhere in society, labor-saving machines did not
so much free us from drudgery as enslave us to our creditors.
Because we raised our own food, it was always in adequate supply; because our fuel was raised on our own land, we were always warm and dry; because we had acquired little, we had little
to lose. We experienced the joys and befell the sorrows that are
the lot of all humanity. Our lives were not idyllic—far from it—
but they were not mean or oppressive either, in the way that the
peddlers of industrialism like to imagine.

The only acute pain that I can recall suffering as a result of
our poverty was the intense humiliation I felt when I discovered,
as an adolescent, that most people lived in another way, and that
there was something shameful, so far as others were concerned,
about the way we lived. I felt a kind of loneliness at not being
able to invite my friends to our house, which I had thought cozy

and warm until I was made to see that it was dirty and tawdry by more universal standards. I particularly did not want my friends to know that we had no plumbing; I had learned enough of the culture to know that the outhouse had become a symbol not only of indigence but of indolence and depravity, the next thing to sleeping in gutters.

But bread was the issue over which we children voiced our new-found shame. Our bread was home-baked, using wheat raised and ground on the farm, leavened with home-cultured yeast, and sweetened with honey made by the bees we kept at the bottom of our garden. It was fabulous bread: almost every year it won my mother a purple ribbon at the Chippewa County fair; the slicing of the first loaf in a new batch, still steaming, its sweet, nutty aroma filling the kitchen, was one of the sacred rituals of our household. But my sisters and I, driven by the collapse of rural culture out of our local school and into the consolidated town school, had tasted the allure of the new world. We had acquired the preference of the age for anything manufactured over anything homemade. We suddenly coveted boughten bread, made from the sort of flour that had been so denuded of its wheatness that its only nutrients came from its artificial additives. We were no longer content to eat hick bread. "Wonder bread builds strong bodies seven ways," we said, proud of our modern familiarity with advertising slogans. We yammered and complained, I am now humiliated to confess, until Mother finally gave up baking bread, and we began to eat, like modern folk, a factory substitute.

The real poverty that we then experienced, but did not recognize, characterizes the impoverishment that befell every aspect of rural culture with the industrialization of farming. It was not only our palates that suffered, not only our bodies that were deprived of wholesome bread, but also our souls, which depended as we had not anticipated upon the sanctity of the labors that brought bread to our table. We had lost all the ceremony and artfulness that had once attended the eating of bread: the planting and tilling, the harvesting and winnowing, the grinding and mixing, the miracle of its rising, the mystery of the transforming fire, the sacrament of the first loaf, in which every member of the family had some vital role. It was a critical element in the purpose of our lives, and one of the ways by which we were literally joined to our land. Nobody has expressed better than Thomas McGrath—in my mind the greatest writer our northern plains culture has yet produced—what we lost sight of when we quit culturing bread and started buying it from the factory. McGrath called this magnificent psalm "The Bread of This World":

On the Christmaswhite plains of the floured and flowering
*   kitchen table*
The holy loaves of the bread are slowly being born:
Rising like low hills in the steepled pastures of light—
Lifting the prairie farmhouse afternoon on their arching
*   backs.*

It must be Friday, the bread tells us as it climbs
Out of itself like a poor man climbing up on a cross
Toward transfiguration.
*   And it is a Mystery, surely,*
If we think that this bread rises only out of the enigma
That leavens the Apocalypse of yeast, or ascends on the
*   beards and beads*
Of a rosary and priesthood of barley those Friday heavens
Lofting . . .

*   But we who will eat the bread when we come in*
Out of the cold and dark know it is a deeper mystery
That brings the bread to rise:
*   it is the love and faith*
Of large and lonely women, moving like floury clouds
In farmhouse kitchens, that rounds the loaves and the lives
Of those around them . . .
*   just as we know it is hunger—*
Our own and others'—that gives all salt and savor to bread.

But that is a workaday story and this is the end of the week.

The Latin word from which our own word *culture* derives has several meanings: to inhabit, to till, to worship; these are, in fact, although we have forgotten it, intimately related actions. To inhabit a place means, if one is attentive to the idea from which it comes, not simply to occupy it, or merely to own it, but to dwell within it, to have joined oneself in some organic way to it; it is the place to which one's heart as much as one's body is attached; and the word *till* derives from an Old English word meaning to strive after, to get; and the word *worship* is a contraction: it was originally *worth*ship, the homage one paid to whatever one valued. So the idea of culture encompasses not only the arts and inventions of a people, but also the place within which they dwell, and all that they strive after, and everything that they find worthy. When we gave up the baking of bread in our household, we abandoned more than a habit of living; in a subtle but very real way, we turned our back upon our culture; and to that extent our lives became less worshipful. The mystery of bread, the sacrament of it, as Thomas McGrath understood, was never in the ingredients, but in the labor, and in the laborers, that transfigured them into bread.

In our lives, this happened at about the same time that farmers stopped being agriculturalists and started being agribusinessmen. The change in language bespoke a profound truth; we really had forsaken the culture in farming, which is why Wendell Berry, that great prophet crying in the Kentucky wilderness, has argued that the trouble with modern farming—which by its wastefulness and destructiveness endangers the future of humanity—is properly described not as technical, or even as ecological, but as cultural.

As for the moral requisites, our new vision will be, above all else, humble. It will be imbued with the sense that the blunder we make today may not be correctable tomorrow. The past can always be romanticized, and the future is forever subject to glorification, but the present, if we are sane, speaks to us literally. The literal is never demeaning, but it is never flattering either; it is merely truthful. Critical vision requires the literal, the humble, truth.

If I awake in the morning in a pathless wilderness, as I sometimes do, and want to know how to set out again upon my journey, I need to know where I have come from, and where I intend to go, but achieving a reliable reading of either depends upon my knowing where I am now. It is the critical coordinate because it is the only point at which my past and future converge. There have been mornings when I could not say exactly where I was, and then I have been condemned to wander fearfully, lost and lonely, in search of some identifiable landmark, some *now*, from which I could confidently surmise the route I had taken and predict the way home.

I imagine that the critical vision we seek will value durability. We will cherish things, places, ideas, persons, because we hope that they will endure, not forever, surely, because we know that change is also natural and in its own way is our hope. But we will want to try to construct the now so that it anticipates and accommodates change. And we will not deconstruct anything—any idea or literature or living community—that we are not quite certain we know how to reconstruct tomorrow, should it prove necessary or desirable. When I am lost in the wilderness, I try to avoid doing anything—as we must in culture—that has the potential to compound my lostness.

And I imagine that our new critical vision will be reverent. In 1928 the naturalist Henry Beston published a report of a year he spent in residence alone in a beach house on the tip of Cape Cod. He called his account *The Outermost House*. It will last as one of the great books of our century, although there may not be two classrooms in the United States where it is regularly read. It is, like almost the whole of natural history—our most distinctive contribution to letters—an underground literature. At the close of it, Beston asks himself what he has learned from a year lived in intense communion with the land, and he says:

I would answer that one's first appreciation is a sense that the creation is still going on, that the creative forces are as great and as active to-day as they have ever been, and that to-morrow's morning will be as heroic as any of the world. *Creation is here and now.* So near is man to the creative pageant, so much a part is he of the endless and incredible experiment, that any glimpse he may have will be but the revelation of a moment, a solitary note heard in a symphony thundering through debatable existences of time. Poetry is as necessary to comprehension as science. It is as impossible to live without reverence as it is without joy. . . . Touch the earth, love the earth, honour the earth, her plains, her valleys, her hills, and her seas; rest your spirit in her solitary places. For the gifts of life are the earth's and they are given to all, and they are the songs of birds at daybreak, Orion and the Bear, and dawn seen over ocean from the beach.

To think in this way is to think in terms of making a home upon earth. The idea of home is the idea of a sacred place where one is safe, where one is sustained; it is the idea of refuge, of the place where circumstances are organized for one's unconditional benefit. "Home," Robert Frost said, "is where when you have to go there they have to take you in." To think in this way is also to think ecologically. The root word of *ecology,* as we need constantly to be reminded, is *oikos*, a Greek word meaning home. Ecology is the science of home-ness.

How will we know when we have arrived at an ecological—a sustainable—way of thinking? We will know it when we have begun to treat this biological house of ours like a home. I suppose that another definition of home is that it is the place we are proud of. It is the place we keep up, improve, show off, defend. It is the place that we regard as an extension of ourselves. The reverse side of pride is shame. We will know that we have begun to think ecologically when we are ashamed for our biological home to be seen in disorder. When our polluted rivers embarrass us, when our eroding soils are a humiliation, when the failures of our relatives—the wood turtles, the maples and basswoods, the dwarf trout lilies—seem an ugly reflection upon us personally, then we will know that we have begun to think ecologically.

We have colonized this land, but we have not yet discovered it. That is the task before us, to find this place, to learn to know it, to discover how to love it. Let us this day begin this great work. Let us make of this place, at last, a home.

Contributors

SHERMAN ALEXIE is a Spokane/Coeur d'Alene Indian whose first novel, *Reservation Blues,* was published in 1995. He is currently finishing the screenplay for a movie, *Lonely Town,* based on his writings.

SUE BENDER is an artist and family therapist who lives in Berkeley, California. Her first book *Plain and Simple* was published by HarperCollins in 1989. She published *Everyday Sacred* in 1995.

PETER C. BROWN is a writer and management consultant living in St. Paul, Minnesota. He is the author of two business books and has published short stories and articles in the *New Yorker* and other magazines and journals.

NAOMI FEIGELSON CHASE is the author of three books of poetry, *Waiting for the Messiah in Somerville, Mass.; Listening for Water;* and *The Judge's Daughter;* as well as *A Child Is Being Beaten, The Underground Revolution;* and numerous short stories. "Politics" won the Fiction Award from *Negative Capability* in 1989. An unpublished novel won the 1996 Hackney Award for Fiction.

COLETTE, or Sidonie Gabrielle Colette, was born in 1873 and died in 1954. In her lifetime her prolific and diverse body of work garnered critical acclaim. Colette produced novels, including the Claudine books, *Chéri* and *Gigi,* and *The Ripening Seed,* stories, plays, film and radio scripts, and a stream of journalism. She performed in the theater and was steeped in Parisian social and cultural life.

HARRY CREWS is the author of several novels and works of nonfiction in addition to a memoir, *A Childhood: The Biography of a Place.*

REBECCA EAGLE lives in Albuquerque, New Mexico, where she received a master's degree in English from the University of New Mexico. Her fiction has appeared in *Blue Mesa Review.* She is presently working on a short-story collection.

A. B. EMRYS's writing has appeared in *Portland, Paragraph, Sun Dog,* the Santa Fe *Sun,* the Chicago *Tribune,* and other journals. She teaches writing at the University of Nebraska-Kearney.

LOUISE ERDRICH is the author of two collections of poetry, *Jacklight* and *Baptism of Desire;* six novels, *Love Medicine, The Beet Queen, Tracks, The Crown of Columbus* (written with Michael Dorris), *The Bingo Palace,* and *Tales of Burning Love;* and a book of essays, *The Bluejay's Dance.*

K. C. FREDERICK was born in Detroit and teaches at the University of Massachusetts-Boston. His short stories have appeared in many literary magazines and have been cited in Pushcart and BASS. He recently finished a novel, *Country of Memory.*

SUSAN M. GAINES's fiction has appeared in several literary journals and in *The Best of the West 5.* She is completing a novel about a young scientist at an oceanographic institute whose research into climates of the distant past gets her into trouble in the present.

Elizabeth Graver's short-story collection, *Have You Seen Me?*, was awarded the Drue Heinz Literature Prize. Her stories have appeared in *Prize Stories 1994: The O'Henry Awards*, in *Best American Short Stories 1991*, and in several literary journals. She teaches at Boston College.

Paul Gruchow is a freelance writer who lives in Northfield, Minnesota. He is the author of five books, including *The Necessity of Empty Places* and, most recently, *Grass Roots: The Universe of Home*.

S. Afzal Haider has published poems and stories in several anthologies and journals. After being employed as an electrical engineer, a psychologist, and a social worker, Mr. Haider is working toward becoming a full-time writer. He is currently finishing a collection of short stories.

Kathleen Houser lives in Minneapolis with her family. She received a Loft-McKnight Award for poetry in 1988. Her short story "Without a Word Between Us" received the Tamarack Award from *Minnesota Monthly* magazine. She is currently working on a screenplay.

Melinda Johns earned M.A. and M.F.A. degrees from the University of Iowa. More than twenty-five of her stories have been published in such magazines as *North American Review*, *Florida Review*, *California Quarterly*, and *Writ*.

Linda Kantner is a social worker, writer, and mother who lives in St. Paul, Minnesota.

Diane Lefer is the author of the short-story collection *The Circles I Move In*. She teaches in the M.F.A. in Writing Program at Vermont College.

LISA LENZO lives in Michigan. Her stories (one of which won a PEN Syndicated Fiction Project Award) have appeared in many literary journals and have received Pushcart Prize nominations. She is at work on a novel and has recently finished a collection of stories, *Self-Defense.*

MIRIAM LEVINE'S most recent book is *Devotion: A Memoir.* She has written three collections of poetry and *A Guide to Writers' Homes in New England.* Her work has been published in several literary journals. She lives in Arlington, Massachusetts, and teaches at the state college in Framingham.

JIM WAYNE MILLER, of Bowling Green, Kentucky, is a poet, essayist, and novelist. His books include *The Mountains Have Come Closer, Brier, His Book, Newfound,* and *His First, Best Country.* An autobiographical essay appears in *Contemporary Authors Autobiography Series, Vol. 15.*

ANN NIETZKE worked for several years in a psychiatric shelter for the homeless. *Natalie on the Street* was a PEN/West Award Finalist in Nonfiction. Nietzke's novel *Windowlight* received a PEN/West Best First Fiction Award. She is currently completing a collection of short fiction.

ELISAVIETTA RITCHIE'S books are *Flying Time: Stories and Half-Stories; The Arc of the Storm; Elegy for the Other Woman: New and Selected Terribly Female Poems; Tightening the Circle over Eel Country;* and *Wild Garlic: The Journal of Maria S.* She edited *The Dolphin's Arc: Endangered Creatures of the Sea.*

SUSAN PEPPER ROBBINS has published a novel, *One Way Home.* She teaches writing at Hampden-Sydney College and lives with her family in a house (ca. 1978) across the road from the farmhouse (ca. 1820) where she grew up. Her dissertation at the University of Virginia was on the search for a new kind of home and sense of family in Jane Austen's novels.

Tim Schmand writes stories at his home in South Miami, Florida.

Hollis Rowan Seamon has published stories in a number of journals, including *The American Voice, Emrys Journal, The Creative Woman,* and *The Hudson Review* and in *McCall's Magazine.* She teaches writing and literature at the College of Saint Rose in Albany, New York.

Annick Smith is a writer of essays and short fiction and a film-maker whose feature film credits include *A River Runs Through It* and *Heartland.* She has written a memoir, *Homestead,* and, with William Kittredge, co-edited *The Last Best Place, A Montana Anthology.*

Mark Spencer is the author of two collections of short stories, *Spying on Lovers* and *Wedlock,* and a novel, *Love and Reruns in Adams County.* He is currently at work on a new novel.

Sharon Oard Warner teaches creative writing and literature at the University of New Mexico. She is the author of *Learning to Dance and Other Stories* and the editor of *The Way We Write Now: Short Stories from the AIDS Crisis.* She lives in Albuquerque with her husband and sons.

Allen Wheelis has a private practice in psychiatry and psycho-analysis and lives in San Francisco. He is the author of several books in addition to *The Doctor of Desire.*

List of Readings

Alexie, Sherman. "Father Coming Home." In *The Business of Fancy-dancing*. Brooklyn: Hanging Loose Press, 1992. Copyright © 1992 by Sherman Alexie. Reprinted by permission.

Bender, Sue. *Plain and Simple: A Woman's Journey to the Amish*. San Francisco: Harper and Row, 1991, 141–145. Copyright © 1991 by Sue Bender. Reprinted by permission of HarperCollins Publishers, Inc.

Brown, Peter C. "Over Doyles' Drop-Off." *New Yorker* (5 November 1990): 47–52. Copyright © 1990. Reprinted by permission.

Chase, Naomi Feigelson. "Politics." An excerpt was published by Crossing Press in *Word of Mouth*, vol. 1, 1991. Copyright © 1991 by Naomi F. Chase. Printed by permission of the author.

Colette. "My Mother and the Forbidden Fruit." In *My Mother's House and Sido*. Trans. Enid McLeod and Una Vicenzo Troubridge. New York: Farrar, Straus & Young, 1953. Copyright © 1953 and renewed © 1981 by Farrar, Straus, & Giroux, Inc. Reprinted by permission of Farrar, Straus & Giroux, Inc.

Crews, Harry. *A Childhood: The Biography of a Place*. New York: Harper and Row, 1978, 93–98. Copyright © 1978 by Harry Crews. Reprinted by permission of John Hawkins & Associates, Inc.

Crews, Harry. *Blood and Grits*. New York: Harper and Row, 1979, 145. Copyright © 1979 by Harry Crews. Reprinted by permission of John Hawkins & Associates, Inc.

Eagle, Rebecca. "The Baby and the Bathwater." Copyright © 1996 by Rebecca Eagle. Printed by permission of the author.

Levine, Miriam. "Two Houses." In *Devotion: A Memoir*. Athens: University of Georgia Press, 1993. Copyright © 1993 by Miriam Levine. Reprinted by permission.

Miller, Jim Wayne. "A Felt Linkage." *Berea Alumnus* 44 (July–August 1973): 11–14. Copyright © 1973 by Jim Wayne Miller. Reprinted by permission.

Nietzke, Ann. Excerpt from "Natalie." *Calyx: A Journal of Art and Literature by Women* 14, no. 1 (summer 1992): 60–67. *Natalie on the Street* was published by Calyx Books in 1994. Copyright © 1992 by Ann Nietzke. Reprinted by permission.

Ritchie, Elisavietta. "Sounds." In *Flying Time: Stories and Half-Stories*. Chapel Hill, N.C.: Signal Books, 1992. Copyright © 1992 by Elisavietta Ritchie. Reprinted by permission.

Robbins, Susan Pepper. "Red Invitations." Copyright © 1996 by Susan Pepper Robbins. Printed by permission of the author.

Schmand, Timothy. "Crossing Rampart." Copyright © 1996 by Timothy Schmand. Printed by permission of the author.

Seamon, Hollis Rowan. "Middle-Aged Martha Anne." *Hudson Review* 37, no. 4 (winter 1984/85): 557–566. Copyright © 1984 by Hollis Rowan Seamon. Reprinted by permission.

Smith, Annick. "It's Come to This." In *Best American Short Stories 1992*. Boston: Houghton Mifflin, 1992. Copyright © 1991 by Annick Smith. First published in *Story* magazine. Reprinted by permission.

Spencer, Mark. "Home." *Beloit Fiction Journal* 1, no. 2 (spring 1986): 46–55. Copyright © 1986 by Mark Spencer. Reprinted by permission.

Warner, Sharon Oard. "Learning to Dance." In *Learning to Dance*. Minneapolis, Minn.: New Rivers Press, 1992. First published in *Sonora Review*, no. 5 (fall 1983): 1–15. Copyright © 1991 by Sharon Oard Warner. Reprinted by permission of the author.

Wheelis, Allen. *The Doctor of Desire*. New York: W. W. Norton, 1987, 146–151. Copyright © 1987 by Allen Wheelis. Reprinted by permission.

The epigraphs in this book are from the following publications:

Berger, John. *And Our Faces, My Heart, Brief as Photos*. New York: Vintage International, 1991, 57, 64, 67.

Bettelheim, Bruno. *The Uses of Enchantment*. New York: Vintage Books, 1989, 79, 278.

Canfield, Dorothy. "Sex Education." In *A Harvest of Stories*. New York: Harcourt, Brace and Company, 1956, 208.

Chatwin, Bruce. *The Songlines*. New York: Penguin Books, 1988, 18.

Crews, Harry. *A Childhood: The Biography of a Place*. New York: Harper and Row, 1978, 108.

Fromm, Erich. *The Art of Loving*. New York: Harper and Brothers, 1956.

Holm, Bill. *The Music of Failure*. Marshall, Minn: Plains Press, 1985, 3.

Lee, Laurie. *Cider with Rosie*. New York: Penguin Books, 1962, 25, 27.

Mairs, Nancy. *Remembering the Bone House*. New York: Harper and Row, 1990, 146.

Matthiessen, Peter. *The Snow Leopard*. New York: Viking Press, 1978, 44–45.

Vinokurov, Yevgeny. *The New Russian Poets: 1953–1966*. Ed. and trans. George Reavey. New York: The October House, 1966, 53.

Welty, Eudora. *The Eye of the Story*. New York: Vintage Books, 1979, 128–29, 131.

Williams, Barbarajene. *When You Are Cold* (unpublished).

Williams, Michael Ann. *Homeplace*. Athens: University of Georgia, 1991, 135.

Winterson, Jeanette. *Written on the Body*. New York: Vintage International, 1994, 81.

The following material is quoted in this book:

Berger, John. *And Our Faces, My Heart, Brief as Photos*. New York: Vintage International, 1991, 55, 65.

Beston, Henry. *The Outermost House*. Garden City, N.Y.: Doubleday, Doran, and Co., 1931, 220–222.

Crews, Harry. *A Childhood: The Biography of a Place*. New York: Harper and Row, 1978, 21.

Forster, E. M. *Howard's End*. New York: Alfred A. Knopf, 1921, 298.

Frost, Robert. "Death of the Hired Man." In *The Poems of Robert Frost*. New York: Random House, 1946, 41–42.

Hoffman, Eva. *Lost in Translation*. New York: Penguin Books, 1989, 274.

McGrath, Thomas. "The Bread of This World." In *Passages Toward the Dark*. Port Townsend, Wash.: Copper Canyon Press, 1982, 27.

BARBARA BONNER lives in Northfield, Minnesota, where she gardens, paints, reads, and writes. For many years, she worked as a bookseller at the Carleton College Bookstore.

Interior design by Will Powers.
Typeset in Sabon and Eaglefeather
by Stanton Publication Services, Inc.
Printed on acid-free Glatfelter paper
by Edwards Bros., Inc.